Seascape

The Best New England Crime Stories of 2019

First published by Level Best Books 2019

First edition

ISBN: 9781947915497

Editing by Shawn Reilly Simmons
Editing by Verena Rose
Editing by Harriette Sackler
Cover art by SRS

Contents

Foreword

In our fourth year as the editors of the Best New England Crime Stories anthologies, we are pleased to present SEASCAPE: The Best New England Crime Stories 2019. We are continuing our tradition of arranging the stories by state—not alphabetically, but rather like a road trip through New England starting with Connecticut then continuing on through Rhode Island, Massachusetts, Vermont, New Hampshire and ending the trip in Maine.

This year we've decided to do something a little different. While we'll be going through the states and stories in sequence. we're only going to give you a few key words on each story. Just enough to spark your interest. And, so we begin:

CONNECTICUT

WHO DONE IT by Michael Bracken – from today's headlines - human trafficking.

SECOND CHANCES by Tina deBellegard – friendship gone wrong.

ONE NICE THING by Marjorie Drake – the plight of the disabled.

STRINGER by Ang Pompano – it's not always good to take friendly advice.

A TRYST WITH FATE by Lynn Sheft – watch out for disgruntled employees.

THE GHOST WHO READ THE NEWPAPER by Vicki Weisfeld – stranded at a

haunted Inn.

THE SPICE OF LIFE by Tiger Wiseman – good lovin' gone bad.

NEW HAMPSHIRE

NO SECRETS FOR THE DEAD by William Ade – who's Donna?

STOLEN MOMENTS by Shawn Reilly Simmons – a turkey and time travel.

IVY by Katie Tietjen – a rescuer in disguise.

MAINE

TELL ME AGAIN by Woody Hanstein – an attorney's dilemma.

MONSTROUSLY MISUNDERSTOOD by Lorriane Sharma Nelson – are the police at their wits' end?

WHAT LOVE IS by Brenda Seabrooke – a fishing trip gone wrong.

HAVEN by Joseph Walker – the dark side of investigating spousal abuse.

This year's harvest of stories exceeds all expectations. We think they are exceptional and think you will too. ENJOY!

The Editors at Level Best Books,
Dames of Detection, Inc.
Verena Rose
Harriette Sackler
Shawn Reilly Simmons

The Al Blanchard Award

Al Blanchard was one of the original organizers of the New England Crime Bake conference, a president of Mystery Writers of America, New England Chapter, and a member of Sisters in Crime. He was known for encouraging new authors, for being a dedicated writer and mentor, and for being a fan of all things mystery. The popular regional gathering of mystery writers he and a few others conceived of all those years ago is still going strong today.

After his tragic death in 2004, the Crime Bake Committee established The Al Blanchard Award in his memory to honor the best short crime story either by a New England author or with a New England setting. Stories are judged by committee separate from the submissions for the Level Best Books anthology.

Level Best Books is very pleased to be the editors of the Best New England Crime Stories anthologies, and it's an honor for us to continue the tradition of publishing The Al Blanchard Award-winning story. Congratulations to Joseph Walker for winning this year's award with his story "Haven."

Verena Rose
Harriette Sackler
Shawn Reilly Simmons

Editors & Co-Publishers
Level Best Books

CONNECTICUT

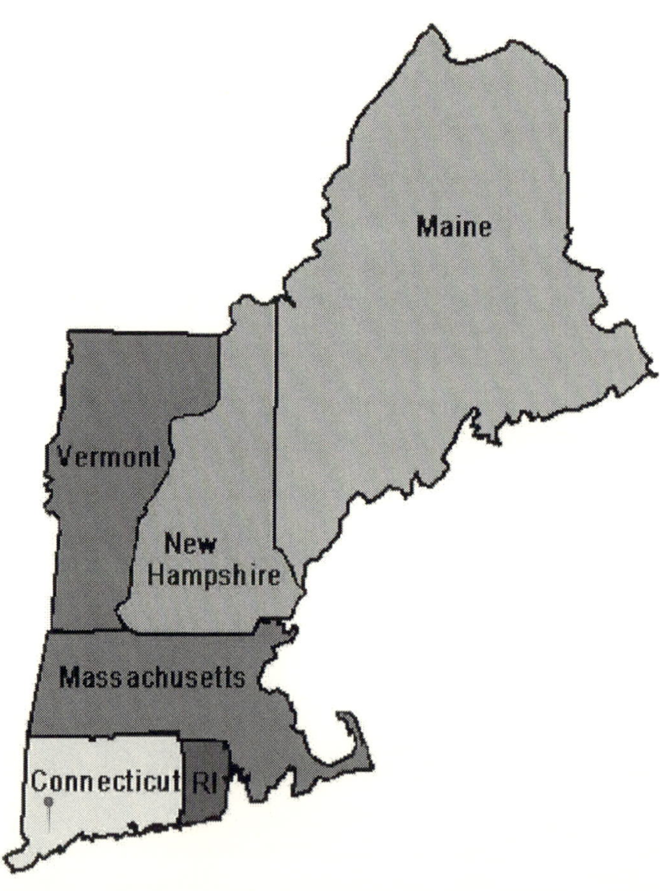

SIGILLUM REUBLICÆ CONNECTICUTENSIS
QUI TRANSTULIT SUSTINET

WHO DONE IT
by Michael Bracken

Wanda Smith stood alone under a black umbrella and stared at the grave of her husband Elmer. Fifty-three years together, fifty-one of them as husband and wife, and she was still numbed by the realization that she would never again feel his strong hand rest on her hip, his warm breath tickle her ear, or the taste of his lips when they pressed against hers. Six months to the day after he was lowered into the ground, she no longer had tears to shed, so the afternoon drizzle dampened her cheeks for her.

"I know who done it."

Wanda turned to see a young boy standing behind her. He wore a soggy white undershirt plastered to his thin frame, cut-off jeans, and muddy running shoes. Wet ringlets of black hair clung to his caramel-colored skin. She had not heard him approach.

"You know who did what?"

"I know who killed Smitty."

She took a deep breath and let it out slowly. Only his friends called her husband Smitty. "The police say it was an accident," Wanda said. "They said he lost his balance and fell down the stairs."

"They lie," the boy said. "He was pushed."

She examined the boy for a moment and saw no guile. "I was going to walk over to the Roadrunner," she said, motioning vaguely toward the diner a block from the cemetery's south entrance. "You want to join me?"

The boy looked around, for what she had no clue, and then he shrugged. "Sure. Why not?"

They crossed the cemetery together, but the boy kept himself well out of reach and would not join her under the umbrella. At the diner, she closed her umbrella and followed the boy inside. He led her to the last booth along the window and sat with his back to the wall. She sat opposite him.

"You hungry?" she asked.

He eyed her warily before nodding.

"Good," she said. "Order anything you like."

"Anything?

"Of course," she said. "Any friend of my husband's is a friend of mine."

A waitress named Mildred, much closer to Wanda's age than to the boy's, squeaked over and poured her a cup of coffee. She had served Wanda many times during the previous six months, but Wanda had always been alone.

As she began to walk away, the boy said, "Hey!"

When Mildred turned back, he upended his cup and tapped on it.

Mildred looked at Wanda, and Wanda said, "Anything my grandson wants."

The waitress filled the boy's cup, returned the coffee pot to its place behind the counter, and came back for their orders. Wanda ordered scrambled eggs and toast. The boy ordered a double bacon cheeseburger with everything, fries, and onion rings.

After the waitress walked away again, Wanda said, "You have a name?"

"Carlos," he said. He didn't offer a last name.

"So, Carlos," Wanda said, "how did you know my husband?"

"From the shelter."

After retiring as a locksmith, Elmer had volunteered three afternoons a week at a shelter in downtown Hartford, a down-on-its-luck hotel that a charitable organization purchased and refurbished to accommodate the city's many homeless children. "You met him there?"

"Yeah. Me and my sister Carmelita. Smitty helped us a couple times."

"My husband was like that."

Carlos ate everything on his plate and then ordered a slice of banana cream pie. When he finished, Wanda asked, "How long has it been since you ate?"

He shrugged. "Yesterday, the day before. I don't keep track."

"They don't feed you at the shelter?"

"I don't stay there no more, not since my sister—" He stopped mid-sentence, his gaze tracking something outside.

Wanda waited a moment for the boy to finish before prompting, "What about your sister?"

"I shouldn't'a' said nothing."

Carlos slid from the booth and bolted for the rear door, brushing past Mildred and causing her to slop coffee on the floor.

As Wanda turned to see what might have caught Carlos' attention outside, Mildred said, "Your grandson's in an awful hurry."

The rain had stopped, and the sun peeked through the clouds. A white panel van with the shelter's name painted on the side occupied a parking spot at the far end of the lot. A thick-bodied man with a ruddy face and a graying flattop approached the diner from the direction of the van.

"Yes," Wanda said as she turned to the waitress. "He was late for practice."

By the time she finished her coffee and approached the cash register to pay the check, the ruddy-faced man had settled at the end of the counter next to it. Though he held a laminated menu in his hand, he paid more attention to Wanda than to the menu, and she felt a chill run down her spine until she was out the door.

She glanced over her shoulder several times as she hurried to the cemetery's parking lot where she'd left her car, not realizing her umbrella remained behind.

Gloria Plummer had long been a friend and neighbor, so Wanda told her about her experience that morning, not mentioning the odd feeling she'd gotten from the van driver.

"You know what those kind of kids are like, Wanda. They'll say anything. That boy used you to get a free meal," Gloria said. "That's all it was."

"I don't think so," Wanda said. "He didn't ask for anything. I'm the one who offered lunch."

"So you believe his story about your husband being pushed down the stairs?"

"I don't know what to believe," Wanda said, "but I can't ignore what the young man told me. If someone killed my Elmer, I want to know who and why."

"You going to the police?"

"They're the ones who told me it was an accident. What could I tell them that would change their minds?"

"Probably nothing," Gloria said.

"I thought I was ready to move on with my life," Wanda said, "but I'm not. Not now. Not after what that young man told me. If there's even a shred of truth to what he said—"

She stopped herself in mid-sentence, uncertain what she intended to say. During the six months since her husband's death, Wanda had been through the five stages of grief—denial, anger, bargaining, depression, and, finally, acceptance—and in her confusion worried that she would go through them all again.

Rain returned the next morning and, on her way out the door, Wanda reached for her umbrella. When she grabbed empty air above the umbrella stand, she realized she had left it at the Roadrunner in her hurry to escape the attention of the ruddy-faced van driver.

Wanda made the diner her first stop that morning and found Mildred working behind the counter.

"Thought you'd be back," the waitress said. She reached under the counter to retrieve the umbrella. As she handed it to Wanda, she added, "That man who came in just before you left asked a lot of questions about you."

"Like what?"

"Your name. The name of the boy with you. Where you live. Anything else I knew about you."

"What'd you tell him?"

"Nothing, because I don't know anything," Mildred said, "but I didn't like the look of him and wouldn't have told him anything even if I did."

"Wanda. My name's Wanda."

Mildred smiled. "Honey, women of a certain age have to stick together."

"Thank you."

"That boy—your grandson—I've seen him around before." She made a face that indicated she didn't believe the boy was related to Wanda. "Why do you think that is?"

"You've seen him in here?"

"Not in here. In the cemetery. He always looked like he was waiting for someone. I'm betting that someone was you."

"If you see him again, call me," Wanda said. She borrowed Gloria's pen and wrote her cellphone number on a napkin. "And if that other guy asks any more questions about him—"

"I'll let you know."

Wanda smiled. "Thanks."

With a firm grip on her umbrella, Wanda returned to her car and drove to the hospital, where she volunteered three days a week, performing her civic duty just as her husband had during his many years at the shelter. Though she served in various capacities at the hospital, she most often pushed wheelchairs around the building, ferrying patients from one place to another.

A recent spate of births had her that day escorting discharged new mothers and their babies from the maternity ward to the circular drive in front of the hospital where new fathers or other family members retrieved them. No one knew what the future held for the children. They might lead healthy lives in happy homes as Wanda had, or they might find themselves living on the street at a young age like her husband had before he was taken in by an older man who taught him a trade.

Two days later, Mildred called.

"I saw that boy," the waitress said as soon as Wanda answered. "That man had ahold of him and was shoving him in the back of that van."

"When was this?"

"About half an hour ago."

"Did you call the police?"

"I did, and an officer came to talk to me," Mildred said. "He seemed interested until I told him who the van belonged to. Then he just closed his notebook and told me it was nothing to be concerned about. He said the shelter picks up runaways all the time. But that isn't what I saw. That youngster did not want to go with that man."

"Did you tell the officer that?"

"Of course I did, but he was having none of it," Mildred said. "He ordered a chocolate-covered doughnut and a black coffee to go and walked out of here as if the only reason he stopped in was to stiff me out of a tip."

They spoke for a few minutes, and Wanda spent several more pondering what she should do about all that she had just learned. She did not have to work at the hospital that afternoon, so she drove to the shelter and asked the unfamiliar young woman behind the front desk if she could see Carlos.

The woman stared at her. "Carlos who?"

Wanda did not know the boy's last name and faltered. "He's one of the young men in your care."

"I don't think we have anyone here by that name."

"Can you check?"

"Are you family?"

"No, I'm—I'm a friend."

"I'm sorry, then, but no."

Remembering the receptionist her husband had introduced to her several years earlier, she asked, "What about Amy Gautman? Could I see her? Is she working today?"

"I don't know anyone by that name, either."

"She doesn't work here anymore?"

"I don't believe so."

An office door opened behind the young woman, and Wanda saw the ruddy-faced van driver staring at her through the open doorway. She shifted her attention from the young woman to the man. "Where's Carlos? What have you done with him?"

He didn't respond, but the young woman behind the counter suggested she leave. "We don't need you upsetting our residents."

"But—"

"If you don't, I'll have Barry escort you out."

The ruddy-faced man's eyes narrowed, and a smile slowly pulled up the corners of his mouth. Wanda didn't like what she saw, and she backed away from the counter. When she reached the door, she turned and let herself out.

Gloria listened to Wanda describe her encounter at the shelter and then said, "So, you were making a nuisance of yourself and they asked you to leave. What's unusual about that?"

"I'm convinced they didn't want me there asking questions. That man was quite threatening."

"So, don't go back. Stop asking questions. Stop being a busybody. Your husband fell down the steps. That's all there is to it."

"Maybe you're right," Wanda said, but she wasn't convinced.

After Gloria left, Wanda walked to the bedroom and opened Elmer's closet. She stared at his clothing and his shoes and all the gimme caps crammed onto the top shelf. She had been unable to part with any of his things, holding onto them for the memories they evoked. She reached in and grasped one of his flannel shirts, touched her face with the sleeve and held it there while she breathed deeply. She imagined the scent of his cologne, the way he smelled after a long day at the shop, his warm breath often carrying a faint trace of garlic and onion, and she knew deep in her heart that she didn't actually smell any of this. What she smelled was a musty closet full of a dead man's clothes.

Elmer would know what to do, though. He always did, but he wasn't sending her any messages from beyond the grave. After a bit she released her hold on his shirt and closed the closet door. Soon she would need to part with his clothes, donate them to the church's resale shop, and move on with her life.

She would have to go through the things in his dresser as well, and not just his socks and underthings, but the doodads and gewgaws he collected over the years and kept in the top drawer along with the zippered leather case containing the tools of his trade, tools he had taught her to use, and which had, more than once, proven useful to open locks when she lost the keys.

After Wanda delivered a patient to radiology the next afternoon, she pushed the empty wheelchair back to the Emergency Room where she had been assigned for the duration of her four-hour Wednesday afternoon shift.

She stopped when she heard, "Mrs. Smitty!"

When Wanda heard her name called again, she followed the sound to find Carlos sitting on a gurney. He was battered and bruised, and his left arm was in a cast.

She asked, "What happened to you?"

He didn't answer. Instead, he said, "You got to get me out of here, Mrs. Smitty."

"But—"

"They know I know. I was lucky to get away, but some stupid cop picked me up and brought me here. Somebody from the shelter's gonna come get me, and then—"

"Get in the chair," Wanda said.

After he did, she grabbed a blanket and wrapped it around his head and shoulders. Then she covered his lap with another.

As she wheeled him away, heading into the bowels of the hospital, one of the nurses stopped her. "Where are you taking this one?"

"Radiology."

"Didn't you just come from there?"

"Been going back and forth all day."

"After you deliver this patient, come back and—"

"I'm sorry," Wanda said. "This is my last one for the day."

She hurried away before the nurse could respond, and she pushed Carlos to the other side of the hospital before she asked, "Can you walk?"

"Yeah, I can."

She left the empty wheelchair near the employee entrance and they hurried across the parking lot to her car. She drove home, parked in the driveway, and led Carlos inside through the kitchen door.

Wanda and her young guest had just settled at the kitchen table when Gloria knocked on the door and then let herself in.

"Is that him?" Gloria demanded. "Is that the boy who said somebody killed your husband?"

"Carlos," Wanda said, "this is my neighbor Gloria."

Gloria dismissed him with a glance and said, "You brought him home? He'll rob you blind!"

Carlos told Wanda, "I ain't going to take nothing from nobody."

"Sit down or go home, Gloria," Wanda told her neighbor.

Gloria glared at her for a moment and then settled onto the chair furthest from Carlos.

Wanda turned to the young man, "So, what happened to you?"

"I was at the cemetery, looking to see if you'd come back, and Barry grabbed me." Carlos held up his broken arm. "He done this when I tried to get away."

"Why did he do that?"

"They don't want me talking to you. They don't want nobody knowing what goes on there. Smitty was going to tell, that's why they pushed him down the stairs."

"What was my husband going to tell?"

"What they do to the girls."

Wanda leaned forward and placed a reassuring hand on Carlos's unbroken arm. "What do they do?"

Carlos told them, using language that burned Wanda's ears.

As he talked, Gloria blanched, but when he finished, she told Wanda, "He's lying. He's making it all up. He's—"

"They done it to my sister, and I couldn't stop them," Carols said. "That's why I ran away. I thought if I didn't say nothing about what they did to Smitty they would leave my sister alone, but I was wrong, and I couldn't do nothing to stop them. They found me, but I ran away again."

"Why were you staying at the shelter?" Wanda asked. "Where are your parents?"

"I ain't got a dad. Just a mom, and one day my mom didn't come home from work," he said. "Carmelita and me, we saw on the news that Immigration raided the factory where she worked, and we think they took her away. We waited for her to come home or to call or something and, when my mom hadn't paid the rent, the landlord came and threw us out. He didn't even let us take our stuff. He just changed the locks on the doors and told us not to come back. We didn't have no place to go, so we was on the streets for a while—"

"Why didn't you go to school and tell your teachers?" Gloria demanded.

"It was summer. There wasn't no school."

"Church?"

"We don't go to church."

"The police would have—"

"The police? Are you crazy lady? It was the police who took my mom. And what would happen to my sister? She wasn't born here. I was, but she wasn't."

Wanda stopped Gloria before she could interrupt with another question.

"We met some other kids on the street, and they told us about the shelter, so we went there. They fed us, gave us a place to sleep, but they had rules, and I didn't really like the rules. Carmelita didn't mind them so much. She thought the people there would help us find a place to live. Other kids found homes. That's what they told us whenever we asked what happened to kids we knew who disappeared. They said they found homes. We were there almost three months before we realized the kids who found homes were almost always girls, girls without no brothers or sisters. So I asked Smitty about it. I asked him why the girls found homes but the rest of us didn't. He said he didn't know but that he would find out. Then they pushed him down the stairs."

Gloria turned to Wanda. "You have to report this."

"I can't go to the police. They won't believe an old lady and a homeless kid," Wanda said. "They didn't believe there was a problem when Mildred from the diner called about Carlos being abducted."

"Then you need to talk to somebody who works there to corroborate this kid's story," Gloria said.

"The only person I knew at the shelter doesn't work there any more." Wanda reached for the directory kept next to her landline telephone and began thumbing through it.

"Are you kidding me?" Gloria said as she unclipped her smartphone from the holder on her belt. "What's the woman's name?"

Within twenty minutes Gloria tracked Amy Gautman, the shelter's former receptionist, to a long-term care facility. Wanda took Carlos with her and they drove across town to talk with her.

A frail, wheelchair-bound woman several years older than Wanda, Amy remembered Wanda's husband even though she did not remember Wanda or Carlos. She smiled when she said, "Smitty was always good with the kids. It's a shame what happened to him."

"That's why we're here," Wanda said, "to find out what really happened to my husband."

Amy sat quietly in her wheelchair and listened to their questions. When they finished, she shook her head. "I can't say."

"Surely you know what went on there," Wanda insisted.

"They got my sister," Carlos said.

"And may have killed my husband."

Amy stared out the window for a moment before returning her attention to her visitors. "They told me if I said anything to anyone, they'd do to me what they did to your husband."

"They threatened to kill you?"

"They said I might have an accident."

"Fall down some stairs?"

"Or worse, they said." She told them how she feared more for her own safety than the safety of the children in the shelter, and how they had used that fear to force her out of her job. "But look at me know," she concluded. "What can they do to me that won't happen soon anyhow?"

She told them what she knew about how the girls were selected and how they were taken to a room on the third floor of the shelter where they were kept until they were taken elsewhere.

"Taken where?"

Amy shook her head. "I don't know. I never knew."

Gloria spent a lot of time on her laptop computer while Wanda and Carlos were away, and when they returned, she asked, "Do you realize there were four hundred and thirty two underage victims of human trafficking in Connecticut between 2006 and 2017, and not one of those cases was ever prosecuted by the state?"

She showed them the *HuffPost* article from which she had learned about the trafficking and sexual exploitation of children in their state.

"We need to see for ourselves," Wanda said. "We need to get inside the shelter and see what's on the third floor."

Before the three of them left Wanda's home late that night, Wanda dug through her husband's top dresser drawer and retrieved a zippered leather case containing some of the tools of his trade, and she grabbed her umbrella on the way out the door because it had begun to rain.

She drove downtown and parked her car so Gloria could watch the alley behind the shelter while she and Carlos approached the building.

Wanda followed Carlos down the alley, shielding them from the rain with her umbrella. Carlos stopped her when they reached a handleless steel door next to a Dumpster and said, "Wait here."

He climbed onto the Dumpster. From there he clambered up the brick wall using barely perceptible niches in the brick wall as finger and toe holds, wincing each time he pulled himself upward with his broken arm, until he reached a second-story window. He pushed the window open, disappeared through it, and a moment later opened the door.

Wanda stepped inside, closed her umbrella, and hung the hooked handle over her arm before following Carlos up the steps to the third floor landing, where they faced another door.

"This is where they keep the girls."

Wanda removed the zippered leather case from her purse, opened it to reveal a selection of lock picks, and soon unlocked the door. The door opened onto a large room containing a dozen beds. Chained to four of them were barely clothed young girls. One was crying softly. The other three stared back at them with dead eyes. None were Carlos's sister.

"We have to get these girls out of here," Wanda said as she began working the lock picks on the first set of cuffs.

She freed them one by one, and as she did, she wrapped each in a bed sheet.

When Wanda reached the crying girl, the girl asked. "What are you going to do to us?"

"Get you out of here." She freed the girl and turned to Carlos. "Take them out to Gloria."

After the girls followed Carlos through the door in which they had entered, Wanda returned the lock picks to their leather case, retrieved her umbrella, and approached the door at the far end of the room. Before she reached it, the door burst open and the ruddy-faced man stood before her.

"What the hell are you doing up here?" He glanced over her shoulder at the empty beds and the door standing open at the other end of the room. "You saggy ass old bitch. You've gone and screwed everything up."

He grabbed at Wanda and she spun away. She wasn't fast enough, though. The ruddy-faced man wrapped his arms around her from behind, lifted her off her feet, and carried her into the front stairwell. She struggled, but she didn't have the strength to loosen his grip, and she envisioned herself being thrown down the same stairs as her husband.

The umbrella was still in her hand, so Wanda thrust it downward, jamming the tip into the top of the ruddy-faced man's foot. He swore and loosened his grip. When he did, she pulled away, stumbling to within inches of the top step before falling to her hands and knees.

Unknown to her, Carlos had returned. When he saw what was happening, he ran the length of the room from the rear door to the front and leapt at the man's back. He swung his cast-laden arm at the man's head and hit him so hard the cast cracked.

The man stumbled forward, knocked Carlos from his back, and didn't see the umbrella Wanda jammed between his legs until he stumbled on it and tumbled down the stairs.

He was struggling to his feet when the first of several police officers bounded up the stairs.

Later, Wanda learned that Gloria had phoned the police when four girls wrapped in bed sheets came running down the alley toward her, one of them yelling for help.

Several days later, Gloria and Carlos joined Wanda at her husband's grave. They stood to the side while Wanda told Elmer everything that had happened since her last visit, from meeting Carlos to the arrests of the human traffickers who had surreptitiously taken control of the shelter. "We did what you tried to do," she said. "We saved all those girls."

Wanda would never again feel her husband's strong hand on her hip or the taste of his lips when he kissed her, but she imagined the warm breeze was his breath tickling her ear one last time.

Then the three of them walked over to the Roadrunner, where Mildred served lunch and peppered them with questions about what she'd read in the newspaper. They told her everything, including that morning's news about the rescue of Carlos's sister Carmelita from a brothel in Stamford and Wanda's plan to reunite both children with their mother.

"They're going to stay with me until then," Wanda said. "Elmer would have wanted it that way."

* * *

Michael Bracken has written several books, including the private eye novel *All White Girls,* and more than 1,300 short stories published in *Alfred Hitchcock's Mystery Magazine, Ellery Queen's Mystery Magazine, Mike Shayne Mystery Magazine, The Best American Mystery Stories,* and in many other anthologies and periodicals. He lives and writes in Texas.

SECOND CHANCES
by Tina deBellegarde

I've had a life of second chances. I suppose it's technically impossible to have more than one second chance but that hasn't stopped me.

When I was a kid I almost blew it, came close to throwing my life away, hanging with the wrong crowd and then jailed on an assault charge after a barroom brawl. Guess I didn't know my own strength. But my grandpa paid my bail, got me a lawyer, then dusted me off and set me on the right path. He said I was cursed with a bad childhood and that I shouldn't have to pay for my parents' mistakes. Grandpa always told me that everyone deserved a second chance.

I had no real skills, just a commercial driver's license, so a buddy of mine got me a job at the Sanitation Department. It wasn't glamorous but it was steady and it paid the bills and then some. Enough to take my son Will to the Mystic Aquarium every couple of months and to take my wife out to play slots at Mohegan Sun on date night.

I grew up in the small seaside village of Uncas, Connecticut. Not much to look at but there were some pretty little cottages scattered around town, their soft grey siding bleached by the sun made me feel that those houses were permanent and secure. I figured they had to have been there awhile in order to get that color. And the entire town had a view of the Sound pretty much anywhere you went. Me and Vinny, that's my buddy from work, we liked to have a drink after work on Fridays at the local hole in the wall, and even from there you got a view of the sunset over the water. But it's a town that will never amount to much because it's not fancy enough for people with money. Besides, they want lighthouses and other mansions to look at, not the view of the power plant like we have.

Anyway, Vinny used to pick me up in his truck every morning. He had a nice truck, vintage he called it. It rattled a bit, and some of the stuffing in the seats wasn't real comfortable but he kept it shiny and brought it to car shows in Wethersfield on the weekends. He pulled up every morning well before sun-up. The deal was he drove and I provided egg sandwiches and a thermos of strong coffee my wife made us every morning. We both figured we got a good deal. We'd drive through those quiet streets each morning and then park in the municipal lot for the county employees. We'd finish our coffee in the dark and wait for just the right time to step out into the cold. New England is as cold as a witch's tit on a winter morning so you don't spend more time than you need to out there. But the timing was complicated, and timing is everything, another thing my grandpa taught me. You wanted to get there before the morning commuter trains started. You see, we needed to walk across the tracks to get from the parking lot to the public works building. If we were running late Vinny would drive like a maniac to get us there before the trains, because once we were stuck at the tracks we would be late to punch in. Vinny told me a story once about a guy who used work there before us. This guy ran around the railroad barriers one morning because he knew if he was late one more time he'd a been fired. So he took his chances and he lost. The train made mincemeat out of him. He never saw it coming.

Anyway, we would down the last of the coffee and walk out of the lot and cross the tracks. Well, I would walk but Vinny had to do double time to keep up with my long legs. I imagine we must have looked pretty funny together. As we punched in we could hear the eastbound and then the westbound trains clatter over the tracks. The old building shook each time they passed, but I found the rhythm kind of soothing. Reminded me of a rocking cradle.

Once we were on the job it was my turn to drive. Me and Vinny, we started together years ago. He didn't have his commercial license so we started with me driving and never changed it after that. We had the same routine every day. I drove, he picked up. It wasn't fair really, but he said he liked being outside and of course I helped him out when there was too much for one guy to handle. Not that he needed my help, for a small guy he could really hustle.

I liked using the driving time to think. I can't say as I remember what I usually thought about, but I found it easy to fill up the time thinking whatever it was I thought about.

The streets were quiet and empty. Only the real early birds would be out in the near darkness. Mostly joggers and dog walkers like Mrs. Stillwell.

"Morning, boys," she'd say like we were children, but at her age I guess we were all children.

After a long morning we would turn in the truck and go for our lunch at Betty's. I loved Betty's, it was the best part of my day. It smelled good and it was welcoming, I knew everyone, and everyone knew me. It was sort of an extended family, at least I think so, since I don't really know what that feels like. But I know I liked it.

I would get my usual, grilled ham and cheese. Vinny would get a turkey club. We'd sit with Tom and George, guys from another truck. Betty treated us like royalty. She was good like that, extra cheese and plenty of coffee refills. When I left she would pack me an extra jelly donut to bring home for later. Man, those were good. She made them herself, light and fluffy with just enough sugar on the outside.

So, like I said, life was peaceful and routine.

But things changed one day, a shift in the universe, you might say.

On our way to work one Tuesday, Vinny rushed to stop at the 7-Eleven to buy a lottery ticket. Once in a while he would get the urge to buy a ticket. Me too for that matter.

"Jackpot today is the biggest pot in Connecticut history," he said to me. "I know we won't win but I kinda feel foolish not trying, you know?"

"Can't let the big one get away, huh?"

I teased him but I bought a ticket too.

With our tickets in hand we rushed to work and parked just in time to run across the tracks. We beat the trains by a minute or two. It was close.

I spent the day driving and daydreaming like I usually did. Navigating the streets of this pretty little town, the sun sparkling on the water, the wind rustling the trees, tapping my hands to the Motown hits on the oldies station. I thought about what I could do with the money. I'd get grandma out of that lousy nursing home and into somewhere nice. I'd buy my wife a new car; she'd been driving an old Buick to work for years. I'd send my son to space camp down south like he always wanted. And on and on.

Most days when I played a ticket I'd check the numbers at night, lose, and go on with my life. Wake up the next morning, start all over again. No big deal, right? This time was different. Because this time I won. And I won big.

I thought I knew myself. I thought that I had practiced winning so many times that this part would have been easy, and at first it was. I got grandma into an upscale place with good people and a nice view of the water. I bought my wife a new car in her favorite shade of blue. And Will went to space camp on his first school break.

But then I quit my job. I didn't just quit, I burned my bridges by telling my boss what I thought of him. Been wanting to do that for a long time. I bought a house in Newport, almost a mansion really, more rooms than I knew what to do with. But my wife didn't want to move too far from her job, and she didn't want to take Will out of his school, especially since he was just coming out of his shell. Eventually all we did was fight. She finally left and took my son with her to live with her mom in New London.

Family I could barely remember, drunk uncles, cousins who had never bothered with me, all started showing up at my door. All looking for money. I gave it to them, of course, they were family after all and I have to admit I liked playing king of the mountain. Besides, grandpa said that everybody deserved a second chance.

By now I'm sure you guessed how this turned out. I spent it all on cars and junk and good for nothing relatives. Before I knew it I couldn't pay the mortgage or the taxes and the house was foreclosed on. The cars were repossessed. I was in deeper than ever. I couldn't even pay my child support.

Well, I'm running the streets with the sanitation truck again. Thanks to Vinny I got my job back. The old boss retired after a heart attack, couldn't of happened to a nicer guy, and Vinny vouched for me with the new boss. This time I'm picking up the garbage and Vinny's driving.

I live alone in a measly two-room apartment off Main Street but I'm glad to have it and I've learned my lesson. Now I know better, I know what matters. I'm dating a sweet lady, Marilyn's her name. She's patient while I get back on my feet. At least I know she's not hanging around because of the money. She's the real deal. I'm hoping to propose next Christmas if I can get a raise.

So every morning before dawn Vinny comes back to pick me up in his beat up old jalopy, clunking down the street, the seat stuffing worse than ever, the heat only working when it wants to.

Every day we punch in then get to work. Vinny drives the truck, the sounds of the same old tired songs drift to the back of the truck where I'm holding on in the cold, picking up someone else's garbage from one old grey dilapidated house to the next. Daydreaming. Sometimes the sun is so bright it hurts my eyes.

After our shifts we go to Betty's for our sandwiches and stale coffee. I say hi to my neighbors, they say hi back but then they put their heads together and whisper. But I'm getting used to it. Small towns and nosey neighbors go together, I guess.

Last Tuesday he picks me up as usual and we stop at 7-Eleven. I get a buttered roll but steer clear of the lottery counter. He gets his ticket every week like religion. Since I won, he believes anything is possible.

That night, don't you know, he calls me at eleven o'clock. He wants me to come over for some beers to celebrate. Who'd a believed it, but he won the jackpot.

We spent the night drinking and planning out his new life. He's a pretty quiet guy, he didn't have grand plans, but then again neither did I at first.

The next morning, he pulls up to my apartment. He's running a little late, I figure the beers must have taken their toll. The dark winter morning is eerie but peaceful, no snow in the forecast. I get in the car.

"Hey, you know your right headlight is out."

"No problem, I won't be needing this truck anymore."

I turn, the look in my eyes startles him.

"Don't worry, don't worry, I'm not going to do what you did. You know I've been looking at cars. I finally decided on something bigger and more comfortable now that I can afford it. I've been promising myself for years. I'm not even quitting my job. But I am going to enjoy going in today to show my ticket off, then I'm leaving early to go put in my claim at the lottery office."

We pull into the parking lot. We rush to beat the train but by the time we arrive at the tracks the red lights start flashing and the bells are ringing. Bad timing, bad luck. We'll have to wait for both trains. It'll be the first time I'm late since I started back. Hopefully, the new guy won't give us a hard time considering the unusual circumstances.

Vinny pulls the ticket out of his wallet and shows it to me, a big stupid grin on his face. "Would you look at that?"

I turn to him. "Hey, let me hold the golden ticket one more time, try to remember what it felt like."

He hands it to me cautiously. "Be careful, don't let the wind take it." He was right, the trains did create a mean draft. The first train finally passes and while we wait for the second train he hands me the ticket. The horns blare and he turns to say something but I can't hear him. Looking at the ticket it all comes back to me, the good and the bad. But mostly the good.

I turn to him but I can't really make out his face in the darkness. He doesn't look like Vinny. He doesn't look like my old buddy. Just someone standing in the dark by the tracks.

I extend my hand to return the ticket, he reaches to take it from me, but I change my mind. He pulls his hand back laughing and says something I can't understand. All I can hear are the bells and the horn of the approaching train. Then I extend my hand again, the same hand, the one with the ticket in it and I give him a shove, just hard enough and just at the right time to place him directly in the path of the train. Timing is everything.

I figure I have a better idea how to do this now. The first time was just practice. After all, everyone's entitled to a second chance.

* * *

Tina deBellegarde's novel manuscript *Winter Witness* was long-listed in the Retreat West and Blue Pencil Agency First Novel Award competitions. She is a member of Mavens of Mayhem, the Upper Hudson Chapter of SinC, Sisters in Crime, Mystery Writers of America, and Hudson Valley Writers Guild. She lives and writes in Catskill, New York. Connect with Tina at *tinadebellegarde.com.*

ONE NICE THING
by Marjorie Drake

The shelter sucked. But there were worse places.

Shavonne had lived with her daughter Jessica for a while, but then Jessica lost her job, and then her apartment, and moved into her in-laws' home. A two-bedroom state-subsidized apartment shared by her abusive soon-to-be ex-husband, Joey, and his alcoholic parents. And that place was already at risk because Jessica and the baby weren't supposed to be there.

Then Shavonne tried a stint with her sister Clarisse, who considered herself almost middle-freaking-class with her insurance company job (customer service rep—big deal) and her apartment in the west end of Hartford.

Clarisse should remember that Shavonne had also had a good job, for twenty years. It was in a machine shop, but she *was* shift supervisor and made more money than Clarisse did. Until the back injury.

No one saw her lift the box of metal parts—it was in the way and she had to finish up—so she finished up and went home, not bothering to tell anyone about how her back hurt until the next day. There were no witnesses, and the company insisted her injury had nothing to do with work, and finally her attorney told her she'd better settle. After paying the doctors and the lawyer, she'd been left with $7500. That was two years ago, and the money was gone.

She'd helped Clarisse with the rent and the heat bill so she could stay there. But she got tired of listening to her crap. After all, she slept on the couch, and bought them both groceries with her food stamps. She wasn't a leech. She'd contributed.

So after she thought about it, maybe the shelter wasn't so bad.

It was a new one, a renovated building behind a Lutheran Church on a side street off Main Street in Hartford. It was a shelter for women and children only, and there were tiny private rooms rather than dormitory style sleeping arrangements. And they didn't make you leave during the day. She had friends who had beds in shelters but had to find someplace else to be during the daytime hours. That was a bitch this time of year. Winter had been hard and though it seemed like it should be over, March continued to be bitter and snowy. Her shelter let her stay inside. Not in her room, but in the common area, after she'd done her chores. They kept giving her the mopping duties, even after she told them about her back, but some of the other women helped her, or traded with her for easier chores, like dusting the books in the shelter's "library."

But she'd been all set to leave and get a place of her own. Because after waiting two years, she'd had her disability hearing, and, she'd thought, if she wasn't disabled, who the hell was?

She'd read the decision three times and it still didn't make sense to her. Her lawyer had explained that the judge found she could still do certain jobs—pencil inspector. Or security monitor.

"Okay," she'd said. "Where can I find those jobs?" She figured even if she lost the job when she missed work because she couldn't get out of bed, it'd be *some* money. Maybe enough so she could help a friend with the rent in return for a place on the couch. Her lawyer explained the jobs were all "theoretical."

"You can't tell me where I can apply for one of those…security jobs, or anything else?"

"No Shavonne, I'm sorry. I can appeal."

"Okay, let's do that."

"But it will take over a year to get a decision, and we aren't likely to win."

Shavonne paused, absorbing the blow. "What else can I do?"

"Well, you can apply again, but you would have to claim you became disabled recently. And it'll take a year or two to get to a hearing."

Shavonne nodded again. The lawyer was a pretty, thin woman in her mid-thirties. Nice-looking suit, looked like it was made of silk. She'd never seen a suit like that. Sometimes Clarisse wore a suit to the insurance company, but it never looked that good. Of course Clarisse had packed on a few pounds recently.

"So, what you're telling me, basically, is...I'm screwed."

The lawyer opened her mouth, closed it, massaged her temples with her fingertips and then looked up and spoke again.

"I'm afraid your options *are* limited. And none are very good." The lawyer paused and picked at an imaginary piece of lint on her black skirt.

"I'm sorry," she said.

"You did the best you could." Shavonne picked up her copy of the decision and headed for the door. She turned back.

"You take care now," she said to the lawyer, who raised her hand in a half-hearted wave.

She waited until after dinner to look at the decision again. Twenty-seven pages.

"I'm not a stupid woman," she thought. "But this keeps repeating the same things over and over. And, for some reason, this judge doesn't seem to believe anything *my* doctors say."

She looked at the last page of the decision, at the judge's signature.

"Maurice L. Flaherty," she said aloud, "What an awful name."

There was a knock on her door.

One of the younger residents stood beaming from the doorway. Shavonne suspected the girl might be high.

"Want to join us for cards?"

"Why thank you, honey," said Shavonne, "I think not, but I appreciate the invitation."

"We'll be in the common room if you change your mind."

Shavonne lay on her cot and tried to stretch her back. She was almost out of the pills from the clinic. They didn't help much with the pain, but they put her to sleep. And being asleep was relief from the pain. She'd been asking for an MRI for the last two years, but her state health insurance wouldn't pay for it. Even the x-rays showed big problems. Her back was falling apart. The pain had started to run down her left leg, and that foot no longer had much feeling. She was tripping a lot, over her own damn foot.

Shavonne picked up the i-Phone her daughter had given her for her last birthday. She'd even taught her how to use it. It wasn't hard. She wasn't stupid. She'd been a lead worker in the end, watching over to make sure everyone did their jobs. She'd cared about that. After all, her company made airplane parts and she sure didn't want to read about some 747 dropping into the sea and wondering if her failure to catch a mistake was the reason.

She opened Google on her phone, where she could look up almost anything. At the hearing, she turned it off as instructed, but it was on the table beside her. The judge looked at it, eyes narrowing, and she'd wanted to explain. But she remembered her lawyer's instructions: *Don't volunteer anything.* Finally, the judge couldn't contain himself.

"And how do you afford an *i-Phone,* if you are in such bad straits?" he'd asked, his ruddy complexion deepening.

"It was a gift," she'd said. "From my daughter!"

Proud. Her little girl had gotten a fancy phone for her mom. She couldn't let her stay with her. But she could give her a phone. It was her one nice thing. Wasn't everyone, she wondered, allowed to have one nice thing?

"Hmmm." The judge had looked up over his glasses, sniffed and pursed his lips. Like maybe he smelled something.

Maurice L. Flaherty. Nerdy little man. Her lawyer told her he had thirty years in "public service." What did that mean? Her lawyer had chuckled. It meant at least two pensions, state and federal. Under either one—lifetime health insurance. Cadillac health insurance. If Shavonne had health insurance like his, she would've had an MRI a long time ago.

"No use hating," she thought. "No use feeling jealous of others."

She thought about the Reverend at her old church. That was one of his favorite themes. "*Yes, there were people who'd been given more than we have.*

Yes, it might seem unfair. But we are rich in Spirit, in Faith, in Love." She hadn't been to church recently. Mostly because the pews were so damned hard. She'd kept having to stand up, sit down, move around.

She wondered where the honorable Maurice Flaherty resided. Certainly he was in one of the suburbs. One of the nicer ones.

Another knock at the door. Everyone's antsy tonight, she thought, not bothering to stand. "It's open."

Ginny from next door stood there, pale and shaky, holding a shoebox.

"Here, you gots to take this and hold it for me," She looked back, simultaneously sliding the box in and slamming the door behind her.

"Ginny, what the hell?"

Shavonne didn't get up right away. She tried, but the pain chose that moment to reach a "ten" and then slid down her leg, into her foot with a special kind of burning in the toes.

"Man," she said, lying back.

Ginny was an odd one. Shavonne didn't know her well, certainly not well enough to be entrusted with some prized possession. Ginny was in her late thirties but looked fifty, and her daily activity was a walk to the methadone clinic. Clean for forty-eight days now, longer than she had been in the last twenty years. Good for her. But she always managed to dodge her chores. Didn't feel well. Had to make a call. The stupid chores took less than a half hour and that was if you were doing them with back pain.

Shavonne sighed as she looked at the shoebox. It wasn't going to be good news.

She knew that before she heard the banging on Ginny's door. The security people were searching her room. Shavonne got up, though she couldn't stand up straight, pushed the shoe box under her bed with her foot, lay back down and rolled over, her back to the door, to wait out the search. When the knock came, she had a moment of panic, which quickly turned to resignation.

"It's open."

Joe from the security desk was an older guy. Tracy, a return resident, accompanied him. Shavonne looked up, her face a complete blank. She'd perfected that look long ago. It had worked well with her ex-husband. He liked to hit women. But he particularly liked it if they were scared and if they hurt when they were hit. The more blank you could look, the less noise you made when he hit you, the quicker it was over.

Joe called out from the door. "You okay?"

She mumbled, "Almost asleep."

"I'm sorry. Tracy here thinks Ginny has a gun."

Shavonne sat up and stared. "Really?"

"I know, Hon," said Joe. "Don't worry. I'm sure it's just a rumor. You get some sleep now."

As the door was closing, Shavonne could hear Tracy. "Dammit, Joe, it's not just rumor. I saw it I told you, I saw it." She couldn't understand Joe's response, but his voice had a deep reassuring sound, as did the sound of their steps retreating down the long hall. She waited a while longer. At least ten minutes. Joe hadn't looked around, or even asked her any questions. She hadn't said anything about the shoebox, but wasn't sure why. She looked at the clock. Not even nine p.m., but most everyone would be in their rooms, lying on their beds staring at the ceiling, or calling relatives begging for a place on their couch.

She sat up and stretched her back. An ache, but no stabbing pain. A good sign. She stood. She was stiff, but not immobilized. Again, good news. It got worse when she bent and pulled the shoebox from under her bed. She lifted it onto her lap. It felt heavier than she'd expected. But then, she hadn't expected it to be a gun, at least not before the visit from Joe and Tracy.

A small revolver. It didn't look that frightening. Metal barrel, a handle of fake wood. She lifted it up, careful not to touch anywhere near the trigger. Where was the safety? She suddenly remembered why the gun was not a completely foreign object. Her dad had a small collection—never used, just for the beauty of the craftsmanship. She rolled the cartridge with her finger, surprised to find a bullet in each chamber. She dropped the gun into the shoebox, heart racing, and slid it back under the bed. Craftsmanship or not, guns were made for one purpose.

She went to her door and opened it. All was quiet. She tiptoed to Ginny's room and knocked softly. She put her head to Ginny's door and listened. Nothing. She knocked again, louder. She was listening, bent over, and jumped when she felt a hand on her shoulder.

"Whoa, Hon, it's okay." Joe again. Shavonne breathed deeply, bent over and waited for her pulse to slow.

"Your pain bad tonight?" Joe asked.

"I'm alright." Shavonne looked into Joe's eyes. "What's with Ginny? She okay?"

"We had to ask her to leave. Rules are rules."

"Did you find something?"

"No gun," he said. "Just a bag of heroin."

"But the methadone...."

Joe walked her back to her room. "Doesn't always work. Not all of the girls have been as hard-working or stayed on the straight and narrow like you."

Shavonne laughed as she opened her door. "And what difference does it make?"

She was about to close the door, but Joe held it open. "*You,*" he said, "you are going through a rough patch and will be fine." His weathered face was frowning and the lines between his eyes and around his lips deepened. He patted her on the shoulder and strode down the hall, the shiny Security badge on his jacket catching the florescent light in the bright hallway, his big ring of keys jingling.

Shavonne shut her door and pulled out the shoebox. She picked the gun up, feeling its comfortable heft in her hand, this time finding the safety easily, clicking it on and off, stroking the dark grey barrel. She removed the bullets from each chamber and slid them into the back pocket of a pair of jeans, shoved the jeans into her backpack and zipped it shut. She guessed the gun was hers now. And there were responsibilities that went with owning a gun.

She lay down and fell asleep more quickly than usual, and she dreamed of a white mailbox set back from a pretty brick sidewalk bordering a pristine green lawn. The name on the mailbox was Flaherty. Big black letters. Below, in smaller ones: Maurice and Mary, Jennifer and Joey, and Spot.

Shavonne woke up early the next morning. The back pain had returned, so she borrowed a heating pad from the front desk and took a pain pill. After an hour or so, she was able to sit and stretch. She played with her i-Phone. She went into the telephone directory, but the Honorable Judge Flaherty wasn't listed. Then she typed his name and "Hartford area." It didn't take long. The judge's picture was on the web page for several local charities, as well as a major golf tournament. He and his wife had attended a ball for the benefit of St. Francis Hospital. He looked like he had sitting there on the bench, but in a black suit instead of a robe and with his arm around a middle-aged woman. Attractive, Shavonne thought, good haircut, nice highlights. But then her eyes dropped to the lower half of the photo and she shook her head. A woman that age had no business showing that much cleavage, especially with that belly hanging out there below the bodice. She chuckled and kept clicking.

It didn't take long to find out that his Honor and his wife lived in Simsbury. No surprise there. It took a little longer to get the address, and it wasn't exact. But there was a public record indicating that he had objected to a neighbor's request for a permit to expand his garage. The neighbor's address was listed. And the judge's letter said he lived on the same street, within a half-mile of the offending property. That would be about two blocks. It would be easy to narrow it down to the undoubtedly lovely and well-maintained Flaherty homestead.

She explored the neighborhood on Google maps. She recognized the name of a pizza place a couple streets away. She'd gone there once, with a co-worker.

Be kind of interesting to see where the little twerp lived. Shavonne leaned back and stretched her legs out. But seeing his place would just be more temptation to the sin of envy. Would it be a sin to covet his house, or just the outbuilding that was likely on the lawn in the backyard? No doubt housing a well-lubricated lawnmower, a clean rake and shovel, a pretty watering can. Push all that stuff aside and there'd still be room for a cot bigger than the one she was sleeping on. The pain meds seemed to be wearing off and Shavonne turned the heating pad on and lay back. She was dozing when her i-Phone rang. It was playing a line from a song—celebrating the singer's "hotness"— which was what Jessica had programmed into it, just to bug her, so that's what she'd hear every time her daughter called. Try as she might, she couldn't figure out how to change it.

"Jessie, you got to change that ring, baby."

"You love it. Like mother, like daughter."

Shavonne couldn't help but laugh.

"So, I haven't seen you in ages, Mama—at *least* a week—and Joey's mom offered to take care of the baby. Couldn't think of a better date than you."

"What's the occasion? And why would she offer?"

"Mom, they're not that bad. And he and I are…better."

Shavonne's teeth clenched but she said nothing.

Jessica continued. "He got a job. Night security at the Travelers. So, what do you say?"

"I say—awesome." Shavonne paused and lifted the top of the shoebox, which was balanced on the end of her bed. She looked at the gun and closed the box. "I've got a craving for pizza. Do you remember that place we went to a couple times, in Simsbury? I mean, if the car is running of course."

"I have a reliable vehicle and a fifty-dollar bill, and I will pick you up at six and you can direct me to wherever you want to go."

"Let's make it seven. I need to take another pain pill and maybe a nap."

And by then it will be dark. Shavonne turned over again, closing the shades.

Shavonne was asleep when Jessica arrived, but the flurry of activity woke her before the knock on her door. She got up, moaning when her numb foot hit the floor, and opened the door to Joe.

"Hey Hon—Jessica's here to take you to dinner."

Shavonne smiled at Joe and felt a momentary desire to reach out and touch him. She was going to miss him. She smiled instead.

"Thank you, Joe. Could you tell her I'll be right down? Just got to fix my face." She winked at him.

He laughed. "Your face is fine, Shavonne. But I'll let her know."

She went to the bathroom in the hall, dipped her head under the cold water, brushed her teeth, and ran a comb through her hair, wishing she'd woken up in time to take a shower. Then she dabbed cover-up over the most obvious of her age spots and applied a thin line of ebony eyeliner on each lid.

Back in her room, she pulled her T-shirt off, and replaced it with a blouse from her backpack. Clean, and an emerald green that everyone said complemented her coloring. She unbuttoned the top two buttons and dropped a necklace over her head. Silver chain, emerald-green stone. She grabbed her big shoulder bag, checked for her wallet, glasses, tissues, and slipped her i-Phone in. Then she pulled out the old pair of jeans and reached into the pockets for the bullets. She rolled them around on her palm. She opened the shoebox and lifted the lid, took the revolver out and slid the bullets into each chamber easily, as though she'd been using guns all her life. She double-checked that the safety was on and put the gun into her purse. There was an inner pocket that had always been too big for her wallet, her phone, or her make-up. It was, however, the perfect size for a small revolver with a dark grey barrel and a fake wood handle.

Dinner was great. Jessica looked happy, alight with the re-discovery of love. Shavonne remembered that feeling. The last time she'd had that feeling was the night Jessica was born, a couple hours before Jessica's father punched her in the face after finishing a twelve-pack of Corona and a half pint of Smirnoff. It was convenient that her labor had started just after the fight. They set the jaw right around when she became dilated to eight centimeters. Instead of an epidural, they'd given her general anesthesia. Two doctors worked on her, one at each end. And when she woke, her jaw was wired shut and she had a baby in her arms. Even crying had hurt as she looked for the first time at her newborn. Her face quivered and ached. The infant cried too. *It's just you and me baby,* she'd thought. Her mind was made up.

She would throw him out.

He never showed up again anyway.

"I love pizza," Jessica said, pulling a third piece onto her plate.

"I remembered this place was good," Shavonne said. "You remember Donna?"

"Yah—she was your best friend at work. And so funny. I liked her." Jessica took another sip of wine. "What's up with her?"

"Don't know. Haven't heard from her since I got let go."

"Well, sheesh Mom, call her."

Shavonne smiled. "Let's get the check."

Jessica paid the bill and they stepped out into the evening. No wind for a change, and the moon was almost full.

"It's nice out," Shavonne said. "Let's walk awhile okay?"

The doctors had told her to try to walk.

Jessica talked about her husband. Everything was different now. He had a job. No drugs in over six months. Life was going to change.

Here it was, the road the judge lived on. They turned and kept walking.

The houses were big and set back from the quiet road. The mailboxes were pretty—all personalized. One had a cardinal perched over it. The others were painted, usually to match the gate in front of the walkway or the front door. Shavonne peered further up a driveway and one of the front porch lights was still on. Yup, the green mailbox matched the front door. As they walked past the next house, Jessica was talking about breast-feeding.

"I did it for six months, Mom," she said, "and I loved it. But then she started getting teeth. And she was so hungry."

"So you gave her some formula," said Shavonne. It wasn't the first time she'd heard the story.

"Well, yeah, but I felt guilty."

Shavonne started to laugh and was about to speak, about to tell her daughter again that if she never had to feel guilty about anything worse than that she was one lucky girl. But the words vanished as they paused at the next house.

There it was. The mailbox looked uncannily like the one from her dream.

It just said "Flaherty" in big black letters though, no first names.

The lights were on in the house. Shavonne stopped and stared. Jessica stopped and stared at her.

"Mom?"

"I know the man who lives here."

"Really? How?"

"He decided my disability case."

"Oh."

Jessica was quiet then and she looked, along with her mother, into the bay windows in the front of the house. There were blinds but they were three quarters up, and you could see a glimpse of dark curtain across the top. Burgundy maybe, or a deep purple.

"Big front yard," said Jessica.

"Yeah," said Shavonne. She stepped onto the lawn and tiptoed toward the house and the bright window, and after hesitating Jessica followed.

"We're awfully close," said Jessica when they were within ten feet of the window—off to the side though, and behind some bushes. They could see His Honor, in dress-down clothes, jeans and a collared shirt, laughing. There were two children, a little older than toddlers. They were hand in hand, spinning in circles, around and around. Finally they tumbled onto the thick rug, laughing. The judge was speaking, calling out, Shavonne thought, to someone in another room. The woman appeared, with two wine glasses in her hands and a plate balanced between her arms. They all made their way to the coffee table, so perfectly centered, so perfectly framed by the big picture window.

Shavonne slid her hand into her purse, into the big pocket that was the perfect size for her gun. As she looked into the picture window she grasped the barrel of the gun. Cold steel. Then she touched the trigger with her index finger. She checked that the safety was on and squeezed the trigger gently. It would be interesting to know how it would feel if the safety was off. If the gun was out of her purse, pointed at something, at someone.

The same four people remained visible in the picture window. It might have been a goddamn play: words exchanged by the couple, heads thrown back in laughter, an affectionate clasp of hands.

Jessica was staring into the window as well, seemingly having forgotten they were on private property, and how close they were to the big house.

"You didn't tell me you got the papers. Did they tell you when you'd start getting checks?"

"Oh yes," said Shavonne. "Never."

"What?"

"I lost. Apparently, I can work."

"What? But how—but what…what are we going to do?"

Shavonne smiled and slid the gun out from her purse. "I don't know, babe. What do you think I should do?"

Jessica stared at the gun. Headlights from a passing car illuminated the pair briefly.

"Mama—"

Shavonne looked down at the gun, as though it was a surprise to her that it was in her hands.

Then she looked at the picture window. The judge and his wife stood blocking the view of the children, arms around each other.

"It's funny," said Shavonne.

Jessica seemed paralyzed, but she responded. One syllable, a squeak. "Yeah?"

"I mean their life. It's not that different from ours, is it? Other than the nice house, and yard and, you know…. all the nice…. *stuff.*"

"Uh huh." Jessica seemed unable to look anywhere except at the gun, held loosely in Shavonne's hand, dangling from her fingers.

"Well," Shavonne added, "*and* the fact that he probably doesn't beat the shit out of them." She chuckled, a deep throaty sound.

"Where'd that come from?" Jessica asked, nodding at the gun, her body stiff.

"Someone at the shelter. She wanted me to hold onto it for her." Shavonne laughed again, a little too loud for the quiet night. Jessica looked around.

"Mama, I think you should put that away. I think we should leave. Before someone comes."

Shavonne kept staring into the picture window. It was hard to believe she was here, standing in the judge's front yard, not ten feet from him, his wife, and his children. Probably everything he cared most about in the world.

She wondered. Was there a dog, too?

They were close enough to hear. Not actual words. But sounds. Tones of voice. It was easy to read tones of voice, even faint ones from behind thick glass. She could tell they weren't the sounds of anger, the sounds she'd heard daily during her married life, the sounds that ended when he went away, and she was left with the baby. She looked at Jessica, her baby, at her stunned face and, suddenly, feeling as though she had awakened from a trance, slid the gun back into her purse. A long shiver traveled down her spine.

"Let's go," Shavonne said, turning toward the street.

When she looked back at the house, the window was dark—the blinds had been closed. She limped to the sidewalk, wincing as she got there. Jessica was close behind.

"Just wanted to check this place out, Hon. Let's get you back to your baby."

Jessica nodded and Shavonne could see tears trailing down her cheeks. They walked toward the car, and Shavonne took her daughter's arm.

A block down there were garbage cans near the sidewalks. Shavonne glanced behind—no one coming. She pulled the gun from her purse, wiped it off with her tissues, lifted the lid and shoved the gun down under the green garbage bag, dropping the plastic cover and watching it land silently. Holding Jessica's arm, she walked, long strides that sent blasts of pain into her back and legs.

"Maybe you could bring me to the apartment tomorrow. I haven't seen my grandbaby in a while."

Jessica squeezed her arm, crying, "Yes, yes, Mama. And Joey and I are thinking of getting a place of our own. But I told him only if my mom has a room there too."

As they got into the car, Shavonne heard the sirens, far away, but not far enough.She touched her daughter's arm. "Let's get out of here."

Jessica turned the key in the ignition.

It caught right away, and they glided into the night, staying well under the speed limit, driving slowly and silently, until they reached the Hartford city limits.

* * *

Marjorie Drake spent over thirty years as an attorney primarily representing injured and disabled people, and that experience informs much of her writing. She recently closed her law practice to write full time and is completing her first novel. She is a member of Mystery Writers of America.

STRINGER
by Ang Pompano

Mattie Mcdowell's phone pinged as she sat in front of the TV eating her lunch. To a stringer, a freelance videographer, that's equal to the cha-ching of a cash register. She hit the Content app on her phone to see the assignment.

BODY FOUND

Hammonasset Beach State Park Campground, Madison, CT

B-roll of Crime Location. Due in 1 hr. 8m., $150

There was a shooting at this location very early this morning. Please get video of the scene plus generic wide shots of this location with the park sign and campground.

She thought about declining. Murder scenes were appalling. But, B-roll meant supplemental footage to be intercut with what a news crew had already taken. The body would have been transported to the morgue hours ago. Now they needed some new footage to update the next report. She thought about her tuition coming due in a few days. She hit the *ACCEPT* button, shoveled in one more mouthful of mac n' cheese, and bolted out to the driveway.

Her tired car had her charged video equipment in the back and a full tank of gas. There was no time to stop for gas or look for your equipment when a notice was received. The media outlets that buy footage from the Content organization want their news copy in short order.

She parked on Route One by the park's entrance sign and popped the trunk to retrieve her camera. You could use a camera phone in a pinch, but a shoulder camera delivered nice steady shots and the long lens was perfect for when the cops keep you behind a line. The more professional the footage looked, the better were the chances that Content would be able to sell it to a media outlet. She found spending money on a good video camera a worthwhile investment. After shooting a few thirty-second shots of the sign from different angles, she drove down the access road to the park entrance station. All lanes to the ticket booths were closed.

When a ranger emerged from the office, she rolled down her window.

"Any chance I can get into the park?"

The ranger looked perplexed. "As you can see, the park is closed. There was an incident."

She had to deal with closed off crime scenes before. Being honest and respectful was always the way to go in this business.

"I'm here to get video footage."

"For which station?"

"I'm freelance. I upload my stuff to an app called Content and they distribute it to different outlets. I have an assignment to get footage of a crime scene. Do you know what happened here?"

"A guy staying over in the campground was killed. The troopers are calling it a random shooting. He was sitting alone at a campfire on his site. I can't believe it. Nice guy. I just brought him a load of firewood last night. You never know."

The ranger sounded like her father. *Be careful. You never know who's out there.* She got it, but still she had no intentions of covering herself in bubble wrap. "I hear you. Is there any chancc that I can drive in there and get a few quick shots?"

"I'm working on the other end of the park by the nature center. There was a trooper here earlier. I don't know where he went, but like I said, the park is closed."

She frowned. "I was hoping I could get in real quick to take some footage and be on my way. I need the cash for my tuition."

"I feel for ya. I've got a kid in college but I can't say it's okay to go in." He looked up and down the road. "I wish I knew where that trooper was. I've got enough to do without playing gatekeeper."

"I can imagine. This is a big park."

"I'll say. Two miles of beaches, boardwalks, pavilions, and the campground. And they keep cutting our staff."

She sighed. "Okay, I guess I'll be going. I could have used this assignment."

The ranger thought a minute.

"I've got to get back down to East Beach. I trust that after I leave you're not going to head down to West Beach where the action is. Cuz if you do, the troopers there are going to kick you out if they catch you."

He got in his car and drove toward Long Island Sound. She could see his car go into the traffic circle about a quarter of a mile down and take the exit to head east. When he was out of sight she drove down to the circle and took the exit to the west.

When Mattie got near the campground, she parked on the road by the yellow-tape barrier of the crime scene. About 200 feet further in she could see a camper marked off with more yellow tape. This had to be quick. She balanced the camera on her shoulder and zoomed in on the RV. She noticed a fire ring with a wisp of smoke trailing from the dying embers. A folding outdoor chair lay on its side. She imagined the victim sitting there just hours before. She followed with action shots of the policemen taking measurements and photographs. She took a longer shot of a group of people huddled by the stack of firewood the ranger had delivered. Witnesses? The police seemed to be taking them aside one at a time for questioning. She took several shots of their expressions and actions from a distance. She tried to be as discreet as possible. The cops seemed too busy to notice her.

If the video was good, and hers usually was, the money would be in her account the next day. Good video was important, but getting the shots uploaded to the website before anyone else was too.

When she became a stringer on the Connecticut shoreline she had no competition. A year later and it seemed everyone and their mother used Content so it was paramount to get the footage in first. Good footage, speed, and creativity could put some decent coin in one's pocket.

A young dude in jeans and a Florida-Georgia Line T-shirt came up to her from the dunes on the other side of the road.

"You must be a stringer." He had a nice smile.

"How do you know?"

"You look like you know what you're shooting. I'm Harper."

"Does that surprise you since I'm a woman?"

"No. But I see you're taking the money shots. You're not some gawker taking stuff for Facebook."

"Okay. You got me. I do this to cover my tuition."

"Me, too. Are you going to tell me your name?"

"No. I suppose you use the Content app?"

He nodded. "I already uploaded my clips to their website. It's all about getting it to them first."

"Damn."

"Hey. Don't let me stop you. Send yours in. Sometimes they buy them all."

"I was going to do that."

She walked over to a picnic table on the other side of the road. She used Bluetooth to drop her video from the camera to her phone. Then she started tagging her clips with keywords.

Harper wandered over and sat. "What school?"

"Why do you want to know?" She wondered if she was being too hard on him. He seemed nice enough even if he was nosey.

"Just talking. Quinnipiac here. I'm in journalism. I get double duty from my footage. I turn it in for a grade and I sell it to Content."

She locked eyes with him. "Seriously? Good for you."

"This is the biggest scoop I've gotten. I was here this morning when they found the body. The pay is good for stuff like that. Then I got this ping for the B-roll and I figured, why not? You got to take the crap assignments along with the 'Breaking News' or it doesn't look good."

A state trooper SUV approached with his car window down.

"What are you two doing here?"

"Just curious," Harper said.

Mattie thought this dude had a lot to learn. Being disrespectful would be a sure way to get kicked out.

"This is an active crime scene." The trooper glared at them. "Be curious someplace else. We have a situation here. You need to leave now."

The trooper started to say something but stopped when his radio crackled to life. "You two get where you gotta go." He closed his window and spoke into his radio.

They both laughed as the trooper headed into the campground.

"My name's Mattie. Where's your car?"

"I hiked in."

They hopped in her car and drove back toward the traffic circle. Neither one spoke. Half way through the circle Harper broke the silence.

"Take the second exit. There's a pavilion on Middle Beach."

"He told us to leave."

"You can't see the parking lot from here and there's nobody around. You've got to get that footage uploaded before it's too late."

He was right. Good shots were useless if the deadline passed. They parked in the lot. As they marched up a path over the dunes a raindrop landed on Mattie's tee shirt and spread out in a big dark spot. They looked to the darkened sky. More drops. They ran for the pavilion. As they ducked under the roof it became a deluge.

"We should have stayed in the car," Mattie said.

"How was I supposed to know it would rain?"

He was right. Actually, it was nice to be under the pavilion with the cloudburst around them. She took a deep breath relishing the smell of the rain on the dry sand. A refreshing breeze came off the water.

"Upload your video before it's too late," he said.

"You're not afraid they'll buy mine instead of yours?"

"I'm not worried. It's all about good composition, framing and the rule of thirds. You know what I mean? I'm good at what I do."

"And so am I." She sat at a table and finished tagging each shot with location and description. Then she began the tedious task of uploading.

"You know they sell these clips for a lot more than the measly commissions they give us." He sat next to her, almost but not quite invading her personal space.

"I need the money," she said.

"I do it mostly for the adrenalin. I hear that ping on my phone and it's like, here we go, get that story."

She looked up from her phone and could see the excitement in his face.

"You get off from CAR vs BUILDING or LUNAR PARADE?"

"More from the due in one hour, or better yet thirty minutes. I'm like going about my business and Ping! I'm in the car and on the way like I'm Clark Kent."

She laughed. "If Clark Kent covered water main breaks and parades."

"Like I said, sometimes you have to take the lame jobs. But there are ways to get around the boredom."

At last her phone gave a beep to tell her the last clip had uploaded.

"Aren't you afraid they'll buy mine instead of yours?" Mattie asked again. "They go by quality instead of speed sometimes."

"I'm good at what I do," Harper boasted.

"Can I see your clips?"

"Why?"

"I want to see if you are as good as you say," Mattie countered.

"Here. Knock yourself out. I don't have anything to worry about."

She watched his clips of the park sign, the campers giving their statements, the police. "Not bad."

"Not bad? Ha! Anybody can take a video. But look how I frame my scenes. Look at my angles, my composition. I know how to set up a good shot," he said.

She huffed. "Yeah, you have some weird angles here."

"What are you talking about?"

"Well, like this one of the fire ring and the camper."

"That's a great shot!"

"It's a decent shot. But you didn't take it today. There's no pile of firewood in the shot."

He looked like a thermometer about to pop as the red crept up from his neck to the top of his forehead. He lurched for the phone.

"Give me that. I took a few stock shots yesterday. It's good business to have shots ready so you can upload first."

She pulled it away as she jumped up from the table. "I don't buy it. Why would you have shot this particular campsite earlier? Because you knew this would be something you could sell? But for what reason? I don't..."

Harper pounced and grabbed her by the neck. Mattie struggled to breathe as his grip got tighter. Her vision blurred. Her arms and legs numbed. She tucked her chin and raised her shoulders in a futile effort to allow air to reach her lungs. Her body wanted to crumple to the floor, but her mind told her that was the easy way out. She needed to hold on until she detected an opening.

A bright flash of lightning and an explosive thunderclap— she felt his grip loosen. She drove her arms up between his, grabbing his head and gouging her thumbs into his eyes. As he released his hold, she hammered her knee into his groin. He pitched backwards to the ground, his hands between his legs.

"I'll kill you!" he yelled.

"I don't think so." The ranger she spoke to at the gate stepped between them radio in hand. "You stay put until the troopers get here."

Mattie stepped around the ranger and aimed her camera at Harper.

"Tell me again about setting up a good shot."

* * *

Ang Pompano's debut mystery novel WHEN IT'S TIME FOR LEAVING was recently published. His short stories include "Diet of Death" in the 2019 Malice Domestic Anthology MYSTERY MOST EDIBLE and "Stringer" in SEASCAPE: THE BEST NEW ENGLAND CRIME STORIES 2019. He is on the board of Sisters in Crime New England and on the New England Crime Bake Planning Committee.

A TRYST WITH FATE
by Lynn Sheft

The blast of the ship's horn signaling the Friday five o'clock departure from the Port of Miami to the aquamarine waters of the Bahamas was matched by the collective laughter of the passengers. Most were senior men and women who were exchanging shy glances or smiling ear to ear hoping for a favorable response. This themed cruise, "These Are the Days," was sponsored by an online dating site aimed at singles over sixty-five. The itinerary was three nights to the Bahamas with a stop at Nassau and the cruise ship's private Bahamas island called Bluebeard's Cay. Appropriately, a steel band played by the pool where many gathered with drinks in hand such as Piña Coladas or bottled beer. The strong ocean breeze whipped women's long tresses around like an egg beater.

A raven-haired woman named Rita Cohen remarked, "There sure are a lot of old people on this cruise." Her sunglasses concealed green eyes and long lashes, the latter artfully applied from a kit. She wore a long cotton dress in periwinkle blue with a floral print scarf fashionably tied around her neck. The only jewelry she wore were diamond stud earrings and a gold watch, a stark contrast to the other women.

"What did you expect, Rita? We're old. You're seventy and I'm sixty-five. That's why we joined the online dating site. At our age, it's slim pickings." Judy said, tying the sleeves of her navy-and–white-striped cardigan around her shoulders. She wore a navy A-line dress and white sandals.

"But I don't feel old."

"Great. Change the subject, will you? We're here to have fun. So stop grousing. You can look forward to the *free* open bar."

"That's a good news, bad news kind of thing."

"What are you talking about?" demanded Judy.

"Good news, I have more money for duty-free shopping. Bad news, we won't know who the cheapskates are."

"Because the men won't be buying us drinks?"

"Yup."

"Let's go find our stateroom. Then we'll come back and sit by the pool."

Rita inserted her key card and entered the room the two friends would share for the weekend. "Oh, how lovely! I'm glad we spent the extra money for a stateroom room with a balcony. We can sit out here and watch the world go by."

"But the idea is to mingle. We won't meet anyone sitting out there by ourselves. That's why I was fine with an outside cabin."

"Now look who's complaining."

"What's this?" Judy held up a small envelope. "It looks like an invitation." She tore the flap open and pulled out a card. "It is. We've been invited to sit at the captain's table for dinner tonight. I wonder if he's single and handsome. I love a man in a uniform."

"Let me see," Judy said snatching the card from Rita's grasp. "I wonder who else is invited. This could be lots of fun."

They both took care dressing for dinner, Rita wearing a coral silk dress with a matching jacket and Judy in a classic black dress with a strand of pearls at her neck. When they entered the dining room, Rita handed the invitation to the hostess. They were escorted to the captain's table offering a magnificent view of the sea. *De rigueur* for cruise ship dining were white tablecloths, fancy-folded napkins, sparkling glass stemware and gleaming place settings. A vivid floral arrangement of red ginger, bird of paradise, and protea took center stage. Subdued lighting and candlelight did wonders for the complexion, including hiding crow's feet.

Rita sat down while Judy hesitated. She was trying to figure where the captain would sit. Just then Judy saw a tall Scandinavian in a white formal uniform with a shock of white hair march toward the table. She smiled at him.

“Good evening, ladies. I’m Captain Steinberger. Please, have a seat.” He pulled out an upholstered chair for Judy next to Rita and she sat down. She was excited to have the chair next to him. She looked at Rita who was controlling her disappointment.

In the next few minutes, the others joined the group. The cruise director, who looked remarkably like Kevin Costner, took the cue from the captain. He pulled out the chairs for the statuesque assistant cruise director (who kept her eyes fixed on the captain) and two sisters from Ohio who were on their tenth cruise. The hilarious comedian going by the stage name of Steve Parsons quipped that he could pull the chair out himself.

After the waiter took their cocktail order, introductions were made. Judy asked, “Do you ever get tired of these beautiful sunsets?”

“Not at all. I grew up in Norway so we had sunlight all day for half the year. And, of course, darkness in winter. I prefer this.”

“I had forgotten how close to the Artic it is. Living in the US, we take sunrises and sunsets for granted,” Judy admitted.

“How long have you been a captain of a cruise ship?” Rita asked with a smile.

“More time than I remember, but I’ve been with this cruise line for eight years. A lot of changes over the years, for the better I might add.”

“It must be hard on your wife with you at sea all the time.”

“Not anymore. I’m divorced.”

“Oh, I’m sorry,” Rita said, the color rising on her cheeks.

“What do you do when you’re not on duty?” Judy asked, toying with her pearl earring.

“I usually play golf. Or read. And what do you do for amusement?” Captain Steinberger asked.

“I love to dance so I go out a couple of nights a week. I like going to the theater and movies. Days, I play pickle ball or take one of the many classes offered in our retirement village.”

“Where’s the retirement village?” the captain asked.

“South Florida, Coconut Creek specifically,” Judy said.

"Have you always lived in Florida?"

"No, I lived in Madison, on the Connecticut shoreline. When I retired from teaching, I realized that I wouldn't have to suffer through a New England winter ever again."

"You want to know cold, you should go where I grew up, Bergen."

"It's all what you get used to," Judy said, running her fingers through her long, wavy blonde hair and flashing her best smile. Their cocktails were served, dinner orders taken, and the captain's focus on Judy was interrupted by the others at their table vying for his attention. When dinner was over, the captain excused himself and handed Judy his business card. "It was delightful meeting you," he said, his blue eyes as bright as his smile. "I look forward to seeing you again."

After he walked away, Judy looked at the card and lowered it to her lap. She turned it over and read, *"Please join me in my stateroom at 11. Starboard side behind the bridge."*

Judy smiled, but felt confused. Through eye contact and conversation, she sensed there was some relationship or bond between the Captain and the assistant cruise director, Ingrid.

Rita said, "What's with you?"

"Nothing. Let's go to the theater now and find some good seats."

"Sounds like a plan." Rita led the way.

They sat down with Rita insisting on the aisle, just in case she had to use the ladies room.

The opening act was an illusionist named Casey Shane who had made appearances at Hollywood's famed Magic Castle, *The Tonight Show* and a variety of casinos. They were also entertained by a female ventriloquist whose puppet was a cranky old man who complained about everything. Rita and Judy laughed so hard they cried. Then a female vocalist took the stage backed up by a quartet. She sang show tunes and within minutes the audience was singing along. Judy wondered if the singer minded.

After the show, they headed to a lively jazz and blues club and sat at the bar. Rita ordered a frozen mango daiquiri and Judy a dry martini on the rocks with an olive. Judy looked at her watch. It was a few minutes after ten. She wondered if she should go meet the captain. She didn't know him beyond what she learned at dinner. *Did he view this a tryst? Or was it an innocent meeting? Probably the first. Can I go just to see what happens? I can always leave if I'm uncomfortable. And what's a little romance at sea? Who am I kidding? A little sex at sea. When was the last time a man held you in his arms? Dr. Oz said sex keeps you young. What am I worrying about? STDs? That's what condoms are for. Should I go to the sundries store and buy them? Then you already decided you're going to sleep with this man? Stop already. Don't think about it. Drink your martini.*

Judy put the glass to her lips and all she got was an olive. She had emptied the drink absently.

"You sure drank that fast, lady," Rita observed. "Where did you go?"

"What are you talking about? I'm been sitting here."

"Yes, your body is here, but not that blonde brain of yours."

"Bartender!" Judy raised her glass jiggling the olive.

A young man in a white shirt, black bowtie, and red vest appeared before her. "Would you like another martini?"

"Yes, please."

He took her glass and returned with a fresh cocktail.

Rita toasted to her friend. "So what's on your mind?"

"I've been invited to the captain's stateroom. I'm just nervous about going." Judy showed Rita the business card.

"I can go in your place, if you like," Rita volunteered, smiling.

"No, I'm a big girl. I wonder if I'm just one of many that revolve through his stateroom door."

"So what if you are. Why can't you take it for what it is? A fling. Two consenting adults. We're here to have fun."

"Yes, but shouldn't I try to mingle with these other eligible senior men?"

"Well, the night is young. The fun doesn't end on a cruise ship. You can always come back when you leave his stateroom. If you spend the night with him, there's always tomorrow."

"And what about you, Rita? Am I abandoning you?"

"No. While your mind was somewhere else, I've been sending signals over to that handsome man over there, the bald one with the blue eyes. I bet you he's a retired cop," Rita said. "And here he comes."

"Hello, ladies. I'm Keith Grimsby. And you are?"

Smiling, Rita introduced Judy and then herself. Judy decided this was a good time to depart. She excused herself and returned to her stateroom to brush her teeth and reapply her lipstick. Even though she'd had a second martini, she was still anxious. Did she dare have another one? She settled on ice water and did deep breathing exercises. She went out on the veranda and sat down. The indigo sky was a mass of dazzling stars and there was moonlight reflecting off the sea's surface. It was too spectacular a view to view alone. She returned to her room, closing the sliding door behind her. She studied the site map of the ship to find the way to the captain's private quarters. She looked at his card and saw his first name was Bjorn. She wasn't quite sure how to pronounce it. She returned the business card to her evening bag for safe keeping.

She found the door to the captain's stateroom just as he indicated, behind the bridge. It was even windier on this level and she was glad she had clipped her hair in a barrette.

She took a deep breath and exhaled slowly. Her hand trembled as she knocked softly on his door. She waited. She still had time to turn and make a quick exit. She inhaled again and slowly let her breath escape.

She knocked again and waited. She opened the door and heard a trumpeter playing "When I Fall in Love." Judy called out, "Captain? It's Judy."

No response. She took a few steps in and closed the door behind her. "Captain?" She walked past his office and into the living room. There was an entertainment system set up with a big screen TV and a stereo, the source of the music. She looked around, seeing the dining room with a table that could seat ten. She walked into the kitchen that was bigger and nicer than the one she had in her condo. "Captain? Are you here?"

Judy walked back to the living room and saw a closed door. She assumed that was his bedroom. Perhaps he fell asleep? She tapped the door with her fingertips. "Captain?"

The door was not latched so she pushed it inward. She saw the captain lying on his side. She walked over and touched his shoulder.

She leaned closer and smelled alcohol. She pushed his shoulder to rouse him from his sleep. He remained immobile. Now worried, she put her fingertips to his carotid artery. Feeling a pulse, she exhaled with relief. *He passed out. I guess this wasn't meant to be.*

Judy left the bedroom, shutting the door. She looked to see if he had been entertaining before her arrival and saw no evidence.

As she stepped out on the promenade, a uniformed officer nodded and rushed past her to the bridge, nearly knocking her over. She recalled seeing him during the safety drill on deck before the ship left port. He was arguing with another officer and stormed off, shouting in Norwegian. Then on the way to the dining room hoots and hollers drew her eye to a cocktail lounge. There she saw him slide off the bar stool to do one-arm pushups. *Crazy Norwegians!*

Not ready to retire for the night, Judy went from one nightclub to another in search of Rita. She found her at Rancheros salsa dancing with Kevin. She waited until the song was over and waved to her. Rita took Kevin by the arm and came over to her.

"What happened to your date?" Rita asked.

"I found him passed out. So here I am. I guess it wasn't meant to be."

"All right then. Can I get you a drink, Judy? Come join us over at the table. There's a guy who saw you earlier and said he wanted to meet you."

"Would you get me an Old Fashioned? It's a drink that suits us, don't you think?"

"Clever girl. I'll see you at the table. Darling, take her over there and make the introductions, will you please?"

Rita winked at him and wrapped her arm around Judy's shoulder, leading the way.

"It's 'darling' now?" Judy teased.

"Yes, and should I call him shnookums?"

Judy laughed. "I dare you!"

At the table, Rita said, "Richie, this is Judy. Slide over, will you, so she can have a seat?"

Richie got up like a gentleman and extended his hand. When Judy offered hers, he kissed the top of it. "Oh my. We are old fashioned." The men's fragrance he wore was enticing, she thought, citrus and floral like patchouli.

As if on cue, Kevin handed Judy her cocktail. They all laughed and settled in at the booth with a view of the dance floor.

"Can you tell the seniors who've had ballroom dancing lessons?" Rita asked.

"I'd say most, except that man in the Tommy Bahama shirt and white slacks. The way he moves, he's probably an instructor," Judy said, raising her glass in a toast.

Judy had finished half her drink when she saw two large men in suits and the ship's officer she recognized as the one she'd passed on the way to the bridge. "There she is!"

The security men rushed to their table wearing body cams. The man with arms the size of fire hydrants reached for her and said, "Madam, will you come with us? Quietly? We have a few questions we'd like to ask."

"What's this all about?" Kevin demanded.

"It's not your business, sir," the muscle-bound man said.

"I'm not going anywhere until you tell me what this is all about. I have my rights," Judy declared.

Muscle Man leaned in close and in a low voice said, "The captain is dead. You were seen leaving his private quarters. We want to ask you a few questions."

Judy gasped. "He was alive when I left. I found him in his bed passed out."

"Why were you in his private quarters?"

"I was invited. Here, I have proof." Judy pulled the Captain's business card from her evening bag. Muscle Man took it from her and pocketed it. Judy didn't know what to say so she sat there silently, waiting.

"I'm asking you to come with me so we can clear this up," Muscle Man said in a gentler tone.

Judy looked around and noticed other passengers nearby had taken an interest. She decided to cooperate. "All right. I'll answer your questions. Rita, do you mind coming with me?"

Rita looked as though she had been asked to jump into the sea without a life jacket. "I suppose so."

Judy caught the change in Muscle Man's expression. The group walked casually out of the nightclub and were taken to an office that had a door marked *Cruise Personnel Only*.

They took seats around an oak conference table except for the security guards who remained standing.

"Let's start from the beginning. What's your name? And tell me how you got this invitation," Muscle Man said indicating the business card he held between his thumb and forefinger.

Judy answered each question, giving him the short version.

"All right. You are free to return to your stateroom, but I ask that you stay onboard when we reach port in the morning. I contacted the FBI so I expect there will be an investigation of the crime scene tomorrow. An agent will want to question you. For now we've secured his stateroom."

"May I ask, how was the captain murdered?"

"Undetermined."

"Is that your way of saying you don't know? Maybe it's alcohol poisoning."

The security detail left along with the officer. Rita and Judy stared at each other and then Judy broke down in tears. Rita hugged her. Judy cried, "I can't believe this. They think I could have murdered him. He was alive when I left. Do I need an attorney?"

"Don't put the cart before the horse. Come on. Let's go back to our room. Have something to drink if you like. We'll sit on our veranda and put this in perspective."

As soon as Rita inserted the key card, Judy rushed past her for the bathroom and got sick. She washed her face, brushed her teeth and exchanged her evening clothes for her nightgown and robe. She drank a bottle of water and felt better for it. Then she picked out a liqueur. She placed ice cubes in a glass, poured Frangelico over it and joined Rita on the veranda.

"Are you all right, Judy?" Rita asked, putting her hand on her friend's shoulder.

"Now I am. I'm glad you're here. I'm hopeful that this mess will be cleared up in the morning. I wonder who would have killed him. I have no reason to."

"That's a good point. Who would have a motive to kill him?" Rita asked, sipping a glass of chardonnay.

The two friends sat in silence, pondering that very question.

Rita said, "I watch a lot of TV and the detectives always look to family first. His ex-wife?"

"I don't know. I assume she's in Norway since they're divorced. Unless she lives in Miami."

"I don't think she'd be on this cruise if they're divorced."

"Unlikely. When I got divorced, I didn't want to be anywhere near that S.O.B," Judy said.

They were quiet again.

"A girlfriend?" Rita asked. "I saw the way Ingrid was looking at him."

"I don't know since I just met him. Possible."

"Too bad we can't get into his stateroom and nose around," Rita said.

"You should know that would definitely be a bad idea," Judy said. "Besides it probably has crime scene tape on it."

"Maybe a friend he had a dispute with?"

Judy finished her drink and said, "I'm not thinking clearly. I'm turning in. Hopefully I'll be able to sleep."

"Good night. I'm going to sit here awhile longer.

After breakfast Saturday, they returned to their stateroom to hearing the telephone ringing. Judy answered the call, "Yes, this is Judy Clark." She saw Rita looking at her with concern. "Give me a few minutes and I'll see you there."

Putting the receiver in the cradle, Judy said, "That was the special agent. He wants to talk to me now. You don't have to wait for me. Go shopping in the Straw Market. I'll find you there."

"Are you worried?"

"Yes, but I'm also concerned that there is a murderer on this ship. I hope the FBI can determine who it is, fast."

When Judy approached the office where she had been interviewed before, the door opened and Ingrid exited, her eyes red from crying. She excused herself and rushed past Judy.

In the open doorway stood an imposing man with brown hair graying at the temples. He wore gray slacks and a white FBI golf shirt.

"Mrs. Clark, come in. Have a seat, please. I'm Special Agent Allan Dumont."

Judy sat down and tried to stifle a cough. The agent handed her a bottle of water. She drank and smiled that she could now find her voice. She waited for the questions.

"I know you'll be repeating yourself, but please recount last evening, beginning with dinner."

When she described the dinner table, Dumont wanted to know who else sat at the table and what she thought of the other guests. "I didn't really talk to any of them as my attention was on the captain and my friend Rita."

"Was the captain flirtatious with you?" Dumont asked.

"No, he was a gentleman and that's why I was surprised he handed me his card with the message to meet him in his room. He mentioned he was divorced so I didn't think too much about it. Quite frankly, I was curious. A handsome man like him could have his pick of women, including much younger ones."

"So why you? Did you say anything to him that would prompt him to invite you to his private quarters?"

"Of course not! I told you I was surprised to receive the invitation."

"All right. I'm sorry if I insulted you. Did anyone else know that you decided to go to the captain's stateroom?"

"My friend Rita."

"Describe what happened when you got to the captain's stateroom."

Judy reiterated the same words she used with the security officers.

"Did you notice anything unusual about the stateroom?"

"No." Judy wiped her hands on her slacks. The image of the captain passed out gave her chills, knowing sometime after she'd left he had been murdered.

Judy cleared her throat. "How did the captain die?"

"It appears he was suffocated. We'll know more after the ME examines the body."

"I'd like to take your fingerprints electronically. We'll need them since a tech team is in his stateroom dusting for fingerprints. Do you object?"

"My fingerprints are in the state of Connecticut's database because I was a teacher there."

"Let's just go ahead and take them now. We'll save time this way."

Judy submitted to the fingerprinting process. It was amazingly fast.

Agent Dumont asked for her contact information which he entered into his laptop.

"You're free to go for now. I'll be in touch. Here's my contact information if you have any questions or you think of something that may help us in the investigation," Dumont said, handing her his business card.

Judy returned to her stateroom so she could take an ibuprofen and lie down. She had a headache that felt like her head would split open.

She kicked off her sandals and laid down on the bed. Her mind flooded with images of the captain. She wondered if he woke up when his air was cut off. Feeling more upset, she got up and grabbed her purse and sunhat to look for Rita in the Straw Market. The distraction would do her good, headache be damned.

Judy found Rita bargaining with a vendor for a straw tote bag. After the purchase was complete, Judy called out to Rita.

"That's a colorful tote," Judy commented.

"And a bargain," Rita said. "How did your interview go?"

"Fine. I'm free to come and go. But when we get back to the ship, I want to take a tour of the bridge. If I remember correctly there's one scheduled after lunch, at two, I think."

"Don't you think they'll cancel it, considering there's an investigation?"

"You're probably right. But I want to go see anyway."

"Why?"

"Just a hunch."

After a morning of shopping the Straw Market and Bay Street, they returned to the ship where they had lunch by the pool. Rita and Judy both had the conch fritters followed by grilled red snapper, coleslaw and French fries. They both drank Kalik, the beer of the Bahamas.

They were joined by Richie and Kevin who demanded every detail of Judy's interrogation. The men invited them to join them to go to Paradise Island, but Judy said they'd meet them there. Judy gave Rita an eye signal reminding her of wanting to visit the bridge.

After the men left, Judy grabbed Rita by the arm. "Let's go."

Rita followed Judy to the bridge where she knocked on the door. They approached it from the port side since the starboard side was crime scene taped. A uniformed officer came to the door. "May I help you?"

"Yes, we're here for the tour of the bridge," Judy announced.

"I'm sorry, ladies. It's been canceled for security reasons."

"Okay, but can I look inside from here?"

The officer moved to one side. The bridge was a large room with windows offering unobstructed views of the sea. There were control panels, computers and radar screens to aid in navigation. She was disappointed not to see a ship's wheel like one on a sailboat.

"That door over there, where does it lead?" Judy asked, pointing to the door at the rear of the bridge.

"That's the captain's private quarters," the officer said.

"Do you take shifts when you're at sea?" Judy asked.

"Yes, we do."

"Okay, we won't bother you any longer," Judy said. She turned to Rita. "Come on, I have an idea."

Judy called Agent Dumont from the house phone. "Mr. Dumont, you may have already thought of this, but there's a way to get into the captain's private quarters from the bridge. Have you looked into the officer I saw last night when I left the captain's stateroom?"

"Not yet, but I have requested all the crew's personnel files. Are you thinking he may have a motive?"

"My husband was in upper management and he often mentioned that employees would be rather upset if they didn't get a favorable review or a promotion. I would guess the captain is his supervisor."

"Good point. I'll check my computer to see if the files came in. Thank you for calling. Oh, please keep this to yourself."

When Judy hung up the phone, Rita said, "I think you missed your calling, Miss Marple."

"What are you talking about?"

"Agatha Christie's sleuth."

"It's my intuition. And a vivid imagination, I'm told by my ex."

"Let's go to Paradise Island while there's still time. The ship departs at five o'clock. We need to be back before then."

They took a taxi to Paradise Island and found Richie and Kevin waiting by the pool.

"You finally made it. Let's go see the marine life exhibits. It got great reviews," Kevin said.

Rita and Judy marveled at the number of sharks.

"It certainly puts Mystic Aquarium to shame," Judy said, referring to the aquarium in Connecticut.

The two couples continued to spend time together back on the ship. Sunday they spent the day at the cruise line's private Bahama island, Bluebeard's Cay. They rented a cabana so they could enjoy a respite from the hot sun reflecting off the white sugar sand and the brilliant aquamarine water. Overhead fans and the balmy breeze kept them comfortable.

When Judy and Rita returned to their stateroom, they saw the telephone light indicating a message had been left. The friends stood looking at each other wondering who should pick up the phone. Judy lifted her eyebrows. Rita smiled with her approval.

Judy listened. "It's Agent Dumont. I'll return his call."

Judy watched Rita pace the floor as she listened to the fed. "So you arrested him?"

Judy bobbed her to indicate to Rita the answer was yes. "Oh, don't mention it, Mr. Dumont." She paused. "Yes, I can be available if need be." Judy smiled and gave the thumbs up sign. "Okay, thank you for letting me know."

Judy hung up the phone and let out a sigh. "Well, that's amazing."

"Tell me. I can't stand the suspense."

Judy waited and took a deep breath. "It turns out the first officer, the man I saw when I left the captain's quarters, received a review from the captain that was not favorable, therefore denying him a promotion."

"And so he killed him?"

"Apparently. But that's for a jury to decide. He's been arrested so he'll be tried in a court."

Rita sat down on the edge of the bed. "What kind of man would kill because he didn't get what he wanted?"

"An unbalanced one, I would say."

* * *

Lynn Sheft spent her long career as a senior copywriter and creative director for South Florida's leading advertising agencies for which she won numerous awards for creative excellence, including the coveted CLIO. Lynn also freelanced for the many cruise lines headquartered in South Florida, including Pearl, Orient, Premier, Royal Caribbean, NCL, and Carnival. She also worked for Florida's leading newspapers, the *Sun-Sentinel* and the *Miami Herald.*

THE GHOST WHO READ THE NEWSPAPER
by Vicki Weisfeld

Nuggets of snow salted the ground around the garage, and the heavy clouds of a Connecticut winter promised more to come—too much more, for my taste. I'd suggested to my employer, J. Middleton Dulcey, that we hire a closed carriage and pair of horses at the livery stable for the drive from New Haven to Boston, but he'd hear no misgivings about the fortitude of his new Model T.

"No, my boy, Mr. Ford's product will carry us there in safety and comfort." He backed the Ford onto the street and we headed away. The hundred-sixty mile trip would require about four hours in fine weather, but we'd had a late start, due to some business of Mr. Dulcey's, and it would be well after dark before we could expect to arrive.

Alas, my trepidation about the weather proved correct. Before we even reached Hartford, great gouts of snow poured down, obscuring the road, and I was kept busy with the new electric windshield cleaners, battling with only moderate success against the blizzard and required frequent attention. Past Hartford, we were the only car on the road, and the tracks of the vehicles that had preceded us were filling rapidly, so that Mr. Dulcey found the driving difficult. He peered into a gloom barely dispelled by our headlamps, trying to make sure we followed the actual road and were not steering into a ditch or worse.

A solid shape flew across our path, startling us both. "What was that!" he exclaimed.

"I believe it was a deer, and there may be more of them."

"That was no deer. It was enormous!"

Although we had been proceeding quite slowly, he slowed more. Then the lamps revealed the forms of perhaps a dozen white-tailed deer ahead of us, stalled in the process of crossing the road. They now stood stock still, trying to work out how two bright moons had come to earth and were now rolling toward them. Mr. Dulcey sounded our Klaxon, and they ran, leaping, away. The road now was as startlingly empty of creatures as it had been filled a moment before.

I noted Mr. Dulcey's hunched shoulders, head thrust forward, eyes straining, and it occurred to me that we would not—we should not—complete our journey tonight. "I'm awfully hungry," I suggested.

Once I'd had the thought, the desire for someplace warm and welcoming ballooned in my thoughts. At my feet was a small carpetbag containing my favorite book, and I looked forward to a satisfying read before sleep. *The Adventures of Sherlock Holmes* had been a companion of years, and I fancied Mr. Dulcey bore some resemblance to Holmes—not in personality, because my employer was an amiable, gregarious man, but in his determination to get to the bottom of things. It was a small, if immodest, leap to see myself, his secretary, as a sort of American Dr. Watson.

"You young people," Mr. Dulcey said. "No staying power." He wisely kept the car in the center of the space between the trees that loomed on either side of us, as there was no knowing where the actual road lay, and it was surely for the best that we met no other vehicle.

At last, I said, "What's that sign ahead? Does it say 'INN'? It looks to be pointing to the right."

"Inn? I don't think so. Not out here in the middle of nowhere." But he regarded the sign longingly too. The weight of the snow stuck to its surface became too much and a clump slid off. INN, for certain.

"I have an idea," he said. "Let's investigate this place. We can eat dinner, have a good night's rest, and make an early start in the morning."

"Yes, let's." I nudged the bag containing my precious book.

He threaded the Ford into a narrow gap between two stands of trees that we presumed was the side road. As it turned out, the inn was no more than a mile distant, yet the blizzard was so fierce and our progress so snaillike, tense minutes elapsed before we saw its lights. Our optimism was rewarded when at last the well-lit, welcoming façade appeared. So grateful were we, I do believe we would have gladly trudged the remaining distance on foot, wearing our city shoes, had it been necessary.

A young man met us under a portico bearing a rustic sign reading "Old Blackwood Inn." The snow had been shoveled away, and before we could properly take in the fact that we had arrived, he unloaded our bags and deposited them inside. He returned with a large broom and began knocking the snow off the car.

"Where should I park my vehicle?" Mr. Dulcey asked.

"I'll do it. You go inside and get warm. Dinner's up."

"I don't know—" It wasn't like Mr. Dulcey to entrust his car to a total stranger, especially one not even shaving yet.

"I'll put it right in that shed over there." He winked at me and pointed. Alongside the shed was a commodious barn, one door standing open.

Mr. Dulcey remained doubtful. "The shed looks—" He would have said "dilapidated," I believe, but was reluctant to offend this minion of our new hosts. "What about the barn?"

"Barn's full of horses," the boy said. "Everyone else came by carriage."

"Did you say dinner is ready?" I asked.

That got us moving again and, realistically, we had no choice about any of this. Nor, for that matter, what came after.

Dinner was delicious in proportion to how welcome it was. Our fellow diners—for the inn was indeed full—comprised two families, a newly married couple, several traveling salesmen, and us. That is, fifteen guests in all.

The two families retired early, and the newlyweds soon followed. The men, and I boyishly counted myself among them, retired to the lounge and arranged ourselves around the large open fireplace. Soon the innkeeper, Mr. Meese, joined us, bringing several bottles of port. I was allowed one glass. The warmth of the fire, the fumes of the wine, the sweet smell of pipe tobacco, all lulled me into a pleasant frame of mind, free of the numbing cold and the terror of the road.

I reflected on how lucky I was to have acquired my position as Mr. Dulcey's secretary and factotum. Born in 1902, I had been too young to fight in the Great War and could not help feeling as if I'd missed out. (That alone tells you how inexperienced I was.) My mother moved our family to her father's country home during the influenza epidemic, and while I was grateful we were spared that catastrophe, still we were isolated from society and the bustle of New Haven for what seemed an interminable period. The only recompense in our self-quarantine was my grandfather's extensive library. There I pursued my education in fits and starts as different interests overtook me.

It was grandfather who learned of Mr. Dulcey's desire for an assistant and recommended me to him. In the summer of 1920 I took up the post and, six months later, found myself at the Old Blackwood Inn, roasting beside the best fire in northern Connecticut. Half-listening to the conversation of the men, I thought, as I frequently did, that every young man should have a sojourn with a Mr. Dulcey. He taught me many things, but most important, how to wring adventure out of life events of every sort.

Reflecting on my good fortune, I must have dozed, because I was startled awake by a log noisily shifting position in the fire. The landlord stood up to poke the blaze, and I saw the lounge had emptied, except for Mr. Dulcey, landlord Meese, and me. Seeing I was awake, Mr. Dulcey said, "Our host here has been telling me we have the best room in the house."

I sat up at this unexpected intelligence. We were, after all, last to arrive.

"Yes indeed," Mr. Meese said. "You have the room of the Old Gentleman."

"Who?" I asked, a bit suspicious, because Mr. Dulcey was not above pulling a joke on me, and this sounded like it might be one.

"We don't know who he is," the landlord said, "but he's haunted this place, gone fifty years now. The woman who sold my wife and me the inn two summers ago warned about making too many changes to your room."

I glanced at Mr. Dulcey. This sounded to me like an excuse for what might be the poor condition of our quarters. He continued to study the fire benignly.

"There's a ghost?" I rubbed my tired eyes.

"Yes. He's why we don't use that room much. Not that everyone who stays there sees him, but he's frightened several of our guests. I usually don't tell people about him, especially the women, so as not to plant the suggestion, but Mr. Dulcey seems a paragon of common sense and asked about the inn's history, so I did mention it."

"What is your history?" I asked. "Was it always the Old Blackwood Inn?"

"Since the day it opened in 1801. Your room is in the original part of the Inn, which offered only a few rooms back then, but did a big business in food and drink, being the only stopping place along this road for twenty miles or more. In the 1880s, the owners expanded, added the second story, and the Old Blackwood became more or less as you see it today.

"Mrs. Meese and I improved the plumbing—a big investment, but it's the way of the future, she says—and refurbished the public rooms downstairs."

"They are exceedingly comfortable," Mr. Dulcey said. "But please tell us about your ghost. How does the Old Gentleman manifest?"

The landlord paced in front of the fire. "People awaken in the night and see a man sitting on the end of the bed, reading a newspaper. He scans the pages and turns them, paying no attention to the bed's occupants. In the morning, he and the newspaper are gone, though my guests say there is a slight indentation at the foot of the bed where he sat. He wears a stovepipe hat and, from their descriptions, I fancy he looks rather like President Lincoln."

"Did the President ever stay here?" I asked.

"Not to my knowledge. In fact, I'm sure not," the landlord said. "The previous owners were all sharp businessmen, especially Charity Farthington, who owned the inn the longest, and she would certainly have capitalized on such a visit."

"Well, it's past our bedtime. If that gentleman visits us tonight, he will certainly be welcome." Mr. Dulcey and I left the lounge and made our way to room #3 at the back of the house. He would have the four-poster to himself, and a trundle bed had been brought in for me and placed under the window. My book lay there enticingly, but I was too sleepy for a long session of reading.

"I, for one, am grateful for our landlady's dedication to modern plumbing," I said, crawling under the covers. The room was chilly, but I was still warm from the fire and soon heated the bed like a live warming pan.

"I could not agree more," Mr. Dulcey said, settling into the massive double bed. "I included her in my prayers."

I'd fallen asleep so fervently hoping that we *would* see the Old Gentleman that I scarcely credited my eyes when at some unknowable hour of the night I awoke and did see him, just as the landlord had described, sitting at the foot of Mr. Dulcey's bed, reading the newspaper. I pinched myself to be sure I wasn't dreaming, but then thought, what if I'm dreaming I pinched myself? With difficulty, though the apparition took no notice of my gyrations, I took my arms out of my nightshirt, turned it around backwards, and stuck my arms through again. If in the morning it was wrong-way-round, I would *know* I had been awake. It would be impossible for me to accomplish that maneuver in my sleep.

As the Old Gentleman continued to read quietly, I eased my feet to the floor. I wanted Mr. Dulcey to see, but he typically woke with such splutter and flutter that I feared the ghost would flee. I approached the wraithlike figure as closely as I dared and discerned that he wasn't exactly transparent, but could be more accurately described as translucent (a distinction I'd learned in one of my grandfather's science books).

I hoped to see his face, which remained indistinct, or some other feature that would lead us to know who he was and why he was there. Alas, although his clothing appeared well-made, it was not distinctive. He wore no signet ring, and when he took out his pocket watch it was of an ordinary type on a fine chain. I feared that checking the time might presage his departure so returned to my cot and lay down. Though gradually suffused with sleep, I watched him through half-closed eyes and woke to a room bright with sunshine. Mr. Dulcey was already awake and dressed.

"You're late abed, my boy," he said. "Sleep well?"

"The ghost—" I stammered. "I saw him. The Old Gentleman."

"Did you now," he said, not prepared to believe I'd done more than dream. "And why is your night dress on backwards?"

I told him the whole story, and, before the others came down for breakfast, we had a whispered conversation with the landlord. They required me to recite my experience down to every detail. It was clear the man's uncertain features and unremarkable dress would shed little light on the mystery. However, I possessed an element of information I had totally disregarded: the newspaper.

I mentioned that the newspaper's masthead was the *Hartford Daily Courant*.

"Interesting," said Mr. Dulcey. He tried to mask his excitement, probably to keep from scattering my vague memories. "Did you happen to notice any headlines?"

"Yes, I did! A long story about the Battle of Gettysburg took up almost the whole front page. Not President Lincoln's speech, but the battle itself. The headline was something like 'Turning Point of War!! Lee Routed!'"

Mr. Dulcey addressed Mr. Meese. "Could your shade have stopped here for the night on his way from Hartford to Boston and brought the newspaper with him? Or did you supply newspapers in the lounge?"

"Either one, I suppose," the landlord said, scratching his head.

"This may narrow down the time of his visit," Mr. Dulcey said. "You wouldn't have records from that era, I suppose? It was nearly sixty years ago."

"Surely we do. Back to the beginning of the inn's existence. They're in the attic along with unclaimed luggage, broken chairs, and a farrago of stuff my wife and I haven't bothered to sort through."

"Well, would you mind...?"

A clatter of children's feet on the stairs led the innkeeper to say, "Certainly, right after breakfast."

We then sat down to the longest meal in the history of mankind.

Mrs. Meese wasn't best pleased that we planned to root around in the attic. Probably she worried we'd kick up a lot of dust and make a mess and, if that was her concern, it was well founded, as that is exactly what happened.

"What is it you're looking for?" she asked.

"Clues, my dear," her husband said.

"Clues to the murders?" She crossed her arms, frowning.

This took Mr. Dulcey and me quite by surprise, and Mr. Meese reddened. "We haven't discussed that, Sarah," he said.

Mr. Dulcey would not be satisfied without the whole story now, though getting it might take some time. He mollified Mrs. Meese by saying we would happily stay another night at least, enjoying her hospitality. True, we didn't have a choice, as the reports on road conditions that we received during breakfast suggested our departure would be delayed a day at least. Several parties who'd arrived in horse-drawn carriages or on horseback were planning to leave, however, and later that morning did so.

At last we climbed the three set of stairs that led us to a low-ceiling space. Even I could barely stand and only under the center beam. Through tiny windows at floor level, beams of sunlight shot across the floor, the effect dizzying in its alternating bands of darkness and light. We crept around like Victor Hugo's hunchback and finally perched on several abandoned portmanteau.

Mr. Dulcey cleared his throat. "Now, Meese, what's this about murders? And are they connected to our Old Gentleman?" His tone clearly would not brook evasion.

"I apologize for not telling you the whole story at the outset. I didn't want to alarm you. You see, not only is the room you're occupying the place where the Old Gentleman appears, it also has been the scene of two mysterious deaths. Mrs. Meese rather exaggerated in calling them 'murders,' as murder was never proven."

Mr. Dulcey waited, his gaze fixed on the landlord, who stood up, wanting to pace, perhaps, bumped his head, and sat down again. "As I said, the room you occupy is not often used, perhaps only one or two nights each month. That apparently was the practice of the previous owners as well. Although every report of the ghost that I know of paints him as a nonthreatening character, both these mysterious deaths occurred *after* sightings of the ghost began."

"And when was that?"

"Right in the middle of the Civil War, when the whole country was full of upset." He combed his mustache with his fingers.

"Perhaps around 1863?" I asked. "That would correspond to the date of the newspaper I saw."

He nodded. "Of course, he may have appeared even earlier, if the occupants of the room were sound sleepers, or thought they had a strange dream, or for some reason didn't report it."

"And the deaths?" Mr. Dulcey pressed.

"The first was of a gentlewoman who was a guest here for several nights in January 1875. She was a Custis and some relation to the Custis family of Virginia—Robert E. Lee's in-laws, you know. She left a half-finished letter on the desk in that room. I was told the letter was full of pro-Confederacy rhetoric and virulent comments about 'the damned Yankees.'" He shook his head.

"How did she die?"

"As I say, that was a mystery. The doctor who examined the body apparently came to no conclusion. Her body was unmarked, he found no weapon or evidence of poison, and the other guests and staff heard or saw nothing amiss. There were no police investigators way out here in those days. Just the coroner's jury, and those worthies deemed Miss Custis's demise as 'death by misadventure.' That was the end of it."

I puzzled over this scanty information. "Is it possible she was in the middle of writing this anti-Union letter, saw the ghost who looked like President Lincoln, and died of fright?"

"A nice theory, my boy," Mr. Dulcey said. "Of course we'll never know, unless her ghost comes back too and tells us!" He guffawed. "And the other death?"

"That one was nearer our time. In 1892, Mr. Jasper Samm from Baltimore occupied the room—a bit of a rarity by then, after all that had occurred.

But the inn was full, and the innkeeper gave him the room. He barely spoke to the other guests and made little impression on them. When he did not appear for breakfast—I heard this second-hand, you understand—the innkeeper was full of foreboding as she approached the door. She found Mr. Samm lying on his back, his face livid, hands clutching his throat, eyes wide open, as if—"

"As if he had just seen a ghost?" I asked.

Mr. Meese pondered this a moment. "Perhaps. Except that the coroner found wedged in his throat his own watch chain. The watch was on the table next to the bed."

"How in the world?" Mr. Dulcey asked.

"You know how some people attach small trinkets to the chain—masonic emblems or the like? Hung on Mr. Samm's chain was a gold-and-enamel replica of the stars and bars, the Confederate battle flag. He choked on it."

Mr. Dulcey looked shocked, and I'm sure I did too. "And what was the coroner's verdict?" he asked.

"Suicide, though I'm told everyone involved thought it a highly unsatisfactory outcome. Yet it was equally hard to conceive how such a tragedy could have come about by accident."

"*Was* he a Confederate?" Mr. Dulcey asked. (Meanwhile, I was triply grateful for my grandfather's service in the Massachusetts Volunteers Second Battalion of Cavalry.)

"It turns out he was. His family had his body shipped back to them in Charleston. You can bet use of the room stopped altogether after that."

Mr. Dulcey's eyebrows asked the next question. "I know, I know," said Meese. "Though, in a storm like the one yesterday, we would have made up pallets on the floor of the lounge if we needed to. And, until the young man saw the ghost last night, no one had seen the Old Gentleman in quite a while, and..."

"Don't apologize!" Mr. Dulcey said. "We are delighted to be part of your adventure! I believe my young friend is correct, and what scanty evidence we have regarding the ghost's identity points to a connection with the Civil War."

"And the Union," I said.

"Let's suppose, for argument's sake, that he's reading a newspaper from near the time he was a guest here. Do you have the inn's records from July 1863, to coincide with the Gettysburg battle? Of course, newspapers covering such a momentous event might have been kept a while, but it seems a good starting point."

After a great deal of looking and pawing and coughing over dusty old volumes, Mr. Meese came up with the guest register from July 1863, and we crowded around, a beam of sunlight offering ample illumination. Perhaps it was the fault of the war, but trade at The Old Blackwood Inn was surprisingly thin that month. Before long, we found several entries we thought promising, including "Calvin Jefferson Haekelmann, Capitol Avenue, Hartford." A penciled annotation read "tailor."

"Unusual name," Mr. Dulcey commented. "And a tailor."

"That could explain the manner of his dress," I said. "Good quality, but sober. Nothing flashy." Meese and Mr. Dulcey frowned at me. "As far as I could tell. In the dark," I amended, realizing I was speaking about a being who had been almost transparent.

From another box, Mr. Meese withdrew a set of ledgers, examining their flyleafs before selecting one. "Now that we have a few candidates, this will tell us what they paid for their rooms." He turned a few pages, and we reviewed the details about the likely guests, none of them noteworthy.

"Look-a-here! Haekelmann arrived July 1 and, yes, indeed, he was given room #3. He apparently kept it several days, but there's no record of payment." He pointed to the lone blank on that page in the "amount tendered" column.

"How could that happen?" Mr. Dulcey asked.

"I suppose someone could have neglected to note the settling of his account," Mr. Meese said, tipping the ledger toward the light, "though these entries were written by Charity Farthington, the inn's previous owner back one. She was a stickler."

"If he died here, would not his bill have been—I don't know the term—voided?" I asked.

"Perhaps," Mr. Meese said, "especially since the register indicates he was alone. And if Charity couldn't ask the family to settle the debt..." He turned over the sheet. "Oh. Here is a note, again in her script: 'Died July 7, 1863. Balance due assigned to Bad Debt. I'd wager that pained her."

"Was there a coroner's inquest?"

"I never heard about one. Haekelmann's death may have died from what we call 'natural causes.'"

"Does your record say whether anyone claimed the body?" Mr. Dulcey asked.

Meese frowned over the page. "No, but Charity's diaries are around somewhere. Perhaps she recorded it." Again a dusty search ensued. When we found the correct diary, Mr. Meese read out a lengthy note describing her unsuccessful efforts to locate family or any business partner, and, it being summer, the urgency of concluding the business. Before too many days passed, for lack of an alternative, Mr. Haekelmann was buried in the cemetery of the nearest town.

"What about his possessions?" Mr. Dulcey asked.

"Nothing about that."

I glanced around the attic at the collection of abandoned suitcases, baggage, and odd-shaped parcels that had accumulated for more than a century. "Your guests forget a lot," I said.

"Most times we know where to forward their belongings. This is just remnants."

I crouched down to look at the cases, each with a paper label tied to it with date and guest's name. Working in concentric circles away from the ladder was a trip back in time. When I reached the 1860s, I studied the labels carefully. Mr. Dulcey and Mr. Meese were content to let me do this on my own, to grind dust into the knees of my trousers and scrape the shine off my boots.

I believe they thought the effort would be fruitless, but my exclamation startled them into attention. "C.J. Haekelmann, July 1863." I picked up the heavy case and carried it to Mr. Dulcey.

"Shall we open it?"

"The owner won't complain," Mr. Meese said drily.

Inside were several shirts and sets of underwear, neatly folded, shaving utensils and hair grooming items, and a leather-bound notebook. It listed appointments with Boston cloth wholesalers for Thursday, July 9, and Friday, July 10—appointments Mr. Haekelmann never kept. The letters confirming those appointments were tucked into the back of the notebook. They discussed the tailor's work producing uniforms for the Union Army.

"Aha!" said Mr. Dulcey. From the bottom of the bag, he lifted out the *Hartford Daily Courant* from July 5, 1863. The headlines identified it as the very edition I'd seen in the Old Gentleman's hands. "Shall we get out of this dust and open it up downstairs? Perhaps we can deduce what the Old Gentleman has been reading all these years."

I suspect we were all feeling a little gritty and in need of a brushing, so we happily agreed to Mr. Dulcey's suggestion.

We carefully spread the newspaper on the big dining table, each of us taking a few sheets. It was brittle and yellowed and smelled of age. Unfortunately, it was I who made the awful discovery. A story about the 14th Connecticut Volunteer Infantry Regiment ended with a list of the regiment's Hartford men who had died at Gettysburg. Among them were three young men named Haekelmann: Calvin, Jr., James, and William.

We three crowded around to read the story through several times. We silently agreed this was the awful news that killed their father. Finally, Mr. Dulcey quietly folded the paper and carried it to our room.

When spring came, Mr. Dulcey proposed a driving trip to Gettysburg, to which I gladly assented. We'd learned a great deal about the 14th Connecticut Volunteers over the winter, including their nickname, "The Nutmeg Regiment." As we stood on Cemetery Hill where the 14th helped repulse Pickett's charge, Mr. Dulcey picked up three small white stones.

A few weeks later, we made a return visit to the Old Blackwood Inn, in much better weather conditions than our previous visit, occupying our old room, #3. Before we went to bed that night, Mr. Dulcey pulled out of his bag one of our books about Gettysburg and a large box. In the box was a set of toy soldiers, outfitted in the blue and gray of the Civil War. We spent some time setting them up according to the maps in our book and using several bunched up green napkins cadged from the dining room for our battlefield.

We went to bed not knowing what to expect, really.

"Could this be risky? Might the ghost think we are baiting him?" I asked.

"I highly doubt that," Mr. Dulcey said. "Perhaps 'seeing' the tragedy in this way will put his mind at ease. We're demonstrating that we recognize his distress and its cause."

I struggled to stay awake, but it was a struggle I lost. When morning arrived, Mr. Dulcey stood, fists on hips, scanning our makeshift scene. "It's just as we left it!" I said, disappointed.

"Not quite." He pointed. Three blue soldiers lay on their sides, surrounded by men in firing position. "Not quite."

Later that day, Mr. Dulcey persuaded the landlord to accompany us to the town cemetery. It took some looking and the help of one of the gravediggers, but we found Mr. Haekelmann's unmarked grave, identified only by a number stamped on a tin disc. Mr. Dulcey took the three fallen toy soldiers and the three stones from the battlefield and laid them where he thought Mr. Haekelmann's heart might be. It was a solemn moment. I recited the *Gettysburg Address*, an inspiring speech Mr. Haekelmann would never have heard.

During the years I remained in Mr. Dulcey's employ, we stayed at the Old Blackwood numerous times, always in Room #3. After Mrs. Meese painted it and made fresh curtains, it became a charming room, though its chief charm for me, the nocturnal visits by the Old Gentleman, were no more.

* * *

Vicki Weisfeld's short stories have appeared in *Sherlock Holmes Mystery*

Magazine and *Ellery Queen Mystery Magazine*; "Breadcrumbs" (*Betty Fedora,* Issue 3) won a 2017 Derringer Award. Find her in the anthologies *Busted: Arresting Stories from the Beat* from Level Best Books, *Passport to Murder, Best Laid Plans,* and *Quoth the Raven.* Online: www.vweisfeld.com; book reviews at the UK website crimefictionlover.com.

THE SPICE OF LIFE
by Tiger Wiseman

Sunday lunch at the parsonage proceeded as usual. The Reverend Peter Willis ate with gusto, pausing only to reiterate the finer points of that morning's lengthy sermon.

"Such a shame Melissa Fenton didn't attend services this morning," he said, helping himself to another roasted potato. "She would have benefitted from my message, don't you think?"

His wife, Lillian, agreed, also as usual. She knew any other response would lead to a lengthy dissertation on the superior intellect of the male species.

The reverend sipped from his wine glass and then took up his soliloquy where he'd left off. "I've spoken to Jonah about counseling, but Melissa seems reluctant.He really should insist. I'll speak to him again. It's a man's God-given duty to lead his wife in her daily life, to correct mistakes, and make sure she avoids the temptation to be slovenly or lazy. I've always tried to act accordingly and look at how happy we are."

Lillian barely managed not to choke on her roll. She swallowed some water before hazarding an opinion. "Not everyone is like us, Peter. Maybe they've just grown apart. It's been known to happen after many, many years of marriage."

"Any marriage can be saved, and it is a husband's—and a wife's—duty to try until they succeed."

"It was different when they were young." She added some carrots to her plate before elaborating. "Twenty-five years ago, I had them both in my senior chemistry class. They were Naughton's own Romeo and Juliet, or

Elizabeth and Darcy, so deep in love that if you found one, the other was never far away."

"Really," her husband said around a mouthful. "I'm afraid I have to lay the blame on Jonah for not taking a firmer hand. He assures me he does his best, reminding Melissa when she falls short, but she doesn't appear to remember, or maybe care. As I said this morning, the husband is the head of the household and he should always be a wife's first priority. That's why the bride agrees to love, honor and obey, while the husband promises to cherish and support. To that end, a wife should always be groomed and, when her husband comes home from work, she must exert herself to make him comfortable. Have him lean back in a comfortable chair or suggest he lie down in the bedroom to rest before dinner, as I do. Have a cool or warm drink ready for him. Arrange his pillow and offer to take off his shoes. Speak in a low, soft, soothing and pleasant voice. Allow him to relax and unwind."

Lillian allowed the reverend's words to wash over her without listening. She'd heard it all before at the morning service, and on many other occasions. Instead, she turned her mind back to 1994, when she was still single and excited about sharing her enthusiasm for science with her students—before she married the reverend and, at his insistence, gave up her career to concentrate on him and the parish. She clearly remembered seventeen-year-old Melissa as a petite, curvy brunette with a quick laugh and a figure all the girls coveted, and Jonah—who at that age had a full head of curly black hair and played full-back on the high school football team—as a randy young man who couldn't resist Melissa, as evidenced by her positive pregnancy test at the end of their senior year, followed by their quickie wedding.

Realizing her husband had stopped talking, Lillian passed him the meat platter while she gathered her wits and decided what to say. "Their marriage hasn't been easy. They lost their first child. That's been known to break up a couple, but they stayed together," she said, adding "although I can't imagine why" in her own head.

"Obviously something must be working in that marriage if it's lasted this long. I can only hope that their marriage is a lot like ours, with the husband taking the lead, serving as teacher and mentor and the wife following his sage tutelage. Jonah agreed to come for one-on-one counseling sessions to help him better manage his relationship and the disappointments he has had to endure. I'm just amazed I had to make the first move. He should have approached me on his own. Did you speak to Melissa as I asked? Offer to help her improve in her wifely duties?"

"Yes, dear, I did. She agreed to meet me for coffee next Thursday, though, she does not seem to be very enamored of her husband. Maybe this is one marriage that can't be saved."

"As they say, love moves in mysterious ways, Lillian. Take strength from my wisdom and we will have those two cooing again. Are there more rolls?"

"They also say that 'No one can hate you more than someone who used to love you'," the reverend's wife muttered under her breath as she stood up to replenish the bread basket.

"And bring back my antacid pill when you come. I hope you remembered to refill my prescription. It's not as if you have anything more important to do than take care of your husband, now is there?"

Melissa Stark Fenton rummaged through the crate of jumbled utensils in the Blue Bell Diner's cramped kitchen. As she sorted through peelers, spatulas, and other kitchen gadgets, she glanced up at the greasy calendar on the wall: May 30. In that moment, her mind flashed back twenty-five years, back to the same day in 1994: graduation day. It was a lifetime ago, she thought. No, it was two lifetimes ago. She remembered anticipating a day filled with friends, fun, and gifts. Her parents had hinted at a new car and she hoped it was the red Mitsubishi 3000GT she'd been dropping clues about all year. The only cloud in her day had been the queasiness in her stomach, but she'd quickly forgotten that in the revelry of champagne, vodka and other stuff at the post-graduation party. She'd gotten pretty wasted, she remembered with a smile; so had Jonah, but that was nothing new. Liquor always made everything so much more fun. Not to mention that double batch of marijuana brownies Jonah had brought. Lord, it had been great to be young and carefree. To have a whole summer before them until they both took off for the Culinary Institute of America, her to study culinary skills, him to master pastry and baking.

All these years later, she could still remember his words that night: "First it's culinary school and then a *stage,* an apprenticeship, in New York, London, or Paris. Ten years from now, you'll be executive chef at The Ritz and I'll be head *patissier,* creating pastry masterpieces at Le Bernardin. We're going to set the culinary world on fire."

"Does this look like The Ritz?" she asked the empty diner kitchen before continuing her rummage through the box and returning to her reminiscences.

Tossing aside a lemon zester, Melissa's thoughts jumped to the month after graduation—June 30th, to be exact—when she'd sucked in her breath and growing waistline as her mother zipped closed the hastily purchased wedding gown. Everything about the wedding had been chosen, booked, and purchased in haste. You can only pass off a "preemie" for just so long. At that point, she was just grateful that Jonah had, reluctantly, given up his place and scholarship at the CIA to seek employment and provide for their once-impending family. With no degree, he'd settled for an entry-level job at a local wholesale bakery.

By August, she'd written all the wedding thank-you notes and lost the baby. She'd been a little relieved when she miscarried. She suspected Jonah had been too. But by then it was too late to reclaim their scholarships. "Now what?" she'd wondered but made no attempt to plan out an alternative future. Nor did she stop eating for two despite Jonah's comments about whales and elephants. She always felt hungry, and since she couldn't fill her life with her dreams, she filled her stomach instead.

With no solid plan, Melissa took the work she could find. While Jonah slogged on at Kellers, "home of Connecticut's best rolls," Melissa moved through the kitchens of various small, undistinguished eateries, starting as a kitchen assistant and moving up through the ranks to prep cook, cook, and finally chef, albeit of a local diner. None of the places she worked offered fancy training like *saucier, rotisseur,* or *friturier.* If something needed saucing, roasting, or frying, she did it. And if the prep guy didn't show, she peeled the vegetables alongside the dish boy.

"Gotcha," Melissa said as she extricated a meat tenderizer from the crate. Anger and disappointment fueled her energy as she held the tenderizer over a thick slab of tough beef. Then she pressed down with all her might and, as the 48 needle-like blades punctured the flesh, she thought of Jonah's sunburnt chest and smiled. She continued to mindlessly perforate the meat over and over, allowing her thoughts to float back over the years.

At first, the teenaged newly-weds muddled on together in a state of confused love. They talked about trying to get pregnant again, about opening their own restaurant in town, or maybe moving somewhere else and starting over. They celebrated their anniversary with a jointly-prepared culinary feast for two and fancy cocktails, a tradition they vowed to repeat until "the end of time."

That was the first year. By their third anniversary, right after Melissa got her first promotion, she and Jonah had settled into a routine and separate bedrooms. Although they had grandiose ideas, tenacity and planning did not feature in their combined gene pool. Small disappointments escalated into insults ("If your butt gets any bigger, we're going to have to install double doors"; "I'm not saying you're going bald, but at this rate you'll find Waldo before you find your hairline") and they lived as roommates more than husband and wife. Resentment grew with each passing year, but on their meager salaries neither could afford to support themselves alone much less pay potential spousal support, so they trundled on under the same roof.

Melissa took up smoking in an (unsuccessful) attempt to curb her appetite and Jonah tried Rogaine, but neither yielded success. Regular sex dwindled to semi-annual booty calls. Jonah had several short-lived affairs that he kept as well hidden as his receding hairline, but Melissa remained true to their vows—if you didn't count that one afternoon with the substitute UPS guy, the one with the cute butt and dreamy eyes. In year eight of their marriage, Melissa decided her life would be happier—and maybe healthier—without her balding Lothario, but after consulting a divorce lawyer she realized that not only would she lose the house she loved if they divorced, but she also could not afford the rents in Fairfield County, Connecticut—or even her attorney himself. Her only consolation came from knowing Jonah could not afford a divorce or the house either. And his lady loves all dropped him like a hot potato when they found out he'd lied about being a master pastry chef.

Life as they knew it went on…and on. Jonah blamed Melissa for getting pregnant (glossing over his part in the event), costing him his CIA pastry arts degree and therefore his destiny of winning, at a minimum, a James Beard award. She blamed him for the pregnancy, her lost figure, the ignominy of "slinging hash" for a living, and not supporting her in the style she'd imagined. She mocked his hair loss with ever increasing venom, while he zeroed in on her weight. Romeo and Juliet had become Petruchio and Katherine.

By year ten, Melissa had switched to e-cigarettes to tame her nicotine cravings—smoking had failed as a diet aid, but she was now addicted to nicotine and had expanded to size 18 pants. Jonah, who had no weight issues and still smoked a pack a day, took to wearing a jaunty cap as his receding hairline could no longer be hidden with a comb-over. Insults became daily events, nastier with every passing year ("Good thing you don't play basketball—your hairline would always be making a back-court violation"; "You just got a notice from DMV—they want you to install a backing-up alarm on your butt.") Still, they remained together out of inertia and economic need, and continued their one and only nod to matrimonial harmony: an annual, one-day anniversary truce during which they prepared, and shared, a special meal—special not only for the food but for the lack of barbs and putdowns. By mutual consent, they stuck to safe topics like a dissection of the latest episode of *Top Chef* and how they could out-cook/bake any of the on-screen chefs. Melissa never mentioned her dreams of a solo life. Or the new, potentially lethal, kitchen utensils she'd discovered over the past twelve months.

While she cooked their celebratory meal each June, Jonah mixed up a special cocktail and baked a fancy dessert. The first year it was a chocolate martini, and a bittersweet chocolate soufflé for after the meal; the next, a Celtic Mule and an Irish Tiramisu. For their twentieth, he concocted a vodka-based Nordic Polar Bear along with a traditional, calorie-laden, Swedish Princess Torte.

"Wonder what theme he'll come up with this year?"' Melissa mused, setting aside the sinewy steak she'd now beaten into a semi-pulp, and attacking the next one. He always chose a theme—ingredients, color, ethnicity, or location—but refused to share it with Melissa, leaving her to guess what foods might go well between his offerings. There had been some interesting pairings, like the year he chose a Japanese Umetini cocktail and elaborate mochi, and she cooked Pakistani.

Melissa held up her part of the annual culinary feasts, creating appetizer, entrée, and sometimes salad, as well as hors d'oeuvres to enjoy as they sipped Jonah's latest concoction. This was the one day of the year when she exerted herself to think beyond meatloaf and tacos, and to rekindle a flicker of her teenaged culinary brilliance and enthusiasm. Since she only aimed for excellence once a year, the results were not always flawless, but there had never been a total disaster and Jonah's cocktails tended to dull one's taste buds. The year she scorched the Oysters Rockefeller (and contemplated the relative merits of a corkscrew versus an oyster shucker when applied to a bald head), she'd redeemed herself with a near-flawless Beef Wellington. And if 2012's paella had been a little too well done on the bottom, last year's *mousseline* of salmon with *sauce verte,* followed by rack of lamb with sauce *à l'erable* had left them both sighing with delight. In fact, they'd had to save the baklava until the next day or imperil their digestive systems—and the seams of her size 3X dress.

On June 22nd, with a week until their silver anniversary, Melissa told Jonah she planned to outdo not only her previous culinary efforts, but also his. Jonah accepted her challenge of one-upmanship. He'd always been so competitive.

Just the day before, Melissa had reviewed her innovative menu with her new friend, the reverend's wife, who gave it her full blessing. While Reverend Willis and Jonah thought the women were meeting weekly to scrutinize Melissa's failures as a wife and decide how to correct her shortcomings when they met each week, she and Lillian were actually commiserating. They bonded over coffee, donuts, and mutual vexation with their lot in life.

Melissa was particularly annoyed that Jonah had begun another affair, this time with an older, but well-to-do, photographer. Like his other dalliances, he wasn't hiding it well. Unlike the other ones, he seemed particularly enamored with this woman. Both things had bothered Melissa enough that she'd begun contemplating divorce again, despite the inherent problems with it. But Lillian had helped Melissa see that divorce wasn't the answer. Instead, she should make the most of her upcoming anniversary—a day when she and Jonah were always nice to each other—to try to get her life on the right track.

June 30th finally arrived, and Melissa planned to follow Lillian's advice. So, to Jonah's obvious surprise, Melissa made a celebratory breakfast. "Eggs Benedict," she announced, "and I made a special peppery hollandaise just for you. I'll have mine without sauce—I want to save room for all the tasting I'll be doing today while I tweak our dinner to perfection."

Thanks to the annual truce, Jacob merely smiled. Not an insult, jibe, or veiled threat was uttered. Melissa was enjoying her anniversary already.

As soon as Jonah left for the bakery where he'd prepare his dessert, Melissa rolled up her sleeves and started cooking dinner. She'd chosen a more elaborate menu than usual. They would start with a cream of mushroom soup finished with toasted almonds, earthy Bushmills whiskey, and cream. This would be followed by asparagus and watercress salad with champagne saffron vinaigrette. She'd added a fish course, this year: poached salmon with *mousseline* sauce garnished with cucumber and fresh dill from her own garden. Then a rose water and mint sorbet to cleanse the palate, and finally, the *pièce de résistance*: pan-seared filet mignon topped with foie gras and truffle drizzled with a cognac, Madeira, black pepper, and red wine reduction, served with potatoes Anna, creamed carrots and stuffed zucchini. Jonah loved his spice, dousing every meal with Tabasco, even before tasting the food. This year, she planned to make the soup extra peppery, just for him. A special soup for a special anniversary, she thought, drawing deeply on her freshly filled e-cig. She'd spent her mad-money stash to pay for the dinner's ingredients, but the look on Jonah's face would be worth it.

Melissa spent the entire day in the kitchen before taking a shower, dressing and fixing her hair. She greeted her husband with a rare smile when he returned, asking how his day had been.

"Same as every other day at the bakery," he said. "Did have a mild case of the runs, but nothing that will keep me from enjoying tonight's meal."

"So glad to hear that." And thanks for sharing, she thought. "I made a super special meal for our twenty-fifth. Hors d'oeuvres are ready, I'll go get them. About an hour until dinner."

"I'll shake the cocktails right now," Jonah replied. "This year I'm making Penicillins, a recipe from Singapore I found online. It's slightly sweet, slightly salty with a distinct whiff of the sea, or so the article said. Come try one."

After a leisurely cocktail hour, the pair moved to the dining room. Melissa served the soup. Her hand shook slightly as she placed the plates on the table. She felt a little dizzy and wondered how much booze Jonah had put in the cocktails. She felt her stomach flutter, but didn't want to admit, even to herself, that she'd sampled more than her fair share of the canapés in the kitchen—she'd been so hungry, and the smoked-salmon blinis and chicken-liver *bruschetta* had looked too tempting to resist...Anticipation, she thought. Excitement is making me light headed, and my heart is racing. Her hand shook as she placed the soup bowls on the table, being sure to give her husband the one she'd topped with extra ground pepper. She couldn't wait to see his reaction. Indeed, she watched intently as he took the first spoonful, and then the next, until he emptied the bowl.

"That was wonderful," Jonah said, laying down his spoon. "A little heavy on the whiskey, but just the right amount of pepper. I can't wait to taste the next course. I'll make us each another cocktail while you get it ready."

Melissa continued to observe her husband through the salmon course, the salad, the palate-cleansing sorbet, and the elaborate entrée, pleased to see him enjoying every bit. Lillian had been right. Working hard to please Jonah was the way to go.

Jonah savored the meal, accepting seconds of the filet with its rich, wine-heavy sauce. He smiled at Melissa as she sipped her third cocktail.

"Good?" he asked.

"Perfect," she replied, draining her glass. "Are you feeling alright? You look a little pale and you're sweating."

"Guess I'm just not used to so much rich food all at once."

"Just let me get clear these dishes and then I have something to tell you, something to mark this special occasion."

"I'll make more cocktails. Maybe scotch, and the candied ginger garnish, will settle my stomach after all that great food. Another Penicillin should do the trick. We can enjoy dessert later."

She smiled as she saw him sway and grasp the table when he stood. For a moment he reminded her of the boy she had loved, full of hair and dreams. "Those drinks really hit the spot, don't they?" she said.

When they'd both sat down again, Jonah lifted his glass in a toast. "Here's to twenty-five years together, through ups and downs, thick and thin."

Melissa's eyes narrowed at those last words, sensing another dig at her weight, but relaxed when no more came.

"Here's to the future," he said. "A happy one."

"Cheers."

They drank in unison before settling back in their chairs. "What did you want to tell me?" Jonah asked.

Melissa saw Jonah sway slightly on his chair. "Are you feeling alright?"

"Actually, I feel like my heart is racing. Guess maybe I should slow down on the Penicillins. But your meal was delicious," he hastened to add.

"I'm so happy," she said.

"Me too," he said.

Melissa started to feel unwell herself. Sympathetic pains or excitement, she wondered. Either way, she needed to have her say now, it seemed, before she ended up sick on the bathroom floor. She couldn't let their wonderful meal end without sharing her big surprise.

"Did you know that liquid nicotine, the kind I use in my e-cigs, tastes like black pepper?" she said, then sipped her sweet cocktail to alleviate a slight metallic taste in her mouth. Her hand shook badly. She was surprised her nerves were getting the better of her. After all, she'd been looking forward to this moment. She nearly rubbed her hands together before she said, "The Internet said it only takes sixty milligrams to kill someone as skinny as you. I added forty to your breakfast béarnaise and another sixty to your soup for good measure."

Melissa was laughing at Jonah's wide-open mouth as she started to rise from her chair. Suddenly she swayed, grabbing the edge of the table in order to remain upright. Her eyes widened. Loss of balance—this was not nerves. At the same moment, her husband convulsed, gasping, but smiling. He wheezed something.

"What?" she asked, breathing heavily. "A final insult?"

"No," Jonah rasped. She could barely hear his words. "I'm just surprised how well suited we are to each other, even after twenty-five years. I laced your drinks with cyanide. Like they use to develop film. Twenty-five milligrams in each of your four drinks. Enough to kill an elephant—or even you."

"It's a tribute to the power of love," the Reverend Wills told his wife at dinner on the first day of July. "While it's a shame—and a bit strange—they both died like that, at least they did live as man and wife for twenty-five years and now the Lord has welcomed them to live—and cook—in love and harmony together for all eternity. It's almost perfect that they passed on the actual day of their anniversary. I'm sure my counseling sessions with Jonah, and whatever little tips you gave Melissa, helped make it the best anniversary ever. Well, until they passed, that is."

"Yes, dear, I'm sure you're right, as always. Don't forget to take your antacid. The pharmacist said the insurance company substituted a new, improved brand. You're supposed to just swallow it," Lillian said as she handed her husband the brown, liquid-filled capsule. "He said they taste disagreeable, very peppery, if you chew them."

* * *

Tiger Wiseman took up fiction writing following a career in software consulting and journalism. With many technical papers and newspaper articles under her byline, this is her first published short story. Tiger lives in Connecticut with her uber-spoiled Golden Retriever, Murphy.

RHODE ISLAND

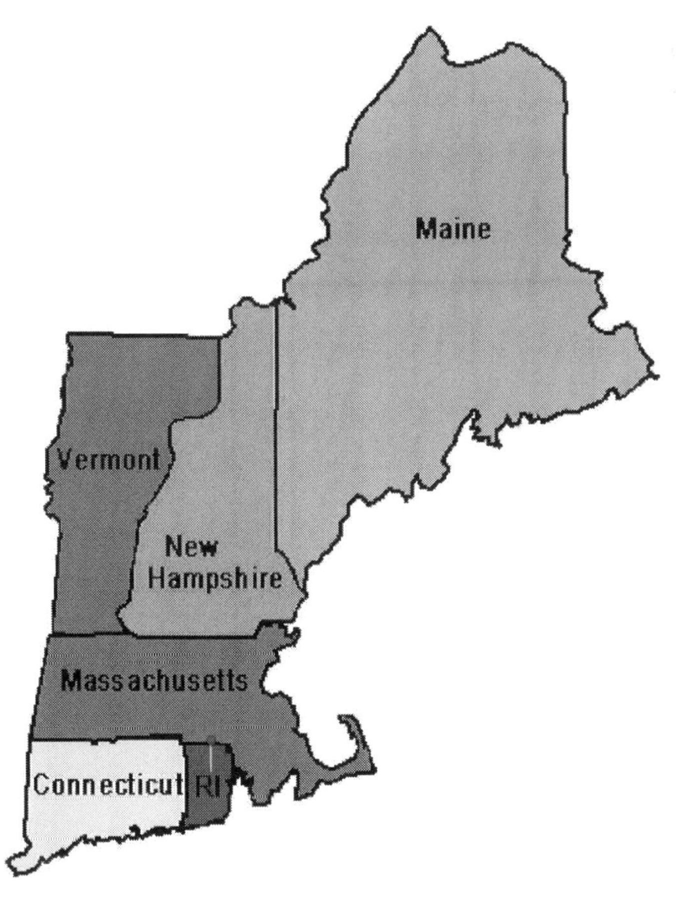

SEAL OF THE STATE OF RHODE ISLAND AND PROVIDENCE PLANTATIONS
HOPE
1636

DREAMERS DODGE DOJO
by Adele Gardner

Kiera stood watching the sunset over Oakland Beach, Rhode Island. She rested a brown hand on her younger brother's shoulder. Orange clouds low on the horizon turned the opposite shore into a blocky silhouette. Contrails streaked through the remaining blue sky. It looked so festive, so appropriate for her brother's big day tomorrow.

"This time tomorrow, we'll be looking out on an ocean bluer than that sky," Donnie said.

"Swimming with the dolphins," Kiera said wistfully.

"You can still come along, Kie. Brett said he could get a group rate. Carry the party over to the Bahamas."

"On your honeymoon? You've got to be joking, Boo." Kiera turned slowly, her eyes drinking in the dark blue waves, their texture as craggy as the Rhode Island shoreline. She missed the soft, sandy Virginia beaches.

Her brother snagged her hand, the gesture taking her back to their childhood walks. "At least I wouldn't be alone."

She gave his hand a reassuring squeeze. "What do you mean, Donnie?" She had suspicions, but felt it best to remain positive. That's what Dad always said. She tried to live up to Dad's kindness, his forgiving nature, his wisdom in giving people the benefit of the doubt—a spiritual wealth of which Anthony Williams had been justifiably proud. Ever since their dad died at forty-three, when they were in their teens, Kiera had worked hard to protect Dontrell.

But Dontrell, who always confided in her, only shook his head.

They headed back to their hotel in Warwick, Rhode Island, where they joined Brett's family in the lobby, then walked to a seafood restaurant across the street. Donnie and Kie sat to Brett's left; Brett's parents sat on his right. Next to Kie was Samantha, Brett's cousin, her platinum blond hair as artificial as Kiera's painstakingly blonde locks. Kiera wondered if Samantha, with her skin as pale as a china doll, got as many questions as Kie did about her 'unusual' hair color.

Brett's friends and relatives talked amongst themselves. Donnie mostly stayed tuned to Brett. Kiera felt distinctly uncomfortable, imprisoned by her shyness. She kept looking up at the others, alert for a chance to join in a conversation, but the few times people spoke to her, they seemed to concentrate on one question: "Where are you from?" For some reason, her answer, "Virginia Beach," didn't seem to satisfy them.

But the locals made up for it. In small-town fashion, the news spread fast through the restaurant about the reason for their stay. An older man and woman came up to shake hands with Dontrell and Brett, congratulating them. Three young men and a teenage girl came over, laughing and patting Donnie and Brett's backs, thanking them for coming to Rhode Island for this important ceremony. Warmth spread through Kiera at this welcome, taking place in a year when gay marriage was still only legal in a few states.

Some diners switched chairs before dessert to talk to others. Kiera seized the chance to sit closer to Brett's parents. Miriam smiled at Kiera through gold-rimmed glasses, her round pink cheeks beaming. She patted Kiera's hand. "It's just wonderful, isn't it? I feel as though the sun's finally breaking through the clouds for my son. We're going to just love having Dontrell in the family."

"You're so kind. I'm glad Donnie has such a welcoming new family. You know, you're the only parents he has now."

Miriam's face fell. "Oh dear. What a shame. With the loving way Dontrell talks about his Mom and Dad, I thought they were still alive."

"They're always with us," Kiera agreed. She tried to hide her dismay that Donnie's new mother-in-law didn't even know the basic facts about their family.

Across the table, Dontrell leaned toward his prospective mate, clearly waiting for a chance to join the conversation. Brett, telling his friends a story, patted Donnie's hand, then held it with absent affection.

Finally, people got up and wandered back to the hotel. In her room, Kiera set up her laptop and kicked off her shoes, logging into the hotel's Wi-Fi so she could get some work done for class. Online graduate education finally made it possible to progress toward a master's degree despite her work schedule, which was erratic, to say the least. Her boss recommended an MBA, but she'd chosen English literature with emphasis in creative writing. A girl can dream.

A faint tapping came at her door. Her tall, graceful brother wrapped her in a hug. "I'm so glad you're here, sis."

"Oh, I'm going to miss you!" With one final squeeze, she let him go.

He sat on the bed, so she returned to her chair. "What's wrong? You can tell me anything, Donnie."

"Yeah. But you're the only relative who came for me. I don't want to turn you against Brett."

Kiera searched for the right thing to say. "Sometimes it's worth taking a step back. You don't want to make a mistake."

"I don't want to call off the wedding. I love Brett. Love is worth making sacrifices for, especially when it's so hard to find."

"Then what?"

"I just found out he's been married a few times before."

"A few times?"

"To women."

"You didn't know this?"

"I guess he was afraid to tell me. But his third wife showed up for the wedding. Tabitha Reynolds. He suspects his mom invited her."

Kiera shook her head, humming her disapproval. "And what ended the marriages? How many?"

"Three. Brett didn't exactly say. But I gather the last one involved money. He's not exactly good with finances. He just can't seem to remember he's not a pro ballplayer anymore."

"Boo, you can't get into that!" she said, aghast. "You had a hard enough time building up the comic business!" A sci-fi and superhero fan since boyhood, he'd persevered past institutional racism to get a coveted spot at the big firms. But when they kept him in too small a box, he walked away to found his own wildly successful indie comic, *Dreamers Dodge Dojo*.

"I know the man's faults, but you can't choose who you love," he pleaded. "He's good to me. I think all he needs is discipline. I can help him with that."

"You think you can rein him in?" Kiera asked skeptically.

Then Brett knocked. "We're practicing a flash minuet," he said. "I thought it'd go well with the ballroom."

"It's not a ballroom," Dontrell said.

"Not this again. It'll look pretty. Don't worry, I've got instructions. We can practice while watching BBC America."

"How about *Doctor Who*?" Kiera suggested.

"I said the minuet, not the drunk giraffe," Brett said with a snarky smile.

"Just as long as you don't invite any clockwork androids," Dontrell said.

At last, close to 2 a.m., Kiera escaped to her room—with Brett's driver's license number. She knew a few things, after the way her marriage ended. But other than confirming his marriages and a troubling financial picture, she found nothing. She slept badly.

At the wedding, they sat under the trees in the Grove at Moses Brown School in Providence, Rhode Island. The beautiful filtered forest sunlight played over shady blooms.

Kiera read a sonnet she'd written for the occasion. Dontrell's high school chum Martina played an achingly beautiful flute solo she'd composed. Brett's mom read scripture. The ecumenical minister reflected on love's true meaning, led the couple to share their vows, and pronounced a blessing.

Despite herself, tears sprang to Kiera's eyes as the couple faced each other, holding hands. Love shone from their faces, pure and vibrant, as they leaned in for the kiss.

Then they all walked into the school for the reception. In the beautiful Sinclair Room, tables ringed the walls, leaving a wide space clear in the center. Shining hardwood floors awaited the dancers. With the grand piano in one corner and the tall arched windows adding gauzy light, it looked like a proper ballroom.

While Dontrell danced with his new husband, Kiera hovered on the periphery, scanning the room. The sea of white faces made her nervous. Aside from Martina and her partner Julieta, with their tawny Mexican good looks, and Lorenzo, whose Dad was Filipino, she and Dontrell were the only people of color in the room.

Front and center, tall Dontrell waltzed with his solid ex-athlete. Brett's normally pasty skin flushed in patches, his silky blue shirt already clinging with sweat. Cool as a cucumber, Dontrell glowed from within, his mahogany skin warm, his grin marking bold lines around his princely nose. "I'm proud of you, Boo," she murmured.

Smiling to herself, Kiera reminisced about Dontrell's "bachelor party." Who but Dontrell would have such a cool sendoff? They'd shared the long road trip up from Virginia, just like old times. Before swinging back to Rhode Island, they'd gone all the way to see the *USS Constitution* in Boston Harbor, a longtime dream.

Walking the boards of that awesome, ancient ship, they stood and listened to it creaking in the wind and the water slapping the wooden hull that famously earned the nickname "Old Ironsides." They chatted excitedly about how much Dad, a through-and-through Navy man, would have loved this trip.

"And Mom," Dontrell added. "She loved this old ship. I remember those songs she used to sing when we were kids."

"I wish they were both here with us. At the wedding, too."

Donnie sighed. Leaning out over the railing, he said, "I don't."

"How can you say that? They'd be so proud of you, Donnie. You achieved your dreams—you're a successful comics creator, and now you're getting married—"

"You know Dad never could have handled it," Donnie argued. "Mom either."

For most of his life, he'd hidden his true self for simple survival. When Donnie was sixteen, she'd found him crying in the bathroom with a knife at his wrist. Only then did she learn his secret. But even with Kiera's support, Donnie waited to come out until both their parents were dead.

Softly, she told him, "I know they'd have been shocked at first. But they loved you, Donnie. They both loved you so much. They'd have come around."

"Tell yourself that, if it makes you feel better," he said with surprising force. "But they'd hate that I'm gay! And how do you think I feel? My grief's compounded by knowing I couldn't be myself while they were alive!"

"Uncle James and Aunt Stefani love you. Our cousins too. They'd have come," Kiera said.

"I'm not out to everyone, Kiera. Let sleeping dogs lie."

As they toured belowdecks—past swinging hammocks, giant timbers, and cannons secured by ropes—sadness stole over Kiera. Dontrell would rather cut out part of himself than cut himself off from his family. But their family loved him. Some unintentional remarks might hurt, but she couldn't imagine deliberate cruelty.

Then Grandma's words rang in her mind: "Your Grandfather would be so ashamed." How Kiera had cried. Five years ago, she'd called to tell Grandma about her own impending marriage—a commitment so serious she'd converted to Catholicism, leaving the AME church. In the end, it hadn't helped her marriage. And Grandma's words still stung.

When they got back up to the deck, she linked her arm through his. "I wish you never had to consider such choices. I'm sorry you were born into such a hard life."

"Oh, it has its moments. Besides, I've got you, sis." He grinned.

Now here he was, wearing the sweetest smile and dancing up a storm with his one true love.

As soon as the dance floor opened up, Kiera hurried out to join him. He held out his hands to welcome her. She smiled up at him, tears in her eyes. "I'm so happy for you."

"I'm so glad you came."

"I'm so glad you found a loving partner in life. You've really got it all," she said softly.

He didn't answer her unspoken question, only gave her that deep, gentle Williams smile as they waltzed, so tall he reminded her of Dad teaching her to dance. "I hope someday you find someone who makes you as happy as Brett makes me.

Kiera woke to a man's low, ragged scream. Still half-asleep, she put a pillow over her head, thinking it was a private moment. Then doors slammed. A woman shrieked. Kiera jumped out of bed, struggling into her robe.

Next door, Brett rocked on his knees, uttering an unearthly moan through gritted teeth, holding her brother's lifeless, bloody hand.

She pushed past the hallway huddle to kneel at Donnie's side. His chest didn't move, his eyes stared and his mouth was frozen open, showing clenched teeth. She checked his pulse, did chest compressions, breathed for him. His lips were cold. No blood flowed.

She stroked Donnie's cheek. His brown skin had an ashy undertone, not warm life. She talked to him softly, sharing memories of Dad and Mom, the way they often did. She blinked away her tears, not letting herself sob. She didn't want him to worry about her.

Then the police guided her away while the EMTs took over. Brett sobbed, curled against the wall, blood smeared on his hands and bathrobe. Kiera found some on her own.

So many questions. She answered while she watched them cover Donnie and strap him to a stretcher.

Introducing herself as Lieutenant Lin, the sympathetic officer asked, "How long has your brother been depressed?"

"No way. No way! Donnie was happy—he just got married! He loved his job! He had everything to live for!"

"It happens that way sometimes," said a burly white officer with a crew cut—Detective Parks. "The family is the last to know something's wrong."

That didn't sound right. She knew Donnie. She tried to convince them.

They wrote things down. Lieutenant Lin gave her a card.

Alone at last, Kiera cleaned up, then paced the small bedroom, wanting to tear everything she saw to shreds. Nothing made sense. Donnie, dead? Dead! Her sobs roared.

Kiera called Uncle James, who promised clear her further absence from work and contact the local funeral home. She declined his offer to send her cousin up to fetch her. She couldn't afford to stay here much longer—but she couldn't leave Donnie like this. Not while his killer roamed free.

Crime scene and postmortem analysis revealed Donnie's prints on the knife weren't in the right places to make that long cut on his left arm—and there were no left-hand prints for the cut on his right. Plus, the second wound suggested equal force applied, not weakness from severed muscles and blood loss.

Kiera volunteered her laptop and her college passwords to prove the times she'd been actively working on her classes. A thin alibi, but she wanted to clear herself quickly so they could find the real culprit.

They brought her laptop back with more questions. "You disapproved of your brother's husband," Detective Parks said.

Desperately searching her memory for any stray words, she said, "I didn't trust him. I worried about my brother. That's true. But that's not a motive to kill Donnie!"

Lieutenant Lin said, "You're Dontrell's sole beneficiary."

"No, that's Brett. They made new wills before they got married. Donnie traveled a lot for comic cons, and he didn't want to leave anything to chance."

Parks said, "Of his life insurance policy. You didn't know about this? A month ago, he took out a million-dollar policy for death and disability."

"He can't afford that!" she cried. Then she remembered that it didn't matter. His death hit her like a blow between the eyes.

Her face serious, her voice soft, Lin said, "He was leaving your life."

"He was my brother, not my lover. Besides, I was happy for him. Worried, yes, but happy!"

Lin said, "I'm sorry. We have to ask."

"What about Brett? Are you looking at him? Two of his wives ended up dead!" Then Kiera remembered how she'd gotten that information. So that's it. She'd encouraged them to examine her browser history.

But Lin and Parks exchanged glances, and Lin said, "We're checking everything out, Ms. Williams."

And they left. Simple as that.

But no way Kiera would let things ride.

Going undercover wasn't going to be easy. She knew she stood out here. Aside from the service staff, she'd seen very few black people at this hotel. Especially compared to home in Hampton Roads.

But even there, at the museum where she'd interned in college, she'd been the only black employee not in the custodial department. She'd rapidly gotten sick of the humiliating questions people asked—requesting that she fix stopped up toilets and scrub down the fridge before they noticed who she was, if they bothered to notice at all.

She unpacked her manager's uniform from the movie theatre. She'd brought it for the trip home, hoping to snag a few behind-the-scenes theatre tours, and possibly some interviews. She wanted to live closer to Dontrell's new home.

She knew from experience that a uniform, any uniform, made her part of the landscape. Whenever she stopped to pick up a gallon of milk or paint after work, people saw that uniform and started asking the price of cheese and where to find the hammers.

She started with the hotel restaurant and bar. Despite the tragedy—or perhaps because of it—a surprising number of people gathered here. She glimpsed Brett sitting at a booth with a white redhead. Using the second entrance, she approached from the rear, choosing a booth that put her back to his.

Brett told the woman, "I wanted you to be happy with someone else, Tabby. You could never be fulfilled with me. You know it's true."

So she was Tabitha Reynolds, the third wife Donnie had mentioned. The contralto pleaded, "I was happy with you! Maybe you didn't do that one thing, but you know we did everything else!"

He sounded apologetic. "I wanted you to be happy. I know my own limitations. There's a reason I never had children. I just can't satisfy a woman in that particular way. Anything else, I'm happy to oblige. I always thought it made me a better lover. I could be more attentive, more focused on your needs. But it was a role I played to fit in. And you were so unhappy. We both were. I finally realized that's just not enough."

Tabitha said sadly, "You'd never let me do anything for you."

He said gently, "Then why do you want me back?"

She exclaimed, "Were all our years wasted?"

Brett said, "I don't know about that. But I never loved you the way you wanted me to. We were great friends, Tabby. I respect you. I admire you, but not like that. I was living a lie."

"You were living off me," Tabitha said pointedly.

"I'm sorry," he said simply.

Kiera heard someone getting up, and hunched into her menu. As Tabitha stormed past, Kiera glimpsed a fiery scowl. Then Tabitha dragged a tissue across her eyes. With chagrin, Kiera recognized that contorted expression as a struggle not to cry.

A server stopped by, and Kiera ordered salad. Probably a mistake. Brett must have recognized her voice. He slid in across from her. "Any port in a storm."

"Why'd you invite her?"

"She invited herself."

"What if she killed Dontrell to get you back?"

"That wouldn't accomplish a damned thing. She's just emotional today because murder's shocking. But she knows I'll never get back with her. And she's got me paying her every month, a hefty sum I can't imagine she'd want to lose."

"I thought you were tapped out."

He looked surprised. "Didn't Donnie tell you? I got a book contract. Six figures. Turns out my baseball career isn't over yet. I loved impressing Donnie for a change. Just in time for the wedding." His faint smile reflected nostalgia and love. Then the smile fell away—killed by the knowledge that kept pummeling them both.

She pounced. "Did you kill Donnie?"

"God, no!" He pushed himself violently back from the table, into the booth wall. His bloodshot eyes were frank with weariness and grief. "I loved Donnie more than life itself. You've got to believe me. Without him—all this is a farce! If it weren't for my parents—"

"What? You'd kill yourself?" she said bitterly.

"That's a real possibility," he agreed, sincerity burning through that glare down his strong hooked nose.

She felt exhausted, suddenly. Wanted nothing more than to lie down. Maybe never get up again. Brett hunched across from her, his shoulders near his ears and his hands over his face. He swiped a cocktail napkin and deftly slipped it behind his shielding hand. "What are we gonna do?"

His unconscious assumption that they were a team—family—stung her with unexpected warmth, like a limb waking up. Donnie's widower. Her brother, now. Donnie himself, sitting across from her. She said gruffly, "You're going to help me find out who did this."

"But how?"

His brown hair, so artfully arranged yesterday, stood up in tangled, greasy clumps. At least he'd pulled on a Boston College T-shirt. "Suspicion has been cast on both of us. I don't think it sticks, though. Right?"

"You believe me?" he whispered.

She wasn't sure, though his grief spoke to her. But this man needed some reassurance or he'd fall apart. "Yes."

He clung to her hand so hard it hurt. "Bless you," he said. "You're just as good a sister as Donnie said."

She freed her hand. "We have to do this, for Donnie."

He put his hand on hers like a Musketeer swear. "For Donnie."

Food and drink. They picked at the stuff of life. And picked apart the possible causes of Dontrell's death.

"The thing is, there's no reason for anyone to murder Donnie," Kiera agonized. "How can the police find the murderer if we can't even find a motive?"

"My brother, Grayson," Brett growled. "He got wind of the book advance and hit me up. Wanted me to invest in his startup. Dontrell didn't think it was a sound deal. He said the reason I wasn't better off financially was all this family pressure. I felt guilty for my own success as a catcher, so I let my family and friends sponge off me shamelessly. He said, 'You'd have a nice living from investments, if you hadn't let them sucker you out of all that cash.' After Grayson found out, he really had it in for Donnie. That's why Gray didn't come to the wedding."

"That kind of rules him out as a suspect," Kiera said. "What about the rest of your family? Was anyone opposed to interracial couples?"

Brett snorted. "No. They're all for it. But being gay? Even outside baseball, there were reasons why it took me so long to come out. I'm my Uncle Sebastian's only heir. He blamed Dontrell for 'what happened to me.' He has this crazy idea I was straight the whole time and Dontrell led me astray. But he's 85 and getting frail. I don't see him overpowering Donnie."

"I think we're dismissing Tabitha too quickly."

"Fine. We can investigate her." He waved a hand. "But we'll be wasting time we could spend catching the real killer."

"What about your other ex-wives?"

"One killed herself with sleeping pills. The other crashed her car. DUI."

"I'm sorry. And I'm sorry to ask this, but—"

"I was cleared. But it ate up the rest of my money, and a lot of my parents' too. And before you ask, Lieutenant Lin said not to leave town." He put bills on the table and stood. "But I'm sure as hell leaving this restaurant."

They stood in the hall, waiting for the elevator. "Who stands to benefit, Brett? I mean, aside from us."

"No one."

"His collaborator on the comic book," Kiera said.

"What? Orlando? No way. Not to sound crass, Kiera, but I'm his heir. We signed the wills when we got the marriage license. And I'm planning to keep his work in print for a long, long time. Maybe even a ghostwriter to carry on *Dreamers Dodge Dojo* and develop his other projects. I already talked to his agent. You know how Donnie protected his image. I figured he'd want damage control."

"You've been busy."

He ran a shaky hand through his hair. The spikes got worse. "It's all I could think about. What I could do for Donnie. Comics were his life. He used to talk about how unfair it was, that print-only authors had a much better chance of longevity. How frustrated he felt when a book went out of print. Like his characters, these people he loved, had been given a death sentence."

Kiera took his arm and boarded the elevator. As three men in suits approached, she stabbed the button to close the doors.

She put her arm around his shoulders, the way she did when she'd walked Donnie home from school. He said, "Don't worry, Kiera. I won't leave you out in the cold. Donnie loved you. He'd want you to be part of it. If you wrote some of the stories, Donnie's fans would be thrilled."

"That's great, Brett. But you're missing the point. Donnie and Orlando had a collaboration agreement. There's only one person who gets to make those decisions now. One person who benefits from the proceeds of the Dojo now that Donnie's dead. And that's his creative partner. Orlando Lemming."

Brett looked as stunned as a schoolboy who expects a field trip and finds a final exam. "Orlando? He loved Donnie. They were best buds. Donnie even went up to see him after the wedding, before we turned in. He said they couldn't talk at the reception, with all those people."

"They were lovers, before you came along."

"Yeah, like *six years* before I came along. Donnie told me after we got serious so I wouldn't get the wrong idea. Believe me, they're just high school chums."

She forced out the words. "Donnie almost died over that man."

The elevator door opened. A girl and boy got on wearing superhero T-shirts.

Waiting for their floor, Kiera thought back. At the wedding, Orlando kept to himself markedly, as if granting Donnie space, offering a pained smile across the distance but shaking his head when Donnie waved him over. Maybe he sensed what only Donnie and Kiera knew: that Donnie felt the relationship getting strained with Brett in the picture. That he felt stifled and held back by Orlando's constrained view of what comics could be.

A few more people got on, wearing shirts for Sandman and Black Panther. Soto voce, she told Brett, "Donnie wanted to end the partnership. He planned to strike out on his own."

The elevator kept stopping. More comic fans got on, some wearing art from *Dreamers Dodge Dojo*. Brett nudged Kiera and gave her a thumbs up. She nodded, but her stomach dropped as the elevator rose. She recognized that art. Donnie showed her the cover of his upcoming book, under tight wraps for the last six months. A favorite character's heroic death concluded a meaningful story arc. Donnie intended to close the series with that triumphant but bittersweet moment. But Orlando argued bitterly against letting the man stay dead.

A young girl wore a purple Dojo T that depicted a black samurai and his cat. She spoke excitedly to her friend. "They pushed up the release date. I heard you can get an autographed copy right now!"

Kiera said, "Nice shirt." The young girl beamed. "I love the Dojo. What's the book?"

The friend's maroon T-shirt showed the bow-wielding princess in her distinctive new lavender armor, which didn't appear until the new book. She passed Kiera her phone. "See? *Dreamers Open the Way*. There's going to be some mind-bending revelation about Leonard!"

The social media post showed the completed art. A quick scroll revealed an embedded podcast whose cover photo showed Orlando holding the book with a tag to Dontrell and a brief "Rest in peace" comment. The timestamp was fifteen minutes after the EMTs pronounced Dontrell dead at the scene. Talk about breaking news.

The elevator stopped. While the girls bounced down the corridor, Kiera pulled out her own phone.

"Orlando didn't say anything about this," Brett said.

Down the hall on the right, music and babbling voices flowed from an open door. Kiera pressed play on Orlando's podcast. He mixed enthusiasm for the book with gratitude to fans and an ostentatious farewell to his friend.

"Did Donnie finish the book without telling me?" Brett looked lost.

"It's possible he wrapped everything up before the wedding and saved it for a surprise."

They stood outside the room. After a few minutes, she pressed pause. Only a quarter done on the status bar. This podcast was close to forty minutes long.

Fans streamed to and fro. "It looks like a comic con party," Brett said. "It's a wonder management hasn't shut it down."

"Good thing I'm wearing a manager's uniform," she said.

Kiera waded in, raising her voice and clearing people out. At the sound of authority, bewildered fans fled, clutching their loot as if signed posters and comics were contraband.

Orlando sat at a table near the window, a cash box on the sill. She strode up, holding her phone toward him as it played his voice praising the book.

"You don't like my tribute to Donnie? I'm sorry. I just couldn't keep my grief bottled up. Such a tragedy," he said.

"It's thirty-eight minutes long," she said flatly.

Orlando blanched. He tried to flee. Brett held him imprisoned in strong arms while she phoned the police.

Then she yanked the extension cord from his sound system and employed what she'd learned from her internship at that maritime museum. She trussed him in a series of sturdy knots.

* * *

Librarian **Adele Gardner** (www.gardnercastle.com) is a professional member of Sisters in Crime with mystery stories and articles in *Mystery Weekly Magazine, Virginia Is for Mysteries II, A Study in Lavender*, and *Magill's*

Choice: 100 Masters of Mystery and Detective Fiction. She's had over 400 stories, poems, illustrations, and articles published. She's literary executor for her father, Dr. Delbert R. Gardner.

STONEMAN HAZARD
by Jim Wright

If you are driving south on the Slocum road back toward the University and down from the sod fields, where the turf is cut and rolled and trucked out to all over New England, and if you are paying attention and not driving too fast, back in the trees a little past the Grange you can see a tiny stagnant pool of water. It isn't more than about 15 feet in diameter, and for most of the year it has a thick green scum of algae and duckweed on the surface. For part of the year, though, right after the spring thaw, you can see the water clear and dark and it will amaze you at the apparent depth. The pool disappears into inky blackness and it seems to be without bottom or end. The stillness of the water and the woods around this pool have a mesmerizing quality, and if you stare at it long enough a feeling of vertigo comes over you. If you don't shake this dreaminess in time, it will reach out into your mind and grab you, toppling you over into the cold watery entrance to what many old-timers around here think must be Hell itself.

There is a road not far from here at the northeast section of what used to be old Henry Arnold's farm called Indian Corner.Most people use this as a back way up to Route 4 and then on up to Providence. They don't give the names of these roads any thought - just thinking ahead to how backed up the highway might be and what meetings they have, or if they can slip away at lunch with that new girl in accounting. If any thought is given to this road, they probably figure that the name represents what used to be a meeting place or a trading site back in the early days.Back in the time after the colonists' war, when the frozen swamp among the cedar trees ran red with the blood of the Indians' massacre, and after which the Narragansetts had to come begging to the English for pots and knives in return for valuable furs and pelts.They'd be somewhat right. It is, of course, named after the Narragansetts. In actuality, it's named after a single Narragansett. But not from colonial times, or even the times near and after the Revolution. The "Indian" in Indian Corner Road was a particular Jonathan "Stoneman" Hazard who lived between here and Little Rest Hill, above a small shop on what is now the Old North Road, where he carved gravestone markers for the marble works in Little Rest—they call it Kingston, now. But this was not back in the early times. The year was 1873 when Stoneman went wild and started his murderous rampage through the woods and fields of Little Rest and Slocumville and even over into Exeter. What happened at the end of that chaos is what connects him to both the road on the corner of the farm and that little black evil pool of water hidden in the trees south of the Grange.

Now, before all this happened Stoneman was liked well enough among the people of the area. He seemed to be an honest man and a fine craftsman. You can still see his work among the headstones of Old Fernwood Cemetery.Even the wealthy Potters used his stones to mark their esteemed remains in the family plot on South Road. He was always spoken of well in the community, but those that met the man himself often came away with a vague feeling of unease.There was something about Stoneman that was a bit strange. Something that you could sense but not accurately describe.

It was thought that he was about thirty-five when the events that are described here took place, but no one knows for sure.He had one of those qualities about him that made his true age almost impossible to guess. He could have been anywhere from twenty to sixty judging from his looks. Stoneman himself didn't know how old he was. If you asked him, he would smile with a strange crooked and wrinkled look and say "Does the granite and marble I carve know how old they are? Does it care?" That was the way with Stoneman. But as long as his work was good and his prices low enough, the people put up with his eccentricities.

Early one spring, right after the snows melted and before the days turned warm enough to bring out most flowers and tree buds, when the earliest of the crocuses bloomed in purple and white and yellow, Stoneman was walking back to his shop after delivering a headstone for one of the Sherman family that had just crossed over to the other side, as the Spiritualists put the matter. He was leading his old swayback horse that pulled the small cart he used to carry the stones across Main Street when he heard a cry from up the way to Mooresfield. Here came galloping down at full speed a youthful chestnut horse carrying the equally youthful Susan Peckham, practically shouting and screaming for life and limb had not her well-bred decorum prevented it.Something had spooked the horse and she was now at its complete mercy and about to collide with Stoneman's cart or anything else that happened to have the bad luck to get in her way.

The stonecutter dropped the reins to his old mare and with a quick step got out in the middle of the way, holding up his arms and making a hissing sound from between his teeth. The chestnut horse stopped before him and started wheeling around in the street, snorting and stamping its front hooves. Stoneman continued closer to it, still with his arms raised and quietly speaking some words that no one that had stopped to watch the episode could understand—even those that knew at the very least what the Narragansett language sounded like.These were no Indian words. They had the exotic sound of an ancient tongue, now all but forgotten. The horse didn't care what language it was, though, but it soon had calmed completely and walked up to Stoneman, nuzzling its head in his outstretched hands.

"By the grace of the Lord, Mr. Hazard," said the young lady Susan when she had gathered her breath and composure."I can't even begin to thank you enough. I can't imagine what would have happened had you not stopped this horse—although I can't say how you had the power to do so! Queer, indeed!" Stoneman looked at her but didn't speak—or, more accurately, couldn't speak. He was a man who lived alone and worked alone and only came into town to deliver his stones. He spoke little to anyone, usually just listening to orders and nodding. What he did speak was either overly humble to the point of whispers and bobs of his head or strangely cryptic and weird like the answer concerning his age. He had not the charms and graces of more social surroundings and his Narragansett blood made him self-conscious even in tolerant Little Rest. Given all of this and coupled with the simple beauty of Miss Peckham, he was out of his place and at a loss for words.

"Well," Susan had said after a short awkward silence, "if you come up to our place I am sure that my father will give you some kind of reward." It was then that she did the act that would forever change the history of this little corner of Rhode Island and lead to dark days and horrible legacies. Susan took Stoneman's hand in hers and kissed it—saying again "Thank you so much!" It was only a small act and done out of pure grace and innocence from a girl that had been saved from danger, but this one tiny event happened to be witnessed by a certain Robert Sweet, son of old Nathaniel Sweet the prosperous dry-goods seller, and the man who said he was courting young Susan - if he could ever get the nerve to do such.

Robert had been known since the days of his schooling as a bully. Tall and broad and handsome, he was the kind of fellow that could talk or charm his way out of anything and also knew that same fact. This, coupled with his family's connections in this area, gave him in his own mind an almost free ticket to do what he pleased. When he saw Miss Peckham kissing the hand of that stone-carver, that Indian, that oddity of human nature that was Hazard, his blood boiled and he swore to himself that he would not let that simple act of honest kindness go unpunished. How dare that Stoneman make advances on his girl - the actual truth and the absence of any claims on his part to her heart being ignored in his anger.

It started as simple taunts from Sweet and his band of friends and graduated to more serious pestering. Soon after, Stoneman would wake up to his shop being vandalized and hateful messages being painted on the walls. Then, windows were broken with rocks thrown at midnight and dead chickens dropped in his well. It was not long after that people in the village started whispering behind hands and into neighbors' ears about the strange stonecutter and his fixation on the young Peckham girl. When these rumors and hear-says evolved into the practical rape of the girl in broad daylight on the streets of Little Rest, the constable and his men were forced to do something. All the while, Sweet and his band of hooligans stood by and smiled.His campaign had worked and revenge would soon be his.

The night of September 10th of that year was exceptionally cold. A wicked chill wind blew in from the northeast and the treetops howled and bent dangerously. Mr. Knowles, the constable, and a group of twenty or so men—including Sweet and two of his gang—met up at the jailhouse down the hill a bit from the Congregational church and set out to take Stoneman into custody for the attempted kidnapping and assault of Susan Peckham. Knowles knew he would try his best to do such peacefully, but he feared the only result would be the hanging of the stone-carver on the dark limb of an oak not far from his shop and home. The town's sentiments had been whipped up to an almost Biblical fervor over this alleged incident and only the death of Stoneman Hazard would bring any peace. Knowles shook his head and regretted his next words, but he called to the boys "All right, let's go get him!"

People say that the clouds swirled into an evil purple cyclone that night and the leaves of all the trees in Little Rest were blown off their twigs, a full month or two before the full onset of autumn would leave the rest of Washington County bare.The band of men made their way up Main Street with torches and lanterns, some with clubs and cudgels and some with rifles and pistols, all loaded and ready. Reverend Wells at the parsonage right up the hill from the jailhouse stood at the iron railing at the curbside and thought to try to stop them, but he knew that his words would have no effect. Blood was called for this night, and blood would run no matter what he said to them.Sadly, he watched the lights from the torches and lanterns go up the street and past the wellhouse at the end of South Road and then disappear around the turn to the Old North Road, to Stoneman's house. He watched as the last flicker of orange and yellow faded away and went back to his fireside to pray for whatever peace or forgiveness his Lord could give to the souls of himself and his village.

Thunder rumbled in the distance and flashes of white lit up the trees on the horizon as they approached Stoneman's shop. All the lights were out and the swing-out doors to the shop below were closed, but young Jimmy Peckham—second cousin to Susan—could swear he heard the clinks of a hammer falling on stone coming from inside the darkened building.

"Stoneman Hazard!" shouted the constable. "Open up them doors—we come to get you for trial on account of the assault on Miss Susan Peckham. "No sound was heard from the building.Some of the men grew nervous and edgy, now that the actual deed was at hand. Brave talk during mugs of beer was one thing, but the thought of taking the strange stone-carver into custody was beginning to play upon their minds. The thunder grew closer and the flashes of white more intense. A cold rain began to fall.

"Stoneman! Open up them doors!" shouted Knowles a second time. He was trying to formulate a plan in his mind as to what he might do.It seemed to him that no one was home and this was all for naught, but now he had an angry and scared mob on his hands that would not return home without some kind of action or vengeance.

"He's in there!" spat Robert Sweet."Did'n you say so, Jimmy?" He took a step toward the building and grabbed one of the torches from a nearby hand. "Let's just burn him out!" Before Knowles could stay his arm, Sweet made to throw the torch to the base of the shop doors. Just as he did so, a sudden lightning bolt with a simultaneous crash of thunder seared the night sky to blinding day and there, standing in the rain, beside the shop and next to the big tree in the side yard was the silhouette of a man.

"Jesus! Did you see that?" hissed one of them in a scared whisper. The night was black again. Nothing in the yard could be seen. "That was him! That was him, right?"

Sweet had been stopped by the sudden crash of thunder and the shock of seeing the figure, but he wasn't stopped long. Before anyone could prevent him, he yelled and threw the torch toward the building. It landed at the base of the doors, which after a short time caught and flames started to lick around the edges. He quickly grabbed another torch, and some of the other men of the gang threw theirs. The carver's shop was soon wrapped in orange and yellow flames.

"Sweet, you damn fool!" shouted Knowles."This isn't what we..." His words were cut short. From behind them, on the other side of the Old North Road came a sing-song voice out of the shadows and rain. Strange words mixed with the howling wind, the same kind of words that people heard Stoneman speak when he calmed the runaway horse in the street those months ago. Words that came from the echos of the distant past, from the shadows of ancient forests and the depths of hidden caves and words that came from underneath the frozen ice of the Great Swamp during that bloody December close to two centuries ago—words from the dead-white lips of the massacred Indians.

The rain blew harder now, horizontal and stinging on the faces of the men. Lantern and torches blew out, leaving them in utter blackness and alone with the meandering melody of the strange voice. The wind screamed mercilessly and the purple clouds swirled overhead with mad rage.When all reached to an almost feverish pitch and the men reduced to almost whimpering in supernatural fright, a huge bolt of lightning crashed out of the hellish sky and struck the gigantic oak that had stood on the streetside for a hundred years or more. A massive limb from this ancient tree ripped apart from the trunk and crashed into the group of men, instantly killing Sweet and three more men and leaving more trapped under its weight moaning in their dying pain. Those that could ran screaming down the road, back towards the village. The strange words were heard no more, and once again the night was dark except for the fire that was consuming Stoneman's house and quiet save for the howling of the wind.

That autumn was spent in fear around Little Rest and Slocumville and Exeter. Constable Knowles had escaped that night of the storm, unharmed except for his nerves.Most of the others weren't as lucky.When he thought about it, and he didn't usually like to think about it, he figured that he was spared because he had tried to stop Sweet and keep some semblance of peace that night. He thought that maybe there was some kind of supernatural justice happening and that only those that had wronged Stoneman were injured or killed. But then his Yankee sense of logic and practicality overcame him and he told himself he was just lucky.

Stoneman disappeared into the blackness that night.No one had seen him since, but they all knew he was still around, hidden in the woods and swamps of the countryside. For one thing, people walking at night on the roads, hurrying back to their houses and the warm fireplaces that gave them a sense of protection, heard whispers and quiet melodies from the shadows that raised goosebumps on their arms and prickled the hairs on the back of their necks.Reverend Wells tried to turn them from their superstitions and overactive imaginations in his Sunday sermons but the people were convinced otherwise by what they themselves heard and felt.

People were turning up dead, too. In the farmhouses of Exeter and Slocumville, and in the parlors of the village houses in Little Rest, men were found expired on the floor with eyes wide in horror and their limbs in contortions of terror.No medical reason could be found for their deaths other than a heart spasm or apoplexy. But everyone in the area knew it was Stoneman. These men had been murdered - perhaps not with knife blade or bullet, but by other means that no one might speak of. All of the men had connections with that night of the storm when the gang went to get the stone-carver from his house. Brothers, fathers, cousins, friends - all had some link to those cursed men.

Old Sol Fayerweather the blacksmith closed up his shop for the season and headed out to stay with family in Jamestown. The marble works closed down also and Mister Clark, the lawyer down the way, hadn't been seen in his office in weeks. Rumors spread to Narragansett, and Shannock and even as far away as Charlestown and Matunuck that Little Rest was damned. People stayed away from the area, and even the locals shuttered themselves in their white houses along Main Street. By dusk, no one could be seen walking the streets. The farmers in Slocumville stayed inside, too. At night they said they could hear whispers outside their walls and some mornings they would come to find their animals in a state of panic. Sometimes the cows and sheep would even be found dead from fright, laying rigid in the hay of their stalls.

By the first of November, over twenty men had been found dead inside their locked houses. All from the same panic-induced seizures. It was November 11 - two months and a day from that fateful night when the Cursed Oak, as it had come to be called, had crushed the men in the Old North Road, when Stoneman Hazard was again seen. Seth Franklin from up on Lafayette Road was walking and leading his horse along the road around Henry Arnold's farm, bringing a package to the post office to be mailed out to his sister in Pennsylvania, when he saw him. The fields were bare now at this time of year, nothing but half-frozen ridges and furrows of mud and dirt. On the corner, though, there were some old withered cornstalks that had not been cut and there in the middle and half-hidden by the whispery yellow and brown leaves was Stoneman standing just as still as a Greek statue. Seth jumped back in shock, dropping the package as a dark chill traveled up his spine.

"N..n..now, Stoneman, I got no troubles with you," he stammered. "I wasn't there that night of the storm and neither was none of my family."Seth took a few steps back, leaving his packet where it lay. Still, Stoneman moved not a single muscle. He was dressed in tatters and the snaky muscles of his arms, hardened by years of wielding the heavy hammers, were cut and scratched by brambles and thorns.His hair hung lankily about his shoulders, greasy and tangled. His eyes stared into Seth's with a cold steel gaze. "I'm just going to back away and head on home," Seth whispered. He stepped back a few more paces and his heart was just starting to slow back down from a pounding drum in his throat when Stoneman suddenly jumped from the stalks and screamed into the sky a sound that came straight from Hell.Never had Seth Franklin heard a scream like this - never since the last Narragansett had been killed in the Great Swamp had anyone heard a scream like this. Perhaps only the damned souls below that black ice would recognize what Seth heard that day on the corner of Hank Arnold's empty corn field. Seth's blood froze icy in his veins and his horse reared up on its hind legs at the sound, ripping the reins from Seth's hands and knocking him to the ground. He watched in shock as Stoneman leapt from among the cornstalks into the street.With a final sharp gaze into Seth's own eyes, he turned and ran down the road towards the Slocum's farm and the railroad tracks.

Almost at once, in a strange sense of curiosity mixed with a trace of fear and adrenaline, Seth leapt to his feet and grabbed his horse. He swung his legs up and over and started after the running figure of Stoneman, already some ways in the distance. He chased him down across the fields, past the post office and around the corner near the Slocum brother's houses, along the railroad line and almost until the white steeple of the Baptist church could be seen. Even though Seth was on horseback, he never seemed to be able to get closer to Stoneman, who ran with an eerie lightness and speed over the semi-frozen fields and dirt roads. Suddenly, the Indian stone-carver stopped in the middle of the road and turned to face Seth.The farmer pulled up his horse to a stop about a hundred feet up from where Stoneman stood. What happened next, and what the farmer saw occur, would pass down into legend in this area. He told and retold the story what seemed like a thousand times that winter to whomever would listen.

"He stood there in the road, just staring at me," he would say. "My horse had gone all crazy and wheeled and snorted there in fright, but I kept my eyes sharp on that devil. It was strange—I was never scared. Nervous, like, and full of energy that ran through my body and then went all stale and sickening, but never scared.We stayed that way for what seemed like an hour, but it was only a minute or so I would think. Then, that creature turned to the side of the road, where that little spring is tucked back in the trees—you know the one I mean, a little ways up from the church. He walked over to it and with one last look at me, he yelled that infernal sound again and leapt into the scummy water.

"Here's the strange thing," Seth would say, leaning in close to the listener and lowering his voice to a whisper."There wasn't no splash of water and that Stoneman disappeared without a single sound or ripple. I'd always thought that pool was no more than a foot or two deep, but I guess I was wrong. That entire six-foot man vanished underneath the surface in a flash and I never saw him come back up again. Drowned I guess, although I can't see why or even how. I heard from a fisherman I know from P'int Jude that a man can't willfully drown himself noways. But that's what I saw, and I swear to that on my very soul. That devil Stoneman just disappeared.

"I've walked that road since. And every time I pass that pool of water—it's all frozen now—I get a weird feeling in my bones and the hairs on my neck stand up.My horse won't go past it at all.She'll spook and jump around and snort like she's seeing a ghost but there's nothing there. Just that black evil pool and those silent trees—you never hear nor see any birds or squirrels around there any more. Just a silent black corner of the world, right there."

When spring came around and the snows melted on the farm fields and the ice left the top of the little pool of water in the trees, some of the more adventurous boys of Little Rest took a trip up the Old North Road and past the blackened ruins of Stoneman's shop. They walked past the schoolhouse and all the way up to the Baptist church. They spent some time daring each other to go further, and finally one was brave enough to walk the final distance to the water's edge. What he saw in the inky depths of that pool he didn't say, but he ran back to the village at a sprint and would never speak about it. They say he was never quite "right" after that day.

What he saw, of course, from under the waters, was the grinning face of Stoneman Hazard staring back at him with an evil burning in his eyes.

* * *

Jim Wright was born in Connecticut and always considered himself a New Englander, but it wasn't until moving to Rhode Island that he really became immersed in the spirit of the region. Inspired by the local landscape, his horror and suspense stories feature the old colonial houses, swampy backwoods, and ancient cemeteries that are found all over southern Rhode Island.

MASSACHUSETTS

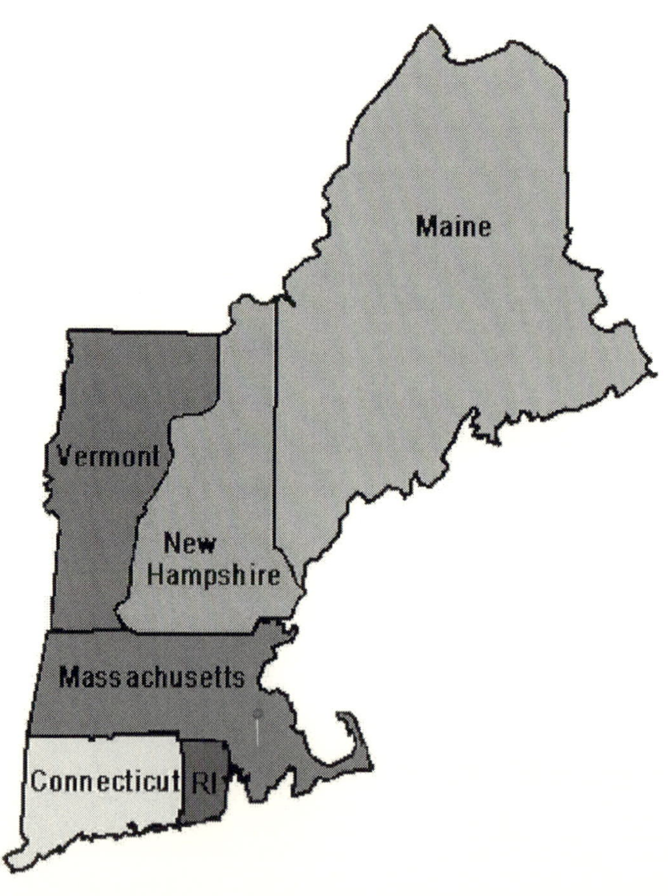

SIGILLUM REIPUBLICÆ MASSACHUSETTENSIS.
ENSE PETIT PLACIDAM SVB LIBERTATE QVIETEM

THE MANICURIST
by Christine Bagley

Every day, the gold-framed doors of Pétale de Rose revolve for the affluent women of Beacon Hill and Back Bay. With their Louis Vuittons swinging on wrists adorned with David Yurman, and the scent of Chanel trailing in their wake, they jockey for appointments with Doreen Fabrizio, the hot, new manicurist at the exclusive salon.

A street-smart kid from a tough neighborhood in East Boston, Doreen began doing nails when she was thirteen. Her artistic talent was evident in the designs she drew freehand for family and friends, who flocked to her three-story tenement after school and on weekends.

At nineteen years old, license in hand, she auditioned for the nail technician position at Pétale de Rose with the same fervor as a budding actress in a Broadway tryout. Hauling her own supply of nail paraphernalia, in a Prada knockoff, she gave the owner of Pétale de Rose, Kathy O'Rourke, a French manicure in less than thirty minutes. Doreen had noticed Kathy's Celtic necklace and copied the design onto Kathy's ring finger. Astonished at the meticulousness of the design and the manicure, she hired Doreen on the spot. Within six months, Doreen was working six days a week, making nearly $1,000 on tips alone. Her petite frame walked proudly through the salon; thick black ponytail twitching like a horse's tail. But Doreen's confident posture was a façade for an unhappy, abusive childhood.

Doreen's stepfather, Armand Felice, was a small time gangster and an alcoholic. Her mother had died of breast cancer the year before, and living alone with Armand had become a nightmare of physical and verbal abuse. The day he tossed a hot cup of coffee in her face because it wasn't strong enough, she'd picked up the pot and swung it at his head. But Armand was too quick and punched her, knocking Doreen into the doorframe. She received eight stitches at Mass General Hospital, and still remembered Sean McDougal, the private investigator who worked with the Boston Police Department on domestic abuse.He knew her mother and the countless times she'd been in the hospital, only to drop charges against Armand because she was afraid for her life.

"Get out of that house, little girl," he'd said. "Go to a family member, or call me and I'll find a place for you. I promise. Just get out of that house." She never forgot his kindness and had kept his business card and telephone number.

Two days later, she moved in with her Aunt Julep.

Doreen wanted a better life, a chance to be somebody, maybe even run her own salon one day. But her aunt thought she was putting on airs.

"Come off it, Doreen, you're no better than anybody else," she'd said, inhaling deeply from her cigarette, long red nails like claws on a falcon. "You're just like the rest of us so knock it off. What's wrong with doin' nails at Tina's anyways?"

Doreen didn't bother to explain. After she landed the job at Pétale de Rose, she moved to a studio apartment over Nina's Ristorante in the North End. She toned down her makeup and stopped wearing tight clothes. She waited for sales at Ann Taylor and bought good leather shoes and handbags from Marshalls and T.J. Maxx. And she stopped chewing gum.

Doreen's first appointment, on a crisp Monday morning in October, was Hattie Van Buren, a Suffolk County prosecutor married to the owner of a biotech company in Kendall Square. They had no children and lived in a four-story brownstone on Beacon Hill. She was classy, smart, and good-hearted.

Hattie was chatting with Gwen Bigelow, who was sitting behind her waiting for Doreen. Gwen was the Managing Director of Rita's Place, a shelter for homeless and abused women, and also on the board of directors at many of the institutes and major hospitals in Boston. A Massachusetts Democrat with flaming red hair, her philanthropic activities ranged from anti-war demonstrations to feeding the homeless. Gwen had been Doreen's first customer and Doreen adored her. She was elegant without trying, and could wear jeans and a T-shirt and still look like royalty. Gwen was largely responsible for the rapid rise in clients that Doreen was now enjoying.

At home in her apartment, Doreen would often imitate the way Gwen Bigelow spoke.

"I *saw* that woman yesterday," she'd repeat in the mirror. Not "I *seen* that woman yesterday," or "Mimi *doesn't* work on Saturdays. Not "Mimi *don't* work on Saturdays."

Doreen's hands were small and nimble her strokes swift and confident as she bent over Hattie's nail beds, applying a soft pink color, and listening to her conversation with Gwen.

"The little punk got off again," said Hattie.

Gwen was thumbing through *Town & Country*. "I know."

"Second time," said Hattie.

Gwen cleared her throat. "Doreen, did you finish painting that accent wall in your apartment?" asked Gwen.

"Yes, it really came out nice. Thanks for suggesting the Tuscany Red."

"You're very welcome," Gwen answered. "Hattie. Do you know anyone who could walk Chelsea tonight? I have to attend a political rally at the Hynes, and my normal dog walker is on vacation."

"I'll do it," volunteered Doreen. "You don't live far from here, right?"

"No, no. I couldn't ask you to do that. You're busy enough here, Doreen."

"I don't mind. I love dogs."

"Well. If you're sure, it would be a huge help to me."

Gwen gave her a spare key, and when Doreen entered the enormous front hall, she gasped. A gold-framed portrait hung over a mantled fireplace, and two floor-to-ceiling windows were framed in royal blue velvet drapes that pooled on the floor. The dining room also had floor-to-ceiling windows and the biggest china cabinet she had ever seen. Doreen looked longingly at the curved staircase leading to the second floor, but Chelsea was wagging her tail and licking Doreen's hand.

After she walked the dog along Comm Ave, Doreen tiptoed up the stairs and entered the master bedroom. The room was done in soft shades of mint green, with a king-size four-poster bed covered with silk throw pillows. The walk-in closet was nearly as big as her apartment. Touching the expensive clothing, she memorized the labels, and then went into the bathroom.

"Whoa," she whispered, admiring the white marble room.

A small velvet pouch caught her eye on the shelf beneath the three-paneled mirror. Though she knew it was wrong, she opened it. A delicate silver necklace slipped out. She could barely make out the design of the charm but she knew she'd seen it before.

She put the necklace back and hurried downstairs, noticing an envelope on the hall table with her name on it. Inside was a $100 bill. She let herself out, hopped into her dinged up Ford Escape, and drove home.

Joannie Napolitano was Doreen's best friend. She towered over Doreen, and had beautiful blue eyes lined heavily with black pencil. In third grade, Joannie had shoved Theresa Gagnon to the ground when Theresa tried to pull Doreen off the monkey bars. From then on, they'd been BFFs. Joannie still lived in East Boston and worked as a waitress at MacCarthy's Bar in Faneuil Hall. Tonight she was staying at Doreen's apartment on a blow-up mattress.

"Don't you need a roomie, Dory?" she asked, snapping her gum and blowing giant bubbles. Doreen was repairing a broken nail for Joannie and drinking ginger ale.

"It's too small for both of us, Joannie. But someday, I'm going to buy a nice big place, and then we can be roomies."

"You're gonna do it, Dory I know you will. Then you can hang all your artwork. The daisies are my favorite, they're so happy," said Joanie, staring at the far wall. "Hey, why you still drinking that stuff anyways?" Joannie asked, pointing to Doreen's ginger ale.

"Queasy stomach."

"Whaddya queasy about, hon?"

Doreen was silent for a moment, unconsciously touching the scar on the side of her head. "I'm afraid Armand's going to find out where I am." Doreen's stomach twisted at the thought.

Joannie reached across the table and put her hand on Doreen's arm. "Aw, Dory, he's probably in Vegas by now."

Doreen shrugged. "What do you think?" she asked after fixing Joannie's nail.

"Looks awesome!"

Joannie hung her tongue out and rolled her eyes. Doreen shook her head, smiling.

"Try wearing rubber gloves the next time you put your hand down the disposal."

Doreen was arranging nail polish bottles on the shelf when Tessa Bulfinch walked in. Automatically, she reached for Raspberry Rapture. Tessa was tall with short blonde hair and a sweet disposition. Kathy O'Rourke told Doreen that Tessa had once been married to Gary Kavanagh, a pitcher for the New York Yankees.

"She never talks about him," Kathy said. "It was a messy divorce and she had to get a restraining order against him. Then she ended up marrying her lawyer. Isn't that romantic? Now she works at the Battered Women's Legal Assistance Project."

"Hi Doreen," Tessa said, sliding into the chair. "I like your hair like that."

Doreen was wearing a French braid that ran down the middle of her back.

"Really? Thanks. I'm never sure if I get it right."

"Oh yes," Tessa said. "It's perfect."

As Doreen opened the drawer of her table, she noticed Tessa was wearing a necklace similar to the one in Gwen Bigelow's bathroom.

"That's a pretty necklace," said Doreen. "What is that?"

Tessa's hand flew to her neck as her face turned bright red.

"I forgot I was wearing it. It's a…um…kind of an abstract design…a funky piece I picked up…I forget where…" her voice trailed off.

Tessa was clearly rattled and Doreen couldn't understand why. Doreen leaned forward trying to see the small, silver design, but Tessa drew back and tucked the chain inside her shirt.

While Doreen shaped and filed Tessa's nails, she wondered why Tessa was so rattled. Maybe she didn't want anyone to know she had the same necklace as Gwen. But Tessa wasn't the copycat type; she had her own classic style. It was odd, but Doreen's next customer was getting fidgety, and her thoughts were diverted elsewhere.

A week later, Joannie walked into Pétale de Rose for the first time. She'd told Dory she wanted to see where she worked but Dory said she'd have to get a manicure because she couldn't stop working to chat. When Joannie came through the door, a woman appeared and stood behind what looked like the pulpit Father Dominic preached from at St. Anthony's.

"May I help you, miss?"

Speaking in an exaggerated polished voice, Joannie said, "I have an appointment with Doreen at two."

She was having a hard time holding her gum underneath her tongue when she spoke. Joannie realized she should've worn the black blazer instead of the turquoise fringed leather jacket. The jeans and spiked heels were fine, but her hair was too big and she'd overdone it with the make up and jewelry.

"Right this way, Ms. Napolitano."

Joannie mouthed the words "Ms. Napolitano" as she followed Kathy O'Rourke to Doreen's bay.

Doreen's head was bent over Tessa's nails.

"Doreen, your next client is here," Kathy announced.

"Be right with you," said Doreen, looking up. When she saw Joannie she grinned.

Tessa turned to see whom Doreen was talking to.

"Hello," she said.

"Hello," said Joannie.

"Tessa, this is my friend, Joannie Napolitano. Joannie, this is one of my regulars, Tessa Bulfinch."

"Oh, hi!" said Tessa. "It's nice to meet you. I'd shake your hand but..."

Joannie smiled. "That's okay, Ms. Bulfinch, I understand."

"It's Tessa, Joannie, please."

Joannie wiggled her head. "Okay. Tessa."

"How long have you two known each other?" Tessa asked Doreen.

"Forevah," said Joannie, dropping the fake voice.

Tessa stood and gestured to the seat she'd just vacated.

"How long is forever?" she asked, looking at Doreen and Joannie.

"Since grammar school," said Doreen.

"Tessa!" called Gwen Bigelow as she approached Doreen's bay.

When Doreen saw Gwen she was surprised because she'd just been in the week before. "Did you have an appointment today, Gwen?"

"No, dear. I just came in to buy that hand cream you used on me last time."

"Gwen, this is Doreen's friend, Joannie Napolitano," said Tessa.

"How do you do, Joannie, I'm Gwen Bigelow."

Joannie and Gwen shook hands as Tessa walked toward the hand dryers.

"How do you know our Doreen?" Gwen asked.

"We've been best friends since grammar school in East Boston."

"Oh, my. I don't remember any of my friends from grammar school. That's wonderful you're still close. Friends mean everything in life."

Doreen looked at Joannie and said, "Gwen is responsible for me getting so many clients."

Joannie opened her eyes wide and looked at Doreen.

"Oh my God. You're the one!"

"Jeez, I feel like a celebrity."

"You are!" said Joannie. "Dory told me all about you and was so excited when you told her how good she was 'course I always knew she was great but when she told me about your beautiful big car and mink coat and how you gave her a twenty-five dollar tip I couldn't believe it it's so awesome to meet you in person!"

Doreen's face turned scarlet.

"Dory? I didn't know that was your nickname, Doreen," said Gwen. "I like that."

"Thank you."

"Well, I have to fly, but it was very nice meeting you, Joannie. Maybe we'll run into each other again."

"Nice meeting you too, Gwen."

As Gwen walked away, Joannie lifted the gum from underneath her tongue and started chewing furiously.

"I'm so glad I got to meet some of your clients. Tessa Bulfinch is wicked nice and Gwen Bigelow is gorgeous! Did you see her diamond oh my God and she's got a Balenciaga pocketbook those things cost like two thousand dollars, holy shit!"

"Keep your voice down," said Doreen.

"Oh, sorry."

"So what color would you like today, Ms. Napolitano?"

Joannie's face turned somber as she leaned forward. "Listen, sweetie. I have some bad news for you."

"Tell me."

"Your Aunt Julep was taken to the hospital last night. Apparently, Armand was drunk and looking for you. Your aunt said she didn't know where you were and he didn't believe her. He broke her jaw, Dory."

Doreen took a deep breath, letting it out slowly between puffed cheeks. "Sweet Jesus," she whispered as she ran the cross on her necklace back and forth. She frowned as her heart pounded uncontrollably. "Was he arrested?"

"No. Your aunt said she fell down the stairs in her apartment."

"He got evicted, you know. He's working as a janitor somewhere in Charlestown."

Doreen turned and took a bottle off the shelf, shook it a few times, then placed it on her table. For once, Joannie kept silent, aware of the tremor in

Doreen's hands.

Back in her apartment that night, Doreen poured herself a ginger ale and wrapped her arms around herself while rocking on the edge of the bed. She was deathly afraid her stepfather was going to find her. Then what? He'd want money? She'd get another beating? Before she went to bed, she moved a chair underneath the doorknob, and kept her cell phone by her side. But she did not sleep the entire night. She stared at the ceiling and wondered if she should call Sean McDougal.

The next day, the man himself walked into Pétale de Rose. Tall and broad-shouldered, McDougal was known to skirt the law, believing in Machiavelli's phrase "The end justifies the means." He was in his mid-sixties and was frequently found reading detective stories at Cate's Cafe in Harvard Square, where he sat outside and fed the pigeons when the weather was warm. It was 7:00 p.m. and the salon was empty except for Doreen.

"Remember me, little girl?"

"Yes sir, I do."

"How are you doing these days? Everything okay?"

Doreen shrugged.

"May I?" he asked, sitting down in a chair and crossing his legs.

"Of course."

"Your Aunt Julep recently suffered a broken jaw, I understand."

"That's what I heard."

"A nasty piece of work, that Armand."

"Yes, sir."

"Has he been in touch with you?"

"No, sir."

"You still have my card?"

"I do."

"Good. Now, I understand that Hattie Van Buren is one of your clients, is that correct?"

"Yes."

"And how about Gwen Bigelow and Tessa Bulfinch?"

"Yes. Why do you ask?"

"Not at liberty to say."

McDougal uncrossed his legs and leaned forward. "Has Hattie Van Buren ever mentioned any of her cases?"

Doreen shook her head. "Not to me."

"What about Gwen Bigelow? She ever bring up her work at Rita's Place?"

"I only know she's the managing director. And she's a very nice person."

"Do you know if she drives a large black Mercedes?"

"Yes, she does."

McDougal looked straight at Doreen. "How well do you know these women?"

"I mean, I'm not friends with them but I like them very much."

"They're a pretty close-knit group, aren't they?"

"I guess."

McDougal's voice grew soft and gentle. Doreen saw the look of compassion that crossed his face, a kindness she remembered well.

"Listen to me, little one. You keep that card I gave you, and if you ever need anything, you call me. Understand?" When he stood up, he put his hand on her shoulder. "I mean it, Doreen. Anything at all." And then he left. Unexpectedly her eyes filled as she watched him through the window.

At 7:00 the next night, Sheila Nussbaum walked into the salon. Sheila was in her late thirties and had long, black hair. Kathy O'Rourke told Doreen that Sheila lived in one of those swanky condos at The Ritz-Carlton. Her husband was much older, and a surgeon at Mass General. Sheila was his third wife. They'd met at the hospital where Sheila had been a psych nurse. After they married, she'd quit, and now answered the hotline at the Boston Women's Crisis Center.

Sheila seemed nervous and kept biting her lip. She asked if Hattie or Gwen had been in the salon that day.

"No, they had appointments last week."

"What about Tessa Bulfinch? Did she come in today?"

"No. She's not due again for another week."

Sheila was quiet while Doreen focused on squaring her nails.

"...said he was pushed from behind. It's a wonder he's still alive..."

Doreen looked up when Sheila twisted in her chair to see who was talking. When she turned back she looked troubled.

Forty minutes later Sheila left the salon but forgot her wallet on the counter. Doreen gave herself a manicure then called Sheila, who answered on the second ring.

"Hello?"

"Is this Sheila Nussbaum?"

"Who is this?"

"It's me, Doreen, at the nail salon."

"How did you get this number?"

"You gave it to me in case I needed to re-schedule an appointment."

"You're re-scheduling my appointment now?"

"No, I'm calling because you forgot your wallet."

"Oh Christ, that's all I need."

"I'll drop it off for you," said Doreen.

"Oh my. Do you mind terribly?"

"Not at all. I'm closing up anyhow and I can swing by on my way home."

Sheila lived on the 23rd floor of the Residences at The Ritz-Carlton. When she opened the door, Doreen could see beyond to a spectacular view that overlooked Boston Common and the Public Garden.

"Come in, Doreen. I'm sorry if I sounded rude on the telephone. I've had a terrible week and I'm just not myself."

Sheila had a glass of wine in her hand and gestured toward the living room. Doreen tried not to appear overwhelmed by the opulence and grandeur of her surroundings. She sat down on the edge of the white sectional couch, opening her tote bag to get Sheila's wallet.

"Would you like a cold drink?" asked Sheila taking the wallet from Doreen's outstretched hand.

"Oh no. I'm fine. Thanks."

"Doreen, you came all the way over here to return my wallet, the least I can do is offer you a Coke."

"Okay, that would be great. You have a gorgeous home," she called out as Sheila headed for the kitchen.

"Thank you. I'll show you around in a minute."

"Really? That would be great, but I don't want to bother you."

"It's no bother. Larry's at the hospital and I'm not going anywhere."

Sheila had refilled her wine glass and brought it with her for the tour. Doreen was impressed by the open concept of the condo. They came back through the kitchen where Sheila poured herself another glass of wine and refilled Doreen's Coke. Doreen could tell that Sheila was getting tipsy. They went back into the living room where Sheila plopped herself down on the couch and started giggling.

Holding out her right hand she said, "I schmudged a nail before I left the shalom but I didn't want to tell you."

"Why not? I would have fixed it for you."

"It wash my own fault. I shoulda been more careful."

Sheila's eyes began to droop and she leaned her head on the couch. Doreen made idle conversation, but Sheila was fading fast. Within minutes she was asleep, snoring lightly.

Doreen found a blanket in the guest room and covered Sheila before heading out. As she passed the kitchen, she noticed something shiny on the counter. She walked over and saw a similar silver necklace to the ones Tessa and Gwen owned. Doreen lifted the necklace to examine it more closely. Looking around the kitchen, gently opening drawers, she found a small magnifying glass.

Doreen glanced in the living room but Shcila was sound asleep. She held the necklace under the magnifier and sure enough, it was the same necklace, only this time she could see a woman holding a set of plates. She forgot what it was called but knew it was some kind of legal symbol. Doreen put the necklace back on the counter and let herself out.

Back at her place, Doreen couldn't settle down. She knew it was none of her business, but it was bizarre to find out that three of her clients owned the same unusual necklace. Yet, the only one she had ever actually seen wearing it was Tessa, who had tried to hide it from her. Did Hattie Van Buren own one too?

The next morning when Doreen opened the salon, she found a copy of *The Boston Globe* folded in thirds, face up, left on the chair that Sheila Nussbaum had sat in the night before. She picked up the newspaper and read the article.

A 34-year old man claimed he'd been pushed off the second floor of a Cambridge Street garage around 2:00 a.m. on Thursday. The man suffered two broken legs, a fractured wrist, and multiple lacerations of the face. He was admitted to Mass General Hospital and told the surgeon, Dr. Lawrence Nussbaum, that he had been pushed from behind off the wall of the Early Bird Garage. The victim, William "Billy" Fergus, had been released from Walpole State Prison three months earlier where he had done time for beating his wife unconscious with a wooden curtain rod. Doreen recognized the name of the surgeon as Sheila's husband.

Doreen remembered Sheila's reaction when she overheard the women talking about a man claiming he'd been pushed. When Doreen called her about her wallet, she'd sounded tense.

What was going on with her clients lately? They were the kindest, most generous women she'd ever met, and now they all seemed suspicious to her. And Sean McDougal had also seemed suspicious of them.

Maybe all the women went to the same law school. But why hide it, unless it was a secret society? And why was Sheila so upset about the man who was pushed off the garage? Did she know him?

Doreen thought about Hattie Van Buren, a Suffolk County prosecutor, who'd been unable to convict a man twice for domestic abuse. Gwen Bigelow was on the Board of Rita's Place, a home for abused women. Tessa Bulfinch worked for the Battered Women's Legal Assistance Project. Sheila Nussbaum ran the hotline at the Women's Crisis Center. All of them were involved with violence against women.

Scenes from the last few days in the salon went roaring through Doreen's head like a passing freight train. Were these four women taking the law into their own hands? Is that why Sean McDougal had been asking about them? Had they pushed Billy Fergus off the garage?

The only way to know was to see them in action.

Starting at eleven o'clock that night, Doreen began parking across the street from Hattie's brownstone on Mount Vernon Street. Hattie was the only one she wasn't sure of. If nothing happened here, she'd move on to Gwen's house.

Two nights later, at 1:12 a.m. in the pouring rain, Hattie came out her front door dressed in black, holding an umbrella over her head, her hair tucked under a dark baseball cap. She walked quickly toward Charles Street then took a right onto Beacon Street, and a left on to Avery, stopping at The Ritz-Carlton. As Doreen double-parked on Beacon, she hardly recognized Sheila Nussbaum, also in dark clothing, wearing a short wig and glasses. In less than five minutes, Gwen Bigelow pulled up in her large, black Mercedes with Tessa Bulfinch riding shotgun. Sheila and Hattie jumped into the back seat.

Doreen followed the black Mercedes to Storrow Drive at a discreet distance. The car crossed over the Charles River and took a right on to Memorial Drive. From there they slowly drove through the narrow streets of Charlestown where the car eventually stopped across from Finney's Bar & Grill.

A few minutes later a man emerged from the bar, staggering as he walked. There was something vaguely familiar about him, but the rain had become torrential and she couldn't see that well. He continued to walk unsteadily and eventually made his way to the Charlestown Bridge. The black car picked up speed and began beeping its horn. The man turned, lost his footing, and fell against the bridge railing.

And that's when Doreen recognized the man as her stepfather, Armand Felice. She watched, mesmerized as the black car screeched to a halt and three doors flew open. Armand was lifted by his feet and shoved off the bridge into the icy, dark waters of the Charles River locks.

"Oh my good God," said Doreen, shocked by what she had just witnessed. Her mouth went dry and she began to shake all over.

Tessa, Hattie, and Sheila ran back to the car, jumped in, and slammed the doors. Gwen sped over the bridge and took a left into the North End and Doreen's neighborhood. But it was not over. Doreen spotted a large, dark car beeping, trying to pass two cars behind. A man was at the wheel and coming up fast behind her. Had he seen what happened? Snapping out of her haze, she stepped on the gas, honked her horn, and waved from behind the wheel.

The black Mercedes was nearing Nina's Ristorante and the smell of garlic filled the air. Gwen looked in her rear view mirror but did not recognize her so Doreen pulled up beside her at the next set of lights.

She leaned over and put down the window, yelling, "It's Doreen. Someone's on to you!"

Gwen looked stunned.

"Just follow me!"

Without waiting for an answer, Doreen passed the black car and took a sharp left. The Mercedes was close behind. After two more sharp lefts and a right, she pulled into an alley and went down a narrow opening between two buildings. She got out of the car.

"Go straight through there and take a right. You'll end up on 93 north. Go! Now!"

The next morning, McDougal stopped by for a chat.

"Late night last night?"

Doreen began sliding the cross on her neck from side to side.

"Not sure what you mean."

"I think you do."

He gave her the same kind look he had before. But Armand was out of her life, and there was no way she would ever rat out the people who had made that happen. Had McDougal been the one following her, or was he just guessing she was at the scene?

"You're playing with fire, little girl. Now mind you, I don't always play by the rules, but you're too young and have too bright a future to get mixed up in something you'll regret."

Doreen knew her flushed face was betraying her but there was something about McDougal that she trusted.

He raised his eyebrows and smiled at her. "Fortunately for you, I don't have any solid evidence."

Doreen waited.

McDougal looked at the cross on her necklace. "Ever hear, 'Vengeance is mine, sayeth the Lord'?"

"Yes, sir."

"Am I right in assuming it's over for you?'"

"Yes, sir."

"Think you can talk your clients into finding an alternative to justice?"

"I think I can."

"Good. You take care now, hear?"

"Yes, sir, I will."

One year later, Doreen woke to the sun streaming through the second floor window of a large Victorian home in Brookline she'd purchased with the help of some "investors," and the money she'd saved working at Pétale de Rose. She rolled over on her back and smiled as she listened to the birds chirping in the tree outside. Six months ago, Joannie Napolitano had moved in with her, and downstairs was her own salon, which she'd named *Femme Fatale*.

Her eyes traveled across the room to the middle drawer of her lingerie chest, where a small velvet pouch held a silver necklace with a blindfolded woman holding the scales of justice. A souvenir from another life.

* * *

Christine Bagley received her MFA from Lesley University and was a fiction contributor to the 2016 Bread Loaf Writers' Conference. She won Honorable Mention in 2012 for the Al Blanchard Award in Crime Fiction and, since 2011, she has been teaching foreign nationals how to improve their writing. *The Manicurist* is her sixth short story publication.

FOR LOVE OF THE DEAD
by Rachel Brown

I massage the corpse's hands, trying to get the fingers to uncurl. It usually doesn't take too long, but this young lady is proving quite a challenge. With her curled mane of bright auburn hair, pale skin and long, delicate neck, she has a bewitching beauty and I wonder whether there is a grisly history. But her records reveal a probable suicide: sleeping pills ground up in alcohol. I shift position to gain a better grip on her hands, and allow myself to think about the girl she might have been. I'm not in any hurry. This is the time I get to cherish my people. Between massage and formaldehyde, I can begin to believe I pump life back into the dead.

The buzzer for the front reception sounds. I ignore it at first. It's after hours, and whoever it is can come back tomorrow, or telephone. By the time things roll around to me, emergencies are generally over. But this caller is insistent, and the buzzer rings for a third time. Reluctantly, since I generally find myself more at peace with the dead than the living, I haul myself up out of my seat and go to see who it is.

As I approach the glass doors I see a woman outside, peering in. She looks to be in her fifties, and she wears one of those brightly colored shawls that women her age often use to conceal loose neck skin. Opening the door causes the woman to start gushing like beer from a draft tap, although the latter would be far more welcome.

"You're Naomi? The one who has my Becca? They told me her body had gone for embalming now the autopsy's done. Is she in there?" She gestures inside.

I raise my eyebrows, but I don't invite her in. "Embalming is part of my job," I say. She wants to see one of the corpses. I often get this sort of request from people who can't wait for me to finish. I always tell them they'd much rather see the deceased after I've practiced my art than before; if necessary I say I'm in the middle of draining organs, a stinky business. That usually sends them on their way.

"My Becca's young. Just twenty-one. You must have noticed her."

So my young angel goes by Becca. Of course I noticed her. She's the only female south of sixty I have downstairs. "How can I help you?"

"I'm her mother. I need to come in. I've heard about you."

I size her up. I took this job for many reasons. One, I hardly ever have insipid conversations that nudge at intimacy; in a funeral home, people either want to go deep, sometimes even deep irreverence, my favorite, or they want focused, shallow small talk, which I can also manage. Hovering somewhere in the middle is what kills me, so to speak. Two, I believe in death. I really do. I have a tagline: *Death is the bookend of a well-lived life.* Third, I want to help people, give them options. When my Grandpa died my mom was angry as hell that she couldn't bury him the way she'd have liked to. He wanted a hole in the ground in the woods; he got a full-barreled procession with fancy cars that he despised. She blamed me because I told her if she buried him without a permit I'd report her. Helping people sometimes means letting them in to vent, but I'm not sure about this lady. Moms generally want to sidle in and cozy up to the corpse. I sigh. "I'm so sorry about your daughter, but it wouldn't help. Best see her when she's ready."

"Sam Pearson said you'd help me."

Sam. Okay, there's another reason I'm an undertaker. I get sucked in. It's such a big thing, death. Your one shot at everything, whisked away. So when death is unnatural I get curious. Can't help myself. I've been known to poke around. I feel I owe it to my corpses. His mother was one of my first, and between us we found out that she'd been killed because she'd been about to blow the whistle on an EPO doping racket at greyhound races.

Sam always credited with me the sleuthing. Rightly so, I suppose, though I try not to get too cocky.

I usher her in and sit her down. "What do you mean?" I ask.

"There was a murder note, you see. Have you ever heard of such a damn thing?" The woman cackles loudly. Some people might find that distasteful, but not me. There are few rules in my parlor.

"I've heard of it," I say, trying not to sound too interested. This doesn't happened often, especially not in a small town like Northampton. But I've read about notes that are supposedly penned by the killer. Usually they're not. Usually those notes turn out to be suicides, the *yet more troubled kind,* I suppose. The ones who can't resist running circles around people even after they're gone. "But wasn't it a suicide?"

"The police think it was *probably* suicide," she corrects.

"And you don't?"

She shakes her head. "I'm her mother," she repeats, as though this ends the analysis. "And I say it's a murder note."

I decide to humor her. "Who do you think killed Becca then?"

"Someone who was jealous of her, I suppose. Or someone she dumped." She thrusts a piece of paper at me, looking furtive. "I'm not supposed to have it, but I copied it out. It hasn't been released, but Sam said you'd want to see it."

I take the note. Of course I want to see it.

For all who loved me, I'm so sorry.

What you don't know is my guilt.

The heartache of living with myself all these years, knowing the person I am.

I am a person who has caused pain to others.

I am a person who has caused harm to others.

I am not a person who enriches the world. I bring sorrow in my wake.

That is why I must proceed no further down this path of life.

I am ashamed of my deeds; I will not tell them here.

For my mother, I love you more than I can say.

For my three musketeers, I blow you each a kiss.

For my girlfriends, say a prayer for me.

For all who loved me, I'm sorry. I hope that in death we can find intimacy of souls.

I look at Becca's mom blankly. What a frickin' travesty of a note. *Intimacy of souls*? Who says that? "Awful," I say, drawing out the word slowly, "but I'm not sure why you'd call this a murder note."

"Oh, I see it's *supposed* to look like suicide," she says, pointedly.

I read it again. It's certainly a bit odd, I'll grant her that, but a person's last words can be. "Who are the three musketeers?"

Becca's mom shrugs, then begins to cry. "She had three roommates. All boys. Maybe it was them? I didn't like that she lived with all boys."

I hand her a tissue. "You said somebody might have been jilted? Was that one of them?"

She dabs at her eyes and gives me a sad look. "I don't know. She never told me, but everyone fell in love with Becca. She can't have killed herself though. She just can't have. So," she looks at me imploringly, "you'll do your thing?"

I'm bleary-eyed by the time I set Becca out for viewing. Open caskets will be the death of me, I like to say, and sometimes I get a giggle, though more often an indignant stare. I stayed up most of the night after her mom finally left, reading up on details about the case. But I didn't skimp on my Becca. No way. Strong foundation, a little blush, mascara, and golden eyeshadow with a hint of green to match her three-quarter sleeve wrap dress. She looks like Botticelli's Aphrodite, but clothed exactly to her mother's specs.

Things don't look good for mom's murder theory. I doubt all of the details of the investigation have been released, but Becca had a prescription for sleeping pills, and friends reported that she'd been upset by a recent romantic break up, though nobody had realized how deeply she must have been affected.

People are beginning to file in. I hover in the background, just behind the casket. People tend not to notice me. It's not my job to interfere with the grieving, but I need to be present just in case something goes wrong with the corpse. One time somebody actually leaned into the coffin and hugged the body. You're not supposed to do that. Corpses can be quite delicately arranged. The whole show went belly side up for a moment. Almost literally.

Today I have another motive for lurking. Becca's family has invited the mourners to leave small tokens of remembrance in the coffin. Photos are common, as are trinkets, or emblems of a shared hobby, such as a chess piece or a knitting needle. In my experience, people tend to deliver something that strokes their own ego. They like to pretend that the deceased cared about them in a particular kind of way. I spot one of our local police sergeants, who is also standing unobtrusively nearby. Sergeant Ray Brown, he's a pro. He's here for the same reason I am. Becca's death may have the hallmarks of suicide, but that doesn't mean he thinks the case is airtight. "Naomi," he says, acknowledging me with a brief nod as I slide into shadow.

I spot the three guys who must have been Becca's roommates as soon as they come in. They're dressed almost identically in cheap charcoal gray suits with white shirts and thin black ties that look like they came out of the 70's. One has floppy blond hair that more or less conceals his face; another is dark-skinned with a spiky haircut shaved above his ears; the third is heavyset and broad-faced with a full, dark hipster beard. The three musketeers indeed. They look a bit awestruck and lost, as though they've been invited to a celebrity's party and don't know how to behave.

The blond approaches the casket first. He mumbles something about how much he'll miss her, and how they'll always have Helsinki. He blows a kiss and as he does so he sweeps back his hair so that I can see his face is handsome, chiseled. He drops in a small knife, which he calls "our puukko." My antennae are raised, naturally. A knife is an unusual choice. Aggressive. Spike comes next. He leans over so close to Becca that I almost have to step out to intervene. Then he whispers loudly, "you selfish fucking bitch. You selfish. Fucking. Amazing. Bitch." I'm outraged and I want to punch him. I get quite protective over my corpses. He drops in a note, which is the worst thing he could have done. It's folded so I can't get a glimpse of it, and the casket will shortly be sealed. The only way I'll be able to read that note is exhumation, and I've never gone that far. Not yet. Hipster comes up last. He's crying and making no bones about it, the tears are a-flowing. "Becca," he says in a choked up voice, "you always meant so, so much to me. You'll never even know how much." He drops in some sort of newspaper. I recognize *The Valley Advocate,* our area's weekly, and I can just catch part of the date—September, 2012. Almost seven years ago.

I watch the other mourners too, but I don't see anything that really piques my attention. A hair band. A sneaker. Apparently Becca was a bit of a runner. Her favorite book. (It's a Jodi Picoult novel. More mainstream than I'd hoped for my Becca. At least the uncle who placed it did so carefully, without messing up my craft.) A small model of the Eiffel tower left by somebody who speaks garrulously in French.

The casket is closed and following a short service, a somber procession leads Becca to her final resting place. I wait for them to return, knowing that the mourners will mill around the reception area for refreshments and camaraderie. When the deceased has completed a long, full life it's usually a good time; today it'll doubtless be somber as a courthouse. There's a film of Becca running in the background and I stare intently at it for a while; it's always fascinating for me to see how my corpses move around, animated. Somehow their motions are rarely as I have pictured.

The boys bypass the coffee table and head straight for the beer. I line up behind them, get a bottle myself, then sashay on over. With my hair tucked into my black engine driver cap, high heel boots, and no makeup, I look quite different than I did earlier in the day. Even if they'd noticed me, which they probably didn't, they won't be able to tell.

I brush up against Hipster's arm and fall a little as though I was jostled into him. "Oops, sorry about that."

"No worries," he says absently, giving me a small smile.

"You knew her well? So awful, right?" I try my best to look distraught.

"We all lived with her," Hipster says, gesturing toward his friends. "We're in college together. At Amherst."

"We fucking loved her," says Spike. "She called us her three musketeers!" His words are loud and slurred and I think he may have had a few already, which I don't care for.

"Wow," I say, looking impressed. "She lived with three guys! Foxy lady never told me that. Cheers to her." I raise my glass. "I don't think I'd be able to hack that, but she could do anything."

"Becca was super laid back," says Blondie, giving a sheepish grin. "Which is why this all feels so surreal. How did you know her?"

"I haven't seen her for ages," I say, "but I used to hang out with her on summer vacation a lot. Our families both lived around here." Becca's mom told me the family was local to western Massachusetts. "I'm a few years older, of course, but there was a time when we were really close." I'm actually ten years older, but I've found that with my face scrubbed clean I can easily pass for mid-twenties. On the flip side, with a bunch of makeup caked on I can look over forty. I take pride in my malleability.

Hipster frowns. "You've never visited our apartment, have you?"

"No," I sigh. "It's funny, I'd just been emailing with Becca, and I was supposed to visit her this week. I suppose I'll just go back up to Vermont early now." I pause to let my predicament sink in. I don't really know what I think I'll discover. I suspect Becca's mom simply can't face the fact her daughter topped herself, but I do find it odd that Becca would have mentioned these boys in the suicide note, when she said less about her girlfriends. "You know what I'll miss most about Becca?" I ask.

"Whassat?" Spike obliges.

"Her electricity," I say, and I extend my arms outward as though in wonder. "It was amazing. Everyone was drawn to her, like a burning fire on a cold night. I've seen it with my own eyes. People meet her, then get this dazed look, as though they're entranced." I laugh. "I'd have been jealous if I wasn't half in love with her myself."

Becca's mum had described her to me this way and it looks as though she was right because Blondie eyes me appreciatively. "Yeah," he says. "That's a good way of putting it."

"I just wish I'd seen more of her recently," I say, and my voice wavers. "I feel so out of touch. All these things she did that I never got to talk to her about. Paris. Helsinki."

Blondie puts down his beer. "I can tell you about some of that. I'd like to. Show you pictures, too. You should come over. Like you were planning."

I look surprised. "Oh, I don't mean...I don't want to impose on you."

"Why not?" he says. "You've got extra time in Northampton. It'd be good for us all."

"That's right," says Hipster, and he gestures at the gathering. "It helps to know how loved she was."

Spike raises his beer bottle, but it slips through his fingers and crashes to the floor.

"Three sheets to the wind," mutters Becca's mother, coming to stand next to me. She glares as Spike's friends escort him out of the hall. "No respect, that boy. None at all."

Two hours later I've locked up my parlor and I'm sitting in their apartment looking at a big photo album stuffed with pictures of Finland. I had time to do a little sleuthing on the internet before coming over, from which I learned that the puukko is a small hunting knife used in Finland. I suppose it could be a memento. I tried to look up the *Advocate,* too, but no dice. There were way too many articles from September 2012, and I didn't have time to sift through it all.

Finland is all bright skies and smiling, healthy-looking people. Of course it would be; Finns are the happiest people in the world, they say. It's just as cold there though and I don't understand why they don't have the sour, hunched look of New Englanders, but they don't. Still, I always think it helps my business that I can make people look more at ease in death than they ever were in life. I'm sure I wouldn't do so well in Finland.

Becca and Blondie—whose name, boringly enough, turns out to be John—feature in most of the photos. Apparently they'd met on a term abroad. When I hear they dated in sophomore year my ears prick up. "Ah, Becca," I say, looking fondly at a shot of my girl in her bikini at a public sauna on the shores of the Baltic Sea. I look slyly from John to Spike, "were you all in love with her, then?"

Spike is holding a wet towel to his forehead, and his voice is slightly muffled. "I reckon so," he says. "Hard not to be. She was so sweet, always had time for everyone. But hot too," he adds, peeking out from behind the towel with a cheeky grin. "She called us her three musketeers."

"Must have been nice for her living here, then," I say. "Never short a boyfriend."

Hipster had been out in the kitchen fetching snacks, but on his return his face falls as though my remark pains him. "I wouldn't say that," he says, offering me a bowl of nuts and a beer, which I decline. "Anyway, Syed never got together with her."

Spike, aka Syed, grinds the walnut he is holding between his fingers so hard that it flakes onto the carpet. "Because *you* wasted her time," he says.

"I'm sorry," says Hipster softly.

Syed doesn't answer. He just sits back in his chair, so rigid and upright that he reminds me of a gravestone.

Hipster turns back to me. "Becca and I dated, but it became obvious we were better as friends. I like my books; she likes her parties. Never the twain shall meet. At least, not after morning coffee."

I notice his use of the present tense, but of course I don't correct it. "So you ended it then? A while ago?"

There's a short silence, broken by Syed. "Answer her, then," he says, ice in his voice.

"Yes and no," says Hipster. "I might as well tell you. I'm afraid I broke it off just a few days before she killed herself." Suddenly, his body convulses and I'm afraid he's going to start sobbing as loudly as he had at the funeral parlor. "But it can't have been that," he says wretchedly. "She didn't like me that much. I had no idea."

"Come on, man," says John, getting up and rubbing his friends shoulder. "It wasn't your fault. You know that. You couldn't have known how she'd react."

I wait to see whether any of them will elaborate, even in speculation, but they don't. They simply look downcast, as though John's words have reminded them that they failed to notice their friend's downward spiral. I murmur something about the bathroom, and John points listlessly toward the hallway. "Right at the end," he says.

It doesn't take me long to ascertain that the first room I've entered is Syed's. I don't have anything specific to seek, so I cast my eyes around looking for inspiration. This is the part of the hunt I love: making sense of a jumble of objects. Why does Syed have so many ill-matched shoes? Why does he have a University of Chicago sweatshirt hanging on the back of his chair? I make mental note of the inventory, but pause only at the desk. Here, I find what I believe are prior editions of the missive he placed in Becca's casket. But there is more. Older letters that he wrote Becca and probably never sent. I read a few lines and take a step back, surprised. I need only a taste to understand that his feelings are far more intense than he expressed moments earlier, to say the least. I snap several photos with my phone, then I steal quietly into the next room. By contrast with Syed's, it's impeccably neat. Even the items that don't fit on shelves or in cupboards—mainly shoes and excess books—are stored tidily against the walls. Because of the order, the bedside drawer that has been left an inch or so ajar catches my attention. I let out a breath I didn't realize I'd been holding when I see it's what I'd hoped for: a September 15 article from *The Valley Advocate*. I take more photographs, stuff my phone into my pocket, and am about to try to find John's room when I hear somebody calling me.

"Rachel, are you okay?"

I kick myself for using the name "Rachel"; it's far too close to "Rebecca" and for that reason was the first thing that came to mind—rookie mistake. I dash into the bathroom and immediately flush the toilet. "Just a moment," I yell.

Leaning against the shower wall I first zoom in on the text of the main newspaper article on my phone. Samantha Keough, just sixteen, had been killed at a tragic fairground accident at the Big E when one of the roller-coaster cars had come off its rails. Her younger brother Justin had been on the ride with her, but he had been flung out and into the air, landing several feet away from the car, whereas it had fallen straight down on top of her, crushing her to death. I can't make much sense of the article, but I stare closely at the accompanying picture. It shows a debris-filled field in which grim-faced people are turned-away from the wreckage. In the corner of the photograph are two teenage girls, one Asian and one with flowing long, red hair. I flip to my next photo and read some interviews with witnesses of the tragic accident. One is Becca.

There's a knock at the door. "You okay?" I think it's Syed.

"Coming," I call, and quickly enlarge one of my photos of his old letters. I scan the words, but it is the line at the end that chills me. *With you I feel an intimacy of soul that signifies true love.* I stop for a moment, letting everything I've just read sink in. Then I press the flush again and type out a quick text while running the faucet, before striding out past Syed and giving him a nod. "All yours," I say.

When I return to the living room I accept the beer that Hipster offered me earlier. As I take it, I look at him askance as though I'm inspecting something. "I feel like I recognize you," I say finally. "There's someplace I've seen you before."

He looks at me wide-eyed and shrugs his shoulders. "Sorry," he says. "I don't think so."

"You grew up here in western Mass., right?"

"Local born and bred."

I stare at him some more and will the color to drain from my face. It's something I'm good at. I imagine a tornado, or coming home to find my mother naked. "Oh my God," I say softly. "I remember. At least I think I do. I was at the big E the day your sister—. She was Samantha, right?"

It's his turn to stare at me, hard. "What do you know about that?" he asks, a little harshly.

"I know she died," I say softly. "I'm so sorry."

"Justin, I never knew you had a sister!" exclaims John, sounding a little wounded.

"I don't really talk about it. Too long ago."

"It's so strange the way fate works," I say. "You'll never believe it, but I was there with Becca that day. I remember it hit home because it could so easily have been us. We'd just ridden the same ride. Becca felt especially bad, I know."

I keep my eyes on Justin's body as I speak, and I see his fists tense and clench. He doesn't believe me. He knows his own news clipping. I have dark hair, but I couldn't be mistaken for Asian.

"I don't remember anything like that," he says tightly. "I'd never met Becca before college."

I leave the apartment and walk around the corner to stand flat against a brick-walled building facing out onto a small lot with a few parked cars and a dumpster. I breathe in the damp spring air, musty in these tight confines. Playing a part takes a lot out of me. Still, I know I'm not done. I close my eyes and think about Becca, robbed of her future. I think about the cold stillness of her corpse. For me, this is energizing. Strange to say, but it comforts me to contemplate the long rest that awaits us all. When I first told my mother I'd become an undertaker she scoffed disdainfully. "Why am I not surprised? You probably get along better with the dead than with the living. Always so weird." She wasn't completely wrong. Remembering my charges makes me feel grateful that I'm not there yet; there will be time enough for endless quiet, but for now I am here and I am strong.

Justin arrives not thirty seconds later, as I thought he would. I can tell he's surprised to have caught up to me so quickly. "What are you playing at?" he asks roughly. "You weren't at the Big E that day."

I'm tart in my response. "You sure?"

"Pretty damn sure."

I lean right up to him. "You've never forgiven Becca for the death of your sister, have you? She cut ahead of you in line that day–she admitted it, it should have been her who died. Then, to top it all, in her interview with the paper she made the whole thing about her. How guilty she felt. How terrible it was to witness, that sort of thing."

"Bullshit," he says, but too quickly. "I don't know what you're talking about."

"You set it up nicely, I'll give you that. Breaking up with her days before luring her back with that laced martini. But you couldn't resist tooting your own horn in the so-called suicide note, could you? Three musketeers!

Still, you figured that if anyone did look at you three, they'd go after Syed. He's the one obsessed with Becca. And he's the one who never even dated her. But let me give you some advice. If you're trying to implicate someone, you've got to do it right. You were lazy. Anyone who speaks of intimacy of soul—as in holistic oneness—would never speak of intimacy of *souls* because that suggests separateness."

That's when he lunges at me, but he doesn't even make contact before Sergeant Brown steps out from behind the dumpster. He wasn't exaggerating when he responded to my text and told me he'd be in position in under five minutes.

"Arms in the air!" he shouts. He's holding a gun, and at the sight of it Justin crumples to the floor, whimpering.

Justin is arrested for attempted assault, but Sergeant Brown assures me that a charge of murder in the first degree will be forthcoming if the corroboration plays out as he's expecting. They'll unseal the casket to get that article. They'll find his prints in the right places—maybe even on some of Syed's letters or on Becca's murder note. They'll probe his alibi for the night she died.

The sergeant asks if I'd like to accompany them to the station, but I decline. I'll provide a statement later in the day. Just now, I've received a message that a new body will be arriving in less than an hour. The sooner I'm back with my tribe the better.

* * *

Originally from the UK, **Rachel Brown** now lives in Somerville, Massachusetts, and works as an attorney for the City of Lowell, an old mill town north of Boston. She loves books, language, and punishingly long mountain bike races. This is her second short story in print. Her debut appeared in *Halloween Party 2019*, published by Devils' Party Press.

A LIGHT IN THE WATER
by Cynthia Drew

Francine Lamb tottered through Logan airport in her new spike heels, her tote atop a matched rolling bag—a parting gift from Ed before he died, allegorically cutting her loose.

The greasy spew of a concourse hamburger quivered in her stomach and she wobbled to a stop at the Departures board, lit green—a large number of flights leaving on time tonight.

Should she point out to them that not de-icing planes had doomed hundreds? She'd be happy to wait an extra few minutes while they shot the bird's wings with glycol. *Maintenance staff must be short,* she thought, *this being Christmas Eve. Someone made this decision without regard for passenger safety. Don't they care what their passengers might fear?*

These things Francine knew about herself before she married: that she was afraid of flying and water and heart disease. Heart disease—a fear so overriding that she'd married Ed, a cardiologist with his own plane and a swimming pool in his back yard.

The jet turned at the end of the runway and paused. Francine gazed out her window, unable to distinguish ice from the gloss of silver paint under a skiff of snow on the wing. She heard the usual clicks and pops as flights attendants locked things into place, followed by, "Flight attendants, cross-check and all-call." Her stomach tightened.

The A-300 lurched forward, laden with passengers, luggage, heavy coats and Christmas presents, and an almost-certain layer of ice on its wings, rolled for fifteen seconds, twenty, a full minute. Hell-bent on velocity it bumped along the runway, accelerating into a light snowstorm.

Francine gripped the armrests, squeezed her eyes shut, braced for the inevitable swerve on frozen tarmac, tires blowing, fuselage breaking apart. She mentally pulled the pilot's wheel to her, wanting to feel the plane's nose lift, holding her breath to lighten their load. The jet's belly groaned and thumped, then a pervasive white noise sprayed through the cabin—the same noise she imagined Ed heard now, the shush of premature death.

She heard a cough, and another from a different direction. She flexed her tensed fingers, covered her nose to avoid inhaling recycled germs, opened her eyes, measured the plane's ascent in a twelve-second count to be sure they stayed aloft. She swallowed and blew into her fist. The plane banked wide. Boston's lights lay beneath like a jeweled garrote.

"Dear God," she murmured, "get me to Atlanta and I promise I will go to Mass every Sunday for a month." *Always,* she thought, *always I make these bargains with God, wanting something in return. Then I break my promises.*

She hadn't loved Ed, had never loved anyone but Coy Davis. After she married Ed she stacked a constant yearning to be single on top of her fears and for fifteen years, until he died, she took Ed's charity and affection without returning them, heartsick she had married at all. And then, five months ago, on a Thursday night, Ed wasting in ICU from thyrotoxic heart disease, Francine walked to a hospital bathroom, pushed two fingers down her throat and vomited her fearful, heartsick soul until she spat blood.

After Ed's funeral she lost herself in volunteer work and book club chatter for a couple of months before she ceased talking altogether—her own voice too full of life to suit her ears. She stopped eating rather than heave blood, dropped forty pounds, half her hair and hundreds of hours of sleep.

She decided to travel at Christmas.

And why not, Francine thought. *Why not go somewhere this first Christmas without Ed? Somewhere as far away as I can think to go. I am sane enough to know what I need to do.*

There was no snow in Atlanta as she changed planes; still her answered prayers provided no comfort on takeoff—she clenched her teeth, lifted her feet to help the plane clear the runway, worried the second flight south to Grand Cayman.

From the balcony of her hotel room, near eleven on a warm, windless Christmas Eve, Francine watched people straggle in and out of a bar on the beach, moving in time to the music. A man walked by below, his blonde hair fastened back in a ponytail, his T-shirt stretched across familiar-looking shoulders.

She caught herself: *Yes, yes, plenty of men have long hair and shoulders that look like Coy Davis's shoulders.* She grew sleepy for the first time in five months, and hungry. She ate a candy bar from the mini-fridge, scrubbed her face clean of makeup, went to bed without throwing up and dreamed of staring into Coy Davis's blue eyes.

Soothed by the ocean rollers' steady whish-whish-whish Francine slept until the maid came at midday to make up the room. She ate shrimp tacos at the pool bar, and then walked to the ocean and got thoroughly wet without a thought for her fear of water. She sat on the sand, looking out to the hazy horizon, thinking about Coy Davis, reliving fifteen years ago for the millionth time. Seeing Coy: hard-muscled and quick-witted, feeling him undress her with those fabulous blue eyes.

He used her name too often in conversation, but she did not correct him, forgiving one shortcoming in an otherwise flawless man. And too late Francine found she loved Coy Davis as much as he did—that only she had given away her heart. She sank into the mud of self-pity, and three months later she married Ed. But Ed died of thyrotoxic heart disease.

Thyro-toxic-heart-dis-ease, thyro-toxic-heart-dis-ease, the ocean whooshed in Francine's ears. She gazed down the beach to the bar. *Life is so profuse here,* she thought, *no one supposes they might die.*

Christmas night the on-shore breezes ebbed again. Francine sketched on some makeup, pinned her brown hair up, pulled it down, pinned it up, took it down again, lotioned her arms wrinkled from losing forty pounds in five months and went to the beach bar to celebrate being single.

Under the bar's thatched roof everyone's tongue had thickened with liquor and humidity. She sat at the far end, away from the crowd, shouted an order for a piña colada over UB40's rap in *Red, Red Wine*. Her voice tasted brassy in her mouth.

The man with a blonde ponytail walked by, toward the restroom. She recognized his shoulders and his rangy gait. She stared at him when he returned.

"What?" he stopped, smoothing his T-shirt over his chest. The slogan on his shirt read *Stick Around, It Gets Worse*. He slid onto the bar stool next to hers, ordered a beer.

Francine said nothing.

He looked at her, considering. "Funny, you look like a talker."

Francine's heart pounded. *Yes!* she thought. *Yes, it's him—and I so deserve this after all that's happened*. "Coy?" she said.

"Me?" he scoffed. "Hardly coy."

"No, I mean your name. You're Coy Davis, aren't you?"

He gave her a sideways glance. "Boy, that's a weird one. How'd you get that close?"

"Close?"

"Name's Con Dyer." He shrugged. "I mean, same initials and all. Three letters in my first name, too. Well, actually, my first name's Connor, but everyone calls me Con." He held out his right hand. "And yours?"

"Francine Lamb," she said, shaking hands. "Visiting for a week or so. You too?"

"I live here."

"Lucky. How long have you been here?"

"Twelve years. Where you from, Francine?"

"Boston. When I left yesterday it was snowing. They're having a white Christmas." She picked up her piña colada. "Merry Christmas, Con."

He tipped his beer bottle toward her then took a swig. "Merry Christmas, Francine."

She knew the timbre of Con Dyer's voice and how he would touch her—his fingertips barely skimming her breasts. She would tremble, wanting more, arching her body to his. She leaned on the bar and cupped her chin in her hand.

"You okay?"

She nodded. The curve of his jaw, the tattoo on his forearm, she recognized those too. "You work nearby?"

Con Dyer gestured again with his bottle. "Dive shop next door. Pays the rent. What do you do, Francine?"

"Nothing."

"Nobody does 'nothing,' Francine."

"Seriously. I haven't worked in fifteen years."

"Wow. You get bored doing nothing, Francine?"

"You know what bores me, Con? Hearing my name. Could you go easy on it?"

He grinned and she noticed the familiar cotton-curtain gap between his front teeth. "Tourist talk," he said. "Most people love hearing their names."

"Not me" she said. "Not...me." She looked out to the ocean. The moon's reflection twisted on the surface of the water.

Con pushed his beer bottle away, stood, threw a five on the bar. "I dive tomorrow, can't be drinking. See you around Fran—uh, sorry. Have a good visit, darlin'."

She went back to the hotel, laid on the bed with her arms outstretched. Tears ran down the sides of her face until she slept. She wakened the following morning thinking about Coy Davis. *Do dreams ever really end?* she wondered.

She walked up the beach to the dive shop and enrolled in diving lessons.

Con taught her about the equipment and how to breathe underwater. Christmas week they dived or met for breakfast or walked on the beach at the end of the day. They slept together. He touched her as she expected he would, and she grew to crave that touch.

The afternoon of New Year's Eve, Con Dyer did not come to the beach bar. She left the bar and went next door to the dive shop. Through a side window she saw Con teaching a younger woman about diving equipment, showing her how to breathe. Fury rippled like spiders down Francine's neck, gathered between her shoulder blades and exploded in her stomach next to her fears of water and flying and heart disease. She would teach the diving teacher. *How breathtaking this will be,* she thought. *For both of us.*

She rented a car at the hotel, drove into town to buy packing tape. Went again to the dive shop. Looked through the side window. Now no one was inside. She pulled the car around to the back of the building. Left the engine running. Dragged Con's dive tank from the rack and taped its air intake to the tail pipe. While she waited she thought about how much she would have liked to stay in the Caymans with Con, how happy their life together might have been. After an hour she peeled the packing tape away from the belching tail pipe, cleaned adhesive from the tank's valve, replaced Con's tank alongside others in the rack and returned the car to the rental stand.

On a warm, blue-sky day in mid-January, the humidity as low as it would be all year, the Cayman Compass reported Con Dyer's death by coronary embolism. The obituary called him "a laid-back Albuquerque native."

That night Francine prepared to leave the Caymans. Then it struck her: the paper had his home town and cause of death wrong—Coy hailed from Minneapolis, he died in a diving accident. She unpacked, notified the front desk she would be staying. Changed her mind and packed once more. Remembered she didn't need to flee. Unpacked. Thought again. Repacked and took a taxi to the airport.

Over the plane's PA system a flight attendant explained emergency measures: "...You can activate a light in the water by pulling the tab on the front of your safety vest...," but on takeoff Francine didn't whisper her usual imprecations to her God.

Finally, she knew, she had freed herself of Coy Davis, and faced down her fears of flying and water and heart disease. As the plane climbed into the night sky, she stared out the window at the moon's reflection shivering off a dark sea and wondered how searchers ever found anyone in that vast blackness. *Coro-nary-embo-lism, coro-nary-embo-lism* the jets whined in her ears.

She closed her eyes, imagining Coy's blue-eyed smile, his face slowly replaced by Con's, then the two faces overlaid: Coy's and Con's. And again, Coy's face and Con's. She wondered why Coy had bothered to change his name, how long it had taken his auburn hair to sun bleach, and how incredible that his blue eyes had, she saw now, turned brown. *That's enough,* she thought. *I'm sane enough to know what I did.*

"Ma'am?" a flight attendant prompted. "Water? Juice? Soft drink?"

Francine knew the timbre of the voice. She drew a deep breath. *Dear God,* she prayed, *I will go to mass for a month if this man's eyes are—*

"Water? Juice? Soft drink?" he repeated.

She turned from the window to glance at his name badge. *Calvin Daly.* Her stomach churned, her heart raced.

"Ma'am? You okay?"

She gripped the armrests and squeezed her eyes shut, listening to the jets roar like the crash of the ocean. In that moment she turned loose of her fears of flying and water and heart disease, and then she looked up again at the flight attendant.

And gazed into Coy Davis's fabulous blue eyes.

* * *

Cynthia Drew's short stories and novels have garnered numerous awards, most recently INDIE Gold for Best Mystery 2018. She is half of the sister writing team of Drew Golden, whose Wynn Cabot Mysteries debut this fall from Level Best Books with the first in the series, *Nouveau Noir.*

THE FAMILY HOUSE
by Victoria Goessling

Childhood memories are tricky things, aren't they? Problems that you laugh at as an adult were oh so scary when you were eight or nine. Then again, at that age anything was possible. You quickly recognize that fallacy when adulthood strikes.

I like to think that we had a wonderful childhood. South Boston was our kingdom, safe as long as you stayed away from the fellows who ran with crims like Whitey Bulger and others like him. Us? We were just the Sullivan kids, five of us, three boys, two girls.

Dad worked on the docks and Mom at the phone company. We had more than some of the other kids, less than others. We went to Holy Mother Catholic School, Mass every week, and mostly did what our parents wanted us to do.

It was the way of our world.

Mom and Dad claimed the backyard of our three-family house, turned it into a beautiful place with mystical flowers and Dad's prized tomato plants. They met at a flower show, of all things, two youngsters from Southie, and spent a lot of time together working in back. We all had to help with the vegetables and yard cleanup, but we weren't allowed around most of the flowers because Mom liked strange things like the castor bean plant and caladium and delphinium. Oh, how could I forget her favorite wisteria? It twisted and curled around the pergola that Dad had built for her when they first bought the place. Mom said that the seeds from these things could make us sick and that we needed to stay away. They'd upset our stomach, maybe do worse. Mom always seemed to know everything, so we listened to her and stayed away from her beautiful, deadly blossoms.

We just figured it meant less time weeding and more time running around Carson Beach, racing through the park and making up stories about Fort Independence out on Castle Island. That was just fine with us. All of the neighborhood kids used to hang out there. Then the bullies moved in, claimed the beach as their own. Pretty soon girls stayed away because of the catcalls and grabs. Even big guys like my brothers started avoiding the area. A clean fight they could handle, but the bullies didn't fight clean. Dad said they were the youngsters of some thugs and to leave the chowderheads alone. Find somewhere else to play.

Like I said, we knew enough to avoid that sort of punk, so we did what Dad told us to do, but it was never as much fun as our times at Carson Beach in the heat of the summer.

We all got a little bit older and things changed. Chuck, the oldest of us, joined the Navy and got killed off the coast of Vietnam. Billy joined the Boston Fire Department and then my little brother Jimmy joined the police. Claire and I went into hospital work, me in the lab drawing blood and Claire as a nurse. We all worked our way up the ranks, lived by our parents' rule of decency and honesty, prospered by anyone's standards.

Mom died first. Her lungs gave out from those Virginia Slims that she just couldn't seem to give up. Dad faded away shortly after Mom. The doctors said it was his diabetes, but we all knew it was a broken heart.

Claire moved into the empty apartment on the second floor. I'd never left the family home, not wanting to leave Mom and Dad alone as they got older. The others helped as they could, but it's hard when everyone works a different shift.

Shortly after the funeral, when we were starting to go through their things, Claire and I had a visitor. Said he was interested in buying the house. We said that it wasn't for sale. Billy and Jimmy were married, had families and homes of their own. I'd never married and Claire, to our parent's everlasting Southie Catholic shame, was divorced. This old three family was our home, and the two of us planned to stay, maybe find a nice tenant for the third floor flat, but updates were in order. The place was trapped in the fifties.

Our parents had paid it off years before, done the basic maintenance, and kept their beautiful garden. It was nice. It was home. The goon persisted, but there are few as stubborn as a Southie girl, and he finally left, his card on the telephone table.

It was fancy, with a slick finish and elaborate script, black with white writing. Brendan Costello, Investor and a phone number were the only things written there. Claire and I agreed that we'd never sell to a pretentious idjut like him, if ever we planned to sell.

Jimmy and his Marci dropped in a few days later. The card was still on the table where Claire had tossed it. Jimmy picked it up, read it, and asked what was going on. Claire told him about Costello's visit. Jimmy got real serious and told us to be careful. Costello was a front man for some goons who were buying up as much of Southie as they could, now that the shoreline of Dorchester Bay was getting to be a popular part of Boston. Gentrification was in the wind. Real estate was going up, but these goons were getting some pretty amazing deals. Houses had been sold for crazy low prices lately.

Claire and I talked long into the night, looking through old high school yearbooks that we'd found and wondering what ever happened to so-and-so. Pointing to a picture in Billy's senior year book, she gave a shriek that made my hair stand on end.

I looked at the picture, and the caption under it. *Brendan Costello. The boy most likely to succeed.* I wanted to scratch the smirk off of his face. He'd acted so rich, and here he was from Southie just like us, had gone to school with Billy.

We got another visit from Costello the next day. This time the price he offered was a few grand less. We told him to take a hike. We happened to be cleaning out the game closet at the time. I had a hockey stick and Claire had a baseball bat. Costello, glaring at what we held, said the price would be going down real soon. We needed to be careful. Southie wasn't a family neighborhood anymore. Problems could happen, if we got the picture.

Oh, we got the picture, all right. It took me a while, but suddenly, as Costello stood there talking about problems, I remembered the bullies who took

Carson Beach away from us. One of them had mentioned how bad things might get, accidents kids could experience, if we didn't give up our stretch of the beach. Costello was grown now, barely recognizable until he sneered and said that he'd be back.

With an even lower offer.

The tires on our cars were slashed the next morning. A few days later, a dead cat was found in our mailbox. Rank smelling fish were tucked into the pockets of clothes on the backyard line. The back fence fell down overnight, a gutter was ripped from the back of the house on a calm day.

We didn't tell our brothers. What could they do? Claire and I had a long talk and decided that we weren't giving up our house, our *family* house, like we gave up the beach. Jimmy was a stickler for the rules and would come up with things like increased patrols by the area cruiser, maybe an alarm system. He'd want us to move out "for safety's sake." Billy could run into a burning building but wouldn't stand up to a bully. He was too much like Dad, too kind.

We were just like Mom's people, Claire and I. Stubborn and tough. We weren't Going anywhere.

Things got busy at the hospital then. Lots of people coming down with a really nasty flu, gastric symptoms you don't even want to think about. Most of the hospitals ran out of rooms. Patients were being kept on beds in the halls with only screens for privacy. Worst flu outbreak in years. Claire and I worked a lot of hours in just a few days, twelve and sixteen hour shifts.

One morning we came home to a scorched front porch.

Not burnt down. It was all fixable damage. The beautiful old leaded picture window that Dad had installed on their first anniversary was broken, probably from the spray of the fire hoses. Billy and Jimmy stood there, both out of uniform, shaking their heads. Their friends had called to tell them about the fire.

Costello came up to us as the fire department hoses were being loaded onto the trucks. Said it was a pity about the fire but his offer still stood, just a little bit lower. The boys stared at him until even Costello had the sense to leave. Messing with a Sullivan kid was a bad idea. Four was downright stupid.

Sean O'Hearn wandered up then, another neighborhood kid who'd inherited his folks' home. Said Costello had made him an offer just the other day and he was thinking about taking it. A little under market value, but fast cash, no banks or loan companies involved. Besides, the neighborhood was getting rough.

Billy said that Sean always was an idjut about money and the neighborhood had always been a little rough, and then it was just the Sullivans standing around again.

Claire and I had another talk while the boys went off to get something to cover the front window. We called in to work and explained that a few personal days were needed due to the fire. Our managers grudgingly gave in, each reminding us that there was something of a flu epidemic going on, or hadn't we heard? There had even been a few deaths. Mostly the old and infirm. Still, it was a bad way to go.

We stood on the back porch, looking at the fall remnants of our parents' garden, while Billy and Jimmy did their best on the front window. Claire reminded me that it was almost time to dig up the elephant's ears and caladiums, store the bulbs until spring replanting. Maybe trim back the wisteria.

We listened to the professional lectures that our brothers delivered. Sell up, move on. Sean was a financial idjut but he'd be alive. We might not be so lucky. The fire department was fairly certain that this was no accident.

Each brother could take in a sister, anytime.

There's nothing like family love, is there? Our brothers were simply worried. We told them that we'd think about it but right now we were too tired to make a decision. We needed sleep after the long shifts and the fire. Promised to give their suggestion serious thought once we'd had some rest.

We slept for a few hours and then sat, coffee in hand, and talked about what to do. Talked about how much we'd lose if we sold out.

Costello came by again the following day. Claire and I sat him down, offered some coffee, good and strong. Southie coffee. He took his with cream and two sugars. Greedy as always, he had several cups to our single cup apiece. Ate most of the scones, lemon with those little poppy seeds in them and lots of butter, since we weren't hungry just then. Claire and I alternated going out to the kitchen to get him refills.

The price was considerably less than we'd expected, even from him. We asked for a few days to talk things over and see about new living arrangements.

Surprisingly, he agreed, finishing off another scone.

Two nights later, Claire called me down to the emergency room to draw blood on yet another flu victim. The place was a madhouse, the least sick and injured on stretchers in the halls. Claire smiled and pointed to room three. The patient was so dehydrated that she'd had to make four tries to establish an IV, and hadn't been able to draw any blood at all.

We entered together. Costello looked simply awful, and the room smelled like someone's dog had been sick from both ends. The smell was Costello,

sallow, sweaty, moaning, and totally miserable. Even using my smallest needle, it took a few tries to get all of the tubes the doctors wanted. He looked like death, and a few hours he was just that. Dead.

It was a rough year for the flu victims.

The following spring was a beautiful one. The fire repairs were done. Claire's second floor flat was airing out as the final coats of paint dried. My place had been completed in March. We sat in Dad's pergola, sipping tea and planning the new garden. Waved hello to Sean O'Hearn's wife as she pegged out clothes on the backyard line.

No caladium, delphiniums, wisteria or castor plants. We'd had them all taken out by professionals who understood the inherent dangers. We didn't want anything poisonous around, you see. No upset tummies, or worse. The boys both had young children. I want a dog. Claire likes cats. We plan to take them all to Carson Beach this summer, to run and play and tell ghost stories about Castle Island.

* * *

Victoria Goessling is a member of the Nebraska Writers Guild and Sisters in Crime. New to writing, her short stories have been published in two NWG anthologies (2017 and 2018) and in Misbehaving Nebraskans. She realized at a young age that the gentler sex is the deadlier sex, and if having great fun proving the point.

PRETTY DREAMS
by Peter W. J. Hayes

It wasn't much as flower shops went, but it was enough for Harry. A single store front in a strip mall on Route 1A, south of Lynn, Massachusetts. Through his large front window, Harry looked across the divided highway onto a Hyundai dealer and a Dollar General store. Thirteen years earlier, when he took over the store, the view was a used car dealer and a roast beef sandwich shop. That was before the highway was widened to handle the endless traffic between Lynn and Boston, before the General Electric plant slashed its work force, housing costs plummeted and the demographics of the area flipped upside down like an hourglass. Harry didn't really mind, although several years earlier his insurance company had required him to beef up his security system and install a silent alarm.

He made one safety improvement of his own. He kept a loaded SIG under the counter near the silent alarm button. He liked the feel of it in his hand, and he was particular about his handguns. So far, he'd never needed either one, which he appreciated. The last thing he wanted was police scrutiny, even if he was just protecting his business.

As six-thirty approached, two customers came and went, ordering corsages for an upcoming prom. They were followed—just before closing—by three women talking in lively Cambodian. The youngest of the three, a woman barely into her twenties, stopped the conversation with a laugh and translated for him. From her quick and lilting words, he learned she was a bride-to-be, there to order flowers for her wedding. The happiness behind her words warmed him. He waited patiently as the three women laughed and talked over one another. Each time they reached a consensus, Harry jotted down the translation. During one long exchange, he provided a folding chair for the oldest woman, whom he learned was the grandmother of the bride. When they finished, Harry confirmed the order and thanked them for coming so far in advance. He promised to order the flowers near the wedding date to keep them fresh. The young woman's brown eyes beamed in gratitude, and after she translated Harry's words, the grandmother rose from the chair and squeezed his hand, her smile wreathed in wrinkles. When they left it was dark outside, and a gentle rain was falling.

Harry flipped the open/closed sign on the door and dropped the deadbolt. He carried the cash drawer into his workroom, placed it in his wall safe and removed his Browning Buck Mark .22. With the safe locked, he shrugged into a navy blue pea coat and pocketed the gun. In the showroom, he studied his inventory through the glass door of his largest cooler, listening to the hum of the motor. He chose a blood-red carnation and pinned it to the collar of his coat. He'd made the mistake, years ago, of wearing a white lily. Its brightness against his dark coat almost cost him his life. He prided himself on not making the same mistake twice.

He eased his nondescript Honda onto Route 1A, headed north. Forty minutes later he turned from Swampscott Road onto a bumpy, dirt driveway leading to a junk yard. He parked behind the closed office next to a rusted Ford, and placed his car keys under the visor. He settled into the Ford's driver's seat.

The keys were in the ignition.

He was lucky about this, he knew. Twenty years earlier, Harry and Stick Man Tony worked on a four man crew led by Yinzer, a Pittsburgh transplant as wide as a Pennsylvania oak. Stick Man Tony earned a four-year sentence for using his favorite stick—actually a baseball bat—to encourage someone to repay an overdue loan. A bit too zealous, the man never walked or talked again. When he finished his sentence, Stick Man landed the junkyard job. He liked the work, and seven years later bought out the owner. It was then Harry approached him with a deal. For the last decade, whenever Harry needed a car for a night's work, Stick Man left him one, the keys in the ignition. The next morning, after Harry returned it, Stick Man would take the two thousand dollars in cash Harry had placed under the visor and drop the car in the crusher. But they had rules. If Harry's car was still at the junkyard when Stick Man came to work, he would report his own car stolen and drop Harry's car in the crusher.

So far, everything had worked like a dream.

Harry drove toward Danvers, familiarizing himself with the old Ford's idiosyncrasies. It pulled to the right, but apart from a rattle near the tailpipe, it ran well. What worried him more was Yinzer's behavior at their last meeting. For almost fifteen years, they'd met on the third Wednesday of every month. Sometimes it was relaxed, two old friends catching up. Perhaps every other year, however, Yinzer gave him an envelope with ten thousand dollars in it, and a slip of paper with a name and address. At the next monthly meeting, the job finished, Yinzer would hand over a second envelope with ten thousand in it.

But the last time they met, Yinzer was oddly short of conversation. His eyes were deep set, his skin pale, and he had the reduced look men get after losing a lot of weight. Every time he shifted on his bar stool he stopped speaking, as if gauging whether something might happen. And when Yinzer handed him the envelope, Harry knew from the feel that it contained the entire twenty thousand.

Harry asked him about that, and Yinzer waved a hand the size of a frying pan. "Jesus, Harry. How long we been doing this? I know you'll do the job. You ain't the kind to skip and take the money. I been thinking for a while that it's stupid to split up the payments."

Harry nodded, but he didn't like the change in their routine. They'd made it this far because they had rules and stuck to them. Changing them set off gentle vibrations in his muscles that made him uncomfortable.

"There's something else." Yinzer leaned in close, his bulk blotting out the people sitting at the end of the bar. His gaze was intense. "You don't question this one. No matter what, you do the job. Understand? You do the job." He jabbed him in the chest with a finger the thickness of kielbasa sausage.

Afterwards, alone in his shop, Harry discovered the slip of paper inside the envelope contained only an address. No name. This second break in the rules bothered him more, because he couldn't fix it. He and Yinzer met only once a month, and they didn't know each other's telephone numbers or home addresses. They were never to recognize one another in public. Mickey Clover, their boss, had made the rules years ago, and they worked. Mickey had a similar arrangement with Yinzer.

Harry had turned the slip of paper in his hands, not liking any of it, knowing he would have to go in blind.

He eased the Ford around the corner on a residential street, checking addresses. Yinzer had warned him to look for a handicap ramp leading to the front door, and he spotted it midway down the block. On a cross street, he parked in front of an unlit house and slid latex gloves from his jacket pocket. Tugged them on. He closed his eyes and focused, fighting back a jangly and edgy feeling, then stepped from the car and eased the door closed with a gentle click. Avoiding the cones of light shining down from the street lights, he picked a path to the back door of the house. A glance through the nearest window showed stainless appliances in a darkened kitchen. Lamplight fell across carpeting on the far side of a doorway.

The back door was unlocked, which worried him. Either someone had forgotten to lock it, or it was a trap. He slid the Browning from his pocket. Holding it by his thigh, he stepped into the house and eased the door shut. A medicinal smell clogged his nostrils. From the lighted room came the low mumble of a television, punctuated by a high-pitched laughter track. Harry scooped a salt shaker from the kitchen table. At the doorway into the lamp-lit room he hesitated a split second.

A man sat with his back to him, watching television. Harry took a breath, tossed the salt shaker past the seated man into the front hall and walked up behind him, his feet silent on the carpeting. He raised the Browning. The man's head snapped around, following the clatter of the salt shaker. Harry was about to squeeze the trigger when the man's profile scorched through him.

"Yinzer!" he gagged, skipping sideways and dropping his arm.

Yinzer twisted his face toward him. "Do it!" he shouted. "I told you to do it!"

"No." Harry scrabbled to take a breath.

"I'm the target! Now do it."

"What the hell are you talking about?"

Yinzer's shoulders slumped. His breath rasped in his throat. He refused to look at Harry, the tilt of his head obstinate. "You have to do it." He sounded like an unhappy child.

"No god damned way."

Neither spoke for a few moments. Yinzer stared at the floor. Harry wiped his mouth with the back of his gun hand, tasting latex. The television flipped to a commercial and the light in the room changed. Music swelled.

"What's going on?" Harry asked.

Yinzer shook his head. He still wouldn't meet his eyes. "I made this call, Harry. Not Mickey. It was my money. You gotta help me out here, Harry. I knew you'd be quick and clean. You wouldn't miss."

Harry shuffled his feet. "Why?" he croaked.

Yinzer glanced at him. "I'm done anyway. Doctors give me three months, maybe four. Another month I won't be able to get out of bed. I don't want that."

"How?"

"Cancer. My pancreas. They diagnosed it a coupla months ago. I been getting ready ever since."

Harry wanted to touch him, to say it would be all right, even though he knew it wouldn't. But what chased that need was the staggering intimacy of what Yinzer wanted him to do. It was so personal, and yet they knew so little about each other. They'd worked on a crew for six years, trusted one another, stayed friends, protected each other over the years by holding to their rules.

But this.

He knew almost nothing of Yinzer. Why he left Pittsburgh, why there was a handicap ramp to his house.

Harry struggled to speak, and what came out of his mouth was, "Why the handicap ramp?"

Yinzer stared at the television screen without seeing it. "My wife. She got MS eight years ago. Last few years, she needed a wheelchair."

Harry thought back and remembered her. Lenora, or some name like that. Short and blond, completely out of synch with Yinzer's height and heft. Energetic and laughing, she'd moved around him like a satellite, his gaze following her as if she was the North Star.

"What about her?" Harry asked. "Who's going to take care of her?"

"I already did."

Something in the words made Harry cold.

Yinzer looked up and met Harry's gaze. "No way some asshole in a home is going to take care of her. Who knows what they'd do. I been feeding her, taking care of her. That was my job and I done it."

"What do you mean you already did it?"

Yinzer didn't blink. "I saved some of her meds. Made a cocktail for her this afternoon. Sat with her after she took it." A tremor ran through his body. "That was my job. I took care of it. She didn't feel a thing, just went to sleep. I knew you were coming for me tonight. I'm good with it."

Harry felt Yinzer's words knot in his stomach. He breathed through his mouth. "Yinzer," he said gently.

Yinzer sat back, stretching the wide muscles of his chest. "You ever think of getting out, Harry?"

Harry felt obligated to be honest. "Yeah. I have. It's stupid, but I like the flower shop. I'd be good just doing that. But I don't know how I get out of this. Mickey would come after me."

"Nah." Yinzer scratched the side of his face. "I'm your ticket out, Harry. If I'm dead, there's no more meetings every month. Mickey ain't going to meet with you. That's why he set it up this way, so he wasn't connected to you. And Mickey has this own problems."

Harry hefted the Browning in his hand. "What do you mean?"

"He told me the FBI got a bead on him. But did you hear what I said? Without me, no one connects you and him, even if he tries giving you up for a plea deal. You ain't seen him in forever. I'm the only one who can say Mickey told me who to take out, then I told you, and you did it. I'm the link. So, Harry." He paused. "You pick your reason. Shoot me because you and I go back, we're friends, we stuck together all this time. Or shoot me so you never get caught, so no one connects you and Mickey. You decide."

Harry went cold again, his palm damp around the Browning.

Yinzer's eyes narrowed. "You're a smart guy, Harry. Like why you wear that flower. It's not because you're trying to look good, it's because no one expects a shooter to wear a flower. It throws them off, they relax, and you got them. Although beats me why you used that .22. That I don't get. That gun links you to every shooting. You gotta get rid of it. But here's a better idea. Shoot me for both reasons."

Harry glanced around the room, at the knick knacks on the shelves, the photos on the walls. The large photograph of Yinzer and Lenora on their wedding day, both grinning.

"Yeah," Yinzer said, and Harry realized that Yinzer had followed his gaze as he looked about the room. "Pretty dreams, ain't they? It always starts that way, but this is where you end up." He swung his hand at the room.

"What did you do before I got here tonight?"

"I told you. Sat with Lenora. Then I came down."

"And watched TV?" Harry's mind drifted and he pictured the outside of his shop, smelled the cool sweetness of being inside it. A certainty settled through him.

"Habit. I just turned it on. I was thinking. About when I was a kid. I was sick a lot, I missed like a year of school. It's why I never done good there. I had trouble breathing. I couldn't sleep at night. I was sitting here thinking about how I used to lie awake in bed in the dark, trying to get a breath down, and I taught myself to wait. Right when the morning started, you'd get this change in the light. Real hard to see, but it was there. I almost felt it more than I saw it. And then you'd hear a bird. Just one. Man, that first bird call was sweet. Pure. It was like the whole world was waiting for it. And I'd hear that and know I was going to be okay." His head bobbed slowly and he smiled, his eyes brimming at the memory of it. "And I knew I'd made it through the night. I knew I was good."

Harry shot Yinzer through the temple the instant he finished the sentence.

He bent over, sure he was going to be sick. Somehow he held it in. His ears ringing, he straightened up. Yinzer was tilted away from him, a single neat hole in his temple. No blood or detritus marred the far wall. That was the real reason he used the .22; most of the time the bullet never exited. He took a breath to steady himself.

Harry's own rules clamored at him to leave, but he couldn't. He stared at Yinzer's thick body, how motionless it was, then turned and found his way upstairs. The first room was empty except for a hospital bed and medical apparatus. The second room was the master. Lenora lay on her back on the king sized bed, utterly still, the comforter pulled up to her chin as if Yinzer had worried she might get cold. Her shoulder-length hair was clean and brushed. Her hands above the comforter clasped a twig with four flowers. He recognized the five white petals and yellow center of the plumeria flower. She held the same flowers in her wedding photograph on the first floor. He wondered if Yinzer understood what the flower meant to Buddhists, how it represented eternity.

He hoped so.

On the drive back to the junkyard he stopped at a convenience store to give his hands time to stop shaking. Normally, he could bury away his shootings inside himself, ignore the memory of them. He couldn't even remember with certainty how many times he'd killed someone. Eight? But this was Yinzer, and more than that, the rules were collapsing. The night was wide open above him. At the junkyard he left the envelope with two thousand dollars under the Ford's sun visor and retrieved his car.

Forty minutes later he let himself inside his shop, turned on the light behind the counter and entered the back room. He placed the .22 in his safe, cut up his latex gloves with scissors and flushed the pieces down the toilet. He stood, knowing he was finished for the night, but feeling unfinished. Dislocated. He couldn't stop thinking that he was sick of killing Mickey Clover's enemies. He'd kept doing it because the rules were there and the money followed, like someone who drinks every night because they always did. All he had left was the hollow habit of it, the zeal long gone.

Maybe Yinzer was right. Maybe the FBI would roll up Mickey and everyone would forget about him, but he knew that wasn't possible. The bodies were all out there, every one unsolved, and the FBI would press Mickey about it. It didn't matter if he threw away his .22. The shootings were his, the order for them came from Mickey, and once the cops understood the link they would smother him. Even if Stick Man kept quiet and the cops couldn't prove anything, his business would fold under the pressure. He'd be done.

He decided to make a new rule.

He would find a way to keep the shop. Whatever came at him, so be it. Over the years, he'd laundered the cash from the shootings through the books. He could afford good lawyers, so he would fight.

He walked behind the showroom's counter. With that decision made, he wanted to do something for the shop, to get started, so he found his notes for the young woman's wedding and wrote up the supplier order. He would call tomorrow.

As he finished the front door opened. Harry jerked upright, stunned that he had forgotten to deadbolt it. Wet from the rain, Mickey Clover stood just inside the door with a lopsided grin, a large handgun hanging at his side. Harry instinctively pressed the silent alarm button.

"Hands on the counter, Harry." Mickey raised the handgun, his eyes bright and jumpy.

"Mickey. Never expected to see you again." He placed his palms flat on the counter. He recognized Mickey's silver, engraved Colt .45. It's pearl grips. A collector's gun, not something a shooter would use. It was usually displayed in his office.

A timer started in his head. Four minutes until the cops arrived? He knew he needed to get Mickey talking. Mickey liked to hear himself gab—if he could get Mickey going it might eat up four minutes. He glanced outside and saw a black Town Car beaded with rain in the light from the front window, exhaust trailing from the tailpipe.

"Making my move," Mickey said. He glanced about. "Still looks like when I sold you the place."

"Coolers are new."

"Yeah." Mickey beamed. "This place is something, ain't it? Old times. All that coke shipped from Columbia in containers of roses. So we needed a flower shop to take the deliveries. When was that?"

"Late nineties. Before the DEA shut that route down."

"And you liked this place so much you bought it from me."

"Yeah, I did." The memory of his first days working in the shop shot through him, how the colors of the flowers amazed him, the surprising contentment when he finished his first bouquets. The sweet smell of it all. The peace he felt. He'd never thought himself capable of it. He pulled his mind back. "You said you're making your move?"

"Yeah. Gotta go. Feds made a case on me. But I got an ace card."

"Yeah?"

"Got warned. I been paying this chief for ten years. All I asked was one phone call. If I was going down, he had to warn me. Never went to him for anything else. Gave him ten thousand every Christmas. Stuck an envelope behind the pipes in this cottage he's got up in Maine. You know what's funny? I knew he'd call. Mostly honest guy like that, he takes money for so long and doesn't do anything for it, he feels he owes you. He can't help himself, he has to make the call. Even when he knows it's bad for him."

"So you got the call?"

"Yeah. And I'm getting out' a town for good. Whitey Bulger always showed me the way. But I gotta clean up loose ends. So I go see Yinzer. Guess what? Someone put a bullet in his head. You know anything about that?" He wagged the silver barrel in his direction.

Under Harry's shirt, sweat skated from his armpit over his ribs. "I saw Yinzer last week. The usual meet."

"Yeah, and he didn't have anything for you. And today he's dead. Just saying."

"Had cancer, didn't he?"

"Yeah?" Mickey took a step closer and blinked his eyes hard, his forehead collapsing into a frown. "Small hole in his temple. Clean shot. Kinda thing a .22 would do."

Harry realized Mickey didn't know about Yinzer's cancer. "Beats me.

Haven't seen him since last week. Sorry to hear it, though."

Mickey grinned. "Saved me the trouble." The gun wavered in his hand.

Harry knew he was out of time. The thought of the SIG under the counter itched in his right hand.

The front door opened and a young guy with a thick, tattooed neck and crew cut stuck his head inside the door. "Boss," he called. "Police scanner just lit up. Cops on their way."

Mickey's forehead cleared and he half turned to the young man. "How?" Surprise and anger fought over how he said the word.

Harry snatched the SIG from the shelf and leveled it. Mickey twisted his head around as if he knew he shouldn't have looked away. Harry shot him twice in the chest and shifted the SIG to the front door, only to see it slam closed. Outside, the kid ran around to the driver's side of the Town Car. In the distance a siren climbed the night sky. The Town Car bumped onto Route 1A.

Harry came around the counter and watched the last of anything that was Mickey leak from his eyes. He stood over him, debating what to do, then placed the SIG on the counter and jogged to his safe, carrying Mickey's silver .45. As he walked back, he wiped down the .22, before bending over to wrap Mickey's hand around it. He pushed Mickey's finger on the trigger and fired once into the counter. He dropped the hand, making sure it held the .22. His cell phone rang. He went behind the counter and answered the call from the security company.

The first two cops on the scene moved him into the back room and bagged the SIG. They learned Mickey's name about thirty minutes later and their tone changed. The older of the two wouldn't stop looking at him. A homicide detective kept making Harry repeat what happened. It was two hours later and on the fourth retelling when another cop entered. This one wore a white uniform shirt and enough brass to forge a saxophone. He nodded the detective and the two uniforms out of the room and sat on the folding chair across from Harry.

"I'm Chief Callahan." He didn't stick out his hand for a handshake.

Harry was sure the Chief already knew who he was, so he didn't pretend otherwise, but he wondered why the Chief chased the other men from the room. He noted that the holster strap over his Glock was unsnapped. "I know," Harry said. "I remember you on the beat. Before you made sergeant."

"And you're Cold Harry." Callahan rearranged himself on his chair. "We'd lost track of you. I heard you got the nickname after that shootout with the Portuguese boys who wanted Mickey's turf. They say you're stone cold. That no one ever sees you coming. And now Mickey Clover's lying on his back in your shop."

Something new connected in Harry's mind. Callahan was the one who pinched Stick Man Tony. That pinch got Callahan promoted to sergeant and launched his career to chief.

Harry shrugged. "Mickey told me the FBI got a case on him. Said he was leaving town."

Callahan's blue eyes glinted. "He did, huh?" His hand dropped near his holster.

The new connection in Harry's mind hardened. How easily Callahan put the pinch on Stick Man. How Mickey gloated about knowing a chief. Why Mickey compared himself to Whitey Bulger. He guessed Callahan and Mickey knew each other very well.

Harry leaned in. "Mickey said he was cleaning up loose ends before he left. Meaning me. He said he'd just been to see Yinzer. I was lucky to get the drop on him."

"I don't think luck has anything to do with it. Like it didn't every time someone crossed Mickey and ended up dead."

Harry ignored him. "Bad timing for the FBI, though. They're gonna wonder how Mickey knew to run right now." He paused. "You still got that summer place in Maine?"

Callahan's face turned to concrete, his stare as hard. "You trying to say something?"

Harry forced his voice to be conversational. "You know what got me when Mickey walked in here? The .22 he was holding. Weird gun for him to carry. You should run ballistics on it."

Callahan's eyes shifted. Every one of Harry's shootings was done with the same .22, and Callahan would know that. The .22 could pin eight unsolved shootings on Mickey. Put a bow on them. The question was whether that was gift enough for Callahan to leave him alone.

Callahan shrugged. "We run ballistics on every gun in a shooting. Just because that's the gun doesn't mean Mickey's the shooter."

"But this is your lucky day. Only Mickey could tell the FBI how he found out about their investigation. I'm sure they'll want to talk to me as well, but you know what? Every day I work in this shop, I forget more about the old days. I only remember a couple of things, and I just might forget them too."

The silence could have frozen a hurricane. This was the trade and they both knew it. If Callahan investigated Harry for the shootings, Harry would rat out Callahan's bribes. It was Callahan's family and their summers in Maine for Harry's flower shop. One pretty dream for another.

Callahan stood. "Let's see what ballistics say. Stands to reason if the .22 was used in the other murders, and the shootings stop now, then Mickey was the shooter."

Harry rose. "See. Your lucky day."

Callahan nodded and snapped the holster strap over his Glock. "Only if the shootings really stop."

Harry watched the chief leave. He remembered the driver of the Town Car, the kid with the tattoo on his neck. Bad idea, that tattoo, he thought. He'll be easy to find.

And after that, the shootings really would stop.

He needed time to get the flowers just perfect for a wedding.

* * *

Peter W. J. Hayes is the author of two Vic Lenoski novels, The Things That Aren't There, and The Things That Are Different. More than a dozen of his short stories have appeared in various publications, including the Malice Domestic Anthologies, Black Cat Mystery Magazine and Mystery Weekly. He can be found at www.peterwjhayes.com.

DO NOT DISTURB
by Linda Leszczuk

"What do you mean, 'five items apiece'?" my sister's words echoed my thoughts.

Marcus Bradford III adjusted his glasses as he looked up from the papers he'd been reading. Although he was close to our age, mid-forties, the gesture was reminiscent of his father, who had been *our* father's lawyer as far back as I could remember. He had even taken over Second's office when the old man retired. That's where we were now, the offices of Bradford and Bradford, Attorneys-At-Law, Westfield, Mass.

"That doesn't make sense," I added to Alicia's question.

He gave us both a withering glance and laid the papers on the massive desk. "Let me explain it to you. Your father was tired of the constant bickering between you, and of the care he *didn't* receive from either of you since he became ill. But rather than cut you out of his will completely, he set up a bequest that you each get to take five items from his home as your inheritance. The rest of his property, including the house, will be sold at auction and the proceeds given to West Granville Congregational Church.

"The church?" Alicia cried. "He can't do that. He's dead. We're his heirs. That house and everything in it belongs to us."

"Not according to the terms of your father's will."

"What items," I asked. "Who gets to choose?" Alicia was still making noises about "unfair" and "that can't be right", but I knew better. It was just like that selfish old man to pull something like this. Just because we didn't dote on him every minute or wait on him hand and foot, as though he wasn't already wasting money on that full time nurse.

My question pulled Alicia up short and she sputtered into silence. Bradford the Third turned his attention to me.

"Any five items, for each of you. A total of ten. There is only one stipulation."

Here it comes. "Let me guess. There's a limit on how much those five things can be worth." *Cheap bastard.*

"Not at all. Dollar value is not a factor. The only requirement is that you have to agree on who takes which item. If you can't agree on an item then it goes to auction."

"Wait a minute," Alicia said. "You mean if I want something and Denise says no, I can't have it?"

"Correct. If either of you want an item, the other must agree." His smug look was infuriating. "Your father said for once, the two of you would have to set aside your constant quarreling or neither would get a thing."

We arranged to meet the following morning at our father's house in Granville. Alicia, me, and some old bat from Bradford's office, who was there not only to let us in—dear old Dad had also left instructions that the locks be changed—but to make sure we didn't steal anything. Lots of trust going on here, folks...although I wouldn't have put it past Alicia to have sticky fingers. We had this one day to get our ten items and get out. Tomorrow everything left would be sold at auction, and that would be that. Good bye, old family home.

I hadn't been there for a couple months. I thought of stopping by a few times but Dad had that full time nurse and those Hospice people and it's not like there was anything I could have done for him that they couldn't. With all the money he was wasting on people waiting on him, I probably should be glad there's anything left for Ali and me to inherit at all.

The house itself wasn't anything to get excited about. A small ranch style, sitting on several acres of mostly grass, with a small pond in the far back. There'd been four of us there when I was growing up, back when Mom was alive. Alicia and I had separate bedrooms but had to share a bath. That was a nightmare. She was so selfish, always blocking me out when she knew I had a date or something to get ready for. Of course, I did the same to her.

As they say, payback's a bitch. And so was Alicia.

We wandered through the rooms, cell phones in hand. Anything that might be of value was Googled for a potential price tag. In a way, we were splitting the work in half because I knew anything Ali researched and didn't claim wasn't worth my effort, and she knew the same about me. The furniture was old and worn, but nothing old enough to pass off as an antique. There wasn't a set of silver or fine china…Mom hadn't been into stuff like that. Same with jewelry. About the only piece I remember that was real was her wedding ring. Alicia and I both wanted it when she died—I remember the fight we had—but the old fool buried it with her. What a waste.

Alicia was studying the paintings on the wall, checking the artists. You never know who might have gotten famous. I was working my way down the wall of bookshelves. Mostly framed photos…family, Ali and me as kids, people I sort of remembered and others I didn't recognize. I found one ornate silver frame with the "925" sterling stamp on the bottom.Might be worth something. There was a little model of Fenway Park, a baseball in a plastic case with a faded signature, and a trophy holding a golf ball that said "Hole in one", with a day and a place. I checked out the model and the baseball. The model was worthless. The baseball, if the signature—Ted Williams—could be authenticated, might be worth a couple hundred.

I moved through the bedrooms, coming last to my old bedroom, which Dad had turned into an office of sorts. One of those put-together-yourself desks with an obsolete computer and an even older printer. I sat at the desk and began searching through the drawers. Jeez, he was a pack rat. I waded through piles of old correspondence, receipts, and other assorted junk, putting each pile back exactly as I found it so Ali would have to waste her time going through it, too.

One thing caught my eye. An envelope, yellowed with age, tucked into a leather notebook. I eased out the paper inside, also yellowed and stiff. It was a handwritten letter, the ink slightly faded but still legible.

Dear Hutch,

I will never be able to repay you for what you did for my son but please accept this gift with my undying gratitude.

I know what a baseball fan you are. More importantly, a Sox fan. So you probably know the date, September 28, 1960. It was Ted William's last game. Twenty-one years. He was forty-two years old and he could still hit 'em a mile. Do you remember? Fenway Park. Baltimore was in town. It was the eighth inning, Jack Fisher on the mound for the O's, and Ted came up for what was sure to be his final trip to the plate. The crowd was on their feet. And he connected. The ball hit the stands in right field and ended up in the bullpen. A home run in his final at bat. What a day that was.

But very few people know what happened then. One of the guys brought the ball in from the bull pen to give it to Teddy. But you know how he was. He took that ball, signed it, and gave it to his bat boy, Billy O'Donnell. Billy treasured that ball the rest of his life. Sadly, it wasn't that long. He got cancer and died in '78. And he gave that ball to his best friend – me.

Now I'm giving it to you. I really want you to have it.

God bless you, Hutch.

Larry

Holy sh…! I pulled out my phone and began to search. There was a lot of stuff on that last home run, and it all matched what this guy said in the letter, but there was nothing on what happened to the ball. If this was for real, that damn ball, with this letter, could be worth a fortune.

I read the letter again. I had no idea who this Larry was or what my father had done for his son but the full name and return address on the envelope should make it easy enough to trace him, or whoever was left behind if he'd already moved on to that big ballpark in the sky.

I slid the letter into the inside pocket of the jacket I'd worn for just that purpose and placed the leather notebook back in the drawer. Alicia was in kitchen arguing with the bitch from the lawyer's office. I hurried out to see what the fuss was about.

"They're a set," Ali was saying. "A set. That should count as one item."

The "set" in question was a trio of figurines that belonged to our grandmother. A collector's item? I pulled out my phone and did a quick search. Yeah. They were worth maybe a couple hundred, *if* she could find a buyer.

"What about that?" I interrupted pointing to the painted wooden box she'd brought from the master bedroom.

"What? It was Mama's. I know it's not worth anything, I'd just like to have it."

"Bullshit." I reach over and opened the top. What little jewelry Mama did have was still inside.

"Oh, come on," Ali complained. "It's all costume junk. You know Mama didn't have any real jewelry."

"Except, perhaps the piece in your left front pocket. Would you place that on the table, please?"

Old Bradford's watchdog had good eyes. Alicia flushed crimson and pulled a necklace from her pants pocket. I didn't recognize it but Ali always had a better eye for jewels than me so I assumed it was worth something.

"How about her other pockets?" I asked, mostly to be annoying. "Who knows what else she's got tucked away."

"It's not a concern. You will both be subject to search before you leave the property today."

Damn! If Alicia finds out about the letter, there's no way she'll let me take that ball.

The day wore on. We each placed a number of items on the table "for consideration". That necklace was evidently worth enough that Ali okayed my putting dibs on the fairly new TV from the master bedroom if I'd sign off on the jewelry. Finally we were each down to our last pick each. There were a half dozen items remaining. I made a show of debating between the silver picture frame and the signed baseball. Finally I chose the baseball. Alicia did one last online search to make sure I wasn't putting one over on her, then agreed I could take it.

The ball was mine. But how could I get the letter out of there?

Alicia was still working her phone, trying to choose between a couple of the final items. I stood up and began to pace around the kitchen. "Hey," I asked our watchdog. "Can I take a walk around the yard while she's deciding? Knowing her, this could take a while."

She studied me through narrowed eyes without speaking.

"Or do you need to search me?" I asked, throwing my arms wide, as if inviting a pat down.

She wasn't amused but she nodded toward the kitchen door. "Go on. Just stay on the property."

I already had a plan in mind when I reached the yard. The March wind bit through the topcoat I'd thrown on over my jacket and the brown grass was crunchy under my feet. As casually as I could, I wandered toward the pond. I'd loved this place, once upon a time. In the summer, there'd be ducks and geese, and fat noisy bullfrogs; but now, things were still.

I walked along the edge of the water, looking for a likely spot. Dad's kitchen had yielded a plastic bag and, carefully keeping my body between my hands and who ever might be watching, I eased the letter from my pocket and wrapped it as securely as I could in the bag. Then I bent down and placed it under one of the good sized rocks that lined the shore. Then I took a smaller rock and scratched the top of the first, leaving myself a marker for when I returned. It couldn't be too soon. I calculated in my head. After the auction, of course. But before the place was sold, just in case the new owners didn't like trespassers. Two, maybe three weeks should do it.

I wandered back to the house. Alicia had made her final selection. True to her word, the old watchdog searched our purses and pockets before we left. We gathered up our five pieces each and said good bye to our last link to dear old Dad.

I waited three weeks. The auction was over and everything had been hauled away. A "FOR SALE" sign hung on a post in front on the empty house. The long narrow driveway extended alongside the house and I pulled all the way in so my car was less noticeable, just in case.

Those three weeks had made quite a difference at the pond. We were just into April and ducks and geese were everywhere. There seemed to be way more than I remembered, they pretty much surrounded the pond. I headed for the spot where I'd stashed the letter, trying to avoid the green goose poop that dotted the lawn. Suddenly, this massive goose charged me, honking and flapping his wings. I could tell he meant business so I turned and ran. He gave chase a short ways then broke off and headed back to the shore. What the hell?

I stood there, giving him a chance to get used to me, then slowly began working my way back toward the pond. He was ready for me this time and charged again, this time chasing me almost all the way back to the house before returning to his post.

Okay, this is getting ridiculous. This was my pond, not theirs. Well, sort of. And I needed to get that letter.

I moved parallel to the pond's edge, thinking I could cross the lawn further down and approach the spot from the water's edge. Kind of an end run. But as soon as I turned toward the water, another angry goose came at me and had me running for my life.

I was pissed now, out of breath, with my shoes covered in goose shit. No stupid bird was going to keep me from getting what's mine. I walked back to my car and opened the trunk. Yeah, a tire iron should work. I could swing it like a baseball bat…one of the few things my father did teach me.

I had just grabbed the iron when the sounds of a car in the driveway stopped me. It wasn't exactly a cop car but it had a light bar on the roof and a green badge type emblem on the doors. The driver was wearing some sort of official looking khakis and I was pretty sure he was checking my license number. I dropped the iron on the floor of the trunk, closed the lid, and waited. Finally, he got out of his car.

"Morning, ma'am."

"Good morning." I gave him my best, friendly but concerned smile. "Is there a problem, officer?"

"Ranger," he corrected me. So I was right. Not a cop. "Can I ask what you're doing here, ma'am?"

Another smile, this time with a little "grieving daughter" mixed in. "I'm Denise Hutchinson. This was my father's house. He passed away recently."

"Yes, ma'am. I knew your father. Nice man. I'm sorry for your loss."

"Thank you." I took a couple seconds to compose myself. "I grew up in this house. It's so hard letting it go. I just wanted to look around the yard, visit the pond, one more time. You understand."

He nodded. "Yes, ma'am. But I'm afraid you're going to have to stay away from the pond."

"Stay away? Why?"

"It's nesting season for the geese."

"Well, I'm not going to hurt their nests. I just want to sit by the pond for a while. There shouldn't be any harm in that."

He shook his head. "Not possible, ma'am. Not now."

"You mean I can't go down by the pond until this bunch of geese have moved on?"

"Actually, it's a gaggle."

I stared at him. "What?"

"A gaggle. Not a bunch of geese. It's a gaggle of geese."

"Fine. Whatever. I just want to know when I can get to the pond."

"Well, they've just nested so you've got about a month to wait. Mama over there has to lay her eggs, if she hasn't already, and then she'll be sitting on them till they hatch. About a month. And Dad over there," he motioned toward the brute who tried to attack me, "isn't going to let anyone disturb her. Besides, these are Canadian geese. They're protected by the Migratory Bird Treaty Act of 1918. It's against the law to bother them during nesting season. Pretty stiff penalties involved. That's why I stopped by. We know the property is empty, so we're watching out, making sure no one disturbs the geese. "

I didn't know if he saw the tire iron before but his meaning was clear. Stay away from the geese. Big brother was watching.

I thanked him, told him I was done there for the day, and followed him down the drive. It was okay. The letter was wrapped in plastic. It would be fine. I'd wait out the stupid geese, then get my letter. This would just give me more time to check out who I should take it to.

Knowing the rangers were watching, I forced myself to wait a full month. It was enough. When I approached the pond, there were goslings on the water and many of the nests seemed abandoned. The new families were congregating on the far side of the pond. Most importantly, the stupid bird that was sitting by my rock was gone. I moved toward it carefully but no big daddy charged out to challenge me.

It took me a few minutes to get my bearings. Several of the rocks had been moved or overturned, including the one I had marked. I spotted some bits of torn plastic, the color of the bag I'd used.

The empty nest sat in the exact spot where my rock had been. I stood there, looking inside it. A comfortable bed lined with twigs, goose down, and bits of shredded paper, old and yellow with faded writing.

* * *

Linda Leszczuk, who also writes as LD Masterson, lived on both coasts before becoming landlocked in Ohio. After twenty years managing computers for the American Red Cross, she now divides her time between writing and enjoying her grandchildren. Her short stories have been published in numerous anthologies and magazines and she's currently working on her second novel.

MRS. MONTGOMERY
by Adam Meyer

Dennis checked his watch and realized that everything would be in motion by now: Teddy Montgomery being led in cuffs to the interrogation room at the Hoover Building up in D.C., the DOJ lawyers fine-tuning their case against him, the head of Boston division putting in a confirmation call to FBI Director Bill Webster and President Reagan's chief of staff. He should've been down at the Union Oyster House enjoying a celebratory seafood dinner, but instead he was back on Marlborough Street, a faint headache pressing at his temples.

The Montgomerys lived in a nineteenth-century townhouse, smack in the middle of a Back Bay neighborhood most government bureaucrats could never afford. But life for Teddy Montgomery was different, and not just because he'd married Harper, though that was a lot of it. Most of it really.

Dennis knocked at the front door softly, as if he wasn't sure whether he wanted to admit he was there, but just as he was about to walk away, he heard a lock click. Turning back, he felt his breath catch. Harper Montgomery looked stunning, her blonde hair pinned up, a sweep of floral print reaching from her neck to her knees. Her only jewelry was a set of pearls as white and neatly-shaped as her teeth.

"Dennis, what a lovely surprise." She drew the last word out into three syllables, though her southern drawl had mostly faded during her time up north. "Unfortunately, Teddy's not here."

Of course not. Teddy was being braced by the FBI's top interrogators, who would soon let him know what was in store if he didn't confess and quickly. But Harper didn't know that, not yet.

"He working late again?"

Harper shrugged. "I tried to call him a little while ago but he wasn't at his desk."

Dennis looked away, afraid of betraying more than he intended. He knew he shouldn't be here, especially now. But he'd never be welcome back once Harper found out what he'd done.

"I should probably go…"

"Don't." Harper moved in, putting a hand out but not quite touching him. "Keep me company for a while."

He followed the swish of Harper's skirt into the cool interior, past the huge gilded mirror and the cherrywood tables into the parlor, where tall built-ins showed leather bound books that had probably never been opened. The real books—volumes about American history, the Russian Revolution, political science—were stashed next door, in Teddy's office. Dennis had a handwritten log of every title and copies of several of the volumes in his basement office at 1 Center Plaza.

"Let me get you a glass of sherry."

Harper crossed to a shelf full of crystal and decanters.

"Isn't Espie here?" he asked, sounding more authoritative than he intended. He knew the schedule of all their household staff—Esperanza the maid, Melvin the gardener, the cooks who worked the Friday night dinner parties—but couldn't admit that.

"Espie had a family emergency. Took the night off." Harper turned, looking slyly at him. "I've got the house to myself, or at least I did."

He tried to remember the last time he'd been truly alone with Harper and couldn't, though the number of times he'd fantasized about it were countless. His fantasies often started like this, with an innocent glass of sherry, and quickly escalated into something far more primal. Dennis knocked back a third of his drink with a single gulp.

As Harper settled in an armchair across from him, he noticed a couple of cardboard boxes beside her. The flaps were sealed with shiny tape. He hadn't heard anything about this on the last set of recordings.

"You've started packing?" Dennis asked, trying to hide his surprise.

"I know it's silly when we're not leaving for another couple of months but I just…I felt a sense of, oh, anticipation."

He didn't have the heart to tell her that the new job in Moscow was a ruse and always had been. All part of the plan he had orchestrated over the last fourteen months to help catch Teddy Montgomery.

The phone jangled deep in the house. Harper turned, a wrinkle of concern on her brow.

"I should let you get that," he said.

"It's okay, we just got one of those, what do you call it, an answering machine."

Dennis nodded like this was news, but of course they'd put a small bug in there so that they could monitor all the calls.

"I told Teddy we didn't need it, there's always someone to answer anyway." Harper's slight shoulders pushed up in a shrug. "But you know how much he likes his gadgets."

"I do," Dennis said, smiling. He didn't begrudge Harper her creature comforts, but Teddy was another matter. Harper had come by her money honestly, by virtue of birth. Teddy was the one who'd apparently decided it wasn't enough to be supported by his wife, so he'd set out to make a fortune of his own.

Faintly he heard the sound of Teddy's voice on the machine—buoyant and friendly, perhaps greased by alcohol—telling the caller that their message would be recorded and someone would call them back "very soon." Not too likely.

"Do you want to see if it's Teddy?" Dennis asked. It couldn't be, of course, but it would've seemed wrong to pretend otherwise.

"If it's Teddy, he's only calling for one of two reasons." Harper showed a grin that made her eyes sparkle. "One, he's coming home and wants to know if I need anything, which I don't, or two, he's going to stay at work for another couple of hours. Either way, that's no reason to let his business interrupt ours."

"I didn't realize this was business."

Harper laughed, a full-throated sound that sent a tingle through him. "You know how it is here in Boston, Dennis. Everything is business, even when it doesn't seem like it. Maybe especially when it doesn't seem like it."

"For you, maybe. For me, this is pleasure."

He took a too-big sip, finishing his sherry. What was he doing, flirting with Harper? She was a married woman, married to a suspected double agent no less, one he had staked his career on unmasking. And yet it felt good to tell her something true, for what felt like the first time in months.

"Let me get you some more," she said, reaching for the decanter.

"I really shouldn't..."

"Nonsense. How many more nights like this will we have? Just you and me, I mean."

None, he thought, as he studied the smooth skin of her wrist and listened to the gentle splash of sherry. He had spent so many hours here and though he'd called it work—diligently writing reports, chronicling every conversation—he had enjoyed most of it, bantering with Teddy about whether the Red Sox would finally break the curse of the Bambino or hearing Harper's tales of life at the family estate in Charleston.

"I must admit, Dennis, of all the people we've met here in town, you've always been my favorite."

"Don't let Mayor White hear you say that."

She shook her head. "If Kevin was half as charming as he thinks he is, he'dbe governor by now."

Dennis laughed. Harper didn't. He thought of those monthly dinner parties, packed full of the city's elite. He hated the crowds but late in the night, when the group had thinned to maybe a half dozen people, he could always count on a moment or two alone with Harper in the kitchen, her makeup starting to wear off, the fresh-faced southern belle she'd once been showing underneath.

"I'm serious, you know. Despite all this—" she gestured at the antique furniture, the crystal glasses, the molded plaster—"I'm really just a simple girl. And there's so many phonies around. It's so nice to have someone to talk to who's just...real."

"I'm sure you'll meet lots of great people in Moscow," he said, forcing the words out between swallows. He hated himself for keeping up the charade that Teddy was going to take on a job as Security Chief at the Russian embassy, but that was the trouble with lying for a living. He never knew when to stop.

"I've talked to some of the other wives who've been over there. They say it's not so bad, really, once you get used to it. The Russian way of life, I mean. Still, sometimes I wish that we could just stay here and everything would be like it is right now."

Dennis nodded.

"Teddy promised he'd be home no later than seven-thirty," Harper said, flipping her wrist to check her Cartier watch. Dennis had known Teddy was going to give it to her for birthday long before she received it.

"You know how it is when you're trying to get ahead," he said. "Besides, Teddy's a hard worker."

That was true. Teddy's rapid rise in the Bureau seemed due mostly to his work ethic and his natural affability. Some of Dennis's colleagues had argued he wasn't bright enough to be a double agent, but Dennis knew it didn't take smarts, just opportunity—and greed.

"I just wish he wasn't so single-minded," Harper said. "I wish he was more like you."

"I can be just as ambitious as anyone." His supervisors had promised that if everything went well with the case against Teddy, he'd be the one getting the promotion. For years he'd thought that was what he wanted: money, respect, an office with a view of the Charles River. But now he knew better. He would've traded it all the life Teddy Montgomery was throwing away.

"I don't mean that you're not ambitious, Dennis. But you don't hunger for things the way Teddy does."

Hunger, the very word threatened to unravel him. Don't look at her, he told himself. He wouldn't be able to trust himself.

"Are you talking about money?" he asked. Why was it that he could never seem to turn off the investigative part of his brain? Teddy Montgomery was in custody already, his role in the case over.

"Oh, Teddy doesn't care about money. What he cares about are all the things money can buy."

Dennis nodded. He had detailed lists of all Teddy's purchases the last few months: a Panasonic color television with remote control, a couple of Brooks Brothers suits, that new answering machine.

"I suppose he and I are alike in that way." Harper looked at Dennis over the rim of her glass. "You get used to nice things and you don't want to give them up."

"And what about the things money can't buy?" he asked.

"Like what? Power?" She laughed. "Teddy likes to be the center of attention but he doesn't care much for power."

"Love, then?"

Her laughter was brittle. "It's been some time since Teddy and I were truly in love. Besides, my husband isn't as good as keeping secrets as he likes to think."

For a second Dennis thought: She knows. She knows everything. Then Harper said, "He's having an affair."

Dennis hesitated. He could've pretended that he had no idea what she was talking about, but admitting to knowledge about Teddy's mistress was safe enough. In these circles, the only thing that traveled faster than the summer mosquitoes was gossip.

"Apparently it's been going on for months, though I only found out a few weeks ago. But then I suppose the wife is always the last to know."

"If someone had told you, would it have made any difference?"

"I just wish someone would've been honest with me. Then again, the signs were so obvious, I should've seen them months ago." She stood up, looking wistfully at the cardboard boxes. "Of course it's a cliché but it's true: love is blind, or maybe it's just that love blinds us."

You said you don't love him anymore, he wanted to point out. But that had probably just been her anger speaking. A decade of marriage, of course she loved him. She would probably keep on loving him, even after she discovered what he'd done.

"Is she pretty?" Harper asked. "Teddy's girlfriend?"

Not as pretty as you, he thought, thinking of the surveillance photos of Teddy and the woman outside her Dorchester apartment. What a fool Teddy was. Throwing away his entire life—and lovely Harper—for what? A few extra dollars, the thrill of being a spy.

"I've never seen her," he lied.

"No, of course you haven't." Harper parted her lips, like she was about to say something more, then shook her head. "He's probably with her tonight."

"I doubt it." Her gaze locked on him and Dennis realized he'd said too much. "I just mean…he's a good man."

Hearing the words leave his lips, he wondered: was it true? Yes, Teddy was selling his own country's secrets to the enemy, but he had lots of admirable qualities. He could hold down amazing quantities of alcohol, he told great dirty jokes, and he never forgot a person's name, even if he'd only met them once. Maybe most important of all, he'd managed to get Harper Farris Montgomery to fall in love with him.

"Dennis, there's something I want you to know…"

Harper sat down beside him, the silk of her skirt swishing. He could smell her perfume, something with jasmine in it, and felt a thrill move through him. You have to get out of here, he told himself. You've made a huge mistake, and you're only going to make it worse.

"Whatever it is, we'll talk about it some other time."

Dennis stood. He felt dizzy from the sudden movement, or maybe he'd had too much sherry on an empty stomach. He put a hand to his head, surprised to realize that he was still sweating despite the cool air from the vents. He needed to go home and rest.

"No, I think this might be our last chance."

He looked at her carefully, suddenly sure that she knew his secrets, that she knew exactly where Teddy was and what he'd been accused of and what role Dennis had played in his capture. But how could she? The operation had been airtight.

"Harper, you don't have to…"

"Yes, I do."

She kissed him then, ever so lightly, her lips barely even brushing his, and if not for the tingling throughout his body he might've thought he'd imagined it.

"I've been wanting to do that for a long time," she said.

Me too, he thought, but the words couldn't seem to get from his brain to his freshly-kissed lips. His thoughts were cloudy, and it wasn't just that the moment he'd been dreaming about for months was a reality. He somehow couldn't focus.

"I really wish we could stay in touch," she said, standing up, backing away. "I'd hate for the friendship to just…fall apart. Unfortunately, I don't see any other way. But I promise I'll think of you often."

"Me too," he said. He was having trouble getting the words out, his lips all rubbery, his tongue a dead fish between them.

She set a hand on his knee and then her fingers rose and snatched the glass from his loose grip. That was good, because he felt like it might tumble from his fingers and smash on the hardwood. He thought: Expensive crystal like that, you don't want to be careless.

"I really wish things could've been different, that we'd met under other circumstances."

Yes, he thought. Yes, he wished that too, and heard the creak of floorboards overhead, like someone was up there. But she'd said when he got there that she was alone. He started to ask about it but his mouth wouldn't form the words. Deep in the house the telephone rang again, and it sounded as far away as the trilling of church bells from St. Cecilia's on Sunday mornings.

"Whuh…whuh…"

What's going on? he meant to ask, but suddenly he knew. The doubters were right, he saw that now. Teddy Montgomery wasn't smart enough to pull off an operation like this, but his wife was. That family money the Montgomerys were living on, Harper must've been funneling the payments from the Soviets to her parents in Charleston, then had them transfer the funds to her. He wondered if Dennis had any idea what she'd been up to, or if she'd just pried the secrets from his grasp without him even knowing.

Harper rose, looking down at Dennis, her eyes as cold as the cut glass in her tumbler full of sherry, her lips pursed in what was only half a smile. "I'm sorry," she said, her southern drawl kicking in. "I could tell you how I had to do it, because my family money had started to run out and my parents were going to lose the estate, or how the life of a bored housewife simply didn't suit me. Maybe if I'd been married to someone like you, a man who truly loved his country, I would've made different choices. I don't know."

She kept talking but the words had stopped making sense. He heard the creak of floorboards again, and this time they were behind him, the heft of arms pulling him up, his brain foggier, and he looked over at Harper, touching the edge of her strand of pearls, and the last thought he had before blacking out was that he wished he could kiss her, just one more time.

* * *

Adam Meyer is a fiction writer and screenwriter who's published stories in *Landfall: Best New England Crime Stories 2018,* the MWA anthology *Vengeance,* and *Chesapeake Crimes: Storm Warning* and other anthologies. He's also written TV movies and series for Lifetime, Discovery, and National Geographic and is the author of the YA novel *The Last Domino.* Visit his website at adammeyerwriter.com.

SINK TRAP
by Rory O'Brien

Brad double-checked the address after pulling into the parking lot. Yes, somebody living on the second floor of the old converted jail building had called in a leaky pipe under a sink. Mills, jails, asylums, they were all getting converted into luxury apartments now. Buildings like this usually had a maintenance man to take care of dripping pipes and clogged drains and whatever else, but it had been slow lately and he was happy enough to take this client's money for what should be a quick and easy job.

Still, he wondered about the kind of people who would live in a building like this. You never really knew what you were walking into in these situations. Do this kind of job long enough, going into one private home after another, and you were bound to run into something weird eventually. You always heard stories. But he could take care of himself; he had a big, new pipe wrench in his toolbox.

There were no names next to the doorbells in the lobby, just apartment numbers. He found the unit he was looking for and pressed twice, hefting the toolbox and the drip bucket when the door buzzed open. When he got upstairs, a gangly guy was waiting for him halfway down the hall, standing outside an open apartment door. The guy was wearing a Coast Guard sweatshirt and smiled as Brad came down the hall toward him.

"I'm Brad from Witch City Plumbing. How ya doing?"

"Better now that you're here," the guy said, giving him a kind of tired smile. "I'm...Adam."

"I hear you have a leak?"

"Yeah, this way."

He guided Brad into the apartment and shut the door behind them. It was one of those luxury units that didn't seem too luxurious, really. It looked like half of the places he got called to these days, with granite countertops and stainless steel appliances. This one had Ikea furniture, and there were bookcases where he would have expected the usual flat screen TV. There was a closed door on the other side of the room and the client gestured vaguely toward it and said, "Bedroom's a mess right now."

There was a woman sitting cross-legged on the boxy, gray couch. Cute and petite. She was reading a book on the witch trials and wasn't paying any attention to him.

It was bright in the apartment. There were tall windows looking out over a graveyard behind the building; he had noticed it when he was looking for a place to park. Old headstones jutted up, crooked and uneven, in the late morning sun. He wondered if they gave a discount for an apartment with that view. Maybe they charged extra.

"Nice view," he said.

"Neighbors are quiet," Adam shrugged. "They don't bother me much."

"So, you got a leak somewhere?"

"Yeah. Kitchen sink. Over here."

He led Brad around a corner into a galley kitchen that looked like it had never been used. He pointed to the sink at the far end, and leaned in the doorway as Brad crouched down.

"Okay, well, let me see what you have going on."

He opened the cabinet under the sink, and saw a half-full mixing bowl sitting under a dripping PVC pipe. Inexpensive Home Depot work, like he usually saw in these units. Expensive apartments had pretty much the same plumbing as the cheap ones. He crouched further down, clicked on a his flashlight, and saw a thin crack in the pipe.

"Yup, your sink trap's leaking."

"My what?"

"That elbow bend, where it comes down and then back up before going into the wall? That's a trap. There'll be some water in there, making a seal, keeps gasses from coming up your drain. It's cracked. Don't usually see PVC crack like that. Weird. When did you first notice?"

"Yesterday."

"I told you about it last week," the woman's voice came from the living room.

"Yeah, anyway…" Adam shrugged.

"You don't have a regular maintenance guy for this building?"

"We do, but he's on vacation or something. Back next week. I think. So you know how it goes. You put in a request, and by the time he gets back he's buried with other requests…just seemed easier to call you."

"Probably could have done it yourself," he smiled. "There's gotta be a video online."

"I'm not real handy. How long do you figure this is going to take?"

"It'll be quick," Brad said, looking up at him. There was something weird going on with this guy.

"This going to be expensive?"

"Nope. Seventy-five should cover it."

"Oh, well, I was expecting it to cost more, you know?"

"I can charge you more of you want," Brad laughed.

"No rush."

"Let me get it out of the way."

Adam took out a work leather wallet, counted out the bills, and handed them over.

"So what do you do for work?" Brad stuffed the money into his shirt pocket.

"Me? I'm … a teacher. Substitute teacher."

That made sense. "I thought you were in the Coast Guard for a minute." He nodded toward the sweatshirt.

"No. I…just wear the shirt."

"It was on sale," the woman said.

"So is it just you?" Adam asked. "One man operation?"

"Yeah, just me. Keeps me busy. Sometimes I think about taking on a partner, but…" he shrugged.

"Yeah, I know what you mean. So it's just a cracked pipe, then?"

"Yeah, it's no big deal."

Adam nodded and took a step back. Just far back enough to not be in the way, but not too far out of the way, either. Brad hated it when clients got underfoot, or crowded him. This guy looked like the type who was going to watch over his shoulder and probably tell him how to do his job. So far, he was just watching and being awkward, which was annoying but he'd had worse. Much worse.

He loosened the fittings and dumped the water out into the bowl, thinking that this really was a nothing job. Even a substitute teacher should be able to do it himself. But you never knew, maybe the guy was a disaster. Maybe the woman on the couch in the other room wouldn't even let him try to do it himself. That seemed possible. More than likely.

"Patching it or replacing it?" Adam asked now.

"Replacing." He brought the short length of elbow-bend pipe out from under the sink. "Not worth patching."

"Let me get you something put that on,'" Adam said.

"I have a bucket for it."

"No, no—it's not a problem, really. Just a sec."

Yeah, he was going to be one of those clumsy, helpful types. One of those who insisted on being useful, even when it just made things more difficult. Even when they just tried your patience. But he was paying, so Brad could probably put up with him for another few minutes. This wouldn't take long.

Adam ducked around the corner and was back an instant later with a newspaper. He put it down on the floor in front of him.

"There you go," he said.

Brad hesitated for a moment when he saw the front page headline.

Woman's Murder Still Unsolved.

"Did you see that story?" Adam asked.

"Yeah." Brad slowly nodded. "Yeah, I saw. Too bad, huh? She...she was a pretty girl."

He put the pipe down on the newspaper as Adam stood over him.

The murder of Jennifer Talbot had been on the front page for a week.

She was a pretty, twenty-five year old dental hygienist who lived in south Salem, not far from the Salem State campus. She shared an apartment with Katy Brennan, a twenty-six year old grad student. Last Tuesday, Jennifer had met some friends for drinks after work at a popular downtown bar, and the evening had broken up around nine-thirty. Jennifer had walked one of the other women to her car, but refused a ride to her own vehicle, saying she was parked just a couple of streets over and it was a pleasant night out.

Her roommate was surprised to wake up the next morning to find that Jennifer had evidently not returned home. Katy thought that she had possibly met someone at the bar and spent the night elsewhere, even though "it seemed unlike her," as she later told police. She called Jennifer's number several times, but the calls went to voicemail. She tried not to worry.

A pair of joggers discovered Jennifer Talbot's lifeless body at seven-forty that morning at the edge of a parking lot at Salem Woods, a one-hundred-sixty acre park known for its extensive hiking trails. The badly-beaten body lay a short distance into the woods; her purse was missing, along with one shoe. Tire tracks and footprints at the scene suggested that she had likely fled from a vehicle. Cause of death was blunt force trauma to the head, and tests showed that her blood-alcohol was 0.07—high, but below the legal limit—and she had not been sexually assaulted.

Police interviewed the women that Jennifer had been out with. None of them reported anything unusual or suspicious. No one had been bothering them at the bar, and there did not appear to be anyone following them when they left. The bartender who had been on duty likewise reported nothing unusual on the night in question. Checking downtown traffic cameras, investigators found Jennifer on foot, proceeding north on Washington Street at nine-forty-four, turning left onto Lynde Street, out of the camera's range. She was not seen again.

Interviews at her place of employment were a dead end. The dentist assured police that Jennifer, who had worked for him for four years, was a model employee, always prompt, thorough, and professional. She had called out sick sometime last month, but he had attached no importance to it at the time, and it did not seem suspicious now.

Her roommate stated that Jennifer had broken up with a boyfriend approximately six weeks before. Contacting the boyfriend, Derek James, twenty-six, he stated that the reason for the breakup was his planned move to Florida for work, and her unwillingness to accompany him. He had since relocated, and the Miami PD were able to confirm his alibi for the night of Jennifer's murder. The Salem PD did not consider him a suspect. Her employer and roommate were also eliminated.

Forty-eight hours passed without a solid lead in the murder of Jennifer Talbot. And then another forty-eight hours. There was a strong possibility that this was a random killing, that Jennifer had no personal connection to whoever had murdered her; a thrill killing. Those cases were the hardest to close. Some stayed open for years, and some were never officially closed at all. The police set up a tipline, and reluctantly appealed to the public for help.

There was a murder weapon recovered at the scene, but police withheld the details from the public.

"Pretty girl," Brad said again. "That was a shame."

"Yeah, yeah it was," Adam nodded.

"Think they'll catch the guy?"

"Hope so."

Brad blinked up at his client now. He was starting to have his doubts about this guy. Serious doubts.

Adam smiled, put his foot on the corner of the paper, and slid it back across the floor.

"How much longer do you think?"

"Ten minutes."

This guy had seemed so harmless, but now ... now there was something weird going on with him. There was something hard in his eyes all of a sudden.

"Cool." Adam picked up the paper by the corners, cradling the length of pipe gingerly. He glanced at Brad and went around the corner, back into the living room.

Brad heard him yell, *"Ready!"* as he went.

That's it. This guy was up to something. Keep going into people's homes like this, eventually you ran into something weird. You never knew what the hell you were walking into. This guy lived in an old jail, with a graveyard out back, and a girlfriend who read books on the witch trials. He should have known something was up the minute he walked in.

He grabbed the big, new pipe wrench from his toolbox and was on his feet. He came into the living room, taking the corner wide.

The guy, Adam—if that was even his real name, he thought now—had put the pipe down on the square coffee table. The short woman had put the book aside and was opening some kind of aluminum case.

"What the hell is going on?" Brad demanded, hefting the wrench.

The bedroom door opened and two uniformed police officers came out, followed by a heavyset man in a short-sleeve shirt and a tie.

The cops had hands on their still-holstered weapons, and the woman was dusting the pipe for fingerprints, with a canister of powder and a little brush.

The client turned and held up a badge.

"I'm Detective Andrew Lennox from the Salem PD. I need you to put down that wrench," he said. "Do it now."

Brad held onto the wrench, and looked from the detective, to the woman now lifting a print from the pipe, and then finally over to the two officers.

The woman handed something over to the man in the tie, and he checked it against something on the screen of the tablet he held. After a moment, he nodded.

"It's a match."

"Put the wrench down now and keep your hands where I can see them," Lennox said.

One of the officers slid her pistol out of its holster.

Brad spun and made it to the windows in two bounding strides. It was a long way down to the graveyard, but maybe not too long. He could probably make it. He'd have to. He raised the wrench to shatter the glass…

"Don't!" the detective shouted behind him.

Now, down below, two more cops came into view, with a tall, dark-haired woman who had a badge pinned to her coat. They all looked up at him. None of them smiled.

The wrench thudded to the floor as he raised his hands.

"Your prints were on the pipe wrench you left at the scene. The one you used to kill Jennifer Talbot," Lennox said. "Only plumbers use wrenches like that."

Brad had meant to go back when he realized he had left it there. But he'd been in too much of a panic. He spent a lot of time imagining what it would be like, grabbing a woman off the street, dragging her into the van, bringing her somewhere quiet. But once he got her to the park, dammit, she'd gotten out of the van and started running and he just grabbed the wrench and went after her. That wasn't how it was supposed to go. That wasn't what he'd been imagining at all. And she screamed and he swung before he even realized it and then…then he was back in the van, her blood on him, and he had to get out of there. He hadn't planned to kill her. He didn't think he'd been planning to kill her, at least.

And when he couldn't find the wrench the next morning, he knew he'd dropped the damn stupid thing, left it there when the plan went off the rails, but it was too late to risk going back for it now. That was how you got caught.

"You are under arrest for the murder of Jennifer Talbot," one of the officers said, as the other one handcuffed him. "You have the right to remain silent…"

"You're the fourth plumber I've had in here in the last two days," Lennox smiled. "I was getting tired of putting that pipe back every time. And you're right, I found a video online."

"This is unbelievable," was all Brad could think to say.

"I'll meet you at the station," Lennox said to the officers. "I have two more plumbers lined up for this afternoon and I should cancel."

The officers brought Brad downstairs and put him in the back of a cruiser.

He sat there for a few minutes, looking up at the blank granite face of the old jail building.

Dammit, he thought. You never really knew just what the hell you were walking into.

* * *

Rory O'Brien grew up in New England, in the long shadows of Poe, Hawthorne, and Lovecraft. He is the author of three novels, Gallows Hill, The Afflicted Girl, and Summerland. He lives in Salem, but left his heart in Rhode Island, where it was burned on a rock. Find him online at www.roryobrienbooks.com

WARD'S CLEAVER
by Alan Orloff

Detective Steven Baker of the Boston Police Department stepped into the kitchen of The Back Bay Bistro and walked over to where his partner, Patrice Cook, was crouched over the body of Chef Hugh Ward. A meat cleaver protruded from Ward's forehead, and there was blood everywhere. Wouldn't be hard for the ME to declare cause of death on this one.

"Anything stick out?" Baker asked. "So to speak?"

Cook rose and shook her head in disgust. "A guy has to be plum crazy to do something like this. Just nuts."

"Yeah, you'd have to be bananas to bury a knife in a guy's melon like that," Baker said. "Or really, really angry."

Cook nodded. "*Really* angry."

"Any witnesses?"

"Not to the incident. One of the kitchen staff found the body."

Baker started for the door. "Okay, bring everyone down to the station. We'll grill 'em there. This place is a mess."

The Back Bay Bistro's assistant chef, Sue Vede, dressed in chef whites, folded her arms across her chest as she waited for the questioning to begin.

"Everything is being recorded." Baker sat across from Vede, his tablet resting on the plain table between them. They were in the less dingy of the Harrison Avenue Station's two interrogation rooms—it had been cleaned sometime in the past month—while Cook interviewed another restaurant employee in the second room.

"Am I a suspect?" Vede asked.

"We're just interviewing witnesses, asking questions, trying to catch a killer. If you'd like to call a lawyer, that's your right."

"No, no," Vede said. "No need for that."

"Great. Then let's get started," Baker said. "You found the body, right?"

"And you cut right to the bone, don't you? I *like* that. Refreshing." She smiled, flashing a gold tooth. "Yes, as I told the cop at the scene, I found the body."

"Walk me through it, okay?"

"Sure. I dashed into the restaurant from the Newbury Street entrance, whisked back to the kitchen, pushed open the door, and there he was, sprawled on the floor. I could tell he was dead—a cleaver in the pumpkin tends to kill people, right?—so I dug my phone out of my purse and called 9-1-1."

"You didn't touch anything?"

"Nope. Nothing." She furrowed her brow. "Actually, that's not accurate. Chef Ward had a couple of sauces going, so I turned off the stove. Moved two pans off the heat. I didn't think anyone wanted a restaurant flambé."

"Good thinking. Anybody else around?"

"No. And I had my eyes peeled, too. Thought the murderer might still be lurking."

"Did anything seem out of place to you?"

"Well, Chef Ward didn't usually keep his cleaver embedded in his forehead." She smirked. "Aside from that—and all the blood—things looked like they always did."

Baker swiped the screen of his tablet, then consulted a report. "You called 9-1-1 at 8:47. Did Chef Ward always come in so early?"

"Every other day. See, we're having this little contest to see who gets the job of head chef, moving forward. Our boss—Mr. Anthony—decided we shouldn't be developing our new dishes at the same time, so we alternated mornings. Today was his morning."

"So why were you there?"

"I forgot my phone charger, and I went back to get it. I thought I could duck in before Chef Ward got there. I was wrong." She shuddered. "If I'd been a little earlier, that would have been me stretched out on the cold floor with *my* brains scrambled."

Baker tried not to picture that scenario. "Tell me about this competition for the head chef position."

Vede uncrossed her arms. "Mr. Anthony pitted Chef Ward and me against each other. Whoever developed the best new menu would be named head chef."

"Let me guess. You're a very competitive person?"

Vede smiled a predatory grin. "You better believe it."

"Competitive enough to kill the competition?"

Her eyes flashed. "No need. I was the better chef, and it wasn't even close. Mr. Anthony knew it. The other chefs knew it. Even Ward knew it. Wouldn't admit it, but he knew. I was going to render him obsolete. I would have shredded him. Reduced him to a pulp. And that's a good thing. Some fresh meat will only improve the restaurant."

"How did you two get along?"

"I wasn't exactly fond of him, but he was my boss, so I obeyed his orders. But... well, he wasn't a spring chicken, you know." She sat upright, cleared her throat.

"Meaning?"

"His skills were obsolete, his menu choices stodgy, and his taste was old-fashioned. So I often did things in more modern, innovative ways. He didn't always take that too well. I also tried very hard to keep our working relationship professional." The color on her cheeks rose. "He might have had other ideas."

"Can you clarify that? And please, don't mince words."

"He was always saying, 'Honey, do this,' 'Sugar, do that,' or 'Cupcake, do the other.' Called me his little dumpling. He once told me he wanted to tenderize my loins. I just ignored the sexist pig."

"Why didn't you report his behavior?" On one level, Baker understood a victim's reluctance to report abuse. But it sure made his job harder.

"I didn't want to stir up trouble, get him in hot water. Besides, I didn't just fall off the turnip truck; it's hard enough to get a job in this industry without getting labeled a bad apple."

"Did Ward mistreat everyone like that?"

"He sure grated on people's nerves, never passing a chance to mix it up. He'd boil over about something, his face would turn beet red, and you could practically see steam coming out of his ears. For the most part, though, his tantrums burned out quickly. Can I go now? I've got places to be. Life as a chef is always chop chop."

The owner of The Back Bay Bistro, Dow Anthony, was a florid man with beefy jowls, and he wore a sour expression as if he'd just been doing vinegar shots.

"Any idea who could have done this?" Baker asked.

"What? Trying to drive a cleaver all the way through the poor sap's bean?" Anthony laughed. "Anyone. Everyone. Ward could be an ass. Pompous. Abrasive. Temperamental, heavy on the temper. And the way he carried on about his prized cleaver was ridiculous."

"His prized cleaver?"

"Yes. He loved that knife. Had a special mahogany case made for it, with velvet lining. Professional chefs use a chef's knife for most things, but he'd use his stupid cleaver. He kept saying it was his *brand*. Some might say it was a delicious irony that his precious baby did him in."

Baker glared at Anthony. It always bothered him when witnesses showed little respect for the dead. "If he was so difficult, why did you keep him around?"

Anthony laughed again, harsher this time. "He was a great chef. Best in Boston. Brought in the customers, a nice blend of casual diners and foodies. This place was always jam-packed. We got a lot of good press, too."

"That sounds like a stock answer. How did you *really* get along with him?"

Anthony's grin disappeared. "Like everyone else, badly. We argued all the time."

"About what?"

He sighed. "You name it. Most recently, he wanted a bigger slice of the pie. Wanted his name incorporated into the restaurant's name, as in *Chef Ward's Back Bay Bistro*. Told him no dice."

"How did he take it?"

"He was cheesed off. Then he asked for more money, a fifty percent raise. I told him no can do. His anger seemed to mushroom from there."

Baker glanced at his tablet. "Was he hurting for money?"

"He lived large, and he was always trying to squeeze me for *more cabbage,* his words. I'd say no way, and he'd threaten to quit. I brushed it off. Who else was going to hire that hothead? He was a great chef, I'll give him that, but oh the headaches. Sometimes I just wished I owned a Denny's. You don't need a world-class chef to whip up a Grand Slam."

"Notice anything out of the ordinary the past few days?"

Anthony shifted, and the chair groaned beneath him. "He did seem extra stressed, and I didn't blame him. I was holding a competition to develop a new menu."

"I heard. Why?"

"Chef Ward was burnt out. Things had gotten stagnant, so I was trying to spice up the menu with a splash of fresh energy."

Baker nodded. "How did Ward feel about your plan?"

Anthony stewed on his answer for a while. "Well, how would you feel if someone made you win a competition to keep your job? At first, he was boiling mad. Understandably. But after a few discussions, I think he simmered down, saw that it could be a sweet deal. Overcoming obstacles can bring out the best in a person. I know for a fact he'd been working diligently to come up with some tasty new dishes."

"Okay." Baker tapped out a few notes, glancing up to see how Anthony was reacting to the lull in questioning. Sometimes silence unnerved a witness. After a minute or so, Baker continued. "Anything else unusual in the last week?"

Anthony leaned back, crossed his arms. "As a matter of fact, there was. Last night, Ginger Haskell—she's an influential on-line restaurant critic—came by. We'd heard through the grapevine that she was planning a visit sometime this month, and that had him walking on eggshells."

"How did her visit go?"

Anthony shook his head. "She's no peach. Tough cookie, in fact. And her visit went terrible, to say the least. After she finished eating, Ward stalked out to her table, asked how she enjoyed the meal. She refused to comment, but I was pretty sure she was going to pan us. He declared that her meal was fantastic—he should know, he cooked it—and that we deserved an excellent review. Things crumbled from there, right down the drain. Angry words were exchanged. Chef Ward was steamed, to put it mildly."

"That kind of pressure doesn't sound appropriate."

"It isn't," Anthony said. "And neither is a food critic returning later that night, right after closing time, to continue her beef with the chef."

"Thanks for coming in, Ms. Haskell," Baker said. Cook had joined them in the interrogation room, and even though they were recording the session, she scratched out notes on a pad of paper.

Haskell wore a cream-colored sleeveless blouse which showed off some impressively muscled arms. Baker had Googled her before the interview and learned from her website that she worked out for two hours every day in order to burn the calories from dining out all the time. She brushed some of her strawberry blonde hair from her face with one hand. "Terrible thing, huh?"

"Yes, ma'am." Baker smiled, aiming to put Haskell at ease. "I understand you dined at The Back Bay Bistro last night."

"That's right. I try to go incognito, but with all the social media these days, it's pretty near impossible. Chef Ward recognized me."

That explained why the only pictures of her on her website were from behind or clearly wearing a disguise. "How was your experience?"

"The fish was dry and the white wine wasn't. The gazpacho was warm and the bacon-wrapped scallops weren't." She frowned, and the lines around her mouth wrinkled like a raisin. "All in all, a substandard meal."

"Did you tell Ward that?"

"Not in so many words, no. But I think he knew the score. I'm sure you heard about the dust up."

"Which one?" Baker arched an eyebrow.

Haskell froze, then her expression thawed. "Yes, I should have realized you'd know all about that. You're detectives, after all. As you've dredged up, I went back to the restaurant later to have a few words with Chef Ward."

"What about?"

"I wanted to apologize. I said a few things I wasn't proud of. The Boston restaurant community is a tight one, and I have a reputation for fairness I'd like to maintain." With a jerk of the head, she tossed her hair back.

"How did he take your apology?"

"Called me a saucy tomato. Said I was full of zest. Then he asked me if I was going to write a rave review. When I told him no, not even close, he was fit to be trussed. He whipped out his cleaver and threatened me!"

"Any witnesses to that?" Baker asked.

"Actually, there was. I noticed a guy in the back cleaning up. Must have seen and heard everything. Young dude, skinny as a string bean, face covered in peach fuzz, eyes like pickle chips."

Rich Robinson was a line-cook-in-training—and one of the cleaning crew—at The Back Bay Bistro. He slumped in his chair as Baker and Cook questioned him.

This time, Cook took the lead, while Baker prepared to jump in as good cop, if necessary. "What can you tell us about last night's argument between Ginger Haskell and Chef Ward?" Cook asked.

"Gnarly. She came in all fired up about something and he got up in her grill and they went back and forth like you do when you don't really want to shout, but you're really torqued, you know?" He rubbed his chin nervously.

The more Robinson talked, the stronger the bouquet of pot—muddled with flop sweat—emanated from the kid. He was fried. Baked. *Marinated.* "Are you high, Rich?"

"Do I have to answer that?" The whites of his eyes were anything but.

"We don't care about that. We're trying to solve a murder."

A sheepish grin. "It's my day off. I was just planning to get toasted and loaf around. Nothing wrong with that, amirite?"

"It's eleven-fifteen in the morning."

He shrugged. "Got a late start. As Chef Ward used to tell me, it's okay if you toke on your day off, but when you wear the toque, you gotta be clean."

"A real kitchen philosopher." Cook consulted her notes. "Okay, back to the argument. What did you see?"

"Well, at one point, he was waving his cleaver around like a madman."

"Was he threatening her?" Cook asked.

Robinson stifled a giggle. "Not really. At some point, he's threatened everyone in the kitchen with it, myself included, but he doesn't mean anything by it. Don't get me wrong, Chef Ward was hard on us, real hard, always demanding perfection, and sometimes things got heated in the kitchen. If you made a mistake, he'd skewer you. Every day was a grind. Lately, I'd been trying even harder to keep things clean and orderly, you know?"

"Commendable. Anything else you'd like to add?"

"When most people looked at Chef Ward, they just saw a crabby, crusty old guy. But he had a tender side, too. At his core, he was just a marshmallow. Like sometimes he'd pretend he was an Iron Chef and ham it up. We all tried not to egg him on, but what can you do? He taught us all so much." A few beads of perspiration formed on Robinson's forehead, and he backhanded the sweat away. "I'm roasting in here. Can't you turn down the heat?"

"Sorry. This room never cools down," Cook said. "Can you try to describe exactly what happened?"

"I didn't hear any blood-curdling screams or anything, just some cussing. And I didn't catch much of their conversation, but I did hear her ask him to fork over some dough. He said, quote, 'How much bread are you talking?' and then she said something I couldn't quite hear, and he said, 'That's way too much cheddar.' Then she said something else I couldn't make out."

"How did Ward respond?"

"He seemed to noodle it through for a moment, then he flaked out and got really mad. He yelled that she was out of her gourd, and he was going to squash her."

"Physically?"

Robinson shook his head, and a few droplets of perspiration went airborne. "Naw. I got the feeling he meant professionally."

"Then what happened?"

"She beat it."

"And what did Ward do?"

"He actually kissed his cleaver, like it was his pet or something." Robinson chuckled softly. "Weird dude, all right. But a hell of a chef." His face glazed over, then his features melted as he went from laughing to crying in an instant. "I know it sounds corny, but I'm going to miss that turkey."

The next morning, Cook pulled up a chair at Baker's desk so they could go over their progress on the case.

"I managed to carve out some time to sift through everyone's statements," Cook said, pulling out her notepad. "Despite a few witnesses waffling, I found some interesting tidbits."

"Go on." Baker had spent a restless night, tossing and turning, mind unable to let go of this case. Maybe Cook had come up with something juicy.

"Evidently, the restaurant is in some financial trouble. There are some unsubstantiated rumors that Anthony is skimming off the top. I guess this head chef competition is a last-ditch effort to turn things around. Probably also explains why Anthony wouldn't give Ward a raise, and why Ward had sent out a few feelers, trying to land a job elsewhere. I also discovered that Anthony was looking to trim some payroll. Evidently, a few low-level jobs were in jeopardy, Robinson's included."

"Maybe that's what inspired his reconstituted work ethic," Baker said. "He's trying to save his bacon."

Cook turned a page, read some notes. "That website? The one Ginger Haskell worked for? According to the Internet scuttlebutt, it's about to fold. Maybe she was trying to extort Ward in exchange for a good review? Funnel a little cash her way? Get her palm greased?"

"Possibly." Baker kneaded his temples with his fingers. "It would be nice if we could pare down our list of suspects. Did you take elimination fingerprints from everyone involved?"

"Yep." Cook reached into a folder stuffed inside her notepad, removed some papers, then passed them to Baker. "Here's the prelim fingerprint report from the lab. The only prints anywhere—on the cleaver, on the equipment, on the surfaces—belong to Ward."

Baker flipped through the information. Very few prints had been lifted from the kitchen, despite the abundance of metal and glass surfaces. Probably because of the fastidious cleaning Robinson did the night before. One particular line item grabbed his attention, and he could hardly contain the excitement bubbling within. "Can you get Robinson and Vede in here again? I think we might be able to wrap up this whole enchilada in short order, Cook."

This time, Rich Robinson didn't reek of weed. And his eyeballs seemed focused. "Let me guess," Baker said. "Today's a work day."

"Right on. Clear head and rarin' to go." He glanced around the interrogation room, as if it was the first time he'd been there. "What can I do for you?"

"Just have a few more questions. About the night before the murder."

"Okay." He sat upright and gripped the edge of the table, eager to please.

"I know you've already told us about your clean-up routine, but could you go through it again?"

"Sure. The last week or so, I've tried to take it up a notch. Show Chef Ward, and the others, that I belong in that kitchen. Here's my routine: I empty every trash can, put in new liners, and toss the stuff into the dumpsters out back. Fill the dishwashers. I wipe down every single surface with a bleach solution. Then I go back and do it again. Door handles, cabinet edges, outsides of all the equipment—the mixers, food processors, blenders, whatever. Mr. Anthony hires some helpers, who I supervise, but I'm the one who stays till the end to see that everything gets finished."

"Do you clean the stovetop?"

"Yes, sir. All the cooktop surfaces, knobs, handles. Clean inside the ovens, too. You name it, I wipe it down and shine it up. Takes me a couple of hours, even with the help. I make sure everything is sparkling clean in that damn kitchen." He paused. "With one exception. Chef Ward's cleaver. He washed that himself. May he rest in peace."

Robinson was excused, and a minute later, Cook escorted Sue Vede into the interrogation room. Today, she wore a white chef coat and black slacks. Her shortly-cropped dark hair was still moist.

"Thanks for coming back in on such short notice," Baker said

"I would say it was my pleasure, but I find this room a bit claustrophobic." She brushed a few imaginary crumbs from her sleeve.

"I know you're very busy, so I'll try to make it quick," Baker said. "First, let me congratulate you on your quick thinking to turn the stove off and remove the pans from the burners after you called in the murder. If you hadn't, the whole place might have burned to a crisp."

Vede bowed her head slightly. "Common sense, really."

"You just walked over to the stove, turned the knobs off, and moved the pans from the heat. Did I remember that correctly?"

"Exactly."

"Excellent." Baker drew his tablet close and made a show of reviewing something on the screen. "You know what? We found a single set of fingerprints on Ward's cleaver."

"They're not mine," Vede said.

"I never said they were," Baker replied. "They belonged to Ward. Which only makes sense. I think we can assume he was using his cleaver to prepare his food."

Vede nodded. "Undoubtedly. He used it for everything."

"Of course, Ward didn't cleave himself in the head, so we have to ask ourselves why aren't the killer's fingerprints on the knife?"

Vede shrugged. "Maybe the killer wore gloves."

Baker pounded his fist on the table. "Yes! Exactly. The killer must have worn gloves. A logical explanation, right? A killer would definitely *not* want to leave fingerprints. With me so far?"

"Yes." Vede clasped her hands together, rested them on the table top.

Baker felt his heartbeat gather speed. Slathering icing on the cake was his favorite part of an interrogation. "We also found one person's prints on the stove knobs and that same person's prints on the saucepan handles—Ward's. Once again, it seems that *only* Chef Ward touched those items. But this is where things become puzzling. Because we *know* that the stove had been on and that the saucepans had been moved after Ward was killed. In fact, you said you did that yourself, right?" Baker paused, stared at Vede.

Vede blanched.

"So can you explain how you turned off the stove without leaving prints on the knobs? Or how you moved the pans without leaving prints on the handles?"

Vede looked as if she'd gotten a whiff of some rancid cottage cheese, but she didn't say a word.

"Something seems fishy, doesn't it? Impossible, really. Unless..." Baker stood, put his hands on the table, leaned forward and loomed over Vede. "Here's what I think happened. You desperately wanted the head chef job, but cooking is so subjective that even if you are the better chef, you couldn't guarantee winning Anthony's competition. And you really hated Ward, what with all the abuse he doled out. So you decided to eliminate him. You came in early, knowing he would be there working on his new menu, and no one else would be around. You wore gloves to avoid leaving fingerprints, as any good murderer would. You attacked Ward and killed him with his own cleaver." Baker tilted his head and made eye contact with Vede. "How am I doing so far?"

Vede remained mum, and her skin had taken on the hue of hollandaise sauce.

"But you made two mistakes. First, you turned off the stove and moved the pans while still wearing your gloves—which is ironic, because leaving fingerprints on the knobs would have *helped* your case. Now, I suppose you *might* have used a towel to grab the hot pan handles—although they probably weren't *that* hot because the sauces were just simmering. But, either way, that doesn't explain the stove knobs, does it?"

Vede opened her mouth to speak, but nothing came out.

"Your second mistake was tossing your gloves in the trash like you always did, figuring they would mix with all the other gloves and garbage already steeping in there. Except you weren't aware that Robinson had upped his game and was now making sure he emptied the trash before going home each night."

Vede looked like she was about to puke.

"And wouldn't you know it? We found a single pair of food prep gloves in the trash. As we speak, our lab techs are taking fingerprints off the inside of the gloves. I think we know whose prints are going to be on them, don't we?"

Vede sat quietly for the longest time as Baker just stared at her. Then she swallowed. "Okay, okay. I killed Ward. But it was self-defense. Like I said before, I left my phone charger at the restaurant so I swung by to get it, and Chef Ward was there. He sandwiched me against the worktable and tried to force himself on me. I grabbed the first thing I could—his prized cleaver—and swung it at him. I swear that's the truth."

"You walked in, he attacked you, and you killed him with his cleaver in self-defense, that's your story?"

"Yes. Yes. That's exactly what happened."

Baker exhaled. Spoke in a soft voice. "Why didn't you just say so before?"

"I didn't think anyone would believe me." Vede gazed up at Baker, blinked a few times, then sent her lips trembling, trying to appear as a sympathetic victim.

A smile slowly grew on Baker's lips, and he waited until he had Vede's complete attention before delivering his *pièce de résistance*. "If what you say is true, then why were you wearing food prep gloves?"

Vede's eyes grew to the size of dinner plates. "Uh, because, I, uh—"

Baker held up his hand. "Can it. You might try to feed the jury some saccharine sob story, and they might just gobble it up, but don't forget, I'll be testifying at the trial," Baker said. "And I'll be sure to let everyone know that what you're serving—any way you slice it—is pure baloney."

* * *

Alan Orloff's novel, PRAY FOR THE INNOCENT, won an ITW Thriller Award. His debut, DIAMONDS FOR THE DEAD, was an Agatha Award finalist; his story, "Dying in Dokesville" won a Derringer Award; and "Rule Number One" was selected for THE BEST AMERICAN MYSTERY STORIES 2018. Next: a PI novel, I KNOW WHERE YOU SLEEP (Down & Out Books, 2020). www.alanorloff.com

DEATH AT BOSTON VIGILANCE COMMITTEE
by Verena Rose

Saturday, July 7, 1860

Boston, Massachusetts

Horace Kingsley had arrived in Boston just in time to attend a meeting of the Boston Vigilance Committee. As he entered the hall where the meeting was being held, he immediately noticed a framed copy of a poster from April 24, 1851. It read:

CAUTION!!
COLORED PEOPLE
OF BOSTON, ONE & ALL
You re hereby respectfully CAUTIONED and
Advised, to avoid conversing with the
WATCHMEN AND POLICE OFFICERS
OF BOSTON
For since the recent ORDER OF THE MAYOR &
ALDERMEN, they are empowered to act as
KIDNAPPERS
And
SLAVE CATCHERS,

And they have already been actually employed in
KIDNAPPING, CATCHING, AND KEEPING
SLAVES. Therefore, if you value your LIBERTY,
And the Welfare of the Fugitives among you, Shun
Them in every possible manner, as so many HOUNDS
On the track of the most unfortunate of your race.
KEEP A SHARP LOOK OUT for
KIDNAPPERS, and have
TOP EYE open.

Two of his father's slaves were on the agenda for discussion and unbeknownst to Cyrus, Horace was in Boston to help in their ultimate escape to freedom. Making his way to the front of the room, he approached a man he took to be a member of the Committee.

"Excuse me sir, are you an officer of the Boston Vigilance Committee?"

"Yes, sir, my name is Edmund Jackson. I am a member of the Executive Committee. How can I help you?"

"I'm Horace Kingsley from Washington City. I've traveled to Boston in hopes of assisting with the release and relocation of two slaves currently in police custody. They escaped from my father's plantation on the Eastern Shore of Maryland and I'd prefer they not be returned to servitude there."

As the two men talked, the room filled with men both white and colored. Presently, a distinguished gentleman stepped up to the podium and banged a gavel calling the meeting to order.

"We'll speak further after the meeting," said Mr. Jackson.

After several items on the agenda had been discussed and dealt with, the chairman announced the next item was the recent incarceration of a slave couple who were arrested as runaways.

"Gentlemen, we have been asked to intercede for a couple who are currently languishing in jail awaiting transport back to Maryland. Their owner, Mr. Cyrus Kingsley, is demanding their immediate return."

"Excuse me, Mr. Chairman, my name is Horace Kingsley. The slaves you're speaking of belong to my father. I've come to Boston with the intention of helping them make their way to Canada. I was in hopes of arriving before they got snatched."

Numerous conversations erupted and the chairman banged his gavel to bring the room to attention.

"Mr. Kingsley, do I understand you correctly? You want to help your father's slaves escape?"

"That is correct, Mr. Chairman. I attended medical school in Philadelphia and while there I became interested in the abolitionist movement. When I returned home, because of my belief that slavery is an evil, my father disowned me. I moved to Washington City along with my personal slave, who I immediately freed, and became the city coroner. The escaped slaves are husband and wife. The husband is the brother of my assistant."

A young man rushed into the hall and yelled, "Everybody come quick! There's been a murder at the jail!"

Later that evening in his hotel room, Horace Kingsley was still trying to come to terms with the events that had happened that day. He came to Boston expecting to help Nathan and Lily get to Canada. Instead he had to figure out how to tell Noah that his brother was dead and his sister-in-law was on her way to being sold down the river.

The next day.

Standing on the platform, waiting for his train back to Washington City to arrive, Horace was approached by two of the members of the Boston Vigilance Committee.

"Mr. Kingsley, we are so very sorry for your loss. We've tried to get more information on the events that resulted in Nathan's death but the police are not being very forthcoming. All we were able to find out is that the man your father sent to transport them back to Maryland showed up while we were having our meeting. The police claim that Nathan put up a fight but we are not inclined to believe that."

"I do so appreciate all you've tried to do for them. I wish I had arrived sooner," said Horace shaking his head. "Now I must get back to Washington as soon as I can. I think I know who came to pick them up and where Lily is being taken to be sold. My best friend is a constable there and I'm sure he'll be happy to help me catch up with Nathan's murderer."

Shaking hands with Horace the two men wished him good luck in his endeavor.

THE END...

To find out who murdered Nathan and whether Lily is saved from being sold to a sugar plantation look for DEATH AT MILLER'S TAVERN appearing in Malice Domestic 15: MYSTERY MOST THEATRICAL due out in April 2020 from Wildside Press.

AUTHOR'S NOTE:

The Boston Vigilance Committee was originally founded in 1841, was reorganized in 1851 and continued its good work until it was disbanded in April 1861. The committee's goal was to protect escaped slaves from being kidnapped and returned to slavery in the South. Members of the committee worked with donors and Underground Railroad conductors to provide the escaped slaves with funds, shelter, medical attention, legal counsel and transportation. They would also keep a lookout for slave catchers and would sound the alarm when any came to town. Some members also took an active part in rescue efforts.

* * *

Verena Rose is the Agatha Award nominated co-editor of *Not Everyone's Cup of Tea, An Interesting and Entertaining History of Malice Domestic's First 25 Years* and the Managing Editor of the Malice Domestic anthology series. In addition to serving as Chair of Malice Domestic, Verena writes short stories and is conducting research for a historical mystery series.

MURDER AT THE BIJOU
by Janet Raye Stevens

Lillian swept spilled popcorn into the long-handled dustpan with a small broom. Greasy butter sopped into the lobby's threadbare carpet, joining a thousand other stains dating back to 1920 when her father and grandfather opened the Bijou Theater in Preston, Massachusetts—a week before Lillian was born. She'd grown up with the place, and though only 31, she'd grown old in some ways too.

Grandpa was gone now, so was Pop, her mother, and Lillian's husband, killed at Iwo Jima. Now she feared she was going to lose the last thing she loved. The Bijou.

She dumped the popcorn into the waste bin near the exit, remembering the crowds that used to swarm the ticket booth and throng the lobby, buzzing with excitement as they pushed through the entrances into the theater itself. Now, it was Saturday night, and a whopping eight people sat in a theater of two hundred seats. Ten if she counted the twin boys of about seven who'd darted ahead of their harried-looking mother into the building.

Lillian could blame the fine late-September weather for so few tickets sold. Or the drive-in theaters that seemed to have sprung up in every suburb like crabgrass. But she knew the truth. Television had upended her world, keeping customers at home with their eyes glued to the miniature monster's 16-inch screen.

Had the Bijou's rival theater uptown, The Rialto, experienced such dismal ticket sales? Doubtful. They had a big Hollywood premiere this weekend, *Showboat.* Lillian looked across the lobby at the poster of their current feature film. A huge robot clutched a scantily-clad woman in its arms while tanks fired at the metal beast willy-nilly. The folks who'd ventured away from their television sets tonight probably preferred "Ol' Man River" and Ava Gardner in Technicolor over an odd, black-and-white science-fiction picture like *The Day the Earth Stood Still.*

Lillian wedged the broom and dustpan into the corner next to the popcorn maker as Bernie, her concessions man, scuttled across the lobby, gripping a comic book.

"Well, you sure took your time," she said. He'd stepped away from his post behind the counter to use the washroom what seemed like ages ago.

"Sorry, Lil," he said, not sounding sorry at all. "But the feature's already started. Who's gonna pop out for Milk Duds now?"

She scowled. "Someone might. One sale might help us break even this week. Help *you* keep your job. I suggest you do your reading on your own time."

He slapped his comic book—*Batman,* she saw—on the shelf under the counter with the rest of his stack, muttering something about lady bosses Lillian didn't care to ask him to repeat. She left and circled the lobby again, looking for more things to tidy up.

She probably shouldn't ride Bernie. She'd already lost three concessions men to that home appliance factory that had opened up two towns over. Bernie could be the fourth, but she couldn't have him slacking on the job. Grandpa and Pop wouldn't have let him get away with it. And neither would she.

Lillian stopped at one of the theater's entrances, the one on the left side. She ran her hand over the swinging door's worn padding and peered through the window, as she'd done since she was a kid. As always, a thrill ran down her back when she looked into the darkened theater.

The actors' voices and music reverberated from the speakers. On the screen, a giant metal man stood like a menacing sentry in front of a flying saucer. Carpeted aisles ran down both sides, with the seats in the middle. Light from the projector flickered over the customers' heads. Far fewer heads than in the Bijou's 1930s heyday, when *Gone With the Wind* had played to a packed house for weeks and weeks.

The familiar sequence of dots flared at the edge of the film, warning the projectionist the reel was at its end and to switch on the second projector. That would make the transition between reels seamless. It didn't happen. The picture faded and a space of white—the tail of the film's first reel—followed. Someone in the audience hooted. Seconds later, the second reel began.

Lillian frowned. Herman had been the Bijou's projectionist for twenty years, except the two years when he was in the army. He'd *never* missed his cue. Was he getting careless, like Bernie? Or discouraged, counting the days until they closed and he had to find another job.

A silhouetted figure seated up front caught Lillian's attention. Slumped to the side, probably asleep. That happened. A *lot*. The customer had paid for their ticket, they could nap through the movie if they wanted to. But sleepers also sometimes disturbed the other patrons with their snoring. She should wake up the snoozer before that happened.

She eased open the door. The smell of popcorn and cigarette smoke rolled out. She crept down the aisle and reached the front row in no time, finding a man slumped down with his head against the back of the seat. He'd dropped his drink cup and popcorn container. Soda puddled around his feet and popcorn speckled the floor.

"Sir," Lillian whispered, getting no response. She looked up. None of the other customers seemed to notice her or the sleeping man. She grasped his shoulder, giving it a shake.

The theater brightened as the movie's scene changed from night to day. Light reflected on the man's face. Lillian stifled a cry. He wasn't sleeping. Not by a long shot.

His eyes gaped wide open. Unseeing. Dead.

Lillian had to read the police department phone number three times before it made any sense. Her hands shook so much as she dialed, her fingers kept slipping out of the number holes. Panic threatened to overwhelm her. And so did worry, as a selfish thought gripped her—what would this do for business? Who would want to come to the Bijou now, where customers died in their seats?

She *had* to call the police, but she also hoped she could keep it quiet.

A brusque voice answered and Lillian asked for Detective Chet Diamond, hoping he was on duty tonight. She'd grown up with Chet. He'd been her brother's childhood friend, a few years older than her, always around their house. And the Bijou. She hadn't seen him since he went to war, but she knew he'd joined the police force when he came home. Chet had always been calm and capable, and that's what she needed now to help her figure out what to do.

She was in luck—Chet picked up the phone. She grew warm hearing his voice after all these years.

"Chet, its Lillian Thornton, I mean Lillian Dow, from back on Clover Street. Do you remember me?"

An uncomfortably long pause followed. "Of course I do. Little Lillian, who pestered me and your brother Dennis without mercy when we were kids. What can I do for you?"

She took no offense to his teasing. She'd been as pesky as a mayfly, always flitting around. She blushed even now to remember what a crush she'd had on him.

"I'm sorry to bother you, but..." She took a long, steadying breath. "I'm at the Bijou. We have a small problem and I need advice on how to handle it."

"Problem?" he sounded suspicious and official at the same time. Maybe it hadn't been such a good idea to call him.

"You see, uh, one of our patrons has, well, expired."

Another long pause. "Expired? You mean *died*?"

She sighed. "Yes, that's what I mean. I'm not sure what to do. Should I call the coroner?"

"Leave it to me. I'll be there in ten minutes. No, make that eight."

Eight minutes to the second later, Chet strode through the lobby door. Tall, broad-shouldered, still slim, still breathtakingly handsome with those dark brown eyes and sandy blond hair. No gray at all. Not true in Lillian's case. Silver shoots had taken residence in her auburn curls like unwelcome guests.

Chet took her hand in his comforting grasp. "Lillian. It's been too long. Sorry to have to see you again at such a time." He released her hand but held her gaze. He cleared his throat. "I heard about your husband. I'm sorry."

"Thank you." She gave him a tight smile, grateful he didn't go into detail or ask questions. She didn't have any answers to give. Doug was reported missing in action at Iwo Jima, presumed killed, leaving her staring into a black, gaping hole where her life used to be.

"How's Sylvia?" she asked. Chet had married Sylvia Dane shortly after she and Doug had tied the knot.

His expression turned brittle. "That didn't work out."

Lillian murmured her regrets but wasn't surprised. He'd married a woman he barely knew only a few days before he shipped out. An impulse, her brother Dennis had said. A hurry-up marriage that wouldn't last, Pop had said. He'd seen too many of those in the first world war.

Chet shifted, drew himself up as if putting all that behind him. "All right, Lil. Where's the dead man?"

She led him across the lobby. He opened the door into the theater and waved her in ahead of him.

"I haven't been here in a long time," he said. He sounded wistful.

"You're not the only one. Attendance has been way down. Well, matinees have been good, but thc evening shows—"

"Shh," a fat man in the last row hissed.

They moved down the aisle side-by-side. On the screen, the film's stars were trapped in a stopped elevator after the electricity had blinked out. They reached the front row and Chet squatted next to the dead man's seat. He took the man's arm by the wrist, checking for a pulse, then dug through his pockets. Lillian stood next to Chet and watched, both curious and horrified by his gruesome task.

"I think I see what killed the poor bastard," Chet said softly, glancing up at Lillian.

"Was it his heart?"

"In a manner of speaking."

He flipped the man's suit jacket open, revealing a small knife—stuck in the dead man's chest.

"Right to the heart," Chet said, sounding impressed. "Not a lot of blood. He died almost instantly."

"You...you mean...murder?" Here in the Bijou? In her home.

He gave her a terse nod and bile rose in Lillian's throat. Cold raced through her veins and pins and needles prickled her scalp. She feared she'd faint, as she had that awful day she'd gotten the Western Union telegram about her husband.

"Hey." Chet stood and gripped her by the shoulders, his eyes firm on hers, warm and reassuring. "We'll have none of that. This is serious, Lil. I need your help. You need your wits about you. Can you do that?"

She nodded, unable to speak.

"Good." He released her, peeled off his own suit jacket and draped it over the dead man's face. He turned to her. "I want you to stop the film and gather everyone in the lobby."

Lillian scanned her customers scattered around the theater—two men, one fat, one thin, seated separately in the last row, a woman fairly close by, her hair tied up in a scarf like Rosie the Riveter, a skinny youngster at the opposite end of the front row, an older couple behind him. And up above, next to the projection booth, the young mother and her twins, watching in the privacy of the darkened quiet room.

Lillian looked back at Chet, finally finding her voice. "Do you think one of my customers is responsible?" she asked in disbelief.

He gave her a grim smile. "That's what I mean to find out."

Chet had called in a report to his station house by the time Lillian had gotten everyone to assemble in the lobby near the concession stand. They created quite a hubbub for such a small group—Lillian, the customers, including the towheaded twins, Herman the projectionist, and Bernie, who put aside his comic books and reluctantly joined the group.

Lillian watched Chet place the contents of the dead man's wallet onto the concession counter, still unable to comprehend what had happened, barely able to think the word *murder*.

"Name's John Sanderson," Chet said, peering at an identification card. "Lives in Palmer. Kind of a hike to come here just to see a movie. He was a veteran, served in the war."

"Who didn't?" Herman said then asked, "What's going on? Why'd I have to stop the film?"

Chet ignored him as he went through the other items from the wallet. A matchbook from the Howard Johnson's on Boston Turnpike, a pack of Lucky Strikes, a few bills and some change, and a coupon for ten cents off the Bijou's evening show.

"We've been sending them out," Lillian said, feeling embarrassed. "Trying to drum up business since Uncle Miltie and his television gang came along and stole our customers."

Chet nodded, and did she detect a slight smile at her weak joke? He'd always been kind to her, even when she'd followed him and her brother to the fishing hole and refused to budge when Dennis told her to scat.

"How long are you going to keep us, mister?" the young mother, a pretty blonde, asked. "I've got to get my kids home. It's already past their bedtime."

Her children barely seemed tired the way they chased each other around her legs and tumbled across the carpet, but she looked exhausted.

"What's your name, ma'am?" Chet asked. "I didn't see you in the theater."

"It's Pat Smith," she said, sounding so unsure Lillian wondered if the name was an alias. "I was in the quiet room with my boys."

Chet raised an eyebrow. "Quiet room?"

"A private room for families," Lillian said. "I put it in last year, hoping to compete with the drive-ins. Converted Pop's office next to the projection booth upstairs, where he used to keep the gin during Prohibition. I had a window installed in the wall to watch the movie through."

"Clever," Chet said.

"Shouldn't really call it a quiet room," Mrs. Smith said, shooting a woeful look at her rambunctious boys. "More like a place to put all the noise and not bother anyone else."

"I see your point," Chet said, chuckling. "Well, Mrs. Smith, you'll be able to leave as soon as I get some answers." His gaze touched on everyone assembled, studying each of them closely for a moment. He held up Sanderson's identification card with a picture of a dark-haired man with worried eyes. "I'm Detective Chet Diamond, and I want answers to why and how this man was murdered. Here, tonight."

Cries of shock and disbelief rippled through the group. Lillian's shoulders drooped all the way to the floor.

"Surely you don't think any of *us* had something to do with it," the fat man who'd shushed them earlier called out.

"Maybe, maybe not." Chet placed the dead man's identification card back on the counter with his other belongings and turned back to the group. "My guess is Mr. Sanderson was killed shortly after the film began. He sat in the front row, to the left. I want each of you to tell me if you spoke to the man, if you left your seat, or saw anyone else get up." He shifted his gaze to the fat man. "I'll start with you."

The man claimed to have been glued to his seat from the minute he entered the theater until Lillian had asked Herman to stop the movie and turn up the house lights. Chet questioned the thin man who'd also been in the back row, and he claimed the same.

Chet turned to Lillian next. "Lil, were you in the lobby the whole time? Did you see anyone leave? Notice anything unusual?"

"Yes. I mean no." She couldn't believe how nervous she was. The way he looked at her with those piercing brown eyes had her wanting to confess to every crime under the sun. "I was in the box office selling tickets until shortly before the newsreel began, in the lobby after that. Once everyone entered the theater, I didn't see anyone come or go. Except Bernie. He stepped away from his post to visit the facilities. He was gone a long time."

Chet swung toward Bernie, who was casually leaning against the counter.

"As I told Lil, I was indisposed," Bernie said and slapped a hand to his midsection. "Tummy trouble."

Lillian nodded in confirmation and Chet asked, "Did you see anyone in your travels, Bernie?"

"Nope. Not a soul."

Chet's attention was back on Lillian. "What about earlier? Did you see the dead man? Speak to him?"

"No. I only spoke to him when I sold him a ticket."

Chet turned to Herman. "You're the projectionist, right? You have a good view of the theater. Did you see anyone speaking to the man, or near him?"

"No, no one."

"You could've turned your back and missed seeing the culprit," Lillian said. "Or you could've left the projection booth. You missed the cue to change film reels. That's something you never do. What happened?"

Herman's expression turned squirrelly. "Oh, yeah, I guess I looked away. I was…boxing up the newsreel to send back to the distributor." He abruptly changed the subject. "I saw the dead man before the film. In the lobby. I saw him with *you*." He gestured to the woman with the Rosie the Riveter scarf. "You were both on line to buy popcorn. You were talking."

Bernie jumped in. "They weren't talking, they were arguing."

The woman's cheeks paled but she straightened and eyed Chet with a defiant look. "I *was* arguing with him. He was behind me in line and got mighty fresh. As a nurse, I'm constantly put upon by mashers who think it their right to pinch my fanny or whisper something crude in my ear." She lifted her chin. "I told him *exactly* what I thought of him."

"Good for you," Lillian said. She'd had her share of run-ins with men like that. "Did you speak to Mr. Sanderson again?" She cut off. "Oh, sorry, Chet. Didn't mean to step on your toes."

His lips twitched. "No, do carry on, Detective Thornton."

Wise guy. She turned back to the nurse. "I noticed you were seated closest to the dead man. Did you see anyone near him during the movie?"

She took a moment, as if scrambling for words. "I don't think so. I'm afraid I snoozed through the incident and most of the movie. I worked a double shift today and am completely worn out."

Chet's eyebrows shot up. "You came to the theater to sleep?"

"Yes. You see, I live at home with my parents. You know that radio program, *The Battling Bickersons*? My folks make them look like a sweet, loving couple. I came here to catch forty winks in peace." She squinted, as if trying to see something far away. "Now I think of it…I might've been dreaming, but I thought I saw someone moving about in front of me."

All eyes followed her gaze as it drifted to the tall, skinny kid who'd been sitting at the opposite end of the row from the dead man.

"Who, me?" the kid squeaked.

Chet studied him. "Aren't you George Winthrop? Officer Winthrop's kid brother? You work at Lou's filling station over on Elm." George gave a reluctant nod. "You usually work on Saturday nights. What are you doing here?"

"I…I—" George swallowed convulsively, his Adam's apple bobbing in a furious cha-cha. "All right, I confess! I called in sick to work. I wanted to see this movie in the worst way." He shot Chet a pleading look. "You won't tell Lou, will you? He'll can me for sure."

Chet's eyebrows rose again. "Don't worry, your secret's safe with me. As long as you answer my questions. Did you get up during the movie? Did you speak to Sanderson?"

"No. I was in my seat the whole time. I never spoke to him at all!"

"That's not true," the fat man piped up. "I saw you talking to him in the lobby."

Chet crossed his arms and tapped his foot, scowling at George. "Out with it, son. What really happened?"

George hung his head. "Okay, I spoke to him. He was in a hurry to get to the concessions counter and bashed into me. I lost half my popcorn! I called the fella a jerk and that's it."

Chet eyed Lillian again and she nodded. She hadn't witnessed the encounter, but that explained the spilled popcorn she'd swept off the carpet.

"I never saw him or went near him after that," George said. He stabbed a finger at Bernie. "But *he* did. Talked to him a long time."

Bernie flushed with anger. "Of course I talked to him," he snapped. "He gave me his order, Detective, popcorn and a drink. He paid, I told him to enjoy the show, and that was it."

George narrowed his eyes, clearly unconvinced, but Chet moved on. He turned his attention to the older couple, a balding man and a petite woman in a sober purple suit. "What about you, Mr. and Mrs.—?"

"Morton," the man said. "The wife and I mind our own business, so naturally we didn't see a thing."

"Not quite, Sam," Mr. Morton's wife said, sounding sheepish. "At one point I bent to straighten the seam in my stocking and happened to glance over my shoulder." She shifted her gaze to Mrs. Smith. "I could swear I saw you slip out the door of the room up above."

Mrs. Smith let out a nervous laugh. "You must be mistaken. I never budged from the quiet room until we were asked to come down to the lobby."

"No, Mommy." One of the twins, the one missing his two front teeth, tugged on her skirt. "You did leave. You said you had to go pee-pees."

"Billy, that's not true," she said and shooed the boy away.

"It is! You said you had to go, and you were gone a long time and Bobby ate all the popcorn."

"Did not!" Bobby cried.

"Did too," Billy countered and chased his brother around the concession counter like Tom and Jerry in the cartoons.

Now all eyes were on the young mother. She looked at Chet and let out another nervous giggle. "I suppose I *did* leave for a teeny second. But I didn't go near Mr. Sanders, or whatever his name is...or, uh, was."

"Then where did you go?" Lillian asked. "I saw no one near the powder room after the film started."

Mrs. Smith flashed a panicky look at Herman. He tugged at his collar.

"Oh," Lillian said, the truth dawning. *That* was why Herman had missed his cue to change the reels.

"I get it," Bernie said, with a blat of coarse laughter. "I wonder what Mr. Smith thinks about you two canoodling in the dark?"

Mrs. Smith's face went beet red. "It's not like that. My husband walked out on us two years ago. Simply disappeared, the louse. I've been struggling to raise my boys alone. Herman's the first decent man I've met. He's kind to me, and my boys, so you can put your judgmental thoughts in your back pocket, mister, because I am having none of them."

Herman smiled and lifted her hand to his lips. "In fact, I've asked Mrs. Smith to marry me," he said, gazing at her with shining eyes.

Lillian's heart lifted at such a happy outcome. Chet wasn't as touched.

"Felicitations," he said, sounding grouchy. "But we still have a mystery to solve. Who killed Mr. Sanderson and why?"

"It wasn't me or my wife," Mr. Morton said, then eyed Herman and Mrs. Smith. "What about the lovebirds? Maybe they did it together."

Mrs. Smith huffed in indignation.

"You're out of your mind," Herman spat.

"What about her?" The thin man pinned his gaze on the nurse. "She sat close to the dead fella. Could've killed him with no one seeing."

"And a nurse would know exactly where to stab a man," Bernie put in.

"That's a lie!" the nurse cried. "I had no reason to kill him. I didn't even know him."

"Well, *someone* is responsible!" Mrs. Morton said.

"Yeah, him." The nurse pointed to George. "I could swear I saw him."

George glared at her. "If you were sleeping, how could you see anyone?"

"How do we know *you* didn't do it?" the fat man growled and jabbed a finger into Lillian's face.

"Hey…!" Lillian said and everyone erupted in shouts, accusations, and finger pointing worse than an unruly session of Joe McCarthy's red-hunting committee.

"Quiet!" Chet shouted, like the stern and commanding platoon sergeant he used to be. The whole mob instantly shut up. "Let me get this straight. No one saw anything. Everyone saw someone." His gaze touched on George, the nurse, and Bernie. "And the three of you had a dust-up with the man."

Lillian gasped as something Bernie had said earlier flashed into her mind.

Something that had given him away. "Bernie, how did you know Mr. Sanderson was stabbed? Detective Diamond never mentioned it."

"You're right, Lil," Chet said. "I'll be damned."

Bernie's eye popped and he sputtered a denial.

"Mommy, look what I found," one of the twins said, coming out from behind the counter. "It's dirty. Got syrup on it."

He held up a *Batman* comic book—smeared with blood.

His mother screamed and tried to snatch it away, but he clutched it to his chest. "No. Mine. Finders keepers."

Chet squatted next to the boy and tousled his hair. "Here, son, let me have a look."

"Okay." The boy handed it to Chet. "It's a *Batman*. I like him."

Chet looked it over, then stood and eyed Lillian. "Blood. I bet if we test the knife handle, we'll find traces of ink."

Bernie edged toward the door, but Chet grabbed him by the collar. "Don't even think about it. I want your explanation, and fast."

Bernie shoved his shoulders back and faced Chet. "Sanderson was in my platoon. One night I made a mistake and a lot of fellas got killed. It was an accident." His words poured out in a cold monotone. "Sanderson didn't see it that way, though. He tracked me down, asked if we could meet. We had a drink at the Howard Johnson's between the matinee and tonight's show. I told him to bug off, the past can't be changed no matter how much we want it to. And I left, thinking it was settled."

He shifted position and balled his fists.

"Then Sanderson showed up here. He threatened to hound me, report me to any of the Army brass who'd listen, tell the families of the men killed what I'd done. I told him to watch the show and we'd talk afterward. I knew I had to stop him. I took a knife from my lunchbox, the one I use to cut apples, and slipped into the theater when Lil wasn't looking. Then I—" He shot Chet a hard look. "Bayonet training came in handy."

Chet went as still and solemn as a corpse. Except his eyes. They glittered, piercing Bernie to the bone.

"You hid the knife in the comic book," Chet said, his voice low, dangerous.

"You kept it wrapped it around the knife to keep your fingerprints off the handle. And then you stabbed that man."

Bernie nodded, his expression flat, emotionless. "I did. And you know what? I'd do it again."

Chet stood by Lillian's side as the police rolled the stretcher bearing Sanderson's sheet-covered body out the front door. Bernie, in handcuffs, followed.

"Poor Mr. Sanderson," she said, dabbing her eyes with a handkerchief. "And Bernie. To be so lost he'd do such a thing. What a tragedy."

"I know, Lil," Chet said, his voice gruff. "For some people, the war never ends."

She sighed and looked toward the customers still in the lobby, talking to the police. Mrs. Smith sat on a bench with the twins nestled against her, asleep. Herman, next to her, slid his arm around her shoulders. George wore a hole in the carpet with his pacing.

"Don't worry about the Bijou," Chet said, following her gaze. "In my experience, folks are drawn to the sensational. I bet they'll be back tomorrow. I bet you'll have a packed house every show the next couple weeks."

She brightened. A little. "And then?"

"I don't know. We'll figure something out."

Her heart fluttered to hear that plural pronoun.

Chet gave her an odd smile. "You know, Bernie had one thing right. We can't change the past. We can only look to the future." He eyed the poster advertising *The Day the Earth Stood Still.* "This looks like a fun picture. Maybe I'll stop by for the matinee tomorrow. It's my day off. Will you be here?"

"I'm here every day, Chet."

"Good. I'd like to see you some time when there's not a dead body involved."

She laughed, feeling young and new again. And hopeful, for the first time in a long time. "I'd like that, Chet. If you don't think I'd pester you too much."

He grinned. "I'm thinking you can pester me all you like, Lil."

"Pardon me?" George said. He'd crept up to them while she'd been gazing into Chet's eyes. "Do you think you could put the movie back on? I'm anxious to see how it turns out."

* * *

Award-winning author **Janet Raye Stevens** writes short stories and full-length mystery, YA, and paranormal/Sci-Fi romance with a dash of adventure and a lot of humor. She lives in Massachusetts, where she spends her time drinking tea (Earl Grey, hot), plotting revenge (best served cold), and creating fictional worlds populated with tough-talking gals and cool-thinking guys. Find Janet on Twitter: @janrayestevens

SOUP
by Cynthia Sabelhaus

I pulled my new catering van into Soup's parking lot. The toes on my left foot throbbed, but I was wise to their tricks. Those particular toes along with the foot and shin they'd been attached to were MIA, shot off over a year ago by a scared-stiff, wounded rookie cop in the midst of his first big drug bust. It was my bad luck to be standing in front of him when he grabbed a semi-automatic from a downed drug dealer and started spewing bullets in all directions. The rookie would live to fight another day. My career as the youngest female detective with the Boston Police Department was over.

Shit happens. I'd already learned that from six years as an Army MP, including three deployments in Afghanistan. After *the foot thing,* I'd had plenty of time to feel sorry for myself, do some rehab, get a prosthesis, resume my martial arts training, and okay, pity myself some more. When I'd *adjusted* as much as I thought necessary, I decided to try something different.

I built Soup, a carryout restaurant specializing in comfort food for workers in all those offices in downtown Boston. We were located near I-90, in Boston's Brighton neighborhood, and en route to many commuter communities, and our large kitchen had four drive-up windows. Our menu changed daily, but there was always chili and Boston bean soup along with three other soups or stews, handmade breads, salads, and a few casseroles like mac and cheese and baked ziti. Most folks placed their orders early in the morning. To wait until afternoon meant risking the availability of our more popular dishes.

It was seven p.m., and the sun had been down for over an hour, exacerbating the February chill. Only a few cars were still waiting at the last open window. I hopped out of the van, relieved that the throbbing had stopped. We were only in the second week of providing catering services, and I'd already decided to hire a couple more people to take over that task.

Inside the building I nodded to Hector, who was at the window, and Marla, my first employee and now Soup's Assistant Manager, who was bagging an order. A ringing phone echoed around me. We had two lines, but each call rang on all six phones staged throughout the kitchen and offices. I grabbed the one at the end of the long prep counter.

"Soup, how can I help you?"

"I want chili, enough for four, and mac and cheese." The male voice was familiar.

I looked at the clock and sighed. "I'm sorry, sir. We're out of chili, and we didn't make mac and cheese today. In fact, we're out of all our soups and casseroles, and we're about to close. I'd be happy to take your order for tomorrow." I reached for the next day's order sheet.

"Do you know who you're talking to?" He sounded like our new mayor, but it wouldn't be the first time a customer put on a phony celebrity accent. Devon Jamison had been mayor for almost a month. He was young, from a rich family, entitled and infamous for throwing temper tantrums. The fact that he ran as an Independent and beat both major party candidates told me the city was looking for a change. Whether it was for the better remained to be seen. Whoever the impressionist on the line was, he was doing a credible job.

I tried for civility. "I'm sorry, sir, but it doesn't matter who you are. We are out of food and we are closing. If you'd like to place an order for tomorrow, I'd be happy to take that for you."

"You will regret this!" His bellow ended in a dial tone.

I noted the *blocked call* on caller ID and went back to shutting down Soup. Because we depend on phone and online orders, the last thing I did each night was download the day's order file and voice recordings. It all fit on a thumb drive that I took home with me. If we ever had some sort of computer malfunction, we'd be able to gather most of our order information from the files.

Marla and Hector had finished and were gone, but Marla always placed a carryout bag for me in the walk-in cooler. I grabbed it on my way out the door and was eating a bowl of chili in front of my TV a few minutes later. *Eat your heart out, Mr. Mayor,* I thought, chuckling.

Monsters clawed their way out of my dream and woke me from a deep, troubled sleep, slithering their way across my bedside table, coming ever closer to my bed. I dug one hand under the pillow beside me, palmed my Sig and snapped it toward the table. At the same time, my eyes adjusted to the low light, and I noticed my cell phone vibrating and dancing toward me. For an instant I thought about shooting it, reconsidered and picked it up.

"Collins," I said. Old habits die hard.

"Meryl?"

I recognized the voice of my old partner from BPD. "Kenny? What's wrong? You okay? Lillian? The kids?"

"Everyone's fine. But your restaurant has been broken into. I thought you'd want to know."

No! I wanted to scream. "You there now?"

"Yep. I'll see ya when you get here."

I pulled on my leg, got dressed in jeans and a tee shirt, shrugged into my warmest jacket and grabbed my keys, purse and gun. I broke a few speed limits but didn't see a single patrol car on my four-mile commute. When I rounded the corner leading to Soup, I realized why. A police convention was in full swing. I parked on the street and walked toward the party.

Kenny Harper met me as soon as I stepped into my parking lot. He looked grim, his jowls hung low, and a roadmap was etched across his fifty-year-old face. I wondered for the first time why a homicide detective was covering a break-in.

"Meryl." He gave me a brief hug. "Sorry this happened."

"Thanks for the call, Kenny." I searched the uniforms around me. "Have you seen anyone from the alarm company?"

"No. Looks like the alarm was disabled."

"Huh. Kids must be getting smarter." I looked around. The building seemed unscathed, at least from the outside. Then I noticed a small group gathered at the far side of the lot. Someone moved, and I saw Father Mike kneeling on the ground. "Oh no!" I said.

Kenny followed my gaze and cleared his throat. "We have one fatality, close enough to your building to suspect it's part of whatever went down here."

"Who?" I did a mental inventory. All my folks were gone before I locked up. None would have been here until three, when the cleaning crew showed up. The cooks followed them around four. I looked at my watch. It was 2:30. "Do you know who it is?" I nodded toward the body.

"A homeless woman. Father Mike says he knows her."

"Carmen," I said, even though I couldn't see her face. "She sleeps near here. When she shows up before closing, we have a meal ready for her. Last night she didn't make it."

Kenny made a note and Father Mike continued administering last rites. I made myself turn toward Soup. From here, I could see the door glass had been smashed. "I'd better take a look at the damage." I moved slowly toward the building.

"Just a quick in-and-out, Meryl. We're treating this as a crime scene—homicide, at least until we find out how Carmen died."

We stood in front of the open doorway. I stuck my hands in my jacket pockets, just to keep them out of contact with anything inside. As I stepped into the building, I wanted to cry. Every piece of equipment, every cabinet, every surface was ripped, dented, scarred, or missing. Walk-in refrigerator and freezer doors had been pulled off and food covered the floor, mixed with broken glass from jars and bottles, all frosted in a mist of flour and other dry staples. The damage extended to our offices where the computers and monitors had been destroyed. I stuck my head into one of the bathrooms and saw water spraying from broken pipes beneath the now-fragmented porcelain fixtures. This went way past vandalism. There were elements of rage, or so it seemed to me. I had never seen anything quite so savage in all my years of MP and police duty. *Who could hate Soup or me this much?*

Fighting back tears, I quickly made my way out of the building. Father Mike was walking toward the entrance. He took one look and wrapped me in his scrawny arms. The priest was seventy, short and thin, but to me he felt like a fortress. He patted my back and I let the tears fall, not sure whether I was crying for Carmen or Soup or both. I wasn't religious and had never been Catholic, but the priest and I had formed a friendship that felt like family. His church was separated from Soup by our two parking lots. Since we weren't open on the weekends, I offered him our parking lot for overflow crowds at mass and the church's frequent weddings, baptisms and funerals. He worked with the homeless when they wandered into the neighborhood and had brought Carmen and many others to my door for a meal. While the others hadn't stuck around for long, Carmen became a regular.

When I ran out of tears, I stepped back and looked across at Carmen. A car with the seal of the Office of the Chief Medical Examiner was parked next to mine and someone was hunched over the body. "What if Carmen came to our door after I left last night?" I asked.

Father Mike nodded. "That could have happened. Or she could have been sleeping in the area and been drawn to the restaurant when someone started trashing it." He gripped my shoulders and turned me away from Carmen. "Whatever happened here, it's not your fault." He gave me a little shake and then stepped away.

Kenny walked up and I cleared my throat. "Any guess how long before we can start cleaning?" I asked.

"It depends. For now, you'd better plan on being out of here for the next two days." He turned from me and headed toward the Medical Examiner who was walking toward her car.

I watched Kenny, thinking about the two days the CSI team would need. It was early Thursday morning. That meant we wouldn't be able to open

Soup until next Monday. It would take a miracle to get it up and running over the weekend.

Father Mike looked toward the church. “Use our kitchen today and tomorrow. I’m sure we have everything you need. We renewed our license with the county last month, passed the health inspection with flying colors, so we’re legal.”

I followed his gaze. The church was cathedral-sized and I knew it had a commercial kitchen. “Are you sure?” I asked.

“Positive. I’ll leave the back door open for you. Let me know if you need any help.”

Kenny came back as the ME’s car drove away. “The doc thinks cause of death is a broken neck, and not the kind you get from falling down the stairs. Looks like her head was whipped around hard. Some kind of commando move. And she says it wasn’t done where we found her.” He paused as two crime scene vans entered the parking lot. “I gotta talk to these guys.” He jogged toward the vans.

I spent another few minutes texting my crew to meet me at the back of the church, and then sending more texts to our food suppliers. After a quick trip home for a shower, change of clothes and to pick up my laptop and portable printer, I was in the church kitchen by the time the first cook arrived.

The kitchen was humming when Kenny came in just before six. I poured two cups of coffee and led him to my temporary office at the far end of the dining room.

“Anything new?” I asked.

“Yeah. We found the spot where Carmen was killed. Just inside the kitchen door. Looks like maybe she tried to stop the vandals.”

A mixture of sorrow, anger, and resolve radiated down my spine, punctuated by a quick stab from my imaginary toes. “I have something I need you to hear.” The thumb drive flashed green at the side of my computer. I played him my last call from yesterday. When it was over, he asked me to play it again.

"That son of a—" Kenny started.

"You can't be sure it was him," I said, although we both believed it was. "Even if we could authenticate the voice with state-of-the-art equipment, there's a decent chance the authentication would be wrong. Even the FBI admits their authentications are occasionally wrong."

"And you know this how?"

"Mr. Google." I smiled sheepishly. "Look, we know the Mayor of Boston did not come to my restaurant in the middle of the night to trash it. We know he was not killing homeless people with his bare hands."

Kenny grinned. "I never met Carmen while she was alive, but I'd bet money she could have taken the little twerp in hand-to-hand combat."

I ignored the comment. "But we do know in addition to his city-provided protection, he kept his private security detail. He even tried to get the city to pay for them, but he shut up fast when the media started reporting on the mercenaries and ex-cons he's hired for his band of thugs."

"Okay, but even if he did order the attack, and I have to say, that seems harsh for withholding chili—even the epic chili from Soup—if it was his private security team, how do we prove it?"

I smiled. "We set a trap and lure them back."

Kenny frowned. "What's this *we* business. You're no longer on the force, Meryl. You can't be part of this."

"Aw, come on, Kenny. I think I know how to get them back here."

The rest of the day went by in a flash. I managed to reconstruct our orders and send texts to inform our clients of the temporary change in pick-up location. By bringing in a half-dozen local teens and purchasing walkie-talkies from a nearby tech store, we were able to meet drivers on their way into the church parking lot, confirm their orders and assign them parking spaces so the young runners could bring their dinners out to them.

When I wasn't helping bag the orders, I hovered near the church phone. Early that morning, I'd left a greeting on Soup's phones asking customers to call us at the church number. For the plan Kenny and I had hatched to succeed, one special customer had to call again. I'd almost given up hope when the call came. The number was blocked, just as it had been the night before.

I waved Kenny over, took a deep breath and pushed the record button on the phone the police had set up. "Soup. How can I help you?"

There was a pause and then the surly voice came on the line. "I want chili for four, a large salad, and a casserole of mac and cheese that serves—"

I cut him off. "I'm sorry, sir. We're about to close. I'd be happy to take your order for tomorrow. The food can be picked up between three and seven, but you'll have to come to the church next door. We've had to relocate temporarily."

"Oh, I'm sorry to hear that." He didn't sound sorry. "What's the problem?"

My teeth were clenched so tightly I had trouble speaking. He knew about the attack on Soup. Otherwise I'd have gotten a repeat of last night's tantrum. "Soup was vandalized last night. It's going to take a day or two before we can cook again."

"Aw, that's too bad."

I cringed and hoped my strained voice would be mistaken for sorrow rather than anger. "Thank you," I said.

"But nobody was hurt, right? So, you'll be able to continue." I could hear the smile in his voice.

"I'm afraid a homeless woman was killed during the attack." *Back to you,* I thought.

This time his emotions weren't fake. "What? That's terrible! Do the police have any idea who did this?"

Gotcha! Now to reel him in. I tried to remember what Kenny and I had discussed. I needed to let Mr. Mayor, or his impersonator, believe there was a security camera on the church roof overlooking Soup's parking lot, but I also needed to soft-pedal the likelihood that a tape from that camera would have caught the break-in or murder. We wanted this to seem like a walk in the park to Carmen's killers, with no need for high-tech tools like heat-detecting infrared devices.

Here goes nothing, I thought. "I'm afraid the police have no clue who might have done this. All Soup's cameras were destroyed. There's a slim chance they might get something from a camera mounted on the roof of the church next door, but in low light from that distance, it's a long shot. The police are sending someone to get the tape from the roof first thing in the morning."

"Well, that's a piece of luck," he said, although I didn't detect much happiness in his voice. "But why would they have to go up to the camera? Don't surveillance cameras send files to a computer somewhere?"

"Yes, sir. But from what I understand, this was an amateur installation by a parishioner who had the old-style VHS tape system. The tape stores about seven days' footage before it begins recording over the old video. The camera is on the edge of the roof pointed at our building, and the priest says a wire runs from the video camera to a small penthouse where the recording device is kept along with HVAC and ventilation equipment. The police won't have to disturb the camera, although it's anyone's guess whether it still works. They'll take the stairs up to the penthouse and retrieve the tape."

Anxious to change the subject, I asked if he wanted that order for chili and mac and cheese the next day. He muttered something noncommittal and got off the phone.

Kenny had been sitting across from me, wearing a headset and listening to my conversation. He shook his head, pulled off his headset and said, "You even convinced me the tape wasn't worth looking at. You think they'll bother showing up?"

I nodded. "Wouldn't you?"

"Yeah." He began using his cell phone to get everyone in place. When he finished, he rubbed his eyes and then stared across the table at me.

"Long day, huh?" I said.

He nodded and watched me fill two mugs from a fresh pot of coffee. "Thanks," he said when I handed him one. "When will you be out of here?"

I hesitated. "I hadn't planned to leave—"

"You'll need to leave as close to your regular time as you can. From this point forward, we have to assume we're being watched."

"Where are you going to be?" I asked.

"I'll be sitting with Father Mike." He looked at me and sighed. "*We'll* be sitting with Father Mike in the priest's house behind the cathedral."

I grinned.

"But first drive home and park your car. And Collins? Watch your back."

It was all I could do to stay close to the speed limit. I stopped for carryout Chinese because it gave me a reason to make two tricky turns that verified my suspicion. I had company. I made a quick call to Kenny to let him know, then parked in my space, carried the take-out up to my condo, turned on the kitchen and living room lights and the TV. I put the Chinese food in the refrigerator and went to my dark bedroom to change into a black hoodie and jeans. Five minutes after arriving home, I was walking out the building's back entrance. I caught a cab in front of a hotel two blocks away, asked to be dropped two blocks from the church, and then forced myself to walk casually to the priest's front door.

It was now close to midnight. I used my cell phone to turn off my TV and living room lights and turn on the bedroom light. I wished I'd brought the Chinese food with me but settled for a cup of coffee and a sandwich from Father Mike. Fifteen minutes later, I worked my phone to turn off my bedroom light.

Nothing happened for almost three hours. When it did, I was shocked. I was watching the alarm app on my phone. It suddenly turned green, showing me that the alarm was disabled. I switched to the app that let me watch the cameras both inside and outside my condo, and I hit the RECORD command, just in case anyone got in. I held the phone's small screen so Kenny, Father Mike, and I could watch as a figure dressed in black entered my living room, rushed down the hall to my bedroom, and fired two shots at my bed before fleeing. I'm not sure which of us was most shocked. Kenny was the first to move, grabbing his phone and squawking orders. Now that he knew the attackers were ready to kill, he warned his team.

All was quiet again as Father Mike began turning off lights on the ground floor of his two-story house. He went upstairs to continue his nighttime routine, although I doubted he'd be sleeping until this was over.

"So, what do you think it means? That attack at your place?" Kenny's voice was barely above a whisper.

"For one thing, Carmen's death was no accident."

I could barely see Kenny in the dark, but I heard clothing rustle as he shook his head. "That was a given," he said. "No one kills someone that way by accident. It takes muscle and know-how to snap a neck. But why come after you?"

"Eliminate the witnesses?"

Kenny blew out some air and gave a resigned nod. "You're the only one who actually talked to the mayor." He made air quotes as he spoke the last word. "If they think they destroyed all copies of that conversation, I guess that makes you some kind of witness."

"Something like that." I glanced at the stairs that led to Father Mike. "I think I'll just go sit outside Father Mike's room. I doubt he's in danger, but he's the only other person who might have witnessed something or seen something on the supposed tape."

"Good. That way we'll know where you are. I don't want my team mistaking you for one of these commandos. Stay near the father until one of us comes to get you."

Kenny left and I climbed the stairs to the hallway where only one door was closed—Father Mike's bedroom, I assumed. I thought about dragging a chair into the hall, but instead went into the bedroom opposite his, left the door open and pulled a wooden chair into the shadows beyond the door. It wasn't exactly comfortable, but it didn't squeak, and I thought the discomfort would help me stay alert.

I entertained myself running every possible scenario through my head. What if they came up the outside wall and got in through Father Mike's window? I kicked myself for not checking out the room in advance or at least making sure the window was locked. What if two or more would-be assassins came into the house? It seemed unlikely, but I'd just have to play it by ear. I tried to think of something else. New menus for Soup entertained me for a while. A "To Do" list for getting Soup back in business got me through another hour. Soon it would be daybreak and I hoped the danger would be over.

I wasn't that lucky. I heard the front door open below me. *Please let it be Kenny.* I saw a narrow flashlight beam swing up the stairs. *Okay, not Kenny.* I picked up my gun, which had been sitting in my lap all this time.

The light reached the top of the stairs and lit the one closed door. If the intruder swung the light behind him, he'd see me. Instead he reached for the door handle.

I stood, took two steps to the doorway and pointed my weapon at his back. "Freeze," I said in my loudest police voice. "Drop your weapon and turn around slowly."

As I expected, he didn't drop his gun, he didn't move slowly. He swung his gun toward me with Kung Fu-like grace. I knew he would pull the trigger as soon as he had me in his sights. I gripped my own trigger, tightened my arm muscles and was taking a quick breath when Father Mike's door slowly opened. I couldn't risk the shot. I turned right, lifted my left leg and reversed direction, swinging it and the rest of me to the left. I kicked his gun arm hard with my artificial foot. He fired just before the gun flew from his hand. The bullet hit my foot. There was no pain, of course, but the force spun me around. I managed to stay upright, the prosthesis twisting but staying attached. I knew I'd have major bruises on the stump. The intruder scrambled for his gun, but Father Mike was quicker. One mighty swing of a fireplace poker and the intruder was down and out.

Father Mike frisked the guy, finding a knife in his pocket and a second gun in an ankle holster. We tied him up, took his weapons and left him lying where he fell in front of the priest's bedroom. We went downstairs in time to hear Kenny knock twice on the front door and then come in.

"I think it's over," he said. "We have six in custody."

I looked at Father Mike. He was still holding the poker. His eyes twinkled when he looked at me. "You want to tell him?"

I couldn't help grinning. "No. You go ahead."

With a priestly nod, a quick look heavenward, and a few whispered words that were probably for God's ears only, he said in his quiet, measured voice, "Number seven is here at the top of the stairs."

Kenny sent two uniforms to bring down the intruder who'd regained consciousness and was yelling about my shooting at him. It took a few moments for me to realize he was insisting that all the weapons were mine, and he was an innocent bystander. After the officers took him away, Kenny rubbed his face. "So, do we have evidence to hold this guy?" he asked.

Well, we have the video from my apartment. I'm pretty sure it was the same dude." I hobbled over to the weapons and pointed out the one that was fired at me. My left foot wasn't working quite right.

"Hey, you're limping," Father Mike said. "Are you injured?"

I looked down at the powder burns and hole in my left shoe. "I think this is our proof. Can we get someone to swab my hands and the intruder's for gunshot residue? I didn't fire my weapon, and I was careful how I picked up his." I wiggled my artificial foot and heard something rattle. "I think the bullet from his weapon is still inside here."

Kenny's eyebrows went up as he bent to examine the neat hole in the outside of the rubber foot. There was no corresponding exit hole in the other side. He looked up at me. "Hey, Meryl. You got a spare leg at home? I think we may need to keep this one."

On Friday, I made my formal statements at BPD-Brighton and gave them the file containing the first call from the mayor. By then, the mayor himself had issued a statement taking responsibility for hiring the thugs and calling Soup, but he claimed he had no knowledge of the plan to vandalize my restaurant or the later attempt to steal the video tape from the church.

Carmen's killer was identified by a single strand of her hair caught in commando number seven's watchband. His fellow mercenaries didn't hesitate to testify against him in exchange for reduced charges. As I'd guessed, number seven was also the person who shot up my sheets before he came after Father Mike. One count of murder and two of attempted murder should put him away for a good long time. While the mayor's private security thugs backed up the mayor's statement, it didn't take the media long to run with the story.

"You think the mayor ordered the attack on Soup?" Kenny asked as he walked me out of the Brighton police station.

I thought about it for a moment. "No, I guess not. It bothers me that he alerted them to the church camera, though. By then he knew they'd killed someone."

"You think we'll find enough to arrest him?"

"Probably not. But I'm not voting for him again."

With the church now part of a larger crime scene, we weren't able to open on Friday, but my staff appreciated a paid day off. I managed to get some sleep in a nice, anonymous hotel while my home was processed for evidence. On Saturday my restaurant became a major construction zone. Members of Father Mike's church helped with the cleanup, and local contractors installed new cabinets, appliances, counters, sinks, bathroom fixtures, paint and drywall patches. They all volunteered to postpone billing until my check from the insurance company arrived. On Monday, Soup opened as usual. We never got another call from the mayor.

* * *

Cynthia Sabelhaus is the editor of *Calliope—a Writer's Workshop by Mail* (www.CalliopeOnTheWeb.org). Although most of her publishing credits have been for nonfiction, mystery fiction has always been her first love. She received the William F. Deeck-Malice Domestic grant for unpublished writers. "Soup" is her first published mystery story. Cynthia and her husband and fellow writer, Ralph, live in Arizona.

MONSTERS DON'T SLEEP AT NIGHT

by Gabriel Valjan

Quinn stood in front of his locker too tired to kill the small rat escaping from it. O'Malley next to him, a mounted police officer, talked to himself. He was angry he had to change out his shirt and angrier still that he had to pay the Replacements Clerk an exorbitant price for another one.

Quinn understood why when he saw blood splatter on the man's collar. Boston Police Commissioner Edwin Curtis enforced strict rules and regulations. Failure to comply with his policies about appearance would result in a fine for O'Malley. The men purchased their own uniforms and the cost of their upkeep and equipment pointed north of two-hundred dollars every year, so every tax hurt. Not a man dared keep spare clothes in his locker, for fear of bringing home vermin and roaches to the family. O'Malley reached into his summer coat for a rag which he then used to wipe down his nightstick. More blood.

"I don't know what'll come first for me, Squint: the asylum from the anarchists on The Common or the poor house because of our beloved Commissioner."

O'Malley called him Squint for the occasional twitch around his left eye. Quinn placed a forefinger to his lips. "Not so loud" and then twirled the same finger. "Ears."

"Bugger'em to hell. I'd ride'em all to perdition on the company horse, if I could."

"Talk like that could jeopardize your standing and wages."

"Some wage when you have a wife and four children." O'Malley threaded his muscular arms through fresh sleeves. "You're a bachelor, and can live off your twenty a week. Get thee married, and see how far my thirty takes you." He fastened the last button now and pulled on his jacket. "Work seventy-odd-hour weeks for six fierce years and there's time yet for me to question the paternity of the rabble I have in me flat." O'Malley, known for his gallows humor, poked Quinn's shoulder with his riot stick. "God's blessing be on your head out there today."

'Out there' for Patrolman Quinn often meant walking the beat on Kneeland Street, where drunken sailors and army men rampaged while on leave or just before they shipped out. He could have it worse. Much worse. He could be back in France surrounded by Huns. Aye, he was content with his lot in Boston for now, despite the low wage, despite the dangers and demands of his occupation, and despite the ways the Protestant elites rigged advancement against Catholics in Boston.

He closed his locker. Let O'Malley enjoy his Brookline and West End anarchists from the comfort of his saddle and crack their heads if he must. He'd police the excesses of youth in military uniform, the drunks, and inept pickpockets.

Time for him to report to the whip and receive his assignment for the day. He looked about; no sign of the rodent.

He couldn't believe where the desk sergeant had assigned him today. His shift was the somewhat posh acre between Harrison Ave. and Washington Street. Warehouses on one end; residents, bars, and jazz clubs on the other. He had heard both locations, however, were cesspools for graft, theft, and sexual congress in dodgy alleys.

Quinn's late mother said the Devil could hide in a moonbeam and monsters don't sleep at night. He didn't complain, though. He could've been assigned the dreaded North End, where the pale horse cantered and was carrying off Italians and others with the Spanish flu.

The sergeant did the unexpected. He wagged his finger to invite Quinn into his confidence. "You might happen upon Lonergan in your travels today," he said.

Quinn had learned to defer to authority in the military so he waited for the subjective to bleed through and there it came, plain as poverty. "That Lonergan. Nothing like a pure shanty Irish who fancies himself lace-curtain Irish. Know the man?"

"Lonergan? By reputation only, but I've not had the pleasure. Why?" Quinn asked.

"Some pleasure. Rumored to be a Bolshevik, with all his palaver about starting a union amongst the rank and file. Christ in heaven, even the coloreds know better than to test that foul bucket of workplace politics, but I digress. You've been given an opportunity, so don't let me hear you've soaked the merchants, or mitched off to a red house."

"I won't, Sergeant."

"I don't get you, Quinn. Nobody gives out the stink about you. Every man has at least one vice from Adam. Indulge the occasional pint at Foley's after your tour?"

Tread this path with caution, Quinn told himself. He needed the job, no matter what it paid, and he had labored to avoid any ink next to his name, or the cliché of another drunk Irishman. The ordinaries on the force drank at Foley's and voted Democrat, while the whip and the brass above him voted Republican and imitated the Brahmins on the Hill. Commissioner Curtis himself kept three Irish servants to manage his household.

Admit to tipple and the sergeant might suggest moral turpitude to his superiors, but deny drink altogether and he was both a snob and a liar. Loyalty and slights within the Department were remembered for as long as a donkey's ear.

"I enjoy a Guinness now and then, Sergeant. Who doesn't?"

Convinced or not, the whip eased back. Though the sergeant had advised him not to accept money from businesses, the truth was that merchants feared hooligans and paid patrolmen and ward bosses for protection. This 'opportunity' could be a test. His bit about the brothel was just as forked and could mean, Go enjoy a lass but don't get caught.

"Luck of the clover on you, Quinn. No reserve duty for you this week or next."

Another unexpected turn, this largesse of no reserve duty surprised Quinn. All patrolmen were required to serve as reservists and bunk overnight in the filthy backroom. The brunt of the obligation fell hardest on the newest and most junior men.

"I'd suggest you visit Foley's later. Never know who you might meet," the sergeant said and reached for a pen near his ledger. "Now, top of the morning to you and off you go into the wilds."

"And the rest of the day to you, Sergeant."

Quinn suspected the sergeant expected intelligence on Lonergan in trade for all his recent fortunes. He had not lied about Lonergan; he knew the man as an acquaintance. Both men were one year out from War's end, and both men worked Boston streets to prove they were trustworthy and reliable, and yet both men were still in No Man's Land. The bosses considered the Irish one step above the Negro, and the city's Irish resented veterans for stealing a job from their brother, cousin, father, or uncle.

There were differences between the two men. Three years and another summer ago, Quinn had nearly gone deaf from listening to German lead in France, at Bealleau Wood as a Marine. Machine-gun nests and bayonet charges by day in the wheat fields, and artillery and gas shells at night in the woods. Around the same time, Lonergan of County Tipperary volunteered for the Irish Regiment. Gassed at Hulluch, he survived that and the subsequent horrors at Somme and Passchendaele. Germans in front of him and British officers, who thought of the Irish as nothing more than pets worth less than their pocket change, behind him.

Quinn's shift started as a friend of promise. Most often, the beat was a form of the Twelve Stations of the Cross. Not this time. Quinn found a 'T' token on the ground after he completed his first walk-through. He flipped the token for the transit system like a penny and whistled while he walked.

Here in the hubbub of horsecars converted into streetcars and pedestrians about, he watched the wires above the electrified trolleys spark, and heard the Washington Street elevated railway screech. As he made his rounds, he acquainted himself with shopkeepers and other characters to establish a rapport and presence in the community. Aside from the unpleasant business of the recent May Day Riot in Roxbury, when the police suppressed the violence between Socialists and Catholics, the men in blue were tolerated.

He'd complete umpteen circuits of his territory and, at some point, meet with a supervisor, who'd sign his journey book. A senior patrolman audited beats to assure conformity to the Commissioner's protocols. Quinn passed Vose & Sons Piano-Forte Manufacturing. The establishment produced 300 pianos a week. One of the company strongmen nodded to him. He was working his way down towards Waltham Street, where The Grover & Baker Sewing Machine Company stood when he heard the short bleat of a whistle.

His supervisor was an officer, a Protestant, who treated him as if he were Sinn Féin and a suspect in the Easter Uprising. The tall man snapped his fingers, demanding Quinn's notebook. Not a word. No eye contact. He paged through the booklet and read the entries, like a stern schoolmaster. When he retrieved his pencil at last, he consulted his gold pocket watch instead of reading the clock on a nearby tower. He pushed the small notebook into Quinn's chest.

"Where to next?" the officer asked.

"I'll proceed down Washington towards Harrison to complete the circuit, Sir."

"On this side of the street?"

The question surprised Quinn. "I suppose," he answered.

"You suppose wrong, Patrolman. You are on the lax side of the street. Cross over and carry on." Impatient, the man huffed and pointed to alleys. "Most of the devilry is there and there." He indicated places without street signs. "Where maggots fester."

"Aye," Quinn said. The man walked off, shaking his head, as if he wondered why God had created the Irish. Sooner than later, Quinn would've canvassed both sides of Washington Street. He had ten hours left. The one benefit to these new orders is that it placed him on the same side of the street as the Power Station, a feat of engineering and ingenuity Quinn admired. The Station trumpeted itself as the world's largest electric power plant, the source for the current running through the city's numerous trains. This same side of the street was where the Boston Social Club met at Foyle's.

Down one alley and nothing, save for a few lads truant from school. They had legs and lungs and Quinn hadn't the bother to chase them. Their crime was robbing themselves of an education. When Quinn resurfaced on Washington, he spotted the supervisor a ways up on the next block, on the opposite side of the street and across from another unnamed lane.

The man touched the brim of his hat, which Quinn interpreted as a signal since it served no other purpose. There were no ladies near him. The boss then put his hands behind his back, turned and left, likely to go and admire the cast-iron railings of the Union Park residences. Sure enough, on Quinn's side of the street he saw four burly types dip into a side street.

Quinn's eye twitched. Trouble.

He blazed through the crowd. He clipped a man's shoulder as he wended his way through a thicket of delivery boys, a swarm of lady shoppers and mothers with baby buggies. He turned the corner and found the four men circling a patrolman.

Lonergan.

The man from Tipperary said nothing to his welcome committee. His stick in one hand, a handkerchief in the other, he waited, keeping the wall to his back. Quinn moved with the stealth he had learned at Quantico and perfected against Germans. Lonergan had seen him, but didn't betray his presence. Lonergan held the front line, while Quinn maintained the rear.

One of the goons stepped forward. Lonergan snapped the handkerchief to sting the lout's eye and distract him long enough for him to crack his skull with the walnut nightstick. Lonergan ducked and pivoted to bat the next man's ribs to his spine.

Quinn surprised a tough from behind, spun him around, and knocked the air out of him. The last man understood the field, the odds against him, but persisted with his target. He sought out Lonergan, this time with a knife drawn.

Lonergan dropped his stick, when his assailant lunged and attempted to slash him with a backhand to his ribs. Lonergan swept his right arm and moved himself off the arc of the attack. Aside the man now, he captured a wrist and used his other hand to drive the man to the ground.

Lonergan looked up. Quinn could tell from Lonergan's eyes, the coldness in them, that he had done this imminent act of violence countless times. Only difference is that another day, in another place and time Lonergan would've snapped the man's neck. Instead, he pressed his knee into the man's shoulder and, holding the wrist, he pulled up hard with enough force to divorce the shoulder from the socket, the sound similar to separating the wing from the chicken.

Dazed and horrified, the other three thugs fled, but not before Quinn clapped one of them across the back of the head, thinking of O'Malley on his horse. Lonergan had a man and Quinn had a question.

"Flip the gurrier over," Quinn told Lonergan.

"You want to work away at him?"

"Not quite what I had in mind, though the thought of it is lovely."

On his back like a worm, the criminal writhed. Hands to his face to protect it, he pleaded for mercy. Quinn pinned him to the ground with his nightstick. The man squirmed in pain and gasped for air.

"Who sent you?" Quinn asked and leaned some more on the pole. The man groaned.

Quinn asked again and eased off some to allow an answer. None.

"Then I shall be your prefect of pain." Quinn stepped on the injured shoulder, mashing bone underfoot. "I've got the patience of Job, but I'll make it simple for you. You're scundered and the lot of you have botched the job. Pure as dirt you are, and don't lie to me. Who hired you?"

"I can't say."

"Can't or won't?" Lonergan asked.

"He'll kill me, I swear it," the man said, wild panic in his eyes. "He'll know it was me."

Quinn reached down and grabbed the filthy shirt collar and peeled the bruiser off the dirt. Their faces were close enough the man could smell a trace of Myrsol shave cream on Quinn. "Was it the tip of the hat?" Quinn asked.

The man clenched his eyes and sobbed.

Quinn had his answer. He dropped the wounded fool to the ground. Lonergan nudged his almost assassin with a foot to the ribs. "Feck off and leave the knife. You'd be needing it about as much as a snake needs shoes. Off with you and stay out of hospital, so there's no record of you for the boss."

Quinn watched the damaged man stagger away. He waited until he was out of earshot before he asked Lonergan, "Why did you let him go?"

"Because he's telling the truth. The other three will rat. Arrest him and the Devil'll know he's dead before God or the judge sees him."

"You alive at the end of your tour only adds coal to their determination," Quinn said.

"And it seems I'm not alone in that, am I? I saw how you moved, friend. Service?"

"Marines."

"Sound wood for the cross you'll bear in this life. Sixteenth Regiment myself, one of Lord Kitchener's unwanted brats." Lonergan tapped Quinn's shoulder as a thank-you. "Finish your shift and, if you're still alive, a Guinness awaits you at Foley's, Dover and Fay Streets."

Quinn sidled up to the stool, looking about for Lonergan. He had survived the day and hoped the same for his new friend. His first time inside the pub, the room turned quiet as a convent as the rest of the lads sized him up. They returned to their conversations after a long hard minute. Quinn recognized faces from around the precinct.

A hand went up. Lonergan excused himself from a small group of patrolmen and motioned to the barkeep, a man in a crisp and immaculate white shirt and apron, his tie tucked into his shirt, to pour two pints of the Black Stuff. A word from the bartender, and Quinn bet he could name the county of origin in the Old Country.

When he had passed through the thick front door, he saw hardwood floors swept clean, and each framed window of glass out to the street, spotless. The likes of the help behind the counter and manning the tables said family place, father and sons. A small placard, a coat of arms, and the Foley name faced Quinn. A small sign announced the birthdate of the pub as 1909. A decade old and the bar already exuded ambience, masculine and practical, and gravitas without pretension. Pint of Guinness placed in front of him, he thanked the server and listened to Lonergan while he waited for his drink.

"I vouched for you," Lonergan said and explained that he told his closest friends about what had happened in the lane. Quinn could identify them because when he surveyed the room, they raised their pint glasses.

Lonergan had received his pint and indicated a lean and severe man with thick eyebrows with his drink, "That there is John McInnes, president of the union. Man is a veteran of the Indian Wars and the Spanish-American War, and rode with President Roosevelt in Cuba. He's delivered a list of grievances to Commissioner Curtis, although he's made it clear that he does not want a strike."

Quinn shook his head. Guinness, properly poured, awaited them.

"All well and good, Lonergan, but McInnes is a politician, like any leader. Curtis talks to the mayor, and Mayor Peters will have Governor Coolidge's ear. Did McInnes use the word 'strike' or not?"

"He had."

"Then Curtis knows it's a possibility, and I'm afraid strike is where we're headed."

"We'll see," Lonergan said. "McInnes has eighteen union reps and the rank and file behind him."

"And the politicians have the newspapers, the militia, but you know what, you're right. We should wait and see." Quinn raised his glass for the toast. "Sláinte."

A few fellows approached Quinn and Lonergan at the bar, introduced themselves. Quinn enjoyed the stout, enjoyed the camaraderie that he had not had since he was a soldier. He missed the bond of faith and reliance on each other for survival against a common enemy. Quinn had not had that, any of it, since he departed from the theatre of war, and he suspected Lonergan harbored the same ache, the want for meaning when he returned to an amnesiac and thankless world.

He drank, he listened, he watched, and he took in all the faces around him, knowing that many of them would be ruined, many of them battered in the weeks to come, and some among them might die merely because of the uniform, and he understood that for most of them nothing would ever be the same again. He knew all this because his left eye was twitching.

Like the August Madness years before, war prevailed but unlike that conflict thought to end by Christmas, theirs this August would cease in September with defeat, a cold bitter contempt and retaliation from the upper echelons of power. The mayor and the reformer James Storrow fashioned a compromise over demands, recognizing the union and insisting that no action be taken against McInnes and his men. The American Federation of Labor backed off, four Boston papers endorsed the plan.

Commissioner Curtis rejected it. Governor Calvin Coolidge rejected it.

Most of the men around Quinn worked seventy hours a week, and as such seventy percent agreed to strike in September. On the ninth day of that month and for three days, looting and lawlessness ruled the streets. The violence reigned until the state militia crushed the insurrection. In the end, there were nine dead and thousands of dollars in damages.

Quinn reported to work, to remove his personal effects from his locker. He had been dismissed, along with all the men who had chosen the strike. Curtis had replaced them, offering the new hires better pay, more vacation time, a pension plan, and subsidies for their uniform and equipment.

As Quinn was about to close his locker, he saw a small rat sitting inside it. The rodent's black eyes stared back at him, its whiskers twitching, as if it understood all that Quinn had experienced as a patrolman. He left the door ajar.

"Goodbye, friend," he said to the creature he knew as an honest comrade in the trenches, then and now.

Postscript

The strike, the strident anti-union stance and the subsequent retaliation, bolstered Governor Coolidge's reputation as a hardliner and secured for him the Vice Presidency in 1920. So devastating was the legacy of the Boston Police Strike of 1919 to the morale of law enforcement everywhere that not one police union was formed until after World War II and no police officer in the United States dared to strike until 1974.

* * *

Gabriel Valjan is the author of the *Roma* and the *Company Files Series* with Winter Goose Publishing. The first novel, *Dirty Old Town,* in the Shane Cleary Series with Level Best Books is scheduled for publication in January 2020. Gabriel is a member of Sisters in Crime, National, New England chapter. He lives in Boston's South End.

PECCATA MUNDY
by CJ Verburg

Being Christopher Mundy at fifty-two is a tragedy I would gladly wish on my worst enemy. I don't, because I have no faith in wishes, and (I'm reliably informed) no worse enemy than myself.

I say *tragedy* in the sense the Greeks defined it: the fall of a person of consequence to disaster. Oedipus, blinded by arrogance, unwittingly slays his father. Othello, blinded by jealousy, murders his innocent bride. Would that I could blind myself to the fall that jeers at me daily from the bathroom mirror. Whose are those sagging jowls, leathery pouches under the once-penetrating eyes, hair sprouting from ears and nostrils but not the crown of the head? I'm accustomed to face a rising star in that frame, not a falling one.

Do I sound bitter? No worries, as my students would say. Today's bathroom mirror comes attached to a plush hotel room near the harbor in Hyannis, Massachusetts. I am a guest of honor at the Cape Cod Literary Festival. A grand display of my oeuvre welcomed me into the lobby: four novels, two books of short stories, and an essay collection. Tomorrow afternoon I will appear on a panel with three other New England luminaries to discuss the timeless question *Is Publishing Dead?* Saturday night I will be interviewed onstage by a stripling from the local TV station who's authored (his verb, not mine) a best-selling guide to social media. Throughout the weekend fans, aspirants, and the curious will pounce on me in hallways and elevators begging for my advice or my autograph. More of my books will sell in these three days than the entire previous month. Yes: I might get lucky.

Or not. My phone is playing the ringtone for a call I'd rather not take.

"Hello, Berta."

"Christopher. Where are you?"

"On my way to the welcoming reception. Talk later?"

Berta Rathbun is the surviving partner of Richard Rathbun, my literary agent and friend for thirty years. Age has not withered her; on the contrary. Her hair, which once coiled at the base of her neck like a sleeping mink, now spikes like a startled porcupine. Her smoker's rasp has become a jackhammer.

"Where's that book proposal you promised me?"

"I want to run it past one more set of eyes."

"Christopher! Schmooze it or lose it. I'm meeting with Simon on Monday. You want to stay in the game, get your ass off the bench. *Finnegans Wake* or *The Three Little Pigs*—just hold your nose and hit Send."

"Tomorrow, Berta. Sunday at the latest."

"Tomorrow, Christopher. The clock is ticking. The perfect is the enemy of the good. And your worst enemy—"

"Oh, there's my escort. Gotta go."

I hang up. And as if a wish-granting genie has popped up from my iPhone, I hear a rat-ta-tat on my door.

"Professor Mundy?"

The vision silhouetted before me dispels the wrath of Rathbun. This angel can't be much past twenty: tawny-cheeked and willowy with a nimbus of bronze curls. Her eyes are outlined in black so that I cannot ignore their flickering emerald depths. Her full lips glisten as if her tongue moistened them the moment before I opened the door.

But she calls me Professor.

"Christopher," I say. "Please."

She holds out her hand. "Katlin Collins." Such soft fingers!

"Katlin. Are you a writer?"

"Me? No. Well, maybe. Not yet." Her cheeks flush. "You ready to go?"

I tamp down the temptation to invite her in. I am a man on a mission, a Lewis (or Clark) ready to follow my Sacagawea anywhere, tracking the fluttering flag of her skirt above those slim legs in their platform sandals. If we're attacked, how can she run? She can't. I'll have to scoop her up and carry her over my shoulder.

"Your books are amazing." She slows so that we can walk side by side.

"Thank you." Gold glints in her earlobe. "Any particular favorites?"

"I was just reading your stories. The one with the squirrel and the pigeons? Omigod."

"Park-Slash-Bench."

"Right. Exactly. Like, it's all there in the title. But I didn't even suspect."

"Good." I chuckle. "So, not too...macho for you?"

"Oh, well." She chuckles back politely. "I really wanted to meet you. I took a writing class at Four C's, but I really want to learn how to do what you do."

We enter a wide carpeted hall. I know where we're going as clearly as if GPS were murmuring in my ear. I'll ask her what she's written; she'll pour out her soul. I'll graciously offer to take a look. Her manuscript will be dreadful: having taught there, I can testify that Cape Cod Community College is no literary spawning ground. But I won't tell her that. I'll invite her to my room for a private conference. No arm-twisting. My sympathetic critique will melt her heart, perhaps enough to make me a happy man.

It doesn't go like that.

"Love and murder," she answers, pausing outside the Iyanough Room. "A romance where somebody gets killed? Two so far."

"You've written two romantic suspense stories?"

"Yeah. Well, books. The Wave-Makers series. Two that I finished, three more that I started. Before my schedule got jammed with work, my kids—"

She flings the door open, allowing me to mask my gasp with a cough.

"You want to see one?" she asks me.

I'm blinking at a brightly lit room full of chattering faces, while the tarnished blossom beside me extracts a phone from her absurdly tiny shoulder bag.

"Do I want to see...?" I echo dumbly.

"My writing. What's your email?"

The crowd engulfs us, carrying Katlin and me in separate directions. Within minutes I'm holding a glass of Chardonnay, plunging into a sea of adulation like a producer at a Hollywood pool party. As a writer, I'm a solitary creature by nature and necessity; but even I have only so much tolerance for being unrecognized.

It would kill me to give this up.

And why should I? I can feel my resolve stiffening. I'm Christopher Mundy, the most ground-breaking literary voice since John Barth. This is my métier. In two days I can damn well come up with something.

I confide to everyone I meet that only the joy of seeing old friends tore me away from my laptop. When you're hot.... No, sorry (finger to lips), my agent swore me to secrecy. All I can say is, this one's a radical change from anything I've ever done.

I scan the room for Katlin Collins and don't see her.

I ask the bartender. He shrugs. "Ask the hostess?"

The skinny woman in a bright blue dress, bright red hair, and sparkling white teeth flashes me a welcoming smile. Everything going OK?

"The young lady who brought me here," I say. "Miss Collins. Or is it Mrs.?"

A cloud dims her patriotic face. "Mrs. Collins. Poor Katlin. Lost her husband last winter."

"Lost him how?"

"Oh, well, I don't like to gossip." A claim I've never found to be true. "Tragic! Leaving his lovely wife and two darling babies."

"What happened?"

"Accidental poisoning." She raises her hand against questions. "That's all I can say."

I improvise. "I wondered about, you know. Tipping her."

"Not allowed, I'm afraid. Do you have breakfast plans tomorrow? Perhaps you could take her out."

I tell myself it's because my heart bleeds for widows and orphans that I spend the night hunched over my iPad like an owl over a mousehole. I tell myself it's because Katlin Collins admires my writing and wants to learn how to do what I do. Because she needs the money. Because I owe her more than an omelet and home-fries. Not until daylight, when I take a razor to the slack, stubbly jowls in the mirror, do I face the truth: It's because, goddammit, I want to learn how to do what she does.

She picks me up at the side entrance in a beat-up blue Chevy. "So you like my Wave-Makers? How much did you read?"

"Both books. Cover to cover." I sweep snack wrappers and plastic toys off the passenger seat. "They're a little rough, but you've got strong plots and some terrific characters." The car door creaks. "How long to write these?"

"Two, three months?"

"A whole book in three months? Start to finish?" If this is true, it's staggering. My fastest novel, *The Clockmaker's Mistress,* kept me nose-to-grindstone for a year.

"Three months for both of them. Like, one month for *Tsunami,* and then *Undertow* took longer because I got jammed with work and stuff."

She parks on the main street of downtown Hyannis. Where is she taking me? I see *Egg* on a sign, and *Brunch*. I'm too stunned to care.

We sit facing each other across paper place mats. Katlin's saying that if she could get some money up front, like a couple thousand bucks, and then royalties coming in, she'd be OK when her night job at the drugstore ends after Labor Day. What kind of a deal can she expect for two finished books plus plans for three more? I tell her I have no idea. She says that since everybody she saw me talking to last night was an author or an editor, can't I find out? And will I introduce her to my publishing friends?

I lift my eyes from her left hand, with its pale band where a ring used to be. "Tell you what, Katlin. I have a better idea."

If there's anything that fills two people with more intense curiosity about each other than sex, it's business.

Obviously, before this goes any further, I want to know what happened to her husband. Katlin balks: too awful, too recent, too painful. So I try an indirect approach: how did he feel about her writing? Oh, he loved it! Devon was her inspiration: acting out the bedtime stories she told the kids, working overtime at We-Can-Dig-It Landscapers so she could take a class at Four C's. She still can't believe he's gone. Almost every night she wakes up in a sweat from the horror of finding him dead in his truck on Valentine's Day, frozen stiff at the wheel. The police said his hands and mouth, and the beer cans and sandwich wrappers beside him, were covered with pesticide.

I dutifully coo over cell-phone photos of Ramona, three, and Devo, two. I learn that Katlin's sister Sharalin helps with babysitting so she can juggle part-time work at the drugstore, Four C's (she quit her writing class), and the Festival hotel. I learn that Devon's life insurance covered his credit-card debts and their overdue rent, but not the loan for the Chevy.

Some inspiration! No wonder *Tsunami* and *Undertow* overflow with rage, deceit, treachery, and violence.

As for what Katlin has learned about me, I can only hope my guest-of-honor status blinds her to the humiliating reality that I too am living on fumes. After an earth-shaking literary debut, my later novels have been a roller-coaster. I've kept up my reputation and my mortgage payments with book reviews, essays, and stories, teaching fellowships at small colleges around New England, of which fortunately there are hundreds, and gigs like this one. Each blip on the radar refreshes my Google search status, ensuring enough minor awards and honorary degrees to prevent Berta from dropping me before novel #5.

At the end of breakfast, Katlin and I come to an agreement. We will publish The Wave-Makers together: her manuscripts transformed to income by my clout and expertise.

We're too giddy to wrangle over details. She's smitten by the bright future I'm giving her: a ticket out of poverty, a share of my stardom. I'm smitten by the bright present she's giving me: satin cheeks and rosy lips, eyelashes as luscious as the black-plumed fans of an exotic dancer, the bare leg that my leg keeps accidentally brushing under the table. Anyway, I tell her, wrangling over details is Berta's job. Ours is to toast our new collaboration with mimosas. Back at the hotel I'll print up a simple pre-nup contract;

and while Katlin heads off to work, I'll dive into *Tsunami.*

Talk about wrangling. It takes me two and a half hours to extract a book proposal from this wild beast of a manuscript. I hit Send and dash out the door.

The Cape Cod Literary Festival gives its guests of honor one meal per day on our own, and I've had mine. For lunch I'm co-hosting a table of fans and would-be authors with Professor Roderick Deam of Cape Cod Community College, AKA Roddy the Snake.

"Oh, you naughty boy!" he hisses in my ear.

I arch my famous Frigid Eyebrow at him.

Roddy sidles closer and murmurs: "Wasn't that our Sun Maiden I saw you flitting off with this morning? No worries, Christopher. Discretion is my middle name. Only, be warned. You wouldn't be the first Icarus to fall out of the sky flying too close to that flame."

Our guests are finding their seats. I murmur back: "What on earth are you driveling about, Roddy?"

"Did Her Hotness tell you about the Valentine's Day tragedy?"

"Yes."

"Ah. Then I need not point out the red flags." He adds with a venomous smile, "To a man of your broad experience."

That's a blow below the belt. During my year as an adjunct professor at Four C's, I was the victim of a malicious prank which even now I seethe to recall. Two female students in my Intro Lit class, outraged by their poor grades, accused me of "inappropriate behavior." No charges were brought—it was absurd; the girls had no evidence, and their motive was obvious—but my reputation took a hit, and I've never been invited back.

Across the table Roddy wriggles into his chair, chatting, dodging eye contact with me. *What red flags?* I silently demand. *What's Katlin Collins to you that you should warn me off?*

I rise the instant our dessert plates are cleared, to catch him before he can slither away. My phone intercedes.

I step behind a rolling dolly stacked with chairs. "Berta. Are you pleased?"

"I'm shocked. I'd be grinning like a Cheshire Cat if I believed you.

Christopher Mundy coauthors The Wave-Makers? Tell me if this rings a bell. Quote: *I'd go back and drown myself retroactively at birth before I'd dip a toe into genre fiction.*"

"And you answered, quote: *Get off your white male high horse and join the twenty-first century.*"

"I didn't say jump in up to your neck, Christopher. With a girl you met yesterday?"

"Irrelevant."

"Not to anyone who's familiar with your history. Starting with Simon."

"I refuse to dignify that with a response. Did you read my proposal or not? Tell me if it strikes you as genre fiction."

"Yes, I read it, and no. On the contrary. Your sample chapters are so dark that I was impelled to look into your coauthor. Katlin Collins. A life more shadows than sunshine, yes? What can you tell me about her late husband?"

"Devon. Charming and feckless. Worked for a landscaper until he accidentally poisoned himself in the parking lot."

"Happy Valentine's Day," says Berta.

"You knew this already."

"I do my homework. Your homework. Devon Collins's boss says he had a violent temper and liked to break the rules. No drinking on the job. No tripto-dio-whatever in the cab. Highly toxic; they spray it on cranberry bogs. Remind me next Thanksgiving."

"Where are you going with this, Berta?"

"It's a tight community. Everybody knows everybody. A difficult husband, a beautiful long-suffering wife, two adorable kids. A $100,000 life insurance policy. Nobody wanted to screw that up. On Valentine's Day? Are you kidding?" She clears her throat. "Your Katlin's sister is married to a cop. There was a feeling that, anyone else, they might have looked closer."

The giddiness from my breakfast mimosa collides with the buzz from my lunchtime Chardonnay. I cling to the molded arms of two plastic chairs for support. The dolly doesn't budge. Sometimes having your back against the wall is an advantage.

"So," I rejoin. "As my agent, your professional opinion."

"Good news and bad news. You must see this, Christopher. A husband who died so unusually is catnip for the media. An invitation to pester and pry and dig up skeletons in your closet. Trample on your privacy. Hang out your dirty linen—not a small load."

"What's the good news?"

Berta chuckles. "There's no such thing as bad publicity."

I give a bravura performance on the *Is Publishing Dead?* panel. With the wind of a new project filling my sails, I'm restored to myself. Every remark exudes authority, insight, wit, and a dash of roguish charm. My listeners are thrilled to hear that novel #5 is coursing through the pipeline. Forgotten are the ravages of age. Mirrored in those rapt faces I see the real Christopher Mundy, the ground-breaking American writer once rumored to be short-listed for a Pulitzer.

I've done it before, and by God I'll do it again.

When I've finished signing books and smiling at everyone's compliments and confessions (evidently they've forgotten my answer to "Where do you get your ideas?"), I text Katlin. We decided this morning—giggling like schoolkids—that she needs to meet Berta more than I need to attend tonight's private dinner. She balked at coming to my room: if the Festival finds out, they'll fire her. I promised absolute secrecy. Where else can we hold a conference call?

So while my fellow honorees hack into their surf-and-turf and each other, I sit on my queen-size bed watching Katlin at the desk. Such delicate hands! Such concentration as her thumbs dance over the screen! O to be thy iPhone . . .

"Are you there?" Berta's voice barks.

"We're both here," says Katlin. "Hi, Berta."

"Yes," I second, warmed by the embrace of that "both."

"So, you're serious about this collaboration?"

"We are," I say.

"Yup," says Katlin. "Will you help us?"

"Here's the deal," Berta says. "I will act as agent for the project, representing the two of you as one party. Christopher, you can explain about rights and such. You've already decided your royalty split, and if either of you withdraws for any reason, the other may choose to continue alone or not. Regarding credit—"

"When do we get paid?" Katlin interrupts.

"If we're lucky, first advance check within a year," says Berta.

"A year?" Katlin glances over as if hoping I'll step in. "I heard, now there's e-books and Amazon, they start paying you right away."

"That's self-publishing. Whole different ballgame." I'd pat her shoulder if I could reach it.

"Different how?"

"Like running a bake sale versus a bakery. I'll explain later. Berta, you were saying?"

"Regarding credit. Yes. I can tell you now, Simon or any other publisher will insist on Christopher as lead author."

Two multicolored fingernails tap the desk. "What does that mean?"

"To begin with, his name above yours on the cover, and bigger."

"Why?" Katlin is frowning. "I'm the one who wrote the books."

"You both write the books, yes? It's about recognition. Christopher Mundy is a name well known and respected among readers and reviewers, therefore publishers. Katlin Collins is not."

"Not yet." I lean forward in case a reassuring hug is called for. "Soon."

"What do you mean, we both write the books?"

The sharpness in her voice causes Berta's to soften. "You tell the stories, and Christopher polishes them."

Katlin's frown shifts to me. "Did you change what I wrote?"

"That's what collaboration means," I say kindly. "What you wrote is amazing. But to stand out from the crowd—to be a true wave-maker—that takes spectacular."

"What did you change?"

Other girls before this one have thrown roadblocks in my path. Sometimes you kick them aside; sometimes you pick your way over them. "It's like weeding a garden. I cleared away some dead stuff, and made the live parts stronger."

"Like what?"

"Stop," Berta says in her bullhorn tone. "Katlin, read Christopher's proposal. Christopher, call me back when you two reach an agreement."

"We're past that." It's kick-aside time. "We signed an agreement this morning. I announced this project to my panel audience. We both want The Wave-Makers to quit wasting space on Katlin's computer and start supporting her family."

"I need to read the proposal." Katlin's arms are crossed on her chest.

"Call me back," says Berta, and hangs up.

My first impulse is to remind my rookie partner that she's in the major leagues now. I squelch it.

"Do you want me to go over the changes with you?"

"I want to go home. My kids are starting to think Sharalin's their mommy." She rises. "Email it to me?"

"No problem." I go to my computer. Our shoulders brush, and the electricity from her bare arm melts the edges off my irritation. "Listen, Katlin. Just one or two things—"

But when I turn, she's gone.

Meet for coffee 8 AM? I text her.

That done, suddenly I'm famished. Tonight's dinner started twenty minutes ago. Still enough time to squeeze some mileage out of my freshly shaved face and Egpytian-cotton shirt.

On certain occasions I've been known to wedge in a chair to get myself a place at the luminaries' table. Not anymore. I'm a guest of honor. My colleagues arc buzzing about my hush-hush new project, repped by the legendary Bertha Rathbun. A tanned hand with a Rolex and an Ivy League ring beckons me to a seat.

No way will I ever give this up.

Ironically, I'm sitting back to back with Professor Roderick Deam from Four C's. Now's my chance to demand an explanation for his red flags. I don't, though. Frankly, I don't care. I'm too seasoned a player to require advice from Roddy the Snake. In fact, as chowder makes way for steak, I back off my idea of building cred for Katlin's and my collaboration. For this audience my role is maverick: half cowboy, half Shakespearean prince, seizing my long-awaited moment to grab literature by the horns and flip it on its head.

I return to my room feeling quite cheerful for a man who didn't intend to spend tonight alone. Replaying each verbal volley from dinner, then the hotel bar, I'm so tickled by my comeback(s) that I forget to check my phone until I'm undressing.

Katlin's text says *No coffee your booked I'm working. Lunch?* Inarticulate girl! What does she mean? Aha—tomorrow is Author Speed Dating, an all-day gauntlet of one-on-ones. Our unscheduled meal is lunch. I've already got her into the Festival Banquet, featuring my interview for Cape Cod Community TV.

Did she read my proposal? She must have. No outrage; that's a good sign. For this deal to fly, I need her to appreciate how much depth and nuance I've pumped into her chirpy prose. Maybe she does. If not, maybe a hard day of minimum-wage drudgery will open her eyes.

I sleep like a rock. When I wake, an idea impales my brain like the Sword in the Stone.

What if Katlin rejects my revisions of *Tsunami?* Her loss! Per our pre-nup, either we collaborate or one of us drops out. If she withdraws for any reason—death, disability, or plain obstinacy—I become sole author, free to proceed however I like.

She'd be upset, but not for long. I'm no monster; I'd make sure she was generously compensated. She could spend more time with her children. Berta I suspect would have no problem drafting a termination and offering Simon a clean deal.

Not that I have any wish to lose my new partner. If I were a wishing man, I'd wish for our collaboration to flourish exactly as we planned.

Still…

Between my last two speed-dates of the morning, I take my phone outside into the Cape Cod sunshine: *Lunch 12:30 meet here?*

"Busy busy!" a sardonic voice remarks.

"Sharp as ever, Roddy."

"And you, Christopher. Congratulations on your new enterprise."

"Thanks." My phone dings. "Excuse me."

Working through lunch, sorry. Later.

An expletive must have escaped my lips, for Roddy winces in feigned shock, followed by feigned solicitousness. "Bad news?"

"Nothing serious. Congratulations to you, by the way, on your paper in *Scholarship Monthly.* We never can know enough about Lord Byron and his circle, eh?"

"Seriously, Christopher." Roddy removes his tortoise-shell glasses. "Stay away from wax wings, won't you?"

"What's that supposed to mean?"

"I taught Katlin Collins's writing class at Four C's. I know what she's capable of. And what she isn't."

"Aren't you mysterious."

"Much as I adore melodrama, I can't bear watching my fellow scriveners crash and burn. Our Sun Maiden needed sanctuary and found it in storytelling. That's all she wants, you know. To keep her head above water, and her kids afloat, and her friends entertained. The desire of the moth for the star? That's you, not her."

"And your role here is what, Roddy? The literary Coast Guard?"

Roddy's lip curls. He re-positions his glasses on his nose. "Yes, well. You laugh, but still you play with matches. Shall we?"

And in we go, walking down the hall together like old friends.

My mind is roiling. Good God, how could Katlin not be fractious, with Devon the Dead for a husband and Roddy the Snake for a guardian?

And Christopher Mundy? What's my role here? The knight who's come charging up just in time to fill the hole in her life? Or a babe who's wandered into a minefield and picked up a pretty toy?

I text Katlin: *Drinks in my room 5:30? Toast Wave-Makers before I announce on TV.*

That's the tone. Kind but firm. Flirt with her, flatter her, charm her, until

I can make sure if this is a Barbie doll or an unexploded bomb in my hand.

Flashing my Festival badge, I liberate a bottle of champagne and a plate of hors d'oeuvres from the Iyanough Room. When Katlin knocks on my door, I greet her with an air-kiss on each cheek. "Dahling, you look fabulous."

She giggles, scans the hall for spies, and slips inside.

"To The Wave-Makers!" We raise our plastic cups.

The wide neck of her dress slips down over her bare shoulder. No straps, no tan lines. I curb my renegade thoughts. "So, did you have time to look at the proposal?"

"Christopher! Yes. Of course. I read it last night. Not, like, all at once. I couldn't. It was too…." She's moving around the room, pulling absently at her neckline and her tiny shoulder bag. "So this morning I read it again, and I kind of got what you're doing. Not totally, I have to say. Like, why a knife fight instead of the beach party? And Jameson is Jago's father? I mean, you've turned my story into your story." Her emerald eyes glance off mine. "But, like I said when I met you. I want to learn how to do what you do."

My sympathy face mellows to a smile. "Yes."

Yes, this just might work. We drink champagne; we nibble scallops on toothpicks. I excuse myself to wipe tartar sauce off the chin of a rising star.

I've agreed to answer her publishing questions over dinner. My question won't be answered until we come back here afterwards: Does Katlin Collins honestly, wholeheartedly accept me as her lead author? But that's two hours away. For now, I'm satisfied—indeed, gratified—to walk into the Festival Banquet with the loveliest woman on Cape Cod.

Once again we're separated as soon as we step inside. TV underlings whisk me to a backstage dressing room for visual tweaking. A scrawny leather-jacketed young man, name-tagged Ryan, shakes my hand. Can he call me Chris? No. Should he say something about my new book? No. I'll handle it.

Katlin presumably has found her seat at our table. I'm escorted to my seat onstage: a blue armchair under a battery of lights that could melt cheese.

As I sit listening to Ryan recite my biography to eight hundred people, an odd sensation comes over me. My chest starts to tingle, then my head, then my arms and legs. I try to stand up and nothing happens.

What is this? A stroke?

The oddest part isn't that my life is passing before my eyes—that's Ryan, reading off his iPad. It's that the lights have dimmed, while my mind is alighting on random images like a drunk firefly.

Katlin's gritted teeth when she described finding her husband frozen in his truck.

Her turbulent frown when she asked if I'd changed what she wrote.

I want to learn how to do what you do. I should have trusted Roddy the Snake's translation. She doesn't want to become a major-league novelist. She wants to get paid for her stories.

The flash of alarm in her eyes when I came out of the bathroom and found her refilling our champagne cups.

Red flags. Devon racked up debts and died. I made her sign an agreement to publish The Wave-Makers my way or not at all.

I can't feel my feet anymore.

What's that noise? Bacon frying? No. Rain beating on a roof? No. That's applause. Then a faraway voice: *Christopher, in your essay "The Tragic Fall," you argue for a narrower usage of the term "tragedy." Can you talk a little about that?*

No. I wish.

* * *

CJ Verburg is an award-winning playwright, director, and author. A longtime New Englander, she collaborated with artist Edward Gorey on diverse theatrical adventures, inspiring her multimedia memoir **Edward Gorey On Stage** and her Cape Cod mysteries **Croaked, Zapped, Disarmed,** and (soon) **Scalped, or The Toastrack Enigma**. Read more of CJ's stories in **Fault Lines** and **Sherlock Holmes Mystery Magazine.** *http://cjverburg.net*

VERMONT

Maine
Vermont
New
Hampshire
Massachusetts
Connecticut
RI

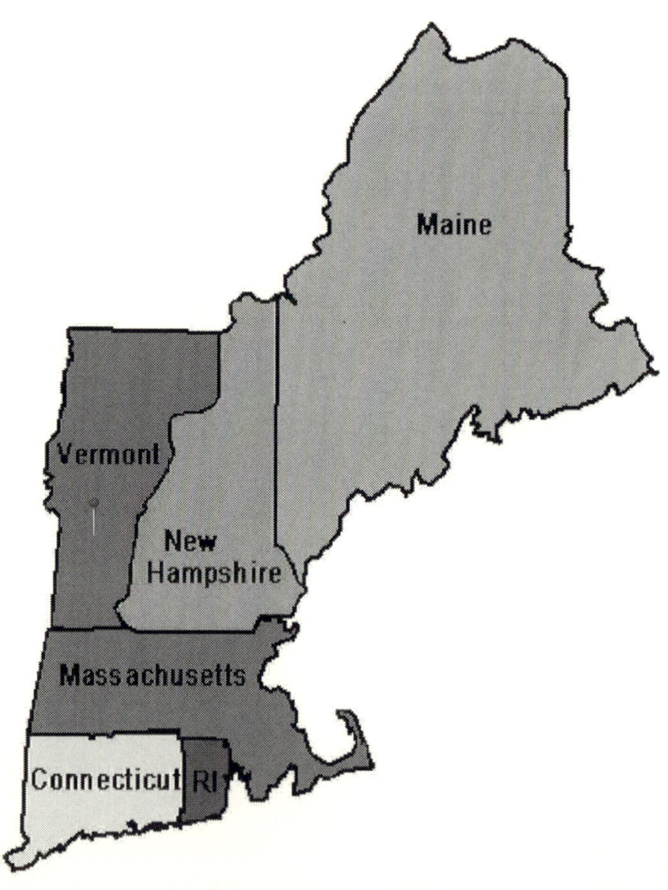

VERMONT
FREEDOM
& UNITY

IF I SHOULD DIE
by Harriette Sackler

When Cassie opened her eyes, she had no clue where she was. The room was dim, with only a sliver of light seeping through a shaded window. She was in a bed covered in clean white sheets, not like the colorful linens that adorned the bed in her room at home. An IV line ran into her and a bunch of machines beeped and flashed numbers.

Cassie's head felt ready to explode and every bone in her body ached. Her muscles were knotted, her stomach cramped, and there was no part of her that didn't feel like crap.

What had happened to her? Why couldn't she remember? She knew the memories were there, but just out of reach.

A knock on the door alerted Cassie to a visitor.

"Come in," she softly said with a scratchy voice. Her throat was dry and painful.

"Miss Anders, how are you feeling?" An unfamiliar man approached her bed. He was an imposing figure, well over six feet and solidly built. What struck Cassie were his eyes, emerald green and kind.

"Please call me Cassie. Truth is, I feel like I died and went to hell."

"I can imagine. You've had a rough time of it, I know. By the way, I'm Detective Steve Burton, St. Francis Police Department."

Cassie didn't know why a detective had come to see her. Hell, she didn't even know where she was.

"Detective, can you tell me where I am and how I got here? I just can't remember what happened to me."

The detective looked at Cassie with pity in his eyes and spoke to her in a soft voice.

"Well, Miss Anders, you were found in an alley in town. You were unconscious, and it was obvious you'd overdosed. The paramedics administered Narcan and, although you were brought out of danger, you were still in pretty bad shape. They transported you here to County Hospital for treatment."

Cassie was silent for a moment as she absorbed the information.

"Can you tell me, is Tommy here, too?"

"Would Tommy be the young man you were found with?"

"Yes. I just met him a few days ago, and he's a really nice guy."

"Cassie, I'm so very sorry to tell you that Tommy Deaver didn't make it. You were lucky. Tommy wasn't."

Cassie was stunned.

"Cassie, I'm going to let you rest now, but I'll be back tomorrow. I know your parents are in the hall waiting to see you."

Cassie lay in bed and thought. Life had been different before the accident. She lived with her parents at home in St. Francis. They struggled to get by. Her dad worked on the assembly line in a local factory, and her mom waitressed at Dee's Diner downtown. They loved their daughter and always encouraged her to do her best. Cassie was a good student at Northwest High, but the best part of her day was afternoon cheerleading practice. When she thought of life after high school, she dreamed of someday going to a really big city, like New York, Boston, or even Los Angeles. She'd leave St. Francis and head for a place alive with promise.

Then one day she fell from the top of the pyramid the squad had formed. Her right leg was shattered by the fall and, after several surgeries to repair the multiple fractures, she'd spent months in rehab to bring life back to her leg. Finally, she was able to regain partial mobility.

But Cassie was left in pain. Lots of pain. Even when in bed or sitting in a chair, she couldn't find any respite from the relentless agony. There were times when she wished she would die, just to get relief. Her doctor, who did not believe in having his patients on pain medication except in the most severe circumstances, prescribed an opioid called OxyContin, which, according to its manufacturer, had a very low incidence of addiction with continued use.

And, blessedly, Cassie found relief. The medication allowed her to return to school and finish her senior year with her friends. She'd never be her old self, but at least the constant agony abated.

However, in a relatively short time, Cassie found that the prescribed dosage was no longer effective. She took more and more pills to find relief, until the day her doctor refused to renew her prescription.

Cassie panicked, but soon discovered she could buy the pills on the street. But not for long. She didn't have the money. Her panic increased whenever she felt the first stirrings of withdrawal from the medication that were not supposed to be addictive. She thought more often of ending her life.

And then she met Tommy. While she sat on the steps of the library in downtown St. Francis, where she'd spent the day, a guy came up to her.

"Hey, pretty girl, haven't seen you around here before. Looks to me like you can use some help."

Cassie didn't know this fellow, but she was emotionally drained and vulnerable. She burst into tears and told him about her situation and her fears.

"Look, babe, I might have a solution to your problem. Street Oxy is gonna cost you plenty, and unless you have loads of cash, you're up a creek. Don't know of any pill mills around here, but we've got a lot of users. No wonder we've got so much crime. Who wouldn't do whatever to keep from jonesing. Shoplift. Break into a house. Whore. Rob. Whatever."

Cassie was getting more upset as Tommy talked. She was scared of what was going to happen to her.

"But there's a way to feel better. A way that's cheaper, but still will take away the pain."

"Tell me," Cassie begged.

"Dope. Smack. H."

"What?"

"Heroin. It takes the place of Oxy, but it's cheap."

Cassie was appalled. "But that's used by drug addicts! The kind of people you see begging on the streets."

"Yeh, that's true," said Tommy. "But do ya know how many of them began using because they couldn't afford Oxy anymore?"

"This is all scary to me." Cassie wasn't that type of person.

"Look," Tommy replied."Why don't you just try it? See how you feel. One hit won't hurt you."

"I don't know. Maybe I could get into a rehab program, and then I won't need any drugs at all."

"You poor kid. Don't you know what kind of hell withdrawal is? You'd rather be dead. And if you survive, you'll be back on Oxy as soon as you walk away from the program."

Cassie was so confused. She just didn't know what to do.

"Let me think about it."

"No problem. I'll be around."

Several days later, Cassie ran into Tommy on the street.

"Hey girl. Did you think about what I told you?"

"I did." Her fears fought against the promise of relief from her pain. Finally, she heard the words escape her lips. "I think I'll give it a try."

"Alright, let's go into that alley across the street, and you can give it a try. I'll help you out."

Tommy made the preparations while Cassie kept her eyes tightly closed. She felt the painful sting as he injected the drug into a vein in her arm. It took Cassie just seconds to feel the effects of the heroin. She would never be able to describe the overwhelming euphoria. But only for a moment. Then she blacked out.

The following day, Detective Burton returned for a second visit.

"Cassie, how are you doing today?"

"A little better, I think. They're giving me something to make sure the effects of not taking the Oxy aren't too bad. It helps with withdrawal."

"That's good. Suboxone helps."

"Detective, can you tell me what happened to me?"

Detective Burton lowered his large frame into the chair next to Cassie's bed.

"Well, I can only tell you what I think happened to you. Unfortunately, I've seen this many times before to too many others who haven't lived to tell."

Cassie shuddered. She was beginning to realize how lucky she'd been.

"Okay, then. The heroin Tommy injected into your arm, and then his own, was laced with fentanyl, another opioid that's fifty times more powerful than heroin. Most of the fentanyl we see up here comes in from China and is used to give an extra kick to an already dangerous drug. It only takes the smallest amount to cause a fatal overdose."

"Oh no! Do you think Tommy knew about the fentanyl?" Cassie just couldn't wrap her mind around what she was hearing.

The detective shook his head.

"No, I don't think Tommy had any idea that the heroin was laced. After all, the hotshot he gave himself was deadly."

It didn't escape Cassie's notice that she had believed that death would have been better for her than living as an addict. Now, she was relieved that she'd survived the overdose.

"Cassie, you might be able to help me with something. Do you know of anyone who might have been supplying Tommy with dope? Anyone he met with on the street? Anyone he mentioned or talked to on the phone?

"No, I'm sorry. As I said, I only met him a few days ago."

"Well, we retrieved his phone from his jacket pocket, and we'll follow up with calls he made or received. Hopefully, we'll get some usable information from that."

Cassie hesitated before asking the detective the question that was on her mind.

"Can you tell me if anyone else overdosed on that bad heroin?"

"I'm afraid that we've had four other fatalities. That's a lot for such a small town. We've got to trace the source now or else there'll be more deaths. Cassie, I'll keep checking in on you when I can."

Steve Burton had been a cop for the past twenty-two years, following his father and grandfather onto the St. Francis police force. He loved his work and really did believe he was making a difference. But times had changed. Years ago, crimes were infrequent, mostly vandalism and the occasional burglary. But now, St. Francis was considered one of the most dangerous cities in Vermont. Sadly, as factories closed and employment became harder to find, residents became desperate and, sometimes, went outside the law to survive. Many of the city's younger residents left, heading for larger cities where they had opportunities to find jobs and live a better life. And who could blame them? St. Francis had little to offer them.

And drugs. The panacea for those who had no prospects. The moments of escape, followed by the need for more, withdrawal, and the pursuit of money to buy more drugs to keep the sickness away. Damn the drug companies and doctors, the prescribers. Every day, Steve saw the results of hopelessness. Right now, he needed to find the people who were selling the deadly opioids that were killing St. Francis residents.

Records indicated that Tommy's next of kin was a Sarah Engle, his maternal grandmother. She'd been awarded his guardianship when he was eight and his parents had abandoned him and left for parts unknown. Tommy's cell also showed that he called his grandmother on a regular basis. It was Steve's duty to inform Mrs. Engle of her grandson's death, a task he always dreaded, but had to be done.

Mrs. Engle lived just inside the city limits, in an area where houses were few and far between. For anyone who valued privacy and didn't appreciate neighbors poking their noses into your business, the isolated area was ideal.

Steve drove up a dirt road that must have been a bitch to navigate in the snow and ice of a New England winter. Up ahead stood a dilapidated house that hadn't seen a coat of paint or exterior repairs in years. To the right of the house, a garage, with doors wide open, housed several old cars and a tractor that must have been parked in there since the turn of the century. The front yard was covered in junk—car parts, tires, and detritus that should have been disposed of long ago. The property was surrounded by trees, bushes and overgrown weeds. Steve wondered how people could live like this.

He knocked on the door and a few moments later, it was answered by a tiny woman. She reminded Steve of his own Granny. Mrs. Engle certainly didn't conform to her surroundings. Neatly dressed in a flowered housedress and spit polished shoes, with her white hair put up in a bun, her kind face welcomed him.

"Good morning. How can I help you?"

"Mrs. Engle?"

"Yes," she smiled. "That's me."

"I'm Detective Burton of the St. Francis Police Department. May I come in for a moment?"

"Of course," she said, stepping aside.

The interior of the house was as neat as a pin. The furniture had seen better days, but looked well cared for. The walls were covered in scenic prints, and knick-knacks were displayed on the surfaces of the tables, tastefully placed around the room. Steve felt that he'd been transported to an entirely different place.

"Mrs. Engle, I'm here to talk to you about your grandson, Tommy."

The smile on her face disappeared, and the look in her eyes hardened.

"Is he in trouble again? Lord knows, I've tried my best to do right by him and give him a good home."

"I'm so sorry to inform you that Tommy is dead. He died of an overdose of heroin laced with fentanyl. We're working around the clock to locate the source of the drug. We've had four other fatalities to date."

Mrs. Engle's face settled into an angry scowl. Steve had seen this response to the death of a family member before. It sometimes took awhile for shock to transform to grief and tears.

"I've told that boy time and time again to stay away from that poison. But he never listened to me. Just like his mother."

"Mrs. Engle, when was the last time you saw Tommy?"

She thought a minute before replying.

"About two weeks ago, I think. He came home to shower, get a good night's sleep, and ask for money. Lord knows where he lays his head when he's not here. But wait, let me ask my son, Gregory, if he'd run into Tommy in town."

She left the room, and Steve heard a door open. Mrs. Engle called out to her son, who entered the room a few minutes later. Gregory Engle was a hulk of a middle-aged man. He wore dirty jeans, a torn tee shirt, and greasy hair tied up in a ponytail.

"Greg, this is Detective Burton. He's come to tell me that Tommy overdosed and died. Fentanyl in the heroin. Have you seen him at all in the past few weeks?"

"Nah, only been to town once and didn't see him. Damn shame he's dead." He turned and left the room.

Steve was getting a funny feeling in the pit of his stomach about these people. After all, he wasn't talking to them about the weather. A member of their family was dead. Something was off here.

Over the next few days, the usual suspects were brought to police headquarters and questioned about their involvement in drug trafficking. Some of them made frequent trips to Virginia, Ohio, or West Virginia, accompanied by a carload of friends or family who posed as patients, to purchase stashes of Oxy or other prescription opioids from pill mills that were only interested in bringing in cash, with no thought to the damage they were doing to human lives. Others had heroin delivered directly to them by a guy from parts unknown. And, several of them talked of a local source, but refused to divulge any additional information. They feared reprisals.

It eventually became evident that the drug fatalities resulted from heroin purchased from a common source. And, not surprisingly, Tommy Deaver, was the dealer.

Steve knew he had to return to the Engle home. He was as sure as the sun rose in the sky that there were answers to his questions there. Steve met with Police Chief Wilson and alerted him to the suspicions he had about the Engles. The chief suggested that Steve take backup in case his visit went south. But Steve insisted that he go alone, assuring Wilson that he'd call for backup, if needed. He also asked the chief to put Judge Turner on alert to issue a warrant to search the premises.

It made more sense to him to head for the Engle property after sunset. That would give him the chance to surveil any suspicious activity without being observed. It would be hell to navigate the road to the house in the dark, but at least he wouldn't be seen.

When he entered the property, Steve turned off his lights and could barely see past the hood of his car. With great caution, he was able to park in a copse of trees, which was no small feat, considering the amount of junk that littered the property.

There were a number of vehicles haphazardly parked near the house. There was business being conducted here under cover of dark, and Steve would bet it wasn't above board. He called in for backup, no lights and sirens, and the warrant. When three patrol cars arrived with officers dressed in riot gear, Steve gave them instructions to stand down until he gave the signal to move in.

Showtime.

Hand on his weapon, Steve softly knocked on the front door. A woman's voice whispered.

"Who's there?"

"Mrs. Engle, it's Detective Burton. Please let me in."

Locks disengaged and the door opened to a very frightened looking Mrs. Engle. She put her index finger to her lips and let him into the house

"We know there's illegal activity being conducted on this property. I'm asking you what it is."

"It's Gregory. He sells drugs. He's the reason my grandson is dead. He lets me live in my house unharmed as long as I keep quiet. He works out of the basement and leaves me alone. I'm an old woman with nowhere else to go, so I have to do as he asks."

"How do I get to the basement?"

I keep the door in the kitchen bolted shut, but there are outside steps in the back. That's where his people come and go. Please, be careful. Gregory is a dangerous man."

"Mrs. Engle, you go into your bedroom and lock the door. I'll come get you when it's safe." Steve handed her the warrant.

When the team was in place, an officer kicked in the door and, weapons drawn, police stormed the basement. The occupants were taken by surprise and complied with orders to drop to the floor. After being frisked, they were handcuffed and taken outside to the police vehicles for transport to headquarters. On a metal table in the center of the room, a large amount of product was being weighed and bagged. It would be analyzed at the forensics lab, but Steve had no doubt that it was heroin spiked with fentanyl. Thankfully no more would hit the street, at least from this source. Gregory Engle and his partners would be put away for a long, long time.

When Steve returned to the first floor of the house, he let Mrs. Engle know that she was safe. Maybe she could now live in peace. He knew that he could enlist some of his buddies in the department to help him clean up her property and do repairs on the house, should she want to remain here.

The following day, Steve went over to the Anders home to give Cassie and her parents the good news. She'd been released from the hospital and had been referred to a drug rehab center that had demonstrated a good deal of success with its opioid addiction program.

"Detective, I'll be entering rehab in two days. I know it won't be easy, but I need to succeed. If I had known what those pills would do to me, I don't think I would have taken them. But, then again, the pain in my leg was so unbearable, I'm not sure I could have survived. But I'm hopeful now. When I was in the hospital they did an MRI that showed a lot of scar tissue pressing against nerves in my leg. The surgeons are confident they can remove it, so I won't be in pain anymore."

"That's great news. I know you can come out of this. You're a smart girl with a good future ahead of you. And, I know your parents will be with you every step along the way."

Steve climbed into his car, feeling good. Not every investigation ended on a positive note. Truth be told, fewer and fewer of them did. But this case motivated him to continue his work. As his radio came to life, alerting him to another officer-assistance-needed call, a corny thought ran through Steve's mind: If I should die today, I know I did good.

* * *

Harriette Sackler is a multi-published, Agatha Award-nominated short story writer whose work has appeared in numerous anthologies of mystery fiction. Harriette has served on the Malice Domestic Board of Directors for many years and her position as Grants Chair allows her to choose the recipients of the William F. Deeck-Malice Domestic Grant for Unpublished Writers in the traditional mystery genre. She is a member of Mystery Writers of America, Sisters in Crime, Crime Writers Association, Historical Writers of America, Short Mystery Fiction Society, and Historical Novel Society of the U.S.

NEW HAMPSHIRE

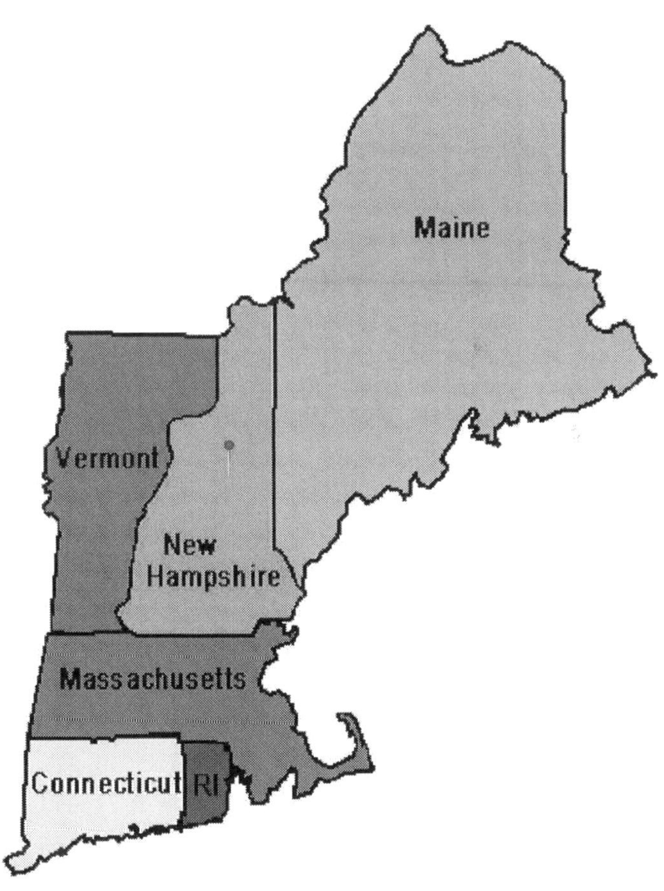

SEAL · OF · THE · STATE · OF · NEW HAMPSHIRE
1776

NO SECRETS FOR THE DEAD
by William Ade

There's one thing I hate about dead people. When it comes to keeping secrets, they've got an unfair advantage. You're getting nothing out of them.

Okay, maybe with some effort and a little luck, you might piece together enough clues to figure out the mystery they took to the grave. But you'll never learn the why behind it all. That's the hardest nut to crack. That's what was on my mind as I sat in Beverly Lyell's kitchen.

"So you found this in your mother's papers?" she asked.

"Right," I said. "It was in her personals, as she liked to call them."

Beverly was chief of the Wolfeboro, New Hampshire, police department. We attended high school together years ago. She then graduated from the police academy, went to work for the local department, and in two decades became the first female chief. I was employed at the Winnie Year-A-Round Market as a butcher. I was the first union female meat cutter ever hired there. We connected over the distinction of being the first women in our jobs at the previous month's twenty-fifth high school class reunion.

Beverly read the typewritten note aloud. "'I've tried to write this message a thousand times and failed. But I no longer can wait.'"

She glanced up at me. I wasn't sure what she wanted. I was uncomfortable when people stared at me. She lowered her head and continued reading aloud.

"'I'm responsible for the death of the young lass named Donna. I've not had a carefree day since then. She lies in Lake Winnipesaukee off of Puffs Cove.'" She paused then asked, "Who's Donna?"

"I don't know."

"Why's this in your mother's possession?"

"I don't know."

"Who wrote it?"

I flopped forward, emptying my lungs in one long hot breath. "For God's sake, Beverly, I...don't...know."

My friend silently reread the message, her lips slipping over each word.

"Was there an envelope?" she asked.

"Yeah, but it wasn't addressed."

She held the letter to the sunlight coming through the kitchen window.

"If I had to guess, I'd say this letter was written a while back."

Good guess. The dry texture of the paper and faded ink clued me in on that fact. I needed Beverly to apply some of her police skills, not tell me the obvious. I mean, she's the professional. I'm just a freaking butcher.

"What are you going to do?" I asked her.

Beverly took in some air, her lower lip protruding. "The first step is determining who Donna was. That's where we need to start."

"And then you'll have divers searching the lake?"

The chief shook her head. "Naw, there's no bones left if it's more than a year in the water. And I'm guessing we're talking decades at least."

"How about looking for teeth?" I asked. I knew teeth were even stronger than bone.

Her nose turned up. "You think you're gonna find teeth sprinkled across the bottom of the largest lake in New Hampshire?" She snorted. Her reaction made me feel stupid, but it wasn't enough to shut me up.

"What if the corpse was wrapped in plastic, something water resistant?"

Beverly cocked an eyebrow and sucked in her lips. I don't always pick up people's facial clues, but I was pretty sure she was irritated with me. I'd keep quiet and follow her lead. Like I'd said, she's the professional crime solver, not me. I just wanted to figure out my mother's secret.

"I'll send this letter off to the lab in Concord for an analysis. Maybe they can narrow down the age."

Beverly stood, looking down at me. "I'll also order a search of the state's missing persons database."

I didn't know what she wanted me to do, so I stayed sitting.

"You know it could take some time before I know anything. Why don't you see if there's anything else in your mother's papers."

"I can do that," I said, relieved to have a clear idea what she wanted me to do. "It won't require much of an effort."

My mother had lived in a small trailer parked off Route 28, back in the pine trees. When she passed away, I carried everything I cared about out in a cardboard box.

"Why don't we meet again in a week," Beverly said as she folded the letter, tapping it against her open palm. "I'll give you a call."

I nodded and quickly stood. I had to admit my feelings were hurt. I'd thought Bev and I had hit it off at the reunion and that she liked me. Now she was rushing me out of her house. I guess she wasn't my friend.

"Sure, I'll wait for your call," I said, shuffling my feet toward the front door. "See you later, Chief Lyell."

Back at my apartment, I shifted the materials still in my mother's box. There was the title to the trailer. Too bad we never owned the lot; I could've sold it. Included were ownership papers for her Chevy, a car needing more repairs than it was worth. There was my dad's death certificate. Cause of death: cirrhosis of the liver. That was no secret. Pa was a drunkard. Fortunately, he wasn't one of those nasty bastards who came home and beat on his family. His drama was to grow morose and turn his rage inward.

"Well, isn't this something," I said to myself as I pulled a folded sheet of paper from between the pages of an old almanac. It was a letter dated fifty years ago. It was from Pa to my mother.

My Dear Willie, it began. Mother's name was Wilhelmina, and I never heard anyone, even Pa, call her anything different. I guessed their relationship was still full of affection when he wrote it.

I hope my letter finds you in a better mood than when I last saw you. I will be coming to Ogunquit once I am done working for Maloney. I know you are angry with me, but please give me another chance. I swear on my momma's grave, I will not drink again. I will be the type of husband you want. Love, Edgar.

"Well, Mother, it seems Pa was better at writing than he was speaking," I said to the empty room. The vocabulary I recalled him using with me was grunts and slurred nonsense. "And his promises weren't worth a damn, either written or spoken."

A yellowed envelope tied with a piece of blue yarn hugged the bottom of the carton. I could tell by the feel that it contained photographs; snapshots, they used to be called. Most all of them were in black and white, and some were turning brown from age. I recognized Mother. Even as a child, her face carried the same disappointed expression she was wearing when she took her last breath two weeks ago.

The one picture that confused me was an image of much younger versions of my parents, another woman I didn't recognize, and a young girl. The other woman was the only one smiling.

It was a week later, and I sat in Beverly's office. She'd insisted we make the meeting a formal police visit. I guess she had to make clear to me that we weren't friends. When you grow up isolated, as I had, you tend to be socially inept. Nonetheless, her brushoff hurt. If I didn't need to know the secret of the letter I found in Mother's box, I'd probably be off soaking my wounded feelings in self-pity.

"The analysis of the paper type, as well as an estimate of the age based on the chemical changes in the ink, suggests the letter was written between eight and ten years ago."

I stroked my forearm, thinking about what was going on with my parents at that time. My dad was sick nine years ago and died early the next winter.

"I also had the team dig through all the missing persons records going back to the 1970s," Beverly said. "I'm guessing this might have been a deathbed confession for an unsolved crime committed long before I started my career."

Beverly reported that there had been twenty disappearances over the last five decades in the Carroll County area. Half the missing people were female. Of those ten, three were murdered by a man called the Ossipee Chopper. He took a shiv to his heart in prison in 1987.

"So I doubt he was writing letters of apology," she said. "The remaining cases were cleared years later. Some were runaways who resurfaced as murder victims in other states or women who'd gone broke and were trying to reestablish family ties."

"Was anyone named Donna?"

"Nope, no Donna. Not even as a middle name."

Beverly looked at me, her brown eyes unblinking. I didn't know what she wanted from me, so I pulled the odd photo from my mother's belongings and slid it across the desk. "I found this. I recognize my folks but not the woman or the girl."

Beverly studied the photo before returning her gaze to me. "You think this might be Donna?"

I hunched my shoulders so high my head almost disappeared. "I don't know. We have no family around here."

"Do you mind if I take this photo over to Children, Youth and Family Services?"

"Why?"

"The smiling woman looks like she's holding a briefcase, like she's an official or someone. I wonder if this Donna was a foster kid. Maybe an old-timer in that department might recognize the woman or girl."

"What was she doing with my folks?" I asked, rubbing my palms together to wipe away the sweat. "I never heard of them fostering a kid."

Beverly's eyebrows rose, and she shrugged. "Maybe your parents had more than a few secrets."

The next day came, and Beverley was on the phone with me. Her hunch had paid off, to some degree.

"No one recognized the girl," she said, "but a retired staff member who now volunteers in the office is certain the woman was Dahlia Jackson, a former social worker."

When I asked if she was going to find this Jackson woman, Beverly muttered some excuse about better things to do than chase a half-century-old cold case. When I protested, she got snarky. "You're a smart girl," she said. "I bet you can hunt her down."

There she goes again, treating me like a pest.

"Yeah…I'll look into it…*Chief*."

A spitting sound came through the phone. "Don't get huffy with me," Beverly said. "All you've given me is a letter written by someone talking about killing a girl no one ever heard of. I have the summer people showing up soon, plus we have Bike Week later this month. I can't go chasing every oddball thing people bring to me."

The phone connection broke off before I could reply. Not that I had a snappy comeback. The heck with her. She's probably too busy answering calls from the rich folks up from Boston, whining about their cottages and motorboats. If her father hadn't been the previous departmental chief, I bet Beverly would've never gotten on the force. Yeah, even in Wolfeboro, it was who you knew.

"I'll show you," I said, slamming the phone down, even though Beverly had already disconnected.

And I did show her. I paid a visit to Children, Youth and Family Services and learned more about Dahlia Jackson. The retiree who recognized Jackson was pretty sharp. She recalled Jackson moving to Manchester, going to work for their social services. I made phone calls to the city of Manchester's human resources department but struck out. Then I had an idea. My meat cutters union kept detailed member records going back decades. So I contacted the New Hampshire chapter of the National Association of Social Workers. I sweet-talked a phone listing service for a retired member named Dahlia Jackson. I was pretty proud of myself for solving a tough problem.

A week later on my off day, I tooled up Route 125 to Rochester, where Jackson was living in a nursing home. I'd spoken to her on the phone, and she said she'd be happy to meet with me, although she couldn't guarantee the reliability of her memory.

The visit lasted thirty minutes, with twenty-eight minutes spent on Jackson's life and times. The other two minutes brought me closer to breaking my mother's secret.

"I worked for child welfare in Carroll County back in the early '70s," she said, looking at the photo. "I remember that child...oh, yes. But her name escapes me."

"Is there any chance that folks called her Donna?"

"You know something—you're right. That girl was Donna. Yes, Donna was her name."

"What can you tell me about the people who fostered her?"

Jackson stared at the photograph, the lips of her toothless mouth squirming.

"You know, I don't remember anything special about those folks."

That wasn't a stunner. Why would I expect my parents to have enough personality to be remembered? But still, I'd hoped that maybe they were different before I was born.

The woman slapped her hand against the arm of her wheelchair. "But I do remember the girl as a difficult child. She was always running away from foster homes. Yeah, she was a troubled one."

I'd only been home an hour after meeting with Dahlia Jackson when a police car pulled into my apartment complex parking lot. I was surprised to see Beverly step out and walk toward my unit. She was in uniform, so I assumed she was there on business.

"May I come in?" she asked after I'd half opened the front door.

I stepped back and waved her in. She entered my living room and, without asking, sat on the sofa. The woman either lacked manners or thought she was above them. If that was the way she wanted to act, then I wouldn't offer her a glass of water.

So it was a surprise, too, when she said, "I want to apologize for my rudeness last week."

Her face seemed to convey sincerity, but my difficulty in reading other people's emotions made me hesitate. I gave her a simple nod, just to be safe.

"I think I can free up some resources to find Dahlia Jackson."

I know I should've buried my urge to gloat, but the impulse was too powerful. "I already found her."

Beverly's eyebrows arched in a steeple. "Oh, really, you talked to her?"

I folded my arms and nodded. "She remembered the girl. Her name was Donna."

"That's all you learned?"

I was in no hurry to be friendly, since she'd been such a snob toward me. But I didn't want to slow down any investigation by acting all mad.

"Mrs. Jackson couldn't recall the girl's last name or the exact dates, but it had to be the late '70s because she left the area soon after. Told me Donna was a difficult kid, always running away. She'd been in and out of foster homes all her life."

"So as far as she knew, no one kept track of the placement?"

"She didn't know anything," I said. "She found another job in Manchester less than a month after placing her with my folks."

Beverly blew out a deep sigh. "The poor girl probably fell through the bureaucratic cracks. I wonder why her disappearance was never reported."

"That's another mystery, huh," I said.

Beverly stared down at her feet and seemed to be mulling something over. She'd already apologized, so I assumed that wasn't what she was pondering. Whatever it was, I had a feeling I wouldn't like what she was going to say.

"I have an idea about what might have happened, if you want to hear it," she said, locking her gaze on mine.

"Yeah, tell me."

"Now, I'm not pulling this out of thin air, you understand. It's based on more than twenty years of seeing a lot of bad human behavior."

I folded my arms and pressed my knees together. "Go ahead."

"Let's start with the facts," she said. "Your parents fostered a child known as Donna. As the case manager said, Donna was difficult, probably the type of kid who made an even-tempered adult want to slap her."

"Are you saying my folks were abusive?"

"No, no." Beverly shook her head. "It's just I've seen the best parents lose their temper with a difficult child."

"My parents never hit me."

The chief tilted her head, a smirk on her face. "I knew you through twelve years of school. You were scared of your own shadow. So, honestly, I doubt you could make anyone angry enough to pop you."

I wanted to throw her opinion of me in her face, but I held back, mostly because she was right.

"So what are you saying?"

"I'm speculating here, but maybe your parents needed the money that fostering a child could bring. The social worker was anxious to get a tough delinquent off her hands. It was a great match for both parties."

I nodded.

"Your folks take the child in," she continued. "Donna's not happy, causes a lot of trouble, and maybe tries to run away. Someone loses their temper and hits the girl. It was an accident, but who'll believe poor folks living in the pines? Her body gets dumped in Lake Winnie. There's no follow-up by the child welfare people because Jackson has moved on. Your folks don't report her missing. The police never look into it because they don't know the girl exists."

"That doesn't sound possible," I said, my temper climbing before dropping off a cliff. "I mean, *does it*? Could a girl actually disappear just like that with no one knowing?"

"People living on the edge of society often don't get noticed, you know what I mean?"

Tears clouded my eyes. As much as I hated listening to Beverly's theory, I despised that it made sense to me. Maybe that explained why Pa was such a mess. Perhaps Donna's death was the reason for his depression and drinking.

"So you think my dad killed her?"

Beverly bobbed her head. "The letter was typewritten so we can't say whether it was a man or a woman. But most times domestic abusers are men."

That may be a fact, but I never saw Pa beat anyone except himself.

Beverley continued, "It could have easily been written about the time your father passed, am I right?"

"Yeah, he died nine years ago in March."

"It was probably a confession pounded out on a typewriter right before he died. It's not unheard of, you know."

"So how did it end up in my mother's personal stuff?"

"Most likely your mother intervened before he could mail it to the police. You can't blame her. She'd suffer the consequences if the authorities found out and started investigating. She probably wanted to protect you, as well."

I couldn't keep the tears from washing down my face. My throat was too thick with emotion for me to talk. I just sat there as Beverly stood and handed me the confessional letter. "There's nothing to be done about it now," she said, her voice soft and comforting. "Maybe we should just drop any further investigation."

I nodded, unable to speak. I sat there crying, really cutting loose when Beverly left through the front door.

Why didn't my mother destroy the letter? Why did she leave it to me? I didn't want her damn secret.

I had the fire going good in the fifty-gallon barrel behind my mother's trailer. The box full of her personals was at my feet. I studied the pieces before tossing them into the flames. I was incinerating a little bit of my parents' past with each item I burned.

I held the confession in my left hand, stating an admission of murdering a girl named Donna. My dad's love letter was in my right, committing to a righteous life. They were two sheets of paper serving as bookends to the sad life of a guilt-ridden man. One was full of promises, the other despair.

I stood there, my eyes bouncing back and forth between each letter. As a butcher, I'd learned to glance at a hunk of meat and read the marbling, the fibers, and the color to identify the kind of cut it was. I'd developed an eye for spotting tiny telltale differences. Something wasn't right about those letters.

My brain finally made connections. My father's love letter was stilted

supervised the less-experienced officer. Dad's career would have been over, even if he didn't get charged with involuntary manslaughter."

"So they recognized Donna as the missing kid," I said, proposing the obvious, "and dumped her in the lake."

Beverly slowly nodded.

"How'd you find all this out?" I asked. "Seems like the two of them kept the secret for a long time."

"My dad told me the day before he passed," she said. "He didn't want to die with that horrible knowledge on his conscience."

My mouth creased. "So your dad gave you the secret to own, huh?"

She sniffed and clutched her hands until the knuckles turned white.

"And you decided to pass it off to me."

"No, no, I wasn't trying to do that," she said, finally looking at me. "When you showed up with the letter, I got spooked. I couldn't let you take it to someone else. I…wanted the girl's death to remain a secret."

I sat there in the dimly lit room, juggling my feelings. It seemed that Beverly was a lot like her old man. They had no second thoughts about letting my family suffer. What would the authorities think about the chief's loose hold on ethics?

"I should report you to the state police."

Beverly didn't react. She must have thought through the consequences before I came over and had a plan. More likely, she assumed she could play me again.

"You could," she said, "and where would that lead? My father's reputation, posthumously destroyed. Maybe I get reprimanded. Would that make you happy?"

I refused to answer. She'd forfeited that courtesy by being a manipulating liar.

"What about people like my family and Donna, folks living on the edge. Are you saying we should just remain quiet, and continue letting people like you treat us like crap?"

Beverly stared back, her eyes wide. I think I surprised her by not rolling over.

I stood to leave. I felt dirty being in the same room with her.

"This is what I want," I said, stabbing my index finger at her face. "You're going to issue a statement that a cold case had been solved. You can say a dying convict admitted to the crime. I don't know, you're good at lying."

Beverly laughed. "Why? Everyone who even knew about the missing girl is dead or so old they've forgotten. You'll bring more attention to something that's long been buried."

A tight smile broke across my face. "And you'll also make a point in the statement that my parents were completely exonerated."

Beverly raised her hands, palms up. "Who'll care?" she shouted, squinting. "No one remembers your folks or that girl."

"You have forty-eight hours…Chief."

As I walked out of the house, Beverly screamed at me, but I ignored her. I climbed into my car and headed out toward Route 109. I planned on arriving at the Witten Cemetery in twenty minutes. I would stand over the slab of stone with my parent's names, telling their spirits or souls or whatever was present that there were no more secrets.

* * *

William Ade lives in Burke, Virginia with his wife, Cynthia. In the past year, he's had short stories in the 2018 Best New England Crime Stories (Level Best Books), Re-imagining Classics (Left Hand Publishers), and *Transcend Literary Magazine*. His story, "Nic Knuckles – Hard Luck Detective," won first place in *Ageless Author's Anthology*'s humor category. Check him out at Billade.com.

STOLEN MOMENTS
by Shawn Reilly Simmons

I felt the car coming before I saw it. A deep rumbling grated the back of my throat as the engine picked up speed. I looked out the front window and watched the car blow through the stop sign on the corner and fishtail, skidding toward the curb across the street. My finger tensed around the handle of my coffee mug and my shoulders crept toward my ears. I dropped the mug a second later, hot coffee splashing my ankles, when I heard the thud of metal on metal.

My heart pounding, I grabbed the cordless phone from its cradle on the kitchen wall and hurried out my front door, dialing 911 as I stepped onto the porch into the dazzling morning sunshine. The Dodge Charger was pinned against Mr. Hathaway's old Cadillac. He was on his porch in his thin blue robe, shaking a fist in the air and shouting at the driver who was slumped forward against the steering wheel.

Mr. Hathaway's voice changed, his yells becoming higher in pitch, his words rushed and panicked. He stumbled down his porch steps and hurried toward the cars. I watched him with the phone pressed tightly to my ear, shouting at him to hold tight, that I was calling for help. Mr. Hathaway fell to his knees and I took a few more steps, a shaky hand rising up to cover my mouth.

"911. What's your emergency?" A woman spoke calmly into my ear.

My vision blurred and I lost all the air in my lungs. "Come quickly," I gasped, "there's been a terrible accident. A child is hurt...please hurry!"

I didn't hear anything the operator said after that. I dropped the phone on the porch and staggered into the street, falling to my knees near the front tires of the stranger's car, unable to look away from little Oliver Parker's Batman sneakers.

The first time I stole a few moments, it was by accident, and I wasn't sure what had really happened. It was the morning of Thanksgiving and I woke to find the turkey I'd so carefully chosen two days before was still frozen solid. In a panic, I headed to the Shop-and-Save, hoping the only local grocery store in our small New Hampshire town would still have a few thawed turkeys left. Although the November air was crisp, my underarms were damp with sweat as I rushed inside, grabbing a squeaky-wheeled grocery cart on my way to the butcher counter. The humiliating thought of Bill's parents showing up and us not having a turkey on the dinner table twisted in my stomach like a damp kitchen rag. I kept picturing my mother-in-law's face, curled in disappointment with a hint of smug glee at my mistake. She made it her business to point out all of my shortcomings, especially when it came to what she thought of as my incompetence as a housewife.

The fact that she'd allowed us to host the holiday dinner in the first place was huge. We'd only been married a year, and we'd started out on the wrong foot with everyone by eloping without the blessing of either set of parents, and by not having a big church wedding. To be fair, my family didn't mind, but the Nelson clan was much different. They made it seem like becoming a member of their family was on par with getting into Harvard, or becoming an astronaut.

Roy Parker, the owner of the Shop-and-Save, shook his head when I asked if there were any turkeys left. I thought I caught a glimmer of satisfaction in his eye, too. Roy and his wife were our neighbors from down the street, and he'd told me on more than one occasion to get the turkey at least a week ahead of the big day, and to get it into a brine by the Tuesday before Thanksgiving. He'd rattled off a long list of ingredients I'd need, but I had just smiled and nodded, knowing the whole time he was talking that I was going to follow the recipe from the Julia Child cookbook Mother had given me as a wedding present.

Roy was only a year older than me, in fact he and Bill had gone to school together, but he insisted on speaking to me as if I were a child. When he took over the Shop-and-Save after his father died of a heart attack while re-stocking the dairy case, his head swelled up that much bigger. I suppose he did have a lot of responsibility, being so young with a wife and a business to run. But I couldn't help thinking that Roy wanted to see me fail too, right alongside my mother-in-law.

"I'm sorry, Pauline, the last one walked out of here five minutes ago," Roy said, wiping his rough hands on his blood-stained apron. "I suppose you could drive to the city and get one," he glanced at his gold watch, nestled in his thick black arm hair, "but you'd better hurry."

My heart sank as I thanked him, and my eyes drifted to the empty refrigerator case in front of me. Roy disappeared through the meat locker doors behind the counter, the rubber edges slapping closed. A cold rush of air from the back room raised goose bumps on my arms and I rubbed the sleeves of my wool coat.

I stared at a small pool of pink blood on the bottom of the cooler, picturing the turkey that had been there just minutes before I arrived. I closed my eyes and counted backwards, picturing signposts drifting toward me in the blackness, like mile markers on the side of an desolate highway. The space between my shallow breaths grew longer as pictured the signs, and the tinny holiday music crackling from the speakers mounted on the ceiling faded, then grew louder again. The song that had been playing when I'd first walked in the store started up again.

I opened my eyes and my stomach did a quick turn, as if I'd just spun through a loop on a roller coaster.

"I think we have one more turkey back there." The sound of Roy's voice floated down the aisle from the front of the store. I blinked twice and shook my head slightly. A turkey encased in tight white plastic lolled in the case in front of me. I snatched it up and put it in my cart.

"Oh, Pauline," Roy said, pulling up short when he saw me. "I didn't see you come in." His eyes fell to my shopping cart and the last turkey inside. The woman who had followed him planted a fist on her meaty hip.

"Do you have another turkey or don't you?" she asked tersely.

Roy's cheeks reddened. "I'm afraid not, Mrs. Nolan. Sorry, I—"

"Never mind," the woman huffed. "That's why I always get over to the city when we want something nice. Not this rinky-dink place." She turned on her heel and marched away. I pretended to study a display of instant stuffing at the end of the aisle.

"Anything else for you today?" Roy asked tightly. I smiled and picked up a box of stuffing.

I hadn't stolen a lot of time, as I came to think of it, too often over the years. And I rarely stole more than five minutes at a time. I was afraid of getting lost in that dark field inside my mind, or running out of sign posts to follow and wandering around in there forever, forgetting my way back to the present. I didn't want to stray too far from the time that I knew, because I wasn't sure what would happen if I came back and everything was different. I'd seen those movies where one person can mess up everyone else's lives by changing something in the past. I figured if I kept myself close, I couldn't mess up anything that badly. What harm could five or ten minutes do?

The ambulance came and put the little boy on the stretcher. Oliver had been knocked out of his shoes, and his Superman lunchbox had slid under Mr. Hathaway's car. The police had come and pulled the driver out of his car, and I watched as they made him try and walk a straight line, and lit up his eyes with a pen light. They pushed him into the back of the cruiser and sped away with sour looks on their faces, like they couldn't stand the smell of the man in the back seat. Roy, Oliver's father, had already been at work at the Shop-and-Save for hours. I squeezed Lizzy's shoulders helplessly as they loaded Oliver into the ambulance, then helped her inside before they tore off for the hospital.

I sat on my front steps with my head in my hands, thinking about Lizzy and Oliver on the way to the emergency room. Lizzy had just been over to visit me a few days earlier. I'd asked her in for tea when she'd stopped by to see if I wanted to buy any baking pans or some such thing, as a fundraiser for Oliver's school trip. She was head of the PTA, in charge of getting the ball rolling on all their new fundraising efforts that year. We sipped chamomile and I ordered some tin measuring spoons I didn't really need.

I liked Lizzy, even though some of the neighbors hadn't exactly welcomed her with open arms after Roy's first wife died the night she took too many sleeping pills. Lizzy and Roy had taken things quickly, especially considering the fact she was seventeen years younger than him. Some of the neighbors had even whispered that Lizzy had married Roy for his money, that the only reason she was interested in old Roy was because she had her eye on the business that had been in his family for decades. All of that could be why I felt a kinship with Lizzy, having been an outsider in the neighborhood myself for many years.

I could tell the first time I met Lizzy that she was a sharp cookie. And she doted on that baby boy, and Roy too, from what I could see. Bill raised his eyebrows over his morning paper when I mentioned Lizzy was pregnant just a few weeks after her and Roy's hasty courtship and no-fuss nuptials down at the courthouse. But he stopped short of making any comment. My husband wasn't the kind of person to lay judgment at anyone's door.

"Oliver is doing so well this year," Lizzy had said that day at my kitchen table. "I'm happy to say he's near the top of his class. And he's joined the chess club too."

"They play chess in second grade?" I asked.

"Oh yes, and he's very good. He loves reading too. And math of course."

I nodded and smiled, making humming noises of approval.

Bill and I had tried for children in the beginning, but it turned out it wasn't meant to be. My mother-in-law started giving me the side eye a few years into our marriage, trying to figure out what might be wrong with me, staring at my midsection when she thought I wasn't looking. I'd robbed her of grandchildren, and she made sure I knew how disappointed she was about that until the day she finally passed away.

When Lizzy left with my order written on her fundraising sheet, I sat for a while and tried to picture what our life would've been like with a child or two running around, losing myself in thoughts of baby blankets, temper tantrums, homework, and graduations. When I eased myself up from the chair I was surprised my cheeks were damp. It had been a few years since I'd wondered about any of that.

When Bill got cancer, I thought about trying to steal that time back and bring us back to before it got a hold of him. But I didn't know how much time would be enough, and I was too scared to take a chance. I figured it had to be months at least, if not a year back to when his pancreas was healthy. I had never attempted to steal that much time, and I didn't know what damage I might cause by trying. My mind spun with possibilities. What if Bill fell out of love with me? What if my selfish need to keep him with me harmed other people? And even if I could steal back the last year, how could we prevent the cancer from taking hold of him again? I couldn't watch him go through the shock and grief of getting the diagnosis all over again.

I'd lie awake at night and listen to Bill's ragged breath on the bad chemo days, gently wiping the sweat from his forehead, and fret about what to do.

I did steal one day back for us, a particularly bad one at the clinic when the chemo grabbed him from the minute he got hooked up to the IV then broke him down completely by the time we left. Bill's doctor couldn't quite meet my eyes with his own when he told me to prepare myself, and to be sure my husband was as comfortable as he could be at home.

Back home, I got him tucked in bed and took his hand, rubbing my thumb across his papery skin.

"Let's take the day off," I said, closing my eyes. Bill's were already closed as he dozed against the pillow, his skin a faded yellow against the pale blue sheets. There was a vibrating sensation where our hands met, and I began counting the signposts in the dark field in my mind. Just one day, I told myself as I counted. We could afford to steal that much.

When I opened my eyes again it was morning.

"I have an idea," I said, after my stomach settled. "Let's skip the clinic today and go for a drive. I think the fresh air will be better."

Bill gazed at me and nodded, his eyes already tired even though he had just woken up. I got him dressed and helped him into the car, then drove to the lake where we used to go for picnics when we were first courting. Back then we'd lounge on a blanket and talk about our future, of what our life would be like together. We'd sip wine and pick out shapes in the clouds, my head cushioned by his strong arm, never imagining the hollowed out shell it would eventually become.

We stopped visiting the park as often ten years into our marriage. Bill got his promotion and started working at the head office in the city. A long commute and even longer board meetings wiped him out, and there was always a long list of things to do around the house on the weekends.

I helped Bill to a bench at the edge of the lake and we watched the ducks circle around the water, their webbed feet working furiously beneath the surface as they glided by, leaving wide Vs in their wake.

Bill died that night in his sleep, right next to me in the bed. His breath stopped coming, and a calm silence filled the room.

The procession of family and friends with casserole dishes in their hands began five days after the accident. Oliver Parker's obituary had appeared in the paper, as well as a front page article about the accident. Even though I'd been a witness to what happened, seeing his little face in black and white pried a loud gasp from deep in my chest. I sank down in the kitchen chair and wept into my hands. After the initial flood of tears, I sat back and crossed my arms at my chest, staring at the paper and the mug shot of the drunk driver next to Oliver's sweetly smiling face.

Upstairs I pulled on my dark blue dress and fixed my eye makeup before heading over to Roy and Lizzy's to pay my respects, a tuna noodle casserole gripped tightly in my hands.

The house was full of folks from town and church, all dressed in dark colors. Roy stood in the corner of the living room with a dazed look on his face and a tumbler full of amber liquid clenched in his fist. Lizzy was on the couch, her shoulders sagging forward as she stared at the coffee table in front of her. Pastor Fred sat near her, his hands folded in his lap, glancing at her between greeting guests as they came through.

I slipped into the kitchen and put my casserole on the counter next to the others, nodding hello to a group of youngsters, all Roy's employees from the Shop-and-Save.

"Hi, Mrs. Nelson," Amber Dunham said. She looked at me quickly then darted her eyes back to her coworkers, huddled in a group near the refrigerator. They were all holding brown beer bottles. Amber wore a black slouchy sweater with one shoulder exposed, a small pink purse with a silver heart-shaped keychain running a groove in her puffy skin.

"Hello, Amber," I said, stopping short of asking the group if they were old enough to be drinking those beers.

"This is the saddest thing ever," Amber said, her eyes glassing over. She pointed to a school portrait of a grinning Oliver on the refrigerator. He was beginning to look like a young boy, but still seemed more like a baby to me.

I bit the inside of my lip and nodded. "I can't think of anything worse for a parent to go through."

"What is going to happen to them?" Amber asked.

"Who?" I asked, pulling my gaze back to her eyes, rimmed with dark eyeliner.

"The Parkers," she said in a rough whisper. I couldn't imagine Roy closing up the store, but it also wasn't an appropriate topic to discus at their son's wake.

I put a hand on her bare shoulder and squeezed. "Let's all of us just make it through today, okay?"

Amber nodded and swiped a hand at her cheek as she stared past me toward the living room, then took a swig of her beer and turned back to her friends.

Pastor Fred was standing when I returned, talking with one of the neighbors, leaving Lizzy alone on the couch. Roy was sitting in the wingback chair by the fireplace, staring at his drink. I sat down gingerly on the sofa and slid close to Lizzy.

"Lizzy, honey," I said quietly. "I can't tell you how sorry I am."

She looked at me with red rimmed eyes and didn't seem to recognize me at first. A tear slid down her cheek and I dug out a tissue from my purse, tucking it into her fist.

"Why did he walk to the bus stop by himself?" Lizzy choked. "It's my fault."

I sat and listened quietly as her words began to tumble out.

"I'd forgotten to put his art project in his backpack. It was still on the kitchen counter. I told him to wait for Mommy on the porch...that I'd left it out to dry the night before and that I'd be right back...that I'd just be one second. Why didn't he wait for me? How could I have let this happen?"

She looked at me, her eyes pleading with me to understand.

"Shh, honey, it's not your fault," I said.

Lizzy broke down in sobs. "Of course it is. It was my job to keep him safe."

"You're an excellent mother, Lizzy," I said. "What happened was a terrible accident."

Lizzy shook her head and stuffed the tissue under her running nose. "It's my fault. I don't know how I'm supposed to go on living after...after..."

I reached out my hand to her. She grabbed it tightly, like a drowning woman who had been thrown overboard. I closed my eyes and brought forward the dark field.

"Close your eyes," I said quietly. "Let's pray together."

To be honest, I'm not much of a church-goer, or even a praying person for that matter, but it felt like the right thing to say in the moment. I sensed Lizzy calming next to me and secured my grip. I bowed my head and the first signpost floated by in the darkness. My breathing slowed and I counted backward, everything falling away except the humming connection between our palms. I felt her hand slip away when I got to the last sign, then went a little farther just to be sure.

When I opened my eyes a few minutes later, my stomach was going through its familiar rolls and I was by myself on the couch in the Parkers' empty living room. I leaned forward and propped my elbows on my knees to steady myself before standing up. Rocking slightly on my feet, I headed toward the kitchen to slip out the back door.

A floorboard creaked over my head and I looked up at the ceiling, the hair on my forearms standing up. I had stolen seven days, carefully counting the signs in the field to bring things back to the afternoon before the accident. If I'd managed it right, it was one o'clock in the afternoon last Tuesday, and no one should be home. Lizzy worked every weekday as a teller at the bank, and Roy was almost always at the Shop-and-Save.

One of the doors upstairs opened. I stepped out of my shoes and picked them up before ducking inside the kitchen entryway.

"I have to get back to the store." It was Roy.

"Come on, we have another twenty minutes at least." That wasn't Lizzy.

I stood in the doorway with my shoes in my hand and leaned further toward the stairway to listen.

"Don't talk back to me," Roy said, an edge in his voice. "Get back to school before you're missed."

"I'm on my free period," the girl said. "And then lunch. I don't have to be back until the fifth hour bell."

The sound of a toilet flushing floated down toward the kitchen.

"You know you can never say anything about this, right? Not at the store, not at school, definitely not to your mother."

"I know," the girl said quietly. "But...you said maybe we...you know, when Oliver is old enough to understand—"

"Enough," Roy said sharply. "Let yourself out the back door and do like I said. Stay behind the fences till you've gone five houses."

Sounds of clothes rustling and more floor boards creaking convinced me to duck out quietly before Roy and his guest made their way downstairs.

Easing open the kitchen door, I caught a glimpse of a pink purse hanging on the back of one of Lizzy's kitchen chairs, the silver heart shaped keychain glimmering in the afternoon light.

"I'll be damned," I muttered before stepping onto the back porch and clicking the door softly closed behind me. I put my shoes back on and walked down the alley toward my house, shaking my head, anger churning in my gut.

The next morning I sat in my porch swing sipping coffee, waiting for Oliver and Lizzy to appear. When they finally stepped outside, I headed toward them, watching Lizzy say something to Oliver then pop back inside the house. He waited a few seconds then started down the steps.

"Oliver," I called to him. "Did Mommy say to wait on the porch?"

Oliver waved and flashed his toothy grin, his Superman lunchbox banging lightly against his bony knee. "Yes."

"Well, let's just wait for her then, okay?"

I felt the engine coming, then heard the rumble of the tires getting closer. I hurried up the porch steps to knelt down in front of Oliver, hugging him tightly.

"It's going to be okay," I whispered to him right before the crash.

"Oh my word," Lizzy shouted from inside the screen door. "Oliver!"

"He's safe," I called to her. "Looks like a bad accident out in front of Mr. Hathaway's. Call 911, honey."

Later that afternoon, I made my way down the canned vegetable aisle at the Shop-and-Save. Amber was kneeling on the floor, stacking cans of green beans into a cone-shaped display.

"Mrs. Nelson," Amber said, looking up at me. "Can I help you find something?"

"Yes, dear. Can you reach some corn for me?" I pointed to the top shelf.

"Sure," Amber said, picking herself up from the floor and reaching for the can. "Here you go."

"Thanks," I said. "Say, I saw your mother earlier today at the bank. She says you got accepted to State. Congratulations."

Amber hid a smile behind her hand and shrugged. "Yeah, I did. But..."

"But what?" I asked.

Amber crossed her fleshy arms across her chest. "It's just, I'm not sure about being so far away from my mom."

"Oh, dear," I said. "Your mother will be just fine. She's excited for you to go and get your degree."

Amber trained her gaze toward the back of the store and shrugged again. "No one else I know got into State. All of my friends work here."

"Amber," I said firmly. "You'll make friends there, and have so many more opportunities when you finish. There is more to this world than Roy Parker's Shop-and-Save."

At the sound of his name Amber's face went pale.

I held her gaze. "It might not seem like it right now, but you'll see once you get out into the world, the things that seem big here are going to be pretty small by comparison."

She nodded and cleared her throat. "You sound like my mom."

I rubbed her forearm rapidly when it looked like she was about to cry. "You're going to do great things very soon. Trust me, I know."

I pressed the buzzer on the butcher counter and watched Roy approach through the foggy plastic windows of the meat locker doors.

"Pauline," Roy said with a sigh. "What can I do for you?"

I put a finger to my chin and studied the beef in the display case. "I feel like a nice steak tonight. What do you recommend?"

Roy raised his eyebrows. "I know you've eaten steak before, Pauline."

I flipped my hand at him and continued to browse. "I know, I was just asking your professional opinion."

"A filet is always a safe bet," Roy said, selecting one from the stack and holding it up for me to see.

"Yes," I said with a nod. "That looks good. Can you wrap it for me?"

"Sure," Roy said, placing the meat on a wooden cutting board.

"A professional opinion is always good to have," I continued as I watched him peel off a sheet of butcher paper. "Just like earlier, I was at the bank asking Lizzy her professional opinion on wills."

"Wills?" Roy said, pausing in his work to look up at me. "She's a bank teller, not an attorney."

"Oh, I know," I said. "But lots of people keep wills in their safety deposit boxes, and she's seen more than a few of them."

Roy snorted a sharp laugh and continued wrapping the steak. "You ready to make a will, Pauline? Who have you got to leave anything to?"

I ignored the sting from his words. "And then Lizzy and I got to talking about…what are they called? Prenuptial agreements? Lizzy says she never signed one of those."

"Those are for rich people, Pauline," Roy said dismissively.

"Really?" I asked. "I'm pretty sure they work for everyone. Well, I guess especially for people who have a lot to lose if their marriage goes south."

Roy looked up at me over the display case and glared. "What are you on about, Pauline? You're not married anymore, remember?"

"You're right, I'm not," I said. "I'm all taken care of by Bill's life insurance, and the money we saved over the years. And the house, of course."

"Bill's family's house," Roy muttered. He wiped his hands on his apron.

"That's right, but I'm the only one left and it's mine. So even I, a childless widow, have something to lose. But not as much as you, with a grocery store that has been in your family for generations. That would be a terrible thing to throw away…" I leaned toward him and placed my hand on the cool glass, then whispered, "…for a few moments of passion with a barely legal employee."

Roy's cheeks flared and he took a step backward. "I don't know what you're talking about."

"Yes you do," I said evenly.

Roy huffed and put his hands on his hips.

"Is my steak ready?" I asked.

Roy glared at me for a few more seconds then handed the steak to me over the counter. Without another word he turned and pushed his way back through the meat locker doors.

"Check mate," Oliver said when he beat me for the second game in a row.

"I give up," I said with a smile. "Have some more lemonade."

Oliver picked up the glass with both hands and gulped, a drizzle spilling down the front of his shirt.

"Oliver, Mommy's got supper ready," Roy shouted from his porch.

"See you tomorrow," I said. Oliver hugged me and trotted down the steps, following the sidewalk close to the grass on the way back to his house like I'd shown him.

After Roy ushered Oliver inside, he turned back to me and nodded.

I raised my hand in a wave and watched him go back inside.

* * *

Shawn Reilly Simmons is the author of the Red Carpet Catering Mysteries published by Henery Press and of several short stories appearing in various anthologies. Shawn serves on the Board of Malice Domestic, and is a member of Sisters in Crime, Mystery Writers of America, International Thriller Writers, and the Crime Writers' Association. Connect with Shawn on TW & IG @ShawnRSimmons or visit www.ShawnReillySimmons.com

IVY
by Katie Tietjen

I saw her before I pulled off I-91.

It was 2:00 in the morning. I steered my rig into the truck stop, gripping the wheel so tight my fingers tingled. I parked in one of the extended spots, leaned back, and watched her in the rearview mirror. Wrapped in a dirty fur coat, she wore high-heeled sandals and her legs were bare. The streetlamp she waited under acted as a spotlight in the cold November night. Her hands clutched the coat around her middle. Every few seconds, she raised one of them to swipe at a part of her face: first her lips, next her nose, then her eyes. Her blond hair looked greasy, even from this far away, and I could see her face twitch every few seconds.

She was jonesing.

Her pimp would be around somewhere. Maybe out of sight, but here. I scanned the mostly-empty lot, noting a beat-up Ford and an older model Corolla. No other rigs. Good.

I grabbed my wallet and climbed down. My legs protested for several seconds when my feet hit the pavement, and I lurched in that stereotypical trucker walk, legs bowed and knees wobbly. Sailors called it getting your "sea legs" when you finally got used to walking on the pitching, rolling deck of a ship in motion. Truckers didn't have a name for this sensation of feeling unbalanced—unwelcome, even—on solid ground.

I turned away from the girl and made my way towards the building. The neon lights on the sign buzzed. As I passed under it, the "i" in "convenience" hissed and went out. I pushed open the door. Bad, saxophone-laden jazz played in the background. A bored teenager sat behind the counter. She barely looked up from her phone when the bell chimed, announcing my entrance. A wiry man leafing through magazines was the only other person there. He eyed me over the top of *Newsweek*. His small black eyes studied me up and down. His nostrils flared.

I'd found the pimp.

Turning my back on him, I headed straight for the coffee machine in the corner, filled a cup, and brought it to the counter. She still didn't look up. Her thumbs flew across her phone's screen, nails clacking. I pulled two crinkled dollars from my wallet and threw them on the counter.

"Keep the change."

My voice sounded rusty. It occurred to me I hadn't used it all day. I'd been driving since Georgia, and there was still a long way to go. I turned to leave. The pimp put the magazine back and watched me without pretense. I made eye contact and held it as I opened the door, the cheerful chime sounding once again. I had the sense he was sizing me up the way a snake does its potential prey.

"Stay safe out there," the teenager said incongruously, eyes still glued to her phone.

The pimp cocked his head and raised his eyebrows. I shook my head once and stepped back out into the cold. I felt the door catch and knew he was right behind me.

"What? You don't like her?" His voice was raspy.

I kept moving, taking several paces down the pavement before I stopped and turned around.

"How old?" I asked, looking him right in the eyes.

His beady eyes jumped from my face to my belt buckle to my boots and back again.

"Eighteen," he said with a smirk.

I squeezed the styrofoam cup. Coffee sloshed out and seared my left hand.

"Eighteen," I echoed.

I reached towards my back pocket with my right hand, and he moved closer, just as I'd known he would. By the time I pulled my hand out, he was six inches from me, ready to close the deal, making it easy for me.

He didn't see the gun until it was too late.

I squeezed the trigger once. He groaned and crumpled on the sidewalk. I backtracked several steps and glanced over my shoulder to make sure the girl at the counter still hadn't looked up. The glass was thick, the silencer was effective, and the bad jazz was loud. She gazed ever downward, the light from her phone screen coloring her skin electric white.

The other girl, the one I'd come here for, watched me from under the street lamp. I tucked the gun back in my waistband and moved towards her. A slight sense of urgency pushed me now; it was unlikely someone else would show up now, but not impossible. I carried the coffee carefully, not wanting to spill any more.

When I got closer, she pulled her coat closer and started shaking her head.

"Why'd you do that?" she said, eyes wide.

She looked like a deer in the headlights. From this close, it was obvious she wasn't a day over sixteen. Thick, cheap pancake make-up attempted, with minimal success, to cover her acne. She badly needed braces. One of her front teeth curved around the other. It reminded me of ivy circling around the trunk of a tree.

"Here," I said, thrusting the coffee at her.

She shook her head more vigorously.

"Naw, mister. I don't want nothin' from you."

She swatted at the coffee, which splattered on the pavement, and took a shaky step back. Her heel wobbled and she nearly fell. I grabbed her arm, which was so thin it felt stick-like, and steadied her. She tried to wrest herself away, but my grip was stronger than her will. I let her struggle for a few seconds.

"Who's gonna take care of me now?" she shrieked. "Huh?"

I tightened my grip and felt defeat overwhelm her fight. Her arm went limp. She started to sob.

"I'm gonna take care of you," I said. "Get in the truck."

"No," she moaned. "No, no, no."

A car, and then another, whipped past on the highway. It was time. I took out the gun.

"We can do this the easy way or the hard way. Your call."

Her eyes widened, and I felt her sharp intake of breath. They flashed as she weighed her options. Her eyes shifted over my shoulder to the store where the counter clerk sat, oblivious. My hand tightened around the gun.

"If you try and get her attention," I said, "I'll kill her, too."

She whimpered, and I could see whatever fight was left drain out of her. She cast one last look at the slumped form of her pimp.

Then she looked up at me. Her eyes were dull, her face a mask.

She said, "The easy way."

I let her arm go and trailed her to the truck cab. She walked less shakily than I'd expected. There wasn't confidence in her step, exactly, but a certain resignation. Once she'd hoisted herself into the passenger seat, I walked around the front to the driver's side. I climbed in, once again stashing the weapon in my back waistband. I knew I wouldn't need it now to control her.

She shrugged off the coat, revealing an electric blue tube top and stick-thin arms riddled with scabs and tracks.

"What do you want me to do?" she asked, her voice dull.

"Buckle up," I said. "And you can leave your coat on."

I pulled the burner phone from my center console and typed in a four word message: *Got her. On way.*

As I put the key into the ignition, a thud sounded from the trailer behind us. The girl looked at me, and I could feel her panic.

"What was that?" Her voice was shrill.

"Don't worry about it," I said.

I turned the key and the big engine flooded to life. I felt a surge of power as I steered the rig out of the parking lot. The girl shivered beside me. She cast one last glance out the window at her dead pimp. I accelerated onto the highway.

A few minutes went by. Voices crackled through the CB radio—truckers alerting each other to the presence of cops, annoying tailgaters, and the like. That and the roar of the engine were the only sounds.

Then, she said, "Do you have anything?"

"No," I said.

The CB crackled more loudly and a voice broke through: "Any word on the Billy Big Rigger who went AWOL this morning?"

Another voice responded, "Good riddance, I say. That guy's a real crackerhead."

I snorted. *Crackerhead* was a term usually reserved for drivers of "four-wheelers," aka non-commercial cars and pickups and the like. That, combined with "Billy Big Rigger," which indicated a driver who was full of himself, told me the guy must be an exceptional jerk.

The girl scratched at her arms. "I need some," she said. "Real soon."

Another voice crackled through on the CB: "He never came back on. Missed his next stop, truck's radar was disabled. I heard there's an APB out on the rig. License plate, description, all of it."

My hands tightened on the steering wheel. I glanced at the cut wires on the GPS tracking device in the console and wondered how much time I had.

"I'm taking you somewhere safe," I told her.

She didn't answer back. She began rocking forward and back.

"Have you ever quit?" I asked. "The life, I mean."

She stopped rocking and turned her head to shoot me a sharp look. I caught it out of the corner of my eye.

"Yeah, I quit. Twice," she said, and then barked out a humorless laugh. "See how well that went?"

"The average," I told her, "is seven times."

"What?" she said.

"The average person quits the life and goes back again seven times before getting out for good," I said.

"What's your deal?" she said slowly, eyes narrowed.

Yet another voice crackled through the CB: "He go rogue? Or did someone truck-jack him?"

A vigorous debate ensued about the fate of the missing trucker. Two thumps sounded from the trailer behind us.

"You ever see ivy wrapped around a tree trunk? Growing around a tree, I mean?" I said.

"Uh, yeah—" she said.

"Well," I said, "it starts out that the tree supports the ivy, gives it somewhere to grow, a stable surface to creep up. But, eventually, the ivy infiltrates the tree. It kills the bark, it prevents the sun from hitting the leaves, it weighs down branches. Little by little, so that you can't even see it happening until it's too late, the ivy kills the tree."

She stopped rocking.

I pulled off my cap and let my long brown ponytail tumble down my back. I peeled the fake mustache off and wiggled my nose, glad to be free of the itchy thing.

"You can call me Ivy," I said.

By the time we pulled off the highway and bounced along the rutted back roads in New Hampshire, the sun was starting to come up. My passenger was asleep. Her head rested against the side window and her mouth was open a little. She looked even younger now. I was so tired, my eyes itched.

My father had told me that used to happen to him on long hauls. He was the reason I already knew my way around a big rig. And he was the reason I'd run willingly into the arms of my first pimp when I was thirteen. And, I suppose, the reason I was where I was now.

I steered us onto an even bumpier driveway. There was no mailbox, no signpost, nothing that would indicate to a casual passer-by that this even was a driveway. But in this particular stretch of New Hampshire woods, there would be no casual passers-by, which was just how we wanted it.

Within a minute, I saw the light on the front porch. Shortly after that, the log cabin came into view. Smoke curled out the chimney. I rolled to a stop and Mama appeared in the doorway, her coffee-colored skin aglow under the light. I grinned, and she grinned back. I hopped out, forgetting about the shock of land after so many hours in the truck, and stumbled. Catching myself, I dashed over to her, barely feeling the ground below my feet.

"I did it," I told her, throwing my arms around her neck.

She fiercely hugged me back. We weren't technically related, but Mama was my family. We'd been in the same stable back when we were in the life. The other girls and I had called her Mama even back then. She always took care of everyone. You had a problem or a question, you went to Mama. She dispensed practical advice, basic medical care, and emotional support.

"Good job, baby," she said as she stroked my hair. I glowed at her praise. "Now, let's get her inside."

We went to the passenger side. The girl was awake now and watching us, her expression guarded. Mama opened the door and offered her a hand. She took it hesitantly and stepped down. I watched her look around and take it in: the pine trees, the cabin, the fresh mountain air. Birds chirped and sang, welcoming the new day. It was a far cry from the concrete and harsh lights of the highway rest stop.

Mama escorted her inside, letting the girl hold her arm the whole time. I heard her explain in her calm, deep voice how we'd built this place as a refuge for girls like her, a place to get clean and get out of the life. Mama was a nurse, she explained, and would be taking care of her. As she guided our very first patient across the threshold, she looked over her shoulder at me and smiled. I smiled back. All our work, all our planning and scouting and scheming, had been worth it.

The sun rose higher in the sky behind the cabin. I closed my eyes and breathed in the fresh, crisp morning air. Beautiful.

THUMP.

I exhaled and narrowed my eyes, thinking of the missing trucker I'd heard about on the CB.

He wasn't missing.

I, at least, knew right where he was. And I knew a few other things about him, too, such as he liked underage girls—the younger, the better. I touched the coat of paint I'd applied to the rig less than 48 hours ago. It had been a hasty job, but had proved a strong enough disguise, as had the license plates I'd stolen from another rig.

But it was time for the truck and its driver to disappear. I walked around the side of the rig, relishing the land—MY land—beneath my feet. I opened the back door. He was more or less right where I'd left him, bound and gagged on the floor. He blinked as the morning light flooded the trailer. There was a dark stain around his crotch where he'd pissed himself.

This one saw the gun, but it was still too late.

Afterwards, I climbed back behind the wheel, pulled the rig around the cabin, and steered through the field and over to the deep quarry that squatted halfway across our property.

I felt a surge of pride as I nudged the truck right up to the edge of the quarry. The engine idled as I struck a match, placed it on the driver's seat, and positioned a rock on the gas pedal. There was a long moment when the truck seemed to hover in mid-air. Then, gravity won. The crash was spectacular. I walked to the edge of the quarry and looked down at the steaming wreckage, the sound still reverberating up the hillside.

The truck actually looked small from way up here, and the quarry seemed vast—hungry, almost.

My stomach growled. I wondered what Mama had made for breakfast. I walked back towards the house, birds chirping to welcome the sunrise. My steps were steady and sure. The land—*my* land, *our* land—was strong and solid beneath my feet.

I could get used to this.

* * *

A lifelong New Englander, **Katie Tietjen** lives in Connecticut with her husband, sons, and cat. She's a Tassy Walden award winner, recipient of the 5th Semester scholarship, and a CRW Stiletto contest finalist. Her favorite fictional characters are Harry Potter and Harry Bosch; hence, you can find her on Twitter @2FavoriteHarrys

MAINE

Maine
Vermont
New
Hampshire
Massachusetts
Connecticut
RI

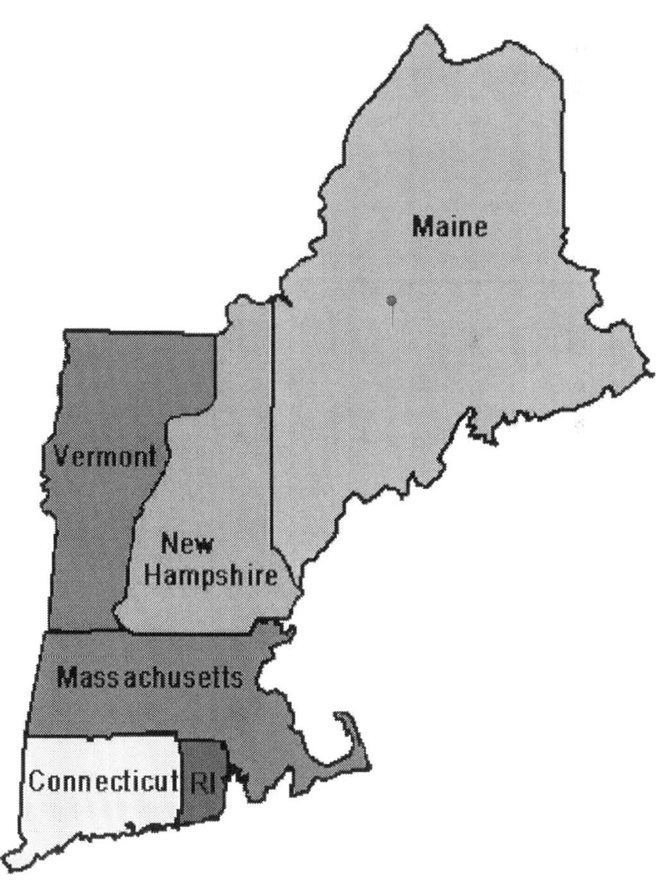

DIRIGO
MAINE

TELL ME AGAIN
by Woody Hanstein

"Tell me again," I said.

"Which part?" the man asked. His breathing was raspy and his skin had a gray tint.

"The part about you wanting to plead guilty to a crime someone else is charged with."

The man rubbed his bald head with his right hand like he was sanding wood. He wore a frayed black suit coat a size too big and dark blue pants spattered with white paint. I tried to avoid staring at the neat stack of $50 bills that he had set down on my desk.He said it was $5,000, and I had no reason to doubt him.

"Does it really matter?" the man asked. He was around fifty years old and had the weathered, wiry look of someone who did physical labor for a living. "I know what I'm doing," he added. "If you won't help me, I'll find a lawyer who will."

None of it made sense, but my law business had been running on fumes ever since the local newspaper ran a story about my reprimand from the board of bar overseers six months earlier.

"You understand that a felony charge like this will mean a prison sentence?" I said."Probably a long one."

The man winced and took a pill bottle and a half-pint of Old Crow out of a side pocket of his suit coat. He twisted the cap off the pills and chased two of them down with a long swallow of bourbon.

"Do I look like I give a shit about a long prison sentence?" he said.

"Cancer?" I asked.

The man nodded but said nothing to elaborate.

"Tell me again how you came to be driving Robbie Kendall's BMW," I said.

The man looked annoyed, but he answered my question in the same flat monotone he'd used since he'd walked in the door. "It's not complicated. It was in the lot beside that tavern. The car was unlocked and the keys were over the visor. I had never driven a Beamer before, so I figured what the fuck. I know I was going too fast, but I never even saw that girl. After I hit her I must have over-corrected because I ended up in a ditch a hundred yards down the road. Why she was walking around so late I got no idea."

"What about the two witnesses who drove by," I said. "From the newspaper it sounded like they were pretty sure it was Kendall they saw standing by the car and jumping into the pickup that came by. How could they mistake a 6'3" former high school football star for an older guy your size?"

The man shrugged. "You'd have to ask them, but it was pitch dark."

"What about the keys?" I asked.

"The keys?"

"The car keys. Why not just leave the keys in the ignition? Why take them with you and then throw them into the woods?"

The man shrugged, his eyes on the bottle of Old Crow standing sentry beside that stack of cash.

"And why not take the laptop?" I asked.

"The laptop?"

"You do that a lot," I said.

"Do what?"

"Repeat my question to buy yourself time."

The man reached for the bourbon and the stack of fifties and looked at me closely. "Mel Doyle said to start with you, but he warned me you might be a pain in the ass," he said. "I've got a right to plead guilty and set things right."

He started to get up but I waved him back into his seat.

"I didn't say I wouldn't help you," I said. "But you can't just walk into court and enter a guilty plea to a felony charge if the evidence won't support it."

The man's eyes narrowed. "That's not what Doyle says."

"Well, Doyle should have explained it better. Before the judge will let you plead guilty, she's got to hold something called a Rule 11 hearing."

The man looked annoyed. "Doyle didn't say nothing about a Rule 11 hearing. He said when the DA sees my notarized statement she'll know she's got no chance prosecuting Kendall. Especially when he has been saying since day one that somebody stole his car and hit that girl."

Mel Doyle was one of the most high-powered lawyers in the state.He had a fancy office in Augusta filled with framed commendations and photos of him golfing with important people.He was also the guy who blew the whistle on me last year to the board of bar overseers after I'd made the mistake of loaning myself $10,000 from my clients' escrow account to pay off the last of my alimony and keep my ex-wife from taking me back to court. I had that money repaid within a month, but Doyle must have known someone at my bank because he turned me in to the board.None of my clients ended up losing a dime, but I knew I was in the wrong and fessed up to the board which gave me the reprimand. The whole thing might have gone unnoticed except that Doyle called the reporter for the local weekly newspaper, and I ended up getting the worst kind of publicity a lawyer can get.

Doyle had been representing Robbie Kendall since he was arrested two days after the accident that nearly killed Julie Marr back in October. Julie was sixteen years old and walking home from babysitting for a neighbor when Kendall's BMW ran her down just before midnight. The accident had been big news in Piedmont, both because Kendall came from such a wealthy family and also because ten years earlier he had been the best high school quarterback in the state—so good he had gotten a football scholarship at the University of Connecticut.

That scholarship, like most things in Kendall's pampered life, ended badly–he lost it his sophomore year after getting into a physical altercation with one of the assistant coaches. Kendall's father was one of the richest men in western Maine, and after that he set his son up in a couple of businesses, but Robbie Kendall ran both of them into the ground in short order.

Julie Marr's pelvis was crushed in the accident, and this past week the local paper ran a story in advance of Kendall's trial which was due to begin on Monday describing her long and painful recovery. The article said she had always loved horses and was still hoping to become a veterinarian, but her doctor still wasn't sure she'd ever be able to ride a horse again.

I looked at the man and let my empty bank account wrestle with my conscience for a while longer. "Let me see your written statement," I finally said.

He slid it across the desk to me and I read it through twice.It obviously had been written by someone else, but it contained enough information about the accident that it would have been impossible to prove he was a liar on the face of it. It was signed *Frederick Wells* at the bottom in handwriting that was firmer and neater than I expected, and the whole statement was sworn to and notarized.

"Why hire a lawyer at all?" I asked. "Why not just take this to someone at the police department and ask them to arrest you?"

"Because Mel Doyle says they'd never believe me. He said they'd just think Robbie Kendall's father paid me off to do it."

That was what anyone with half a brain would think, but I kept that thought to myself and pulled the receipt book out of my top desk drawer."I'll be your lawyer," I said. "But once I give your sworn statement to the DA there will be no turning back."

"I know what I'm doing," the man said.

"I just want to make sure you don't start feeling bad when we get to court and you hear how seriously that poor girl was hurt."

"I got a daughter of my own to feel bad about. When that Marr girl's family gets done suing Kendall, I expect she'll be all set."

"Her civil case is going to get a whole lot harder after you plead guilty to this."

The man thought about that for a while but then shook his head."I got to pay for what I did," he said.

I counted Fred Wells's money and wrote him out a receipt. Then I watched him leave and sat there behind my desk for a long time wondering how I could have fallen so low. I became a lawyer twenty years earlier mostly because I loved the idea of how a courtroom gave even the little man his chance to set things right. It was hard to pinpoint when it started happening but the law for me now was nothing more than a dreary way to pay my bills. I hated the idea of pleading Fred Wells to a crime he didn't commit, but he was certainly competent and would do it with or without my help.

I got up and made a copy of his sworn statement and headed over to the courthouse. On my way I stopped at the bank and deposited Wells's retainer. At the DA's office I asked the pretty new redheaded secretary if I could see Sue Landry.

She shook her head. "She's not seeing anyone today. She's preparing for trial."

"If she's working on Robbie Kendall's case I think you better interrupt her."

The redhead went back down the hall and thirty seconds later she came back out with Sue Landry right behind her.

"This better be important, Gary," she said.

"It is, but you're not going to like it."

I followed her back to her office and after she sat down behind her desk I took a seat myself. I handed her a copy of Fred Wells's statement, but while she read it I wished I were somewhere else. She had been the DA in Hamilton County for the past fifteen years and she had always treated me fairly. When she finished reading she crumpled the affidavit up in an angry ball and bounced it off the trash can two feet from her desk.

"You, Gary?" she said. Then ten seconds later just that one word, "You?"

"I didn't write it," I said.

"I fucking know who wrote it. It's notarized by Mel Doyle's paralegal."

"Well, would you rather find out about it on Monday afternoon in the middle of Doyle's opening statement?"

"I'd rather not find out about it at all," she said. She had short, dark hair just starting to gray and a runner's thin build, and I had never seen her angrier.

"You can pretend this doesn't exist if you want, but from the beginning Kendall did say his car had been stolen and that he wasn't driving."

"We both know this a load of bullshit," she said.

"I don't. Wells told me it's true, and I wasn't there. He knows we'll need to work out some kind of plea agreement before you start picking Kendall's jury on Monday."

Sue Landry looked at me for a long time before she spoke. The look of anger on her face had been replaced with something more like pity which made me only feel even worse.

"So how much is your boy getting?" she asked. "What's the going rate for doing a spoiled rich kid's prison sentence?"

"Sue, all you have is two guys coming from the bar who think they saw someone resembling Kendall get into a pickup. And a crack on the windshield of his BMW that some detective thinks might match up with a bump on Kendall's forehead when he was arrested two days later. "

"I've got more than that," she said. "I got Kendall walking out of Mike's Tavern just before midnight and not running back inside saying 'Holy shit, someone's just stolen my $40,000 car.' Why did he wait four hours to report his car being stolen? And then wait another twelve before he lets the police talk to him?"

"You think he won't have an explanation for all that next week?" I asked.

We sat in silence for a long while.

"I've got to look into this," Sue Landry finally said. "It's only Tuesday, and every cop in this county is going to spend the rest of the week trying to prove your guy is a liar. Mr. Wells better pray I can't because if I do I am going after him and Kendall and even Doyle if I get lucky enough to prove he's involved." She looked down at her desk for a few seconds and then shook her head."Gary, I could have imagined some lawyers doing this, but not you."

"All I know is what Fred Wells told me," I said, but that remark didn't seem to give either one of us any comfort.

"Call me Friday morning if you haven't heard from me before then," she said. "If we can't disprove your guy's statement by then, I'll probably have no choice but to talk to you about some kind of plea."

I waited for the pretty redhead to make me a copy of the police report, and then I walked back to my office. I spent an hour reading through the report and was thinking about heading home early when Mel Doyle called.

"Fred Wells come in to see you today?" he asked.

"That would be confidential," I said. "I'm surprised that you, of all people, would be asking me that."

"Good one," he said, and then he chuckled. "I just wanted you to know that I grilled Wells before he signed that affidavit and I think he's legit. His story is bulletproof as far as I can see."

"Why send him to me?" I asked.

"Because I know how Sue Landry can get, and you won't let her push you around. If Wells feels bad about what he's done and wants to step up to the plate, I don't want that bitch bullying him out of doing the right thing."

"I'd still feel better if I could look into it a bit more," I said.

"How would you do that? There is no forensic evidence at all."

"I'd like to talk to Robbie Kendall. If I could speak with him I'd have a lot more peace of mind."

"Well, that's not going to happen," Doyle said. "As his lawyer I'm telling you to stay away from him, and I mean totally. The bar rules couldn't be any clearer, and if you exchange one word with Robbie Kendall I'll make sure the overseers pull that license of yours in record time."

As much as I wanted to hang up the phone, there was a question I had to ask.

"Mel, it was twenty years ago" I said. "Isn't that a long time to hold a grudge?"

"Roger Bevins was a state senator," Doyle said, his voice suddenly loud and angry. "Do you know how bad that trial made me look?"

I remembered how bad he and Bevins both looked. In 1999 I was a new assistant district attorney, but my cross-examination of Roger Bevins helped his jury see what a liar he was during his Nighthunting trial. It wasn't my fault that Bevin's and his alibi witness couldn't keep to the same script, or that nearly everyone on the jury had their arms tightly folded across their chests and scowls on their faces as they watched Bevins leave the witness stand.All I did was the job I had been sworn to do, but Mel Doyle had held it against me ever since.

Doyle laughed heartily on his end of the phone. "Well, I obviously like you now," he said."Didn't I just send you a $5,000 client?"

I hung up the phone and locked my office and drove home. I fed the cat and made a gin and tonic and then I made a couple more. I made a grilled cheese sandwich and stayed up watching the Red Sox blow a four-run lead and lose to the Tigers. Then I went to bed, but I didn't sleep well.

I got up early and drove in to my office, but I suddenly got the urge to ask Fred Wells a few more questions. He didn't have a phone, but the address he gave me was in the trailer park out past the old shoe shop.

I found his trailer toward the back of the park and saw Wells sitting in the low morning sun at a picnic table. I walked over to him and could see that he was working on a jigsaw puzzle of the Taj Mahal. By his left elbow sat a white ceramic cup of coffee and a fresh pint of Old Crow. He looked up from the puzzle and studied me for a minute.

"You ever seen it?" he asked after a while. "In person, I mean."

"Nope. Paris, France is the closest I ever got."

"Paris must be nice," he said as he fidgeted a blue piece around in a gap amidst a patch of half-finished sky.

"I came to warn you that the DA is going to look into your story."

"Doyle told me she would, but I got nothing to hide."

"Have you thought about how your daughter will take it?" I said.

Wells set the puzzle piece down and looked up at me. "She doesn't think much of me as it is. Her mother hates me and I barely get to see her at all."

"Things weren't good between you and her mom?"

He shook his head. "I gave her a pretty bad time. I can't really blame her for not wanting me in Mandy's life."

"How old is Mandy?"

Wells smiled for the first time since we'd met. "She'll be twelve in a couple of weeks."

"What's she like?" I asked.

"She's a sweetheart. I wish I knew her better. She plays the clarinet, and she's real good, too. She had a solo at the last middle school concert, and I was even there to see it."

"It must be nice to have a talent."

He laughed and shook his head. "She didn't get it from me. She even got invited to the all-state jazz camp when school ends next month."

"She must be excited about that."

He shook his head and drank some coffee. "She can't go," he said. "It cost four hundred bucks, and it was due last week. Her mother's been on disability for the last couple years, and I've never been able to help her out worth a shit."

"Is that why you're doing this?" I asked. "Because you couldn't help your daughter go to jazz camp?"

Wells just shook his head and went back to his puzzle. Then he uncapped his bourbon and poured some into his coffee. I took the hint and told him that he needed to call me on Friday morning if he hadn't heard from me by then. Halfway to my truck I turned toward him.

"Is Clay Knight still the music teacher at the middle school?" I asked.

"He's still there. Why do ask?"

"Just curious. We played basketball together back in high school."

I got into my truck and drove over to the middle school. I went into the office and learned that Clay was probably in the teacher's lounge because he didn't have his first class until second period.

Clay was sitting on a worn-out green couch drinking a diet Pepsi, and on the coffee table in front on him was a half-strung violin. When Clay saw me he set his soda can down and got to his feet and stuck out a hand. He was still tall and lanky.

"Gary, how's the legal business?" he said.

I lied that things were fine and then I asked him about Fred Wells's daughter Mandy.

“She’s a great kid,” Clay said.

“I’m representing her father, and he told me about her jazz camp invitation.”

Clay shook his head. “Yeah, what a shame. She would have loved it.”

“Is it too late for her to go?” I asked. “If you had her $400 today, could you get them to take her?”

He thought for a minute. “I don’t see why not. I’d have to make a couple calls, but it’s the gifted musicians like her they really want.And she’d be ecstatic.”

I took a check out of my wallet and made it out as Clay instructed.“This money is from her father,” I said.

Clay looked at the check. “Can I ask why you’re writing a personal check for her father?”

“No, but you need to let her know about this as soon as possible.Tell her it’s an early birthday present from her father.”

“I’ll see her next period,” Clay said. “Does this have anything to do with what you’re doing for her dad?”

“In a way,” I said.

I drove back to my office and pushed around some papers until noon and went over to the district court to deal with two clients who had traffic infractions. I was back behind my desk late in the afternoon when Fred Wells came into my office.

“Mandy came by my trailer after school,” he said.

When I didn’t respond he sat down in the same chair he’d used the day before.

“I know what you’re trying to do,” he said. “But seeing Mandy so happy just now, makes me feel even worse about how sick I am and what a bad father I’ve been.”

“There’s still time to change,” I said. “You don’t want her thinking you’re like Robbie Kendall.”

“I can live with whatever she thinks for a little while longer.What she needs is something for when I’m gone.” He thought for a minute and then stood up. "It's not Robbie Kendall's fault I stole his car," he said.

Friday morning Sue Landry called me and offered Fred Wells a straight four-year prison sentence for a guilty plea to the charge of leaving the scene of a serious accident. She was still upset that Robbie Kendall would escape justice, but she hadn't found any evidence to shake Fred Wells's statement. I met with Fred that afternoon and couldn't persuade him to change his mind about the whole thing, so I called the court and scheduled his plea for nine o'clock Monday morning.

I spent all Friday evening thinking I should just withdraw from the case and let Wells do it on his own, but I knew that would do nothing to stop things. I went for a run on Saturday morning and stopped by the river to watch a couple carpenters raise a stud wall on the new house that was going up at the end of Twigsnapper Road. I watched them for a long time as they worked, and I envied them more and more as I did.I had done carpentry work summers between semesters of law school, and I had always gotten satisfaction from the progress I could see at the end of each day's work.

I was jogging home when I figured out what I needed to do, and I suddenly felt twenty years younger. I drove to my bank and withdrew the last $4,600 of Fred Wells's retainer.Then I stopped at my office and typed out a letter to the bar overseers and called Brian Crenshaw after that.Brian was surprised to hear what I had in mind, but he said he could easily scare up some business for me. I had helped him out of a sticky legal situation the year before, and we had always gotten along well. The last chore had to wait until Sunday evening.

Sunday after dinner I found Robbie Kendall's cell phone number in the police report and gave him a call after making sure my phone would record it. I introduced myself after Kendall picked up and I told him we had a last-minute problem.I prayed the call would work out like I planned because it was as flagrant a violation of the bar rules as there ever could be.

"What kind of problem?" Kendall asked. "Doyle told me Wells is pleading guilty in the morning."

"Not unless he gets more money, he's not. He's worried that after court tomorrow you are going to change your mind."

"That's bullshit. He got the $10,000 up front money last week just like we promised. He doesn't get the last $30,000 until after the plea is accepted. That's the deal."

"Well, he needs that last $30,000 before he pleads."

"How the fuck am I supposed to find that on a Sunday night?" Kendall asked.

"I don't know, but I think it will be easier than finding another sucker to go serve your four-year sentence down in Windham."

"What if I can't get the money that fast?" he asked.

"Then wear your best suit in the morning, because you probably are going to be picking a jury. Have that last $30,000 in my office at 8:30 a.m. tomorrow or else you and Doyle are going to need another plan."

I got the best night's sleep I could remember having in weeks and put on a pair of blue jeans and a chamois work shirt and drove into town.I had a corn muffin and a cup of coffee in the bagel shop, and I mailed my letter to the bar overseers in the box in front of the post office. Then I went back to my office and called Sue Landry and asked her to stop by as soon as possible if it wouldn't be too much trouble.

Mel Doyle didn't even see Sue when he barged through my office door at 8:20 and shouted "Who in the fuck do you think you are?"

Sue was standing off to the side examining the framed copy of the Magna Carta that my sister bought me right after I had passed the bar exam.

"Do you have my client's $30,000?" I asked.

"I have something better than that," Doyle said. "I have an appointment for one o'clock this afternoon with Helen Wilcox at the bar overseers' office. I spoke with her at home last night, and when she heard you spoke directly with a represented client she was livid."

"Tell her she can calm down," I said.

I handed Doyle a copy of my resignation letter that was already in the mail and handed Sue Landry a CD with the recorded phone conversation

I'd had with Robbie Kendall. The phone call was a grotesque bar violation to be sure, but my guess was it would probably survive Doyle's motion to exclude it at Kendall's trial. Anyone in the state had a right to record his own calls, and since I wasn't a government agent Kendall's Fifth Amendment rights hadn't been violated either.

By noon I'd be banging nails with the crew Brian Crenshaw had working on the new motel they were building out on Route 7, so I didn't think Helen Wilcox would want to waste much time worrying about a guy who had just given up the law. I headed out of my office and from the doorway looked back at Sue Landry who had a big smile on her face and was clutching the CD with both hands. Doyle didn't look quite as happy.

"Could whichever one of you is last out the door please just shut it tight," I said. Then I walked over to the courthouse to give Fred Wells his $4,600 and tell him there had been a change in plans.

* * *

Woody Hanstein has been a trial lawyer for nearly 40 years, and he also now serves as the harbormaster for the coastal Maine town of Georgetown. He is the author of six published mysteries and a number of short stories.

MONSTROUSLY MISUNDERSTOOD
by Lorraine Sharma Nelson

Isha strode down the second floor hallway of the rambling old mansion, ignoring the chill skittering down her back. Dillon Walsh and Liam Kelly, two officers she worked best with, had shared with her the background of Witt's End.

Cursed.

Haunted.

House of monsters.

Those were some of the words they threw out describing the place. And by the looks of it, they weren't too far off. The place looked like a crypt. And the morose atmosphere was intensified by the storm raging outside. Typical Maine spring weather.

At the end of the hall, light spilled out from one of the rooms. Inside, Isha heard sobbing.

"Detective, you made it." Kelly said as she entered. Beside him, a woman wept quietly into a lace-edged hankie. And, stretched out on an enormous four-poster bed that looked like it belonged in Castle Dracula, lay the body of Oliver Davenport Wittley, master of Witt's End.

Correction, former master.

Isha acknowledged Jai Reddy, the medical examiner, and Mike Shannon, department crime photographer, with a nod, then turned her attention to the distraught woman. "Miss Wittley? I'm Detective Isha Naidu,

Misunderstood Police Force." Out of habit, she held out her badge for the woman to see. "I'm so very sorry about your father."

The woman nodded, sniffing.

"May I take a look...?" Isha indicated the body behind her.

"Oh, of course. Please..." Alyssa Wittley hastily stepped away as Isha stepped forward.

As she began a slow perusal of the body, Isha's detective instincts kicked in.

He was dressed in tweed trousers, complete with suspenders. His white shirt was open at the neck, revealing a moss-green ascot haphazardly knotted. Black riding boots completed the ensemble.

To the manor born, Isha thought, staring into Mr. Wittley's wide-open blue eyes. "You done here?" she asked Shannon.

"Yeah. He's all yours."

Isha gently closed Wittley's eyes. As she straightened, hers narrowed.

Something was off.

But what?

Her gaze, calculating now, roamed again over the deceased's body.

"Let's get him back to the morgue," Jai Reddy said over her shoulder.

"Just a sec," Isha said. "Something's not right."

"What?" Walsh asked, moving closer.

A second later, the entire crew was huddled behind Isha, staring at the body.

"What did you find?" Alyssa asked, her voice a gravelly whisper.

Isha studied the corpse.

Nothing.

Frustrated, she turned away, ready to turn the body over to the ME. But then she caught the flash of green at Wittley's throat.

She reached out, carefully untying the knotted ascot, spreading the fabric apart.

Wittley's throat was gouged, the skin split open like a macabre smile.

"I knew it!" Walsh burst out. "It's the Wittley Curse. Come to life."

Back at the station, Kelly fidgeted at his desk, casting furtive glances at Isha.

She sighed, tossing her pen down and turned to him. "Let's have it."

"You don't believe that crap about the werewolf legend, do you?"

"'Course not. But, apart from Wittley's daughter we have no suspects."

"What about money? That's always a motive."

"Read the report, Kelly. There is none. Didn't you notice the sad state of the house?"

Kelly nodded. "I'd say the butler did it, but there were no servants to question."

"They lived alone. Alyssa took care of her dad ..." Isha's voice faded away as she stared out at the rain.

"What is it?" Walsh asked.

"Just wondering what she's going to do now, living there all alone on the outskirts of Misunderstood." On impulse she reached for her phone. "Hello? Miss Wittley? It's Detective Naidu. Just thought I'd see if there's anything you need or—of course. No problem. I'll bring along the officers who were there with me. Yes, right away." Isha hung up and turned to the officers.

They were staring at her.

"Seriously?" Kelly said. "You're dragging us back there in this—" he glanced out the window— "this monsoon?"

"No offense, Detective," Walsh said quietly, "but there is no way I'm going back to that...that..."

"Mausoleum?" Isha supplied, getting to her feet.

He flinched.

Isha looked at both men as she buttoned her raincoat. "You can both come with me of your own volition, or I can pull rank on you. Which is it to be, gentlemen?"

Seventeen minutes later, Isha, Walsh and Kelly were in the living room of Witt's End.

"You don't know what this means to me," Alyssa Wittley poured fragrant Oolong tea into four dainty china cups. "The thought of spending my first night alone in the house was not something I relished."

"Why didn't you book a room at the Quinn in town?" Kelly asked.

Alyssa gave him a knowing look. "Hotels cost money, Officer Kelly."

"Yeah, but aren't you afraid of the curse?" Walsh burst out.

Alyssa set the teapot back on the tray with a clatter, a strangled sob escaping her.

"Are you okay?" Isha asked, leaning forward. "Should we call for a doctor?"

Alyssa shook her head, tears starting to flow down her pale, gaunt cheeks.

"Miss Wittley, please tell me what we can do to help."

"Call me Alyssa, please," she said, with a hiccup. "And there's nothing you can do. He's back from the dead. And he's out for revenge. And I'm next." She looked at Isha, eyes bright with tears. "The curse is real."

Okay, enough.

"Get a hold of yourself, Miss Witt...Alyssa. We're here to help. Please, tell us about it."

Alyssa cleared her throat. "It started over a hundred years ago. One of my ancestors supposedly was cursed by one of the tenants on his land, for...uh... ungentlemanly behavior toward the farmer's daughter. He said the Wittleys would bring forth monsters unto the world forevermore."

Alyssa smoothed out her pleated skirt before continuing. "About a year later, my ancestor's wife had a son. At first, they were ecstatic. You see, they'd been trying for years to start a family, but all the babies were stillborn. Until this little boy. According to my grandfather, the couple lavished their son with love and attention."

Alyssa blew her nose delicately. "But one day when the wife was bathing the boy, she noticed something odd. He was starting to develop hair all over his body. She mentioned to her husband that it was odd to see hair on a five-year-old, but he brushed aside her concerns.

"Well, the hair continued to grow. By the time he was ten he was covered with it. His parents could hardly bear the sight of him. They consulted specialists from all over the country, paying enormous amounts of money for them to examine the boy, but to no avail. None of the specialists stayed long, as the boy's appearance terrified them."

Alyssa leaned forward, her voice rising. "One of them told my ancestor that the boy looked more wolf than human. That was when it dawned on him that the curse had come true. His son was damned."

Alyssa sat back, shaking her head. "I don't know much more about the story. Supposedly, they kept the boy in an attic room, only letting him out at night. Over the years, rumors surfaced about sheep and cattle found with their throats brutally slashed. Of course, some people saw him clearly on nights when the moon was full. Loping through the fields and meadows. Some said they even heard him howl at the moon."

She raised eyes bright with unshed tears to Isha. "And he was just the first, you understand. Every other generation born since has produced a monster. A Wolf Man. It's more than a curse. It's fact. The Wittley family is cursed. My father's grisly death is proof."

The silence hung heavy in the room after she spoke. *Christ,* Isha thought, *this is straight out of a low budget horror movie. How in hell am I supposed to handle this?*

"Alyssa, are you telling me that you think the Wolf Man killed your father?"

Alyssa's cheeks flooded with color, her eyes narrowing. "I *know* he did. This has Elgin's name all over it."

"Your brother, Elgin?" Kelly asked.

"But…it said in the report that he's dead. From a childhood disease," Walsh added, shifting in his chair.

Alyssa waved a hand. "Oh yes, I know what the report says. It was necessary to have everyone think he was dead. Father always said it was for the best."

Isha's patience reached its limit. "Explain yourself, please. We need all the details."

"There's not much to tell, really. Elgin started showing the same symptoms that Wittley men before him have shown. It seems to skip a generation, so my father wasn't affected. But my grandfather was, and he remained in hiding in the attic for most of his life. Oh but, please, don't get the wrong idea about him. He was the kindest, gentlest of men. He didn't hurt a soul…"

"About Elgin?" Isha prodded.

"Yes. Well, Elgin, unlike Grandpapa, was a handful. Once he started sprouting hair everywhere and realized that the household staff was afraid of him, he started acting out."

What do you mean by 'acting out'?" Walsh asked.

"Well, he…uh…he started doing things. Horrible things. First to the household pets. Then to the livestock."

"Like what?" Kelly asked.

"Like smashing their heads with rocks. Or ripping their throats open. "

Isha swallowed the bile rising in her throat. "If he's not dead, as is clearly stated in the police report, where is he?"

"Father sent him overseas to boarding school after Mother died. Under an assumed name, of course. He'd become unmanageable by then. He'd sneak out at night and run around the countryside causing panic. He loved the idea of perpetuating the legend of the Wolf Man."

"But now he's back?"

Alyssa frowned. "That's just it. When Father fell ill, I called Elgin. He lives in a small town in southeast Wales. Anyway, he agreed that there would be no use in his returning since it would only agitate Father."

Alyssa covered her face with her hands. "Oh, this is just too horrible. Why did he have to come back? Why did he kill Father?"

"We don't have any proof that your brother killed him," Isha said softly.

"You don't understand." Alyssa lowered her hands. "A few days before Father died I heard a noise in his room and went to check on him. I…I saw Elgin standing by his bed. There was blood on his mouth. I must have fainted, for when I came to, I was alone. And now Father…" Alyssa shuddered. "Father is dead."

Isha's mind raced. She'd heard of this condition that Elgin suffered; the excess body and facial hair. It was extremely rare but it did exist. "Has he been in contact with you since you last saw him?"

"Why would he contact me? We barely knew each other growing up. He frightened me, you understand? I don't mind telling you that the happiest day of my life was when he was sent off to boarding school."

She clutched at Isha's arm. "You'll find him, won't you? You won't let him kill me like he did Father?"

"No one's killing anyone."

"Promise?"

"Promise," Isha said, patting her hand.

The drive back to the station in the rain was subdued.

When he turned the car into the station parking lot, Kelly shot Isha a questioning look. "What do you make of all this?"

"I think we've entered the Twilight Zone," she said, flipping up the hood of her raincoat. "Let's hope we can find our way out of it with all the answers."

"So you're saying there's nothing we can trace?' Isha asked.

Jai Reddy, the ME shook his head. "Someone's been very careful to leave no clues behind."

"Damn." Isha rubbed the back of her neck. "This is going from bad to worse." She headed back to her cubicle and seeing Walsh and Kelly at their desks, filled them in on the medical report.

"So, what now?" Kelly said. "We've looked everywhere but still can't find the S.O.B."

"Probably waiting for a full moon so he can howl at it," Walsh muttered, tapping away on his keyboard.

"Will you stop with the whole werewolf thing, already?" Isha snapped.

Walsh swiveled his chair to look at her. "Well then, how do you explain the reports we've received of sheep and cattle being mutilated?" He leaned closer. "In each case their necks have been slashed open. What more do you need to believe?"

"How about actual evidence? Until then—"

Isha's phone buzzed, cutting her off. She gave Walsh one last exasperated look before answering. "Detective Naidu." Alyssa Wittley's frantic voice screeched in her ear. "Okay, I'm on my way."

"What is it?" Kelly was already on his feet, reaching for his coat.

"Alyssa. Said her brother just tried to kill her."

"Here, drink this. Tell me again what happened," Isha patted the distraught woman on her shoulder as Walsh handed her a cup of tea.

"I already told you what happened. Why aren't you out looking for him?"

"I have some very qualified officers doing just that," Isha said. "In the meantime, let's go over it again."

Alyssa set her cup down with a clatter. "I told you, I was in the bathroom brushing my teeth, when I heard a noise in the bedroom. I went to check and…and there he was. Standing by the French doors. It was horrible. He looked like a wild animal." Alyssa broke down, sobbing.

Isha waited for her to calm down and tried for a soothing tone. "So, then what happened? You saw him and…"

"He…he lunged at me, his arms outstretched and his fingers curled into claws…" Alyssa hiccupped and reached for her tea.

"But you managed to evade him?"

"Yes. I ran back into the bathroom and locked the door." She clutched at Isha's arm. "Don't you see? With me dead, he inherits everything."

"Calm down, Alyssa," Isha turned to Walsh, on his hands and knees by the French doors leading to the patio. "Find anything?"

He held up a plastic bag. "Found some brown hairs stuck to the lock. I'll take them in to the lab right away."

Isha stared at the cross section of hair under the microscope in Jai Reddy's lab. "So, you're saying these are human?"

"Yep. DNA matches with Oliver Wittley, but they're too coarse to be his."

"Elgin."

"That would be my guess."

Isha pulled into the meadow abutting The Granary, a high-end restaurant that had opened up last year on what was once Andy Miller's dairy farm. The most recent reports of sightings seemed to be centered here.

She waved at the chef, Catriona Dunne, who was in her garden.

Isha checked the angle of the sun, hanging above the hills. She had maybe two hours before darkness fell.

After about an hour of looking for clues, Isha's feet began to hurt. Maybe she could grab a bite at The Granary and then—

She stopped, blinking at an opening in the rock wall before her. It was partially hidden. If she were walking from the opposite direction she'd have missed it.

Her breathing quickened. This would provide a perfect hiding place for someone.

She crawled inside, sniffing at the pungent scent of…what was that? Garlic? Onions? Oregano?

She flicked on her phone flashlight app, waving it around the confined space.

Bingo!

A sleeping bag lay neatly rolled up in one corner. And nearby sat a stack of books and a small canvas bag.

She snapped on a pair of latex gloves and opened the bag. Isha almost laughed. No human remains here. Just a couple of granola bars and half a bag of Oreos. Hardly werewolf food.

So where was that garlic aroma coming from? Something about it seemed familiar. Sighing, she closed the bag.

What now? Clearly, someone was living here. It didn't take a whole lot of smarts to figure out whom.

Elgin Wittley had come home.

She crawled out of the cave.

In time to see a flash of black vanish behind a boulder.

"Who's there?" Isha whipped out her gun, darting behind a bush. She held up her badge. "Police. Come on out."

She heard a scrambling sound and dashed out from behind the bush, following the sounds of footsteps heading away from her.

There. Isha saw someone long and lean run down the slope.

"Stop."

The figure wavered, turning to meet her gaze. Isha saw pale blue eyes coupled with white blonde hair, and long limbs clad in black, before the man spun and darted away from her.

She sprinted after him. He moved faster than she'd seen any human being move.

"Elgin! Wait, please. I want to help."

He slowed, glancing back at her, eyes wide. Terrified.

"Please. Trust me. Look." She made a show of holstering her gun, and held up her bare hands. "I just want to talk, okay? You can't keep running. People are looking for you and they won't be afraid to use force."

He quickened his steps.

"For crying out loud, Elgin. I can't keep up this pace."

He slowed. Stopped.

Thank God.

Isha doubled over, gasping. "About time. Give me a sec and we'll talk, okay?"

"What do you want?"

His accent surprised her. Until she remembered he'd been living in the U.K. from a young age. Of course he'd have a British accent. "Can we sit a moment?" She jerked her head toward a flat expanse of rock near a clump of wild grasses.

He hesitated, his gaze flicking over her shoulder. She glanced back. The roof of The Granary was visible from their location, smoke escaping from the tall twin chimneys. "You have two minutes. What do you want to know?"

Isha sat on the rock, massaging her calves. "For starters, why are you living in a cave like a—"

"Wild animal? Werewolf?"

She shook her head. "That's not what I was going to say. Answer the question, please."

He shrugged, jamming his hands into his jean pockets. "I had nowhere else to go. I'm not welcome at Witt's End and I don't have money for a hotel room."

"Why aren't you welcome there?"

Elgin's pale face tensed. "Ask my sister."

"I did. Why don't you tell me your side?"

"Not much to tell. My parents sent me away at an early age." He stared at Isha. "I'm sure you've heard the stories. Big, bad wolf running around the countryside scaring the natives half to death. Destroying livestock."

"Yes, but I don't believe any of it."

He snorted. "Then you're in the minority. Most folk around here think I'm a monster."

"Well, you can't deny that quite a few of the locals have had their livestock slaughtered since your father's death."

"Since I've returned, you mean."

"I've no idea when you returned. And I'm not in the habit of condemning people until I have proof of their crimes."

"In that case, Officer…"

"Detective Isha Naidu. Misunderstood Police Force."

Elgin grinned. "You're kidding, right?"

She smiled. "Nope. When did you arrive, Elgin?"

His smile disappeared. "Alyssa, sweet soul that she is, called me after he died. If she'd called me when he fell ill, I'd have come home to say my goodbyes. Maybe mend some fences…" He cleared his throat. "Instead, when I arrived she said the house was hers and I had no business being here."

Isha frowned. "She said she called you before he died."

"She lied."

"Well, why contact you about your father's death at all, then?"

"I don't know. That's what Cat—that's what I wondered."

Cat? Interesting. "Did you ask her about it?"

"Yeah. She said she called me in a moment of heartbreak." He laughed, a short gruff bark. "Heartbreak. What a joke. She has no heart."

"She says you killed your father. And that you broke into the house last night and tried to kill her."

Elgin winced. "It's not true. I'm not a murderer." His eyes pierced through

Isha. "I may not have had a good relationship with my father, but I would never kill him."

"Then come with me. Give yourself up until all this is sorted out."

"Go to jail? For something I haven't done." He backed up, his eyes narrowing. "I thought you were going to help me. I thought you were different. But, you're not. You're just like the others." His face flushed. "Do I look like a monster to you?"

"Of course not. Elgin, I'm trying to get to the bottom of this. If you're innocent, I'll prove it. I swear."

He stared at her for a long moment. "And if you can't, Detective Naidu? What happens to me? I rot in your jail?" He shook his head. "No thanks. I'll take my chances out here."

Before Isha could respond, he spun on his heel and loped off across the meadow.

"There you are." Kelly looked up as Isha strode to her desk.

"What's up?" She sank into her chair, tossing her coat onto her desk.

Kelly handed Isha a report. "One of Catriona Dunne's sous chefs reported that he walked into her office to find Elgin Wittley biting her neck."

"Oh, for—o" Isha sprang to her feet, grabbing her coat.

"Let's go." She tossed the car keys to Kelly. "You're driving."

"Isha, I already told you Tyrone was wrong. No one attacked me."

"He insists he saw Elgin Wittley with his mouth on your neck. And you were sobbing."

"Well, he's mistaken." She stood up, adjusting her apron. "It was dark in my office. I was with…someone else. Tyrone called the police before I could stop him. This fuss is all for nothing."

Isha scrutinized the woman for a moment before turning to Kelly. "Would you wait for me outside? I'll only be a moment."

Kelly nodded. "I'll be in the car."

When the door shut behind him, Isha turned to Catriona. "Tell me about your relationship with Elgin Wittley."

Catriona stiffened. "I don't have time for this. I have a full house for dinner tonight and lots of preparation still to do, so if you'll excuse me..." She started for the door.

"I know you've been feeding him. I smelled your Bolognese in that cave. If you know something, please—"

The door slammed shut as Catriona exited the room.

Isha was in bed staring at the ceiling, when her phone rang.

"Hello?"

"Isha?"

She sat up. "Cat?" She checked the time. "It's 2:15 in the morning. What's up?"

"You have to stop Elgin. He's going over to the house. Oh God, he's so angry with her."

"With Alyssa?"

"Yes, please stop him before he does something really stupid."

"I'm on my way. Call the station. Ask for Officer Walsh. He's on the night shift. Have him meet me at Witt's End."

Isha made it to Witt's End in record time. Gun in hand she slid out of the car.

She entered the house and moved quietly through the shadowed hallway. The downstairs area was dark. Empty.

Isha made her way upstairs, where she heard muffled voices coming from the master bedroom. She took a deep breath. "Elgin? Alyssa? It's Detective Naidu. I'm coming in."

Silence.

"I am armed, so please, don't try anything." Isha pushed the door wide and peeked inside.

Elgin had a hand around Alyssa's throat. She flailed, trying to ward him off.

"Elgin, let go of her." Isha raised her gun.

He scowled. "Cat called you, didn't she? Damn it. I told her not to get involved."

"She got involved when she supplied you with food while you've been hiding out. I'm going to ask you one more time, Elgin. Let her go."

"I can't," he said. "It's all her doing, don't you see? She killed Father. Slashed his throat to make it look like I'd done it. She perpetuated the myth that I'm a monster—a werewolf. She wants me to be arrested. Or better yet, killed, so she can inherit everything free and clear."

"That may be," Isha said, "and we'll get to the truth, I promise. But you need to let her go now."

"I can't."

"Elgin, don't make me shoot."

He hesitated, then slowly relaxed his fingers around Alyssa's neck. She tore his hand away, and scrambled over to Isha, sobbing.

"He tried to kill me. You saw it for yourself. Now, do you believe me?" She threw a venomous glare at Elgin, who stood silently by, head drooping, shoulders slumped.

"Well, aren't you going to arrest him?"

Walsh chose that moment to burst through the door, gun raised, breathing hard.

"Hello there," Isha said, smiling grimly. "Nice of you to join us." She jerked her head toward Elgin. "Let's take Mr. Wittley in for questioning."

Isha felt a hand on her shoulder, shaking her.

"Detective? Are you all right?"

She opened her eyes to see both Walsh and Kelly bending over her. "I'm fine," she mumbled, touching the back of her head tentatively. "What happened?"

"You tell us," Kelly said, helping her up.

Isha shook her head, wincing. "I don't know exactly. I was interrogating Elgin. One minute he was sitting across the table from me. The next, I was seeing stars." Isha looked from one man to the other. "I take it he's escaped."

"Looks like it," Walsh said.

"Put out an APB on him," Isha said. "I'll go tell the chief the bad news."

After informing Chief O'Connor of the escape, Isha called Alyssa.

"What do you mean, he's escaped?" Alyssa shrieked over the phone. "How could he escape from a building filled with policemen?"

"Well, he stole one of the officers' coats and—"

"I don't care how he did it. Just find him before he comes for me again."

"We'll find him. Every officer on the force is out looking for him."

"I feel so much better."

"Don't worry," Isha said, ignoring Alyssa's sarcasm. "I won't let the bad guy get away."

Isha stifled a yawn as she checked her watch; two hours and still nothing. She rubbed her eyes and leaned back, scanning the shadowed house and grounds.

Five minutes later, a tall, slim figure in a coat slipped behind the mansion and headed toward the meadow. As she watched, the person switched on a flashlight and scaled the fence with ease, dropping lightly onto the other side. The action caused the hood of the coat to flip back, revealing short, spiky, white-blonde hair that shone in the light of the half moon.

Gotcha.

Isha followed, keeping to the shadows.

The figure moved swiftly, loping through the long grasses. Heading toward Marty Maguire's property.

Isha kept pace, wishing she could see clearly in the darkness. Dawn was still a few hours away and the night was an inky blackness that made it tough to see anything.

Ahead of her, Isha heard a grunt, followed by a thud. The suspect must have scaled the fence bordering Marty's property.

Isha scrambled after the shadowy figure, her heartbeat quickening as she realized they were heading toward the barn.

She watched from a crack in the door as the person lit a lamp, then approached the cow stalls, a wicked-looking knife gleaming in the soft light.

Wait for it. Wait for it.

"Stop!" Isha said, drawing her gun as she stepped inside. The person froze, knife raised, ready to slash down across a poor, unsuspecting cow.

"It's over. Drop the knife."

A low growl issued from deep within the person's chest. Then the knife flashed down toward the cow.

And Isha pulled the trigger.

The figure stiffened for a second, then slumped to the ground.

Isha hurried over, requesting medical assistance on her walkie-talkie. She crouched beside the prone figure, noting the delicate features of Alyssa Wittley and gently removed the wig.

Chief Aidan O'Connor sat back in his chair, hands clasped behind his head. "So, you planned the whole escape, guessing Alyssa would try something else to implicate him?"

Isha nodded. "Yes. Elgin was safely tucked away in our isolation pad the whole time."

"Explain it to me again."

"It's simple. Alyssa killed her father and all those animals in an effort to frame Elgin. With him in prison, she'd own the house and be able to sell it and the land to a developer."

The chief nodded. "Okay. So that whole werewolf story..."

"Perpetuated by Alyssa to make people afraid of Elgin. Some people still remember his childhood affliction." She turned to Jai Reddy. "Want to explain that part?"

"He had a condition called Hirsutism. It's when a person develops excess body hair. Apparently, the Wittley family line has a mutated gene, causing this affliction. It pops up in every other generation. It's why Elgin was affected but his father was not."

"Hmmm. But he looks normal now."

"That's because he's had laser hair removal. It's a permanent way to remove hair. After examining him, Hugh—Doc Sweeney—determined that some areas on his body were a little more resistant to the laser procedure than others. One such area is the back of his wrists, where a small tuft of hair still grows. It's why we were able to get samples at Witt's End. He brushed the back of his hand against the door jamb and left stray hairs behind."

"So, he inherits Witt's End now?" O'Connor asked, looking at Isha.

"Yes. But he doesn't plan on selling. He's turning it into a home for children with unusual medical conditions who are shunned by society."

"Is he? Good for him."

"Yes sir. He's a good man. He's had a rough time of it, but I think he'll be okay moving forward."

"Where is he, by the way, now that he's a free man?"

Isha smiled. "At The Granary. Cat's making him her famous Bolognese."

* * *

Lorraine Sharma Nelson grew up globally, constantly having to adapt to different cultures. Writing was her escape from the reality of always being the new girl in school. Her short stories have been published in sci-fi, fantasy, horror, and mystery/crime anthologies, and usually feature an Indian protagonist. Her Twitter and Instagram handle is @loneriter and at her website: www.lorrainesharmanelson.com.

WHAT LOVE IS
by Brenda Seabrooke

Long dark hair swirls like seaweed around the woman lying face-down half on sand, half in the cold water between the rocks. In the dark she looks like a sea creature with pale appendages flung about, brought in by the tide. A wall of fog hovers off shore.

Dusty Dilton reported her. "I was walking my dog after supper, looking for tide pickings when I seen her." He rushed to a phone booth on the coast road, made the call and returned. The kerosene lamp he uses for a light sheds a soft glow on the scene. "There she is, Deputy."

She's dead but I put a finger to her throat anyway. I play my flashlight around but find no human footprints near the body besides my own and Dusty's dog's. "Good dog."

"Lady's good company since the wife died."

The department budget doesn't allow for radios. Maybe in twenty years, Sheriff McCabe says. Our small county and town are administered by the six-man sheriff's department in Wilson Point, a dot on the Maine coast. No beaches, just rocks except where sand is sometimes dragged in by waves to make a temporary pocket of beach that the next nor'easter could obliterate. The harbor isn't deep enough for a fishing fleet and the water is too cold for swimming. The track that leads to the cove is rocky and bad for the tires. I drive to the coast road phone booth and call in the wash-up.

On my return I widen my search. A single female on a boat would be a rarity in my estimation. Some Maine women might go out alone in iffy weather but more likely she'd been on a boat with others and had fallen off. I scan the rocks on both sides and the water's edge but find nothing to connect to her.

Wilson Pointers are surprised I hadn't come here for the boating or fishing. I might cast a line off a rock but that's as close as I go. I had enough ocean on transports bouncing up and down in the middle of the Atlantic, dodging U-boats. In peacetime the sea is a dangerous and chancy thing without any help from humans. I came here after the war wanting cold and wet as different from the hot dry desert of North Africa as I could find. And small. I didn't want cities or large masses of humans. Or beaches crowded with sweating bodies.

In almost eight years here, I've seen a few wash-ups but they were in worse shape than this one. Most of my job is breaking up fights on Saturday night and finding husbands who haven't come home on time. We don't take those on but keep an eye out. Folks don't know how much a cop knows about them but in a small town like this one, we'd have to be blind or dead not to know Roby Harlow sees Charley Barton on Wednesday nights and Bill Wharton on Tuesdays. Sometimes they mix their nights up and we have to break it up. Each of Ruby's gentlemen who comes for a reading of the cards thinks he's the only one. Ruby thanks us with free readings accompanied by smooth scotch supplied by a friend. Last week she told me I would meet a woman with long dark hair.

The coroner pulls up in the morgue van. "What do you have for me, John?"

Phil Needham's war was in the Pacific. You'd think that ocean had been enough for him but he said Wilson Point sported no palm trees or tropical flowers and that was different enough for him. He was from Boston, meant for a specialty, but like me he chose oblivion. Sometimes I think the town should change its name to Oblivion Point.

Unlike me, he's married and has two boys. He also functions as a medical examiner and in that the county is more than lucky. Most coroner posts don't require training. Phil was happy to take on the job. As head of the local hospital he saw most of the victims before they died. It's a small step to pronounce someone dead at the scene.

Ace Czabo, the newest deputy, drives up in his cream-and-black DeSoto

Sportsman, radio playing Eddie Fisher singing his latest, "Oh! My PaPa." Good the sheriff isn't around to hear it. He hates Fisher. Won't let his teenagers play his records in his house. The girls are lucky he's usually away sheriffing.

Phil unfolds his rangy frame from the van.

Ace follows on his heels. "Whatcha got here?"

"Stay back, Ace. Give him room to work."

"A wash-up? Or a murder?" Ace wants to join the FBI. He's always hoping for important cases that'll look good on his record. So far he hasn't had the balls to apply but plans to any day now though he would first need a serious haircut. Meanwhile he dates every girl on the Maine coast. Once or twice. A good-looking guy, he hasn't figured out what girls want yet. I don't think he knows what he wants either, just what he thinks he wants.

"Did you search the perimeter, Deputy?" Ace asks me as if I'm the green one, not he.

"Ten yards in each direction. Why don't you take it farther?"

The night sheds no moon glimmer on the Atlantic. We hear the waves but can't see them unless we turn a light seaward. Lights from the vehicles and lantern only go so far. When Ace doesn't move, Dusty says. "Here, son, take Lady with you."

Ace takes the piece of rope tied to Lady's collar and clambers over the rocks, his flashlight darting from side to side like an airport searchlight before he takes a step.

The lab's coat gleams white in the dark as she takes the point. The department should spring for a leash to reward her.

"What does it look like, Doc?"

"Female. Dead."

"Drowning?"

"Can't tell till I get her on the table. She hasn't been dead long. No sea creatures been at her yet."

Her clothing looks intact, navy pedal pushers, blue top. Her hair is dark with either flecks of gray or sand caught in the strands along with brown seaweed. In the light her skin looks pearly. "She hasn't been in long."

"Looks that way. She washed up from somewhere nearby." He fetches a bag from the van and eases her into it without my help. She's a little woman, maybe not five feet. One bare foot sticks out. It's small and dainty and the nails are perfectly pink. I wonder if Perfectly Pink is the name of a polish color and I feel sad at the thought of her choosing that perfect shade for the last time.

"Probably off a boat somewhere. I don't recognize her from around here." I know the inhabitants of the county and some from adjacent counties. Especially the ones who get into trouble drinking too much at the Blue Moose on Saturday nights. This is Monday. People drink on Mondays even here but not usually as much as the weekends. Most have to be up early for work during the week. That's not fun with a hangover and alcohol for blood. On Monday they're usually still recovering from the weekend.

I help the Doc carry her to the morgue-mobile as Ace calls it. She hardly weighs anything. I carried my share of bodies in the desert. They were often not intact but weighed more than she does even soaking wet. An immobile body is heavier, no matter the size, but she's an easy carry.

We slide her in and Phil slams the doors just as Ace yells somewhere in the dark.

"Sounded like he said another one," Phil says.

We follow the direction of his shout. Dusty brings his lantern. The rocks are smooth, like the backs of partly submerged whales but here and there a smaller piece has been flung up by the sea. These are easy to trip over but Dusty's light helps us avoid them. We find Ace crouched over a body lying face-down across a rock about twenty feet past where I searched earlier.

"I think this one's alive."

Phil leans down and touches the pulse point on the man's neck. "Yep. He's alive, all right."

I scan the area around him while Phil turns the man's face to the left resting on his arm and pushes on his back above the waist. Footprints wouldn't show on the rock unless they were wet.

The wash-up is an older man, maybe in his fifties. He wears navy shorts and a white pullover, the favored boating attire of a professional man from

Boston or Portland. His legs are pale in the lantern's glow and haven't seen the sun this summer though it's late June already. His face is pasty with an abrasion on his chin.

Phil pushes on the man's back about ten times when suddenly he coughs, chokes and spits sea water. Phil lets him continue for a minute before turning him over and propping him against the rock. Drooping brown eyes under graying brows gaze up at us. He seems confused, understandable after an almost-drowning. Lady walks over and nudges Phil with her nose as if to say well-done human, too bad you couldn't do that to the other one. She lies beside the man as if to warm his thin, cold bones.

Absently the man's hand reaches out to pet Lady's head. I remember hearing Hitler liked his dogs so we couldn't judge him on that but Lady seems concerned for him and that carries more weight. Dogs are excellent judges of humans.

Phil sends Ace back to the van for a blanket as he checks pulse and eye movement.

"Where am I?" The man's voice sounds raw and raspy but that might not be normal. Vomiting salt water can change the timbre of a voice.

I've seen things washed up from the sea but they were always dead long before they reached shore. This is my first experience with a live one. I squat so he won't have to look up. "Do you remember your name, sir?"

"Yes. I'm Dr. Dennis Moxlee."

"Where are you from, Dr. Moxlee?"

"Councilton, Iowa."

"Do you know what state you're in?"

"I was in Maine this morning. I think."

Ace returns with the blanket to wrap around the doctor. He brought a thermos with coffee in it which Phil lets the doctor sip.

The doctor grimaces as the sugar and cream Ace poured in his coffee hit his taste buds. Ace was too young for the war when we drank it with nothing in it, sometimes it wasn't even real coffee.

The sugar revives the man somewhat. His story takes shape. Ace takes notes in the lamplight. Lady puts her head on the man's knee.

"We drove up from Old Orchard Beach yesterday. We spent the night in Whale Beach and this morning rented a boat to take us along the coast. We hired a guide but he took sick and we went on without him. We weren't going far."

"We?"

"My wife Jeanette and me. We always wanted to do that. Jeanette's ancestor Thomas Rogers settled Old Orchard Beach in 1657." He coughs.

None of us look at each other when he mentions Jeanette. We're pretty sure we know where she is.

"Sir, how do you spell Moxlee?"

"Like it sounds. M-o-x-l-e-i-g-h." His cough sounds ragged.

"No more questions, Deputy. He needs to go to the hospital. You take him. I'll follow you. Ace can follow me. Unless you want him to look around any more."

"I think we've seen everything." A camera to take pictures of the wash-ups would be helpful but the budget didn't stretch that far this year either. I have a good memory. I doubt I'll ever forget a single detail of tonight's scene. I haven't forgotten any in Africa.

Ace and I help Dr. Moxleigh up. He staggers a bit as if his knees have turned to jelly but with Dusty leading the way we make it back to the vehicles.

"Do you need to lie down?" I ask the doctor.

"No, I can sit up."

I put him in the front passenger seat of the Ford where I can keep an eye on him if he has a seizure or a heart attack. I climb in and start the engine. No need for the siren. The night is quiet. People are home probably watching *I Love Lucy*.

Dr. Moxleigh seemed almost normal when we reached the car but now he subsides into the seat with a sigh. I drive with one eye on him to the small ten-bed hospital run single-handedly by Phil with the help of nurses. The morgue is in the basement.

Ace pulls up behind me at the emergency entrance and helps me take Dr. Moxleigh inside. He leans heavily onto Ace on his left. "Sorry," he says two or three times.

We leave him with Claire Duquette, the new RN, who hustles him into a shower to remove the sea water and warm him.

"Doc is downstairs," I say with meaning. She catches on immediately and nods. I tell her I'll come back in an hour to talk to him.

I swing by the station to start paperwork and Ace takes the patrol.

When I return, Dr. Moxleigh is in a deep sleep.

"Dr. Needham said to let him sleep. It's the best restorative."

"Did he say anything else, Dr. Moxleigh I mean?"

"No, just 'thank you' and 'that felt so good' after the shower. He crawled into bed and was instantly out."

I nod. Despite the size of the town, I haven't met Duquette before. Her dark hair is in a low bun under the starched white wings of her cap. "The sea is tiring even when one hasn't been in it for hours."

"I'm from inland. I like to look at the sea but I wouldn't like to be in it. It shrivels the fingers." Her nails are clear of polish but I bet she would paint her toenails Really Red.

"Where're you from?"

"Hanover, New Hampshire."

"Dartmouth country."

The phone rings on her desk. "Call me when he wakes up."

She reaches for the receiver. "Will do."

I grab a few hours sleep in an empty cell where the sheriff finds me the next morning. He sends Ace to get breakfast for me. I fill him in on the night's events while he eats my hash browns. His wife refuses to cook any for him until he loses a pound or twenty.

The hospital calls at eleven but it isn't Claire Duquette. I hadn't expected it to be. She had the night shift but I'd had hopes. Miss Carmen O'Reilly is older and local. This isn't her first wash-up patient. The sheriff drives us over.

"He ate a good lunch," Nurse O'Reilly says as we check in.

"Did he say anything?"

"He asked if his wife was here." Her lips tighten to a firm line. "I told him no."

I don't relish what we have to do. Sheriff McCabe slows. "I'll let you do it."

I go in alone. "Dr. Moxleigh, how are you feeling?"

He's sitting up. A smile flickers and goes out. "Like a beached whale."

"I can imagine." I study him. Not a spare ounce of fat. His face seems gaunt, his eyes still droopy but that could be from exhaustion. I try to find a way to tell him about his wife but he beats me to it.

"Have you found my wife?"

"Yes..."

"She's dead, isn't she?"

"How did you know?"

A slow sad smile stretches his mouth. "The nurse said she's not here."

"Actually we found her before we found you. Do you remember the dog last night?"

"White dog?"

"Lady is her name."

"I thought that was a dream. She was lying beside me to keep me warm like a fairy tale animal."

"She found your wife."

A tear slides out of his left eye.

"Can you describe your wife's clothing?"

"Blue pedal pushers. Blue blouse."

The sheriff has been listening outside the door. He joins us. I introduce him to remind the doctor in case he's forgotten.

"You're from Councilton, Iowa. Tell us what you're doing so far from home."

"My wife had never seen the ocean. I'd told her about the Pacific. We plan to go to Hawaii for Christmas but decided to go fishing in Maine this year. She likes to pond fish at home and wanted to try it on the ocean. My wife's family was from Maine but we'd never been to the east coast. We flew to New York and saw the sights. We took a train to Kittery, rented a car and drove to Old Orchard Beach for my wife's family history. We stopped at the hotel in Whale Beach where we booked a boat and guide but he became ill and we decided to go without him. We were only going straight out from shore, to fish and come straight back in. We didn't count on the weather. It was nice when we set out."

He stops and reaches for a water glass off the tray table. His hand shakes as he drains it. He asks me to refill it and drinks more, his hand shaking the whole time.

"I can't seem to get enough water. Ironic isn't it?" Finally he puts the glass down. One eye closes as if he were falling asleep. In a moment he opens it.

The sheriff speaks up. "What happened to put you in the water?"

"I guess it was a wave. I didn't see it. I was trying to turn the boat but it didn't seem responsive. I felt it shudder and then I noticed water around my feet. I thought the cocks or something like that were supposed to drain it but they didn't seem to be working. Jeanette pulled her feet up to get them out of the water but more came in and the boat leaned sideways. Before I could get to the life raft, we were overboard. I reached for Jeanette and found only water. It was cold. So cold."

Tears spill out of his sad sleepy eyes.

"You weren't wearing life jackets?"

"No. Would that have made a difference?"

"Maybe."

"What was the guide's name?"

He doesn't remember. "She said the girls would love this." He chokes up and closes both eyes.

We leave him to his grief. The sheriff spares him from identifying the body. He has no doubts the wash-up is Jeanette Moxleigh.

"Maybe he'll be more chipper tomorrow," I say, "but I wouldn't count on it."

The sheriff goes home for lunch. I pick up a sandwich from the Codfish Café.

Ace left the autopsy report on my desk. I eat as I read. Mrs. Jeanette Moxleigh, 32, died from cardiac arrest. Heart attack. She didn't drown.

No water in her lungs. Five feet tall, slightly underweight at eighty pounds. She had a gash on her arm and a few abrasions from rocks but hadn't been in the water long enough to sustain interference from sea creatures. Doc's conclusion: death brought on by shock and exposure.

I report the findings to the sheriff when he returns from lunch. He listens with his eyes out the window on the sunny Atlantic without a hint of yesterday's weather. If the Moxleighs had waited one more day to go out, they would now be enjoying their vacation.

"It was probably a rogue wave," he says, "and went downhill from there into the deep."

That is the most poetic thing I have ever heard Sheriff McCabe say.

"File it as death by sea," he says finally removing his glasses and pinching the bridge of his nose.

I go back to the hospital to tell Dr. Moxleigh he's free to go but he checked out right after we left the hospital when Phil released his wife for burial.

"How did he leave?"

"In the clothes he'd been wearing. We put them through the wash to get the salt out. No shoes."

"I meant did he call a cab, get on a bus, what?"

"He went over to the garage and got a lift from somebody, I guess. That's what he said he would do."

"How did he pay for things?"

"He had cash in his wallet and a Diners Club card. It had all been wet but dried overnight and was intact. He left this to buy a leash for Dusty's dog or something." She hands me a well-washed tenner.

I glance at my watch. It's after four now. I drive to Whale Beach, stopping at the Stabler Brothers Funeral Home on the way. Arnie Stabler tells me Dr. Moxleigh came by to arrange for his wife to be returned to Iowa.

He'd paid for two nights at the Whale Beach Hotel. He checked out around three and left in the rental car. I ask the clerk about the couple but he says they only spent one actual night and he hadn't been on duty then. I ask to see the room. Somebody is playing an old Billie Holiday record as I walk down the hall, "You Don't Know What Love Is." Her slow sad voice follows me like a dirge to the room which has been cleaned. Nothing to see there. I talk to the maids. Only one had contact with the couple.

"Did they say anything at all when you brought them towels?"

"He wasn't there. He'd gone to rent a boat. She said good morning but that was all. She seemed far away."

"Far away?"

"In her own little world. Oh—she did say one thing. They were going fishing. She said she had never been."

"She'd never been fishing on the ocean or never been fishing at all?"

"I couldn't say. I thought she meant on the ocean. I told her to watch out. The sea can be smooth as glass and suddenly a squall will blow up. She just smiled and said they weren't going far."

She had never been fishing before. Could be ocean fishing or fishing at all. I ask around. Nobody knows of any guides getting sick the day before. Could have been somebody the doctor met in a bar. Or nobody at all. Or another body could wash up. Too flimsy and too speculative for a district attorney to build a case around but I report it to the sheriff the next morning. He agrees with me.

The next morning Dusty comes in wearing a length of rope coiled around his waist. One end is tied to Lady's collar. "Found this ring preserver washed up this morning." He'd tied it to the other end of the rope at his waist.

"Where?"

"Not far from the wash-ups last night."

Without markings, the preserver could be from any boat.

"Look what Lady found." He points to his new belt.

The rope is medium weight, the kind sold in every general, marine supply or hardware store in Maine. I give him the leash and dog food I picked up yesterday along with the change. "The doc left the money for it."

He leans over and unties Lady. "Lady, look what the nice doctor gave you." She sniffs it as he snaps it to her collar.

I scratch her ears. "She earned it. Where did she find the rope?"

"On the rocks near where we found the doctor."

A rope. One preserver. A possible conflict in a comment that the wife made to the hotel maid. A missing guide. A husband who leaked tears as he talked about her. I didn't doubt his sadness or his tears. They were genuine. Despite the slight discrepancies there was still no case to be made. The rope and ring could be from any boat. The victim died from a heart attack. Nothing sinister there. The Coast Guard searches but never finds the boat. It could be washed up on Greenland's empty shore somewhere. The owner collects insurance and retires inland to a lake cabin. He doesn't remember anything about a guide when I track him down.

One January day when snow piles up outside the station and I am not as averse to the heat of the North African desert as I was, the phone rings. Ace answers. "It's long distance. Operator asked for you."

I take the receiver. "Deputy Colton."

Dr. Moxleigh's voice sounds strained and far away, farther than Iowa, maybe as far as Japan. "I need to tell you a story, Deputy. I hope you have time to listen because I may not be able to call again."

"I have time."

"Once there was a happy family, a young doctor with a beautiful wife and three precious little girls. After Pearl Harbor the doctor was sent to the Pacific where he saw untold horrors of what man can do to man. Were you in the war?"

"North Africa. Sicily. Anzio."

"Then you know."

I do. It was a club we all joined and wished we'd been blackballed.

"The young doctor returned, determined to paper over those memories with his family life: birthday parties, Christmas pageants, church dinners, school plays. And to an extent he did. His wife was a member of all the clubs for ladies: garden, book, cards, sewing, missionary, but one by one, she dropped out. The last event was a Christmas open house for the garden club she volunteered their house for. That morning, house and tree were undecorated, the floor needed vacuuming. The doctor who had come home late the night before cancelled appointments and threw decorations on the tree. He called his wife's last friend. She rushed over with garden club members and they prepared the house while the wife stayed in her bedroom, ill, the doctor told them.

"She was ill but not with a disease. She had a habit acquired during the war from an old doctor who still believed in giving laudanum to women to quiet their nerves and stop them from calling him in the middle of the night. She was soon addicted. The young doctor threatened the old doctor but didn't want to report him because he was a pillar of the community and had delivered almost everybody in the town. The doctor's wife continued to see him until the old doctor died. The wife then turned to her husband and he, God help him, provided it."

"Didn't he try to get her clean?"

"He did but every attempt ended in disaster. She was beyond pitiful. He couldn't bear to see her in such pain. He'd seen enough agony in the Pacific. He continued to supply her, keeping her comfortable and healthy while maintaining his practice and taking care of his girls. Between patient appointments he drove them to dance class and music lessons. He bought their clothes in Kansas City while his wife slept her days away in a loopy haze. He braided their hair and checked their homework. He was mother and father to those girls. Everything was under control until he developed a fast-moving and incurable degenerative disease. His girls were in high school. He couldn't leave them responsible for an addicted mother. He couldn't let his wife go through the shame and agony of incarceration and detoxification. She wouldn't survive it and her pain would be intolerable. He found a way to end it without shame or pain. His daughters would be safe. He could die in peace."

"How did he do it?"

"They were drinking Bloody Marys while fishing. When the weather turned, he put a few drops of chloral hydrate in her drink and she became drowsy. He helped her to a bunk where she fell asleep. The last thing she said was thank you.

"He injected her vein with air and held her until her life ended painlessly. He sliced the injection site to look like a ragged cut and threw the scalpel and hypodermic needle overboard. He tied her to a ring buoy and ran the boat in a circle until he managed to swamp it. The increasing waves did the rest. It was getting dark and fog was building up. He got on the ring and towed his wife to shore, depositing her on the sand. He removed the rope and threw it and the preserver into the waves. He found a landing place for himself on the rocks. Then he lay down and waited for discovery."

"Wasn't he cold?"

"Cold, tired, heartsick and grieving. Don't forget grieving."

"No"

"We never forget grieving, even when they aren't dead. We just learn to live with it."

Or die with it but he already knows that.

"I couldn't leave her to suffer and die alone."

The next day the police chief in Councilton calls to tell me Dr. Moxleigh died late last night after the phone call. He left word to notify me. I inform Sheriff McCabe.

"He killed her."

"A mercy killing," he says.

"Still."

"Sometimes life is rough, son."

He hasn't called me son in six years.

"She might have liked to continue living. Maybe she would've cleaned up and looked after her children."

"Maybe." He leaves to buy his wife some flowers.

Life is rough but we have to go on living it. The doctor did what he thought was bestfor his daughters. I didn't think he did the right thing but I couldn't deny his pain. The disease might've affected his thinking. Whatever, he's beyond that now.

I call the hospital. Claire is on day duty. "How do you feel about going dancing tonight?"

"Today is Wednesday not Saturday."

"We can go Saturday, too, if you want to. And Thursday and Friday."

* * *

Brenda Seabrooke is the author of twenty-two stories published in literary reviews, Sherlock Holmes anthologies, and this fourth entry in The Best New England Crime Stories. She is the author of twenty-three books for young readers including SCONES AND BONES ON BAKER STREET: SHERLOCK'S (maybe!) DOG AND THE DIRT DILEMMA and its sequel THE RASCAL IN THE CASTLE: SHERLOCK'S (possible!) DOG AND THE QUEEN'S REVENGE (Belanger Books). She received a grant from the National Endowment for the Arts and Emerson College's Robie Macaulay Award plus awards for her children's books.

HAVEN
by Joseph Walker

Winner of the Al Blanchard Award for 2019

I was sitting with Jess and Angie on the front porch of the big house at Haven, waiting for Mason Barnes to come try to kill his wife. He was running later than we'd expected and my attention was wandering.

"If my legs were a little longer," I said, "I could put my heels up on the porch railing and tilt the chair onto its back legs and pull my hat down over my eyes."

Jess and Angie were sitting together on a swinging bench a few feet to my right. Angie, focused on the long driveway leading down the hill, ignored me. Ignoring me was one of Angie's favorite pastimes. Jess snorted. "Only if by *a little longer* you mean ten inches," she said.

"It would look cooler when Mason shows up," I said. "Just sitting here in an old kitchen chair with all four legs on the floor makes it seem like I'm waiting on him."

"We are waiting on him."

"Sure, but why give him a big head about it?"

"Why do you want to look cool to a wife-beating drunk?" Angie asked.

"General principle of the thing," I said. "Better to look cool than not."

"You forgot how you're dressed," Jess pointed out. "It's a lost cause."

I was trying to think of someone who looked cool in a deputy's uniform when a cloud of dust lifted into the air down where the long gravel drive met the highway. A second later we heard an engine coming.

"Here we go," Jess said. She stood up and cracked her knuckles, stretched her neck back and forth. She was wearing a tank top and a pair of denim shorts and her arms and legs showed a lot of hard, defined muscle. The left side of her head was shaved down to a light blond fuzz, and a curtain of neon purple hair hung down on her right. Sometimes people get distracted by the hair and miss the muscle. That's a mistake.

"Go easy, champ," I said. "We've got fourteen different charges to hang on him."

"He'll walk," said Angie. "They always walk."

That wasn't true, but I let it go. Angie's earned the white-hot anger that keeps her moving through the day, from one crisis to the next. That anger turned the sprawling compound her family had owned for a century and a half into Haven, a shelter for battered women and kids. The house we were sitting in front of had been built by men who got rich when Goldwood was one of the centers of Maine's lumber industry. From what I knew of them, their women and their children were essentially trophies. Every time I came out here, I wondered what they would think of what their fiery lesbian progeny had made.

A fairly new blue pickup I'd never seen before came through the trees where the driveway pierced them, barreling along a little faster than was probably prudent on the loose dry gravel. I might be able to tack grand theft auto onto Mason's laundry list of recent felonies. The truck sliced around the curve and slid to a stop about ten yards off, with the driver's door facing us. It popped open before the truck was completely still and Mason stepped unsteadily out. He hadn't slowed at the sight of my cruiser parked alongside the barn and he didn't seem bothered by my uniform now. He certainly showed no signs of thinking I looked cool, so apparently the vote on that was unanimous. A tire iron dangled from his right hand as he slammed the door and peered up at the three of us, his eyes red and sunken in his pale, bearded face.

"Looking good, Mason," I said. "A credit to your family and upbringing. You're under arrest."

"Fuck you, Wade," he said.

I nodded. "Eloquently expressed, but you're still under arrest." I hadn't moved from the chair, but I'd popped the strap at the top of my holster. Mason was just the kind of slow-thinking asshole to show you a tire iron and then suddenly remember a piece tucked under his shirttails.

"I wanna see Brenda," he said. He took a step toward the stairs. Out of the corner of my eye I watched Jess start to bounce a little, shifting her weight from foot to foot.

"Not a chance," said Angie. "You put her in the hospital last time you saw her, you inbred piece of shit."

"Fuck you too, you dyke bitch," Mason said. He raised his voice to a holler. "Brenda, baby, you in there? C'mon out, honey."

"Honey," said Jess.

"You like that?" I asked.

"Classy."

"Well, you know, Mason's a classy guy. Always has been."

"That's just what I thought when I saw Brenda's X-rays," Jess said. "Mason, that classy, classy guy."

Mason was staring at her, his lip curled. Now that he'd been out of the truck for a minute, I could smell him, even at this distance. Old clothes, dip, spilled beer, unwashed hair. I'd been looking for him for four days, ever since he took the frustrations of his dimming world out on his wife and then ran off into the humid night. From the reek of him he'd spent those four days in backseats and shallow ditches. A couple of hours ago he turned up at the body shop where he worked and beat living hell out of the owner, telling him Brenda was next. His next stop had been the small county hospital, where he broke a nurse's nose and a security guard's arm before being convinced Brenda was no longer there. Mason didn't have much of an IQ, but he'd lived in Goldwood County all his life, and he knew where a woman in Brenda's condition would probably end up. Haven.

Now that he was finally here he stabbed a filthy finger in the air at Jess. "You don't know me, bitch."

"Actually she does, Mason," I said. "She went to school with us, remember?"

"I'm gonna be real fucking hurt if you don't remember me, Mason," Jess said. "I'm the chick who broke a chair on your face one day in the lunchroom."

"It's that shoddy damn furniture they put in the public schools," I explained, directing my comment to Angie. "Shameful."

Angie shook her head, but didn't take her eyes off Mason. She'd moved to the front door of the house and was standing with her back to it and her arms folded across her chest. "Would you please just arrest him and end this?" she said.

Mason didn't like all three of us talking. He had to swivel his head back and forth and he didn't know which of us to threaten. He settled for yelling again. "Brenda! Get your ass out here!"

"Don't forget honey," Jess said. "Get your ass out here, *honey*."

"Oh, fuck you, cunt," Mason said. We'd just about exhausted his vocabulary. He started forward, only a little unsteady, heading directly for the steps up to the porch.

"Last warning, Mason," I said.

"Gonna shoot me, fucker?" He was almost to the stairs, looking at me.

"No need," I said.

Jess vaulted over the porch railing, swinging her legs around in a quick, compact arc. Focused on me, Mason saw the movement too late. He started to raise the tire iron, but Jess's foot in its steel-toed work boot caught him in his left temple and he staggered several steps to his right, fighting for balance. Jess landed easily and followed him and as he righted himself and started to swing the iron wildly at her she stepped inside his reach and brought the heel of her hand up sharp and fast under his chin. The blow crossed his eyes and he fell backwards, sprawling into the grass.

I was standing now at the top of the stairs. My right hand was resting on the butt of my gun. "Stay down, Mason," I said. "She kicked your ass twelve years ago, and that was before she enlisted and really went pro."

Mason was on his hands and knees and didn't seem to be hearing me. Whatever he was flying on was keeping him conscious. Jess stood seven or eight feet back from him and waited as he shook his head and worked his way painfully upward, wobbly as a newborn colt. He still had the iron and as soon as his feet were under him he roared and charged her, raising the iron back behind his head and swinging it in a long circle. Jess caught the iron and stepped to the side as he came, twisting it out of his hand and sticking out a leg to trip him and send him windmilling wildly back to the ground. I winced at the sound of the hard-packed earth knocking the wind out of him. Jess tossed the iron behind her and watched him struggling to get up again.

"I can do this all week, asshole," she said.

"I can't," I said. "I'm gonna have a shitload of paperwork to fill out when I haul him in. Wrap this up, would you?"

Jess grinned. "You never let me have any fun," she said. She tucked her purple hair behind her ear, walked over to where Mason had gotten to his hands and knees, and brought her boot down hard on the fingers of his right hand. I heard several small snaps and Mason let out a howl of pure agony and rage, rolling to his side and pulling the injured hand in tight against his chest. Behind me Angie sucked in her breath. Jess crouched behind Mason and put her hand almost tenderly on his shoulder. "Be a while before you hit anybody with that hand again, right?"

Mason's yowl had settled into anguished sobs. "Bitch," he moaned. "My fucking hand."

"Jess," I said. "Enough."

She looked up at me. We'd been best friends since fifth grade and I'd seen every mood and thought she'd ever had in her life play itself out in her eyes. The way she looked now, I seriously thought for a moment I would have to pull on her to keep Mason alive.

She saw me thinking it and shook her head. "He's not worth it," she said. She held out her hand and I tossed her my cuffs as I started down the steps. She rolled Mason onto his front, not gently, and against his protests pulled his hands back around and cuffed him. Three of the fingers on his right hand were swollen and bent at ugly angles, and though he swore viciously again as the arm was bent behind him, all the fight was gone.

Jess and I hauled him to his feet, but the second we let go he dropped back to his knees, letting his head hang down almost into the dirt. "Bitch crippled me," he said. He sounded like he was about eight years old and whining for justice on the playground. "You saw it, Wade."

I fought down the impulse to pull him up again by his hair. "Gee, Mason, all I saw was you resisting arrest and then Miz Hendrick here graciously stepping in to assist an officer in completing his duty." I looked up at Angie, who'd come down to the foot of the stairs. "That what you saw, uninvolved bystander?"

She nodded. Behind her, the curtain in a front window twitched and I saw Brenda Barnes looking out at us. The entire left side of her face was still the purple and red of deep bruises and there was no emotion on her face that I wanted to put a name to.

I was pretty sure she didn't think any of us looked very cool.

Before I could even get to the shitload of paperwork, I had to take Mason to the hospital, where the entire staff was all too aware of the damage he'd done on his previous visit. They didn't seem to be in any special hurry to get his hand taken care of, or to find the painkillers he kept screaming for. I'm not sure he ever did get the painkillers, actually. They finally got around to setting the fingers and wrapping his whole hand in a cast that made him look like he had a softball at the end of his arm. When they were done with him it was off to the county lockup and then, finally, inevitably, back to the office, well past what should have been the end of an honest working day.

"New postcard on your desk, Wade," Sally said as I came into the building.

"Good evening to you too, Sal."

"Don't shoot the messenger," she said. Sally's been working the reception and dispatch desk for the county cops since my earliest conscious memories. My father used to say that the first settlers in the area came across her sitting in a field one day and built the police station around her.

My father, William Finch, became a deputy in Goldwood County the day he turned eighteen and was sheriff by the time he was thirty. He was forty-seven when he responded to a 911 call from the house of Sean Kelly, a bar owner my dad had known since they were on a Little League team together. Inside the house he found Kelly sitting nude on the couch, drinking straight from a bottle of Jim Beam. Kelly's wife, his teenaged son and daughter, and the daughter's boyfriend were on the floor in front of him. All four of them were naked, hogtied, and shot in the head. Kelly still had the gun in his right hand, held against his naked thigh. The barrel was warm enough that the skin of his leg had blistered a little.

Dad played it by the book. He took the gun away from an unresisting Kelly, cuffed him, and checked the victims for signs of life, though I'm sure he knew that was futile. He found a robe and a pair of sweatpants and put Kelly in them and waited for backup. When three deputies arrived he had them watch and record him while he recited the date and time and read Kelly his rights straight off the Miranda card in his wallet. He put the wallet back in his pocket and squatted in front of Kelly, still sitting on the couch.

"Do you understand the rights I've read to you, sir?" he asked.

"Sure," Kelly said. His eyes were clear and alert, the deputies all agreed later.

"Did you shoot these people, Sean?"

"Yep," Kelly said. He didn't hesitate.

"Why'd you do that?" my father asked.

Kelly smiled. "Never liked any one of 'em," he said. "Cocksuckers talked too much."

There's thirty-seven seconds of silence then. I've timed the recording. It doesn't sound like much but it's a long time to sit through ambient noise. Finally there's the sound of my father letting out air through his nose and the squeak of his gun belt as he stands.

"Secure the scene," he said. "Call the coroner and have Sally ask the state for a forensic team. I'll take Mr. Kelly in."

He put Kelly in his car and drove off and for the next seventy-two hours that was the last anybody knew. The two of them simply vanished.

I'd been on the force about a year at that point and like every other cop in the county I spent the next three days scouring the twenty-three miles between the Kelly house and the county jail, looking for any trace of my father, Kelly, or the car.

It was a state cop who finally found the car in an abandoned sawmill, fifty miles and two counties away. Kelly had been tied to a beam and shot six times. My father's uniform was neatly folded on the hood of his car, next to his badge and unloaded sidearm. A page from his notebook was skewered on the pin of his badge.

"I quit," it said, followed by his slashing, incomprehensible signature.

Now, seven years later, I was at my desk in the sheriff's office looking at the same signature at the bottom of a postcard, inside a clear plastic evidence bag. The picture side of the postcard showed some kind of stork standing on one leg in a swamp. The lower right corner said "Greetings from the Everglades!" in flowing yellow script. The other side was postmarked three days ago in Grand Rapids, Michigan. In blue ink my father had neatly printed the address of the sheriff's office and then, in the space reserved for the message:

Kelly's son was probably going to be trouble in a few years. I busted him a couple of times for vandalism and underage drinking. Maybe he would have grown out of that. I did. Or maybe by now he'd be in prison.

The first postcard had shown up a month after the deaths, after the APBs and the national media frenzy and the county's decision to hire a new sheriff from someplace as far out of town as they could manage. It was a confession, a few sentences confirming that he'd killed Kelly and acted alone, and it was mailed from Texas, though the picture was of the St. Louis arch. I thought that was going to be the last we ever heard of him, but the postcards kept coming, sometimes once a month, sometimes three or four in a week. Never the same postmark twice, never an image that matched the postmark. Never any kind of salutation or greeting. Just a few brief sentences, always about Kelly or his family.

"This one makes forty-seven."

I looked up. Cheryl Hernandez, the sheriff, was leaning against the desk next to mine.

"I don't keep count," I said. "Appreciate you letting me see them."

"A man deserves to know about his father," she said. Cheryl had been a homicide detective in San Francisco before Goldwood County hired her away. We'd never discussed the fact that she'd plainly been hired because she was as unlike my father as possible. "We're done with it, so just get it off to the FBI once you've looked at it."

"Sure," I said.

Cheryl shifted her weight a little against the desk and looked around. Zeke Robbins was the only other person in the big squad room and he was down at the other end, fooling around with the coffee maker and making hushed, urgent noises into his cell phone. She looked back at me. "I hear Mason Barnes had a rough afternoon."

"Wasn't a lot of fun for me either."

"I bet it was fun for Jess Hendrick."

I didn't say anything to that.

Cheryl sighed and stood up. "She's gonna need to come in and sign a statement. Angie too."

"I'm expecting Jess tomorrow morning, Angie probably later in the day. You know they won't both leave Haven at the same time."

"What about Barnes's wife?"

"I don't think she saw anything. I'm dead sure Angie's gonna make sure she stays put out there until Mason's breaking up rocks."

"Christ, Finch," she said. "How fucking long do you think it's been since Maine put prisoners on chain gangs? You need to freshen up your references." She rapped her knuckles sharply on the edge of my desk. "And you need to get that lunatic Hendrick on a short leash before she crosses the line."

I wanted to promise her that Jess would never cross that line, but I couldn't. It's what I would have said about my father, right up until he picked up the phone one day, put on his badge and drove out to Sean Kelly's house. Who the hell was I to make promises?

I got home after dark and found that Ronnie had come by and taken the last of his stuff, mostly winter clothes and the final crate of his treasured vinyl collection. The note he left on the kitchen table was brief and chilly. I crumpled it up and threw it in the trash. Then I pulled it out of the trash, folded it neatly and stuck it in the drawer where I kept my utility bills and bank statements. I poured myself a shot of bourbon and sat on the living room sofa.

The TV was tuned to a reality show about a group of people competing to find a hidden idol on some island. I didn't have the energy to change the channel, and I kept losing track of the rules. After a while it seemed like I was on the island and Mason and Ronnie were taking turns chasing me around. I gave it up and pulled out my phone.

Barrelhouse? I texted Jess.

She must have been awake. It was less than a minute before the screen lit up with a little picture. Thumbs up.

Twenty minutes later I was at a picnic table on the back deck at the Barrelhouse, looking out over the dark waters of Three Pine Lake. The building had been a bar for generations, under a dozen different names and twice that many owners. Once upon a time Sean Kelly had owned it. I was trying to remember what it had been called then when Jess came out the back door. She had a metal pail filled with ice and six bottles of beer.

"What was this place called when Kelly owned it?" I asked.

She sat down across from me and handed me one of the beers. "The Scuttlebutt," she said.

"That's right," I said. I took a pull. "Stupid damn name. Angie asleep?"

"She's in bed, anyway. She doesn't sleep much."

"I get that," I said.

We looked at the lake for a while and the big clear sky. There was a full moon bright enough to read by. We were the only ones out on the deck.

"I feel like there were more lightning bugs around when we were kids," I said after a while.

"Maybe," Jess said.

"Ronnie picked up the last of his stuff today," I said. "Left a note."

Jess blew some air out of her nose. She touched her nearly empty bottle to mine, drained it, and pulled another out of the pail. "That sucks. It's gonna suck for a while. But there will be somebody else."

"Sure," I said. "Gay guys are lining up to date a cop in the middle of nowhere, Maine."

"I found Angie," Jess said. "And everybody loved the cop in the Village People."

I slapped the table. "There it is," I said. "I knew there was somebody who looked cool dressed as a cop."

Jess laughed. I took a drink and thought about telling her about my father's latest postcard. I swear that's what I meant to say, but it's not what came out when I opened my mouth.

"Was there a moment today where you were ready to kill him, Jess?"

She looked down at the bottle and rolled it back and forth in her hands. She was quiet for a long time. I listened to an owl announcing itself from somewhere around the lake off to the left.

"You know what really scares me about assholes like Mason Barnes?" she said finally. She didn't wait for an answer. "It's that on some level I get them. Stuck out here a hundred miles from anything, no money, no real jobs, no hope, nothing to do but drink and fuck around and feel your life going away a day at a time." She took a swallow. "Get to a point where you want to feel like there's somebody on the rung under you. Somebody you get to shit on."

"No excuse," I started.

"I fucking know it isn't," she said. She put the bottle down. "Yeah, I wanted to kill him. There have been a bunch of them I've wanted to kill. You wanted to kill him, too. Don't think I didn't see that."

I half shrugged. I felt like that was as close as I could get.

"Yeah," she said.

"So why didn't you?"

She interlaced her fingers behind her neck and looked up into the sky. "Man, I thought you were just going to be crying in your beer about Robbie. If I'd known you were going to be getting all touchy feely on me I would have stayed in bed with my woman."

I held up my hands. "Okay. Question withdrawn."

"No, listen," she said. "I'm not going to give you any bullshit about law and order or tell you that if I sink to his level and kill him, he wins." She brought her head back down and looked me in the eye. "You were there. Angie was there. And I don't want to end up in a place where all I can do is send the two of you postcards."

I didn't say anything. I looked at her.

"We didn't kill him today," she said. "Take the win."

We sat for a while after that, mostly just looking at the lake and listening to the strange disconnected sounds of insects and birds and distant splashes. We didn't drink anymore.

Eventually Jess stood up and picked up the pail. "I should get back to Haven," she said. "Hey, how about you and me drive down to Fenway this weekend?"

"You're just looking for an excuse to stop at Bob's Clam Hut," I said.

"Guilty as charged," she said. "But you get a game out of it."

"Sox are in Anaheim this weekend," I said. "But we can go get you your clam cake anyway."

"God," she said. "You are so fucking easy." She punched me on the shoulder and walked away.

I stayed out on the deck until the bartender came out to tell me they were closing. Walking the ten minutes home I wondered how long it would be before Mason Barnes had his next beer. I didn't think he'd ever lift one again without feeling an ache in his fingers that he'd never really get used to. That was fine with me. But I didn't kill him today.

When I got home, I took Ronnie's note out of my paperwork drawer and burned it in the kitchen sink. If I dreamed that night, I have no memory of it.

* * *

Joseph S. Walker is an active member of the Mystery Writers of America living in Indiana. Several of his stories have appeared in *Alfred Hitchcock Mystery Magazine,* among other publications. Follow him on Twitter @JSWalkerAuthor and find his website at https://jsw47408.wixsite.com/website.

The Best New England Crime Stories Anthology Collection

THE EDITORS OF LEVEL BEST BOOKS ARE SHAWN REILLY SIMMONS, VERENA ROSE, AND HARRIETTE SACKLER COLLECTIVELY KNOWN AS THE DAMES OF DETECTION.

Landfall: The Best New England Crime Stories 2018

Snowbound: The Best New England Crime Sto-ries 2017

Windward: The Best New England Crime Stories 2016

Made in the USA
Middletown, DE
07 November 2019

78107033R00236